the Boy I Love

the Boy I Love

Lynda Bellingham

**SIMON &
SCHUSTER**

London · New York · Sydney · Toronto · New Delhi

A CBS COMPANY

First published in Great Britain by Simon & Schuster UK Ltd, 2014
A CBS COMPANY
This paperback edition, 2015

1 3 5 7 9 10 8 6 4 2

Simon & Schuster UK Ltd
1st Floor
222 Gray's Inn Road
London WC1X 8HB

www.simonandschuster.co.uk

Simon & Schuster Australia, Sydney
Simon & Schuster India, New Delhi

A CIP catalogue record for this book
is available from the British Library

Paperback ISBN: 978-1-4711-0285-1
Ebook ISBN: 978-1-4711-0286-8

Typeset by M Rules
Printed and bound by CPI Group (UK) Ltd, Croydon, CR0 4YY

A Tribute to Lynda

We are so very proud to be the publishers of Lynda's fiction. Lynda was brimful of ideas born of her lively imagination and her own experiences. She knew instinctively how people of every generation interact and had – of course! – a wonderfully keen eye for drama, and for emotion and love in all guises. She wrote of joy and sadness, conflict and union, old and young, past and present, with tenderness and wisdom. *Tell Me Tomorrow*, Lynda's first novel, has three generations of women at its heart – a grandmother, a mother and a daughter – and Lynda dedicated the novel to mothers everywhere. These wonderful characters shone out on every page, to be joined, in *The Boy I Love*, by an equally memorable and delightful cast. On every page, in every description, in every word of dialogue, readers will hear Lynda's voice loud and clear. How fortunate we are that Lynda completed her second novel this summer so that we can all rejoice in the talents of a truly gifted storyteller.

Suzanne Baboneau
Lynda's editor
November 2014

The boy I love is up in the gallery,
The boy I love is looking now at me.
There he is, can't you see, waving his handkerchief
As merry as a robin that sings on a tree.

George Ware, 1885, sung by Marie Lloyd

Act 1

Enter stage left

Chapter 1

Oh, Mr Porter, what shall I do?
I want to go to Birmingham
And they are taking me onto Crewe.
Send me back to London
As quickly as you can.
Oh, Mr Porter, what a silly girl I am!

September 1982

Sally Thomas swallowed hard and smiled bravely as the whistle blew and the train began to pull out of the station. She gave a final wave to her family, standing at the barrier and already a blur, and sat down with a bump as the train picked up speed.

'Oh, Mr Porter, what shall I do ...' The old Victorian music-hall song rang in her ears as she gazed out at the beautiful cream stone buildings of Cheltenham, her home town. It looked so picture-perfect in the early-morning sun. Traces of autumn tinged the leaves in red and gold, and there were flashes of burnt orange from the creepers that draped themselves over the houses like garlands.

The girl could not help but think how different the landscape would be in Crewe. From gold to grey. Still, she would learn to love the difference between the two and make it her home for the next six months. Her first professional job as an actress! In July, Sally had managed to get an early audition for the upcoming season by physically taking herself to meet the director in Crewe, rather than waiting in line down in London with hundreds of other hopefuls. Her temerity had gained her a place in the company, and now as she fell asleep to the rhythm of the train, she dreamed of bright lights and velvet curtains, and her first introduction to Crewe Theatre just two short months ago ...

July

She was shaken awake as the train shuddered to a halt at Platform One, Crewe station. As she stepped down from the train, Sally was overwhelmed by the size of the place. High above her, steel girders rose in Gothic splendour just like a cathedral. Her ears were bombarded with a cacophony of noise: engines grinding, whistles blowing, brakes screeching and the endless rumble of humanity – a river of people flowing towards the exit or breaking through to platforms to find their trains. Sally began to think she might have misjudged Crewe as just a town 'up north'. The station, at least, seemed to be the centre of the universe!

She joined the other passengers and was swept along to the exit and out to the taxi rank, where things were much calmer and quieter, thank goodness. She hailed a taxi and asked for the theatre.

'Is it far?' she enquired, hoping the answer would be negative as her finances were tight to say the least.

'No, lass, just up the hill. Hop in. You working there?' asked the cab driver, looking at her in his driving mirror as she sat back in the seat.

'I hope to be, yes,' Sally replied shyly. 'I have got an audition today, as a matter of fact. So – fingers crossed.'

'Well, good luck to you, lass. You will do just fine.'

No more than five minutes later, the taxi slowed and stopped outside a beautiful Victorian theatre. It shone like a beacon to Sally. No matter the street was a little shabby, and next door there was a very run-down Chinese takeaway, to Sally it was the gateway to all her dreams. She paid the driver and thanked him for his good wishes, then got out and turned to the front doors. Putting down her suitcase, she pulled on the handle, only to discover that it was locked. She pressed her nose to the glass, shielding her eyes with her hand to peer into the darkness. There were no signs of life.

'Great,' sighed Sally. 'Now what?'

She looked up the street and was greeted by grey stone terraced houses, and a stray dog checking out a lamp-post. Stepping back from the entrance, she told herself, 'There has to be a stage door round the back somewhere.' Sure enough, she spotted an opening at the end of the front of the theatre building, so picking up her things, she set off to investigate. The gap proved to be a narrow alleyway, and halfway down was a battered sign hanging from the wall: *Stage Door.*

With a sigh of relief Sally pushed open the door and stepped into a dimly lit corridor. She ventured further in, expecting to meet a stage doorman – or woman, for that matter.

'Hello? Anybody around?' she called out. There was a small kiosk with a sliding glass window and an empty chair. It was lit by a table lamp with a red silk shade which had long since seen better days in someone's boudoir. Sally thought it looked very incongruous, stuck in this little corner. A two-bar electric fire was glowing gaily and piles of newspapers lay on the floor – but nobody was there to answer her call.

She followed her nose, and then the sign in big red letters painted on the wall leading down the stairs: *to The Stage. Silence!*

The staircase wound round and down, and at the bottom there was a heavy wooden door. Sally pulled on the handle, opened it and stepped into the almost-darkness onstage. She could just make out a dim light in the far corner, presumably from the prompt corner. She tiptoed towards it, keeping an ear out for any sounds of life. She caught the odd word from someone whispering somewhere nearby ... but could not quite make out who was talking. She moved between two black curtains and found herself right out on the stage. Suddenly a light hit her between the eyes like a laser, and she was completely blinded for a few seconds.

'Sorry, sorry,' she called out. 'Is there someone there? My name is Sally Thomas and I have come for an audition. Please take the light off me as I can't see a thing!' She moved towards the front of the stage, trying to get out of the spotlight, and peered out into the auditorium – but could see nothing because she still had spots in front of her eyes.

Then, as her vision slowly adjusted, she felt a presence up to her left – and there in the box, she could make out a figure standing just inside the doorway. There was a red glow burning in the dark and the faint hint of cigar tobacco – but before she could speak, a voice filled the theatre with liquid gold. Sally had never heard such an incredible voice.

'Sorry, young lady. Didn't mean to frighten you. We have trouble with the lighting board. Who did you say you were again?'

'Sally Thomas. Are you Giles Longfellow, by any chance?' Sally was regaining her composure and feeling ready to present herself. After all, she had come a long way for this audition and had no intention of messing it up.

'Yes, indeed I am. Eric, are you still up there?' Giles Longfellow called up to the gods, to where his lighting man was perched on a follow spot trying to adjust the bulb.

A voice wafted out from the darkness. 'Yes, guvnor. All sorted. Be down in a tick.'

'Thank you, Eric. Now, young lady, what are you going to do for me?' The man in the box leaned over the rail towards Sally and she felt she could almost reach up and touch him.

Suddenly, all the house-lights came on and the full beauty of the theatre revealed itself. It was like a wedding cake of pink and white stucco. The red plush seats and the gleaming brass rails set off the intricate plasterwork on the walls and the boxes, rising to a ceiling that was covered in cherubs and flowers. A huge crystal chandelier sent shafts of light down onto the seats below like rays of sunshine piercing a dark forest.

Sally gasped and looked back up to the box, from whence came Giles's richly mellow voice again: 'Young lady, did you hear me? You look like a frightened rabbit.' He stepped back and sat down.

Sally gave him her full attention at once and announced with as much aplomb as she could muster, 'I would like to do

Portia's speech from *The Merchant of Venice*: "The quality of mercy is not strained . . .'"

'Very well, continue.'

The girl walked to the centre of the stage and took a deep breath. This was the moment she had trained for and lived for. Her first proper audition for the professional theatre.

Sally had left drama school six months ago, and had spent the intervening time writing to dozens of repertory theatres throughout the country. Some responded but most never did. It had proved very disheartening in the main, but Sally was determined and driven, and was not going to give up easily. She had managed to get a job at the British Drama League in Fitzroy Square, London. It was an extraordinary place, a cross between a library and advice centre for foreign students, offering drama courses and training for stage management. It also had offices for various departments in theatre, from the technical staff to visiting directors, and was a popular venue for theatres to hold auditions. Sally manned the ancient telephone switchboard, which was like a puzzle for wiring aficionados. Each line had a connection, but oh! – how often did she put the wrong plug in the wrong hole!

'Bear with me, caller,' was her cri de coeur all day long. 'I am so sorry, sir, you have been disconnected.'

By the end of a busy day, Sally would be distraught – but her boss, a lovely man called James Langton, was ever ready to offer her encouragement. James had always been associated with the theatre in some way. Sally was never sure if he had been an actor himself, years ago. He certainly had theatricality about him – and great charm. James ran the Drama League like an historic institution and had taken Sally and another young actor, Jeremy Sinclair, under his wing. Every time a theatre booked the rehearsal rooms to hold auditions, he would ring down and inform them both. This meant that the two actors could ensure that at some point, they were able to insinuate themselves into a position to get an audition.

Sally used to wait until the director had seen everybody, and then she would appear at the door and announce that – what a coincidence! She was an actress and not a telephone operator, after all, and would they please let her audition? Most of the time it worked a treat, but so far she had not managed to get a job. Then one afternoon Mr Langton had come down to her little booth and informed her that Crewe Theatre would soon be holding auditions for its new season, starting in September, and that she should write or phone. Sally wasted no time: she immediately rang the theatre and was told that the director, Giles Longfellow, would indeed be coming down to London to the BDL to hold auditions, but if she was able to come up to Crewe before then, he would be delighted to see her 'in situ' as it were. Seizing this opportunity to get in early, she made an appointment for the following week.

Now here she was, standing on the stage at Crewe, launching into her audition piece with gusto.

Halfway through, however, Giles Longfellow called down from the box, 'Thank you, my dear, that will do. Can you sing?'

Sally was completely thrown by this question. Not because she couldn't sing, but because he had not let her finish her speech. She stammered a, 'Y-yes, I can.'

'Then away you go,' came the response from above.

Sally sang the Victorian music-hall song called 'The Boy I Love', made famous by the great Marie Lloyd. It was a good choice as she could sing it unaccompanied. Her strong, clear soprano voice filled the auditorium with the sweet, affecting melody, and was rewarded by a handclap from the director.

'Well done! Delightful. Stay there – I am coming down.' And Giles disappeared.

Sally admired yet again the elegance of the box and noted that there was a coat of arms on the front. The Royal Box – how very appropriate for the flamboyant Giles Longfellow, she decided. Maybe one day *she* would be singing to Royalty in the box! Her daydreams were interrupted by the arrival of the Director.

'You did well, my dear, and I am very pleased to say I think we can offer you a place in our company next season. You are not experienced enough to play leads, but depending on how well you adapt, and how hard you work, I can certainly promise you some decent roles – and thanks to your fine singing voice I see you in some of our musical productions. It does mean you will have to accept some stage-management work, but at least you will get your forty-two weeks in the theatre, which will make you eligible for your full Equity card. Do you have an agent, by the way?'

Sally had not managed to attract the attention of an agent so far, but she had discussed this with Mr Langton and he had offered to advise her, should the need arise, on the financial side of things. So bearing this in mind, she replied, 'No, but I have a manager called James Langton and he has said he will deal with the fee, if that is convenient to you, sir.'

'James Langton as in the British Drama League?' Giles looked amused.

'Um, yes. Do you know him?' asked Sally.

'Absolutely, my dear! We are old friends. But what is his interest in you, may I ask?'

Sally was not sure which way this conversation should be going, but decided that honesty was the best policy.

'I work in reception at the BDL,' she explained, 'and Mr

Langton very kindly helps me find auditions, et cetera, while I am working there. He has been so supportive, and told me that any time I needed advice, he would help me. So I just thought to mention him to you with respect of salary or whatever. I hope that is all right?'

'Of course, no problem at all. I will talk to him asap. Thank you for coming all this way, dear, and I look forward to welcoming you to the new company in September.'

'Oh, thank you so much, Mr Longfellow, I am thrilled to be working for you and I—'

But he had gone. Disappeared like a magician, without the puff of smoke, although the smell of his cigar drifted across the footlights like a longlost memory. Sally's heart was thumping. She had her first job! Going to the footlights, she took in the auditorium one last time from top to bottom. She loved it! And then she looked up to the Royal Box – and blew a kiss.

Chapter 2

Giles Longfellow was ambitious, but he was also weak. He had talent, but lacked the iron will to pursue his dreams to their ultimate conclusion. All his life he had been led by his heart – well, his nether regions, to be absolutely blunt. He would fall wildly in love and indulge every emotional level of his intellect and physical need. This would last for months, or sometimes only weeks, but it drained him of all his energy and left him reeling. In his youth it had cost him a promising career as an actor because he would lose all interest in a job if the mood for love took him over, and employers soon realized he was a liability. Not only because his stagecraft suffered as his concentration wavered, but on one particular occasion his pursuit of happiness with one individual had led to accusations of rape and he had only just escaped jail.

James Langton was remembering the incident now. He and Giles did not know each other that well, but had agreed to meet after James had rung Giles's secretary to discuss Sally Thomas's contract for the upcoming season.

'You went through a very bad patch a few years back, I

seem to recall,' mused James over a very fine dinner at the Garrick Club.

'Oh God, yes, it was a pretty close thing, but I was bailed out by the lovely Lord Graham. We have been friends ever since.' Giles did not add that they were also lovers, on and off. After the police arrested Giles for indecently assaulting a young man, Lord Edward (Teddie) Graham had stepped in and paid off the boy and his parents and pulled strings with the Commissioner of Police. He and Giles had then had an affair, but unlike most of Giles's romantic attachments it had not fizzled out or ended dramatically, but every now and then had renewed itself.

Lord Graham was married to money and had managed to father three children, most importantly an heir and a spare, as they said in those rarefied social circles. This secured the marriage, and the family seat, which was a beautiful hundred-room stately home in Cheshire. Teddie was able, in the main, to keep his preferences under wraps, but when the need arose he would stay down in London at his club and seek out Giles Longfellow, who after his run-in with the authorities had also had to keep himself in check. Both men enjoyed each other's company and although it was hardly a relationship based on passion it served them both well.

Giles finally started to focus on his career as a director and was offered the post at Crewe five years ago. Edward Graham's country pile was just up the road so it seemed the perfect post – for the time being, at any rate. As he became more confident as a director, thanks to his work at Crewe, so Giles's ambition returned. This season he wanted to make his mark, and head for the West End and perhaps a post with the Royal Shakespeare Company. He had proven himself with several productions at Crewe, and surprisingly, run the financial side at a profit with the help of an Arts Council grant. However, in order to achieve the kind of production that would turn heads in his direction, he was going to need extra cash to lure some exciting talent up to Crewe. Lord Graham was his golden ticket. Teddie had become a patron of the arts, in particular of Crewe Theatre, and had pledged financial support to Giles for his new season. So, Giles was down in London to court a young actor called Rupert Hallam, who was making waves in theatrical circles, to persuade him to come to Crewe to do *Hamlet*. The rest of the cast would soon fall into place if Giles secured the young man. God knows, there were enough actors to choose from, and he had already chosen Sally Thomas.

'I liked her because she showed pluck coming all the way to see me. She gave a consummate performance, maybe not glittering, but she has a good singing voice and I need that in the company, as I am hoping to do two or three music-based productions: a revival of *The Boyfriend*, a Victorian music-hall show, and of course, a pantomime at Christmas. I have told the girl that she will have to do some stage management at first until I can really see her strengths, but I promised her she would get her chance. And, of course, she would be official understudy too.' Giles took a sip of very expensive Bordeaux. As James was paying the bill, he had offered to choose the wine!

James couldn't hide his pride and delight for his protége.

'Oh, believe me she is thrilled, and quite understands the situation. I am very grateful to you, Giles. Actually I have another young actor I would be very pleased if you could audition and give me your thoughts. His name is Jeremy Sinclair and he works for me part-time in the reference library.' James refilled Giles Longfellow's glass.

Giles regarded the other man for a few moments and then said, 'Is it love, James?'

James Langton blushed deeply and spluttered, 'Good God, no! I am not like that, you know I am not. Whatever gave you that idea? I have a wife and I am a respectable married man. Giles, you are outrageous to suggest such a thing.'

Giles burst out laughing. 'All right, calm down, for goodness sake, man. It was just a thought. You don't have to hide things from someone like me . . . ' but James interrupted him.

'Please, stop this at once. I will not tolerate such accusations. I try to help some young actors, male *and* female, because it is such a tough profession, and I see them every day at the Drama League struggling to survive. My interest is purely artistic patronage, if you will, nothing more.'

'Fine, we will leave it at that, and I apologize if I have offended you, James. Now drink up, and let's order another bottle and you can give me some suggestions for a drama.'

Later that evening, James let himself into his neat, suburban terraced house in Finchley. He crept into his tiny study, closing the door behind him, and opened the bottle of brandy on the sideboard. He poured himself a large one and went to sit in his favourite armchair. Taking a generous sip of the golden nectar, he closed his eyes and daydreamed of young buttocks in rugby shorts. Jeremy was a beautiful specimen he had to admit. If only . . .

Sally could hardly contain her excitement when she turned up for work at the British Drama League on Monday morning. She was the first to arrive after Geordie, the caretaker, who could be heard in the kitchen at the back of the building whistling a Beatles tune. She called out to him, 'Geordie, did you pick up the post?' She switched on the light in the hallway as it was always dark. The combination of Victorian tiles and dark green paint made the whole place very depressing, and a tad Dickensian. Sally imagined Uriah Heep appearing in a doorway, smiling unctuously at her and rubbing his hands!

Instead, she was greeted halfway down the hall by the rather portly figure of Geordie in his russet-brown overalls and flat cap.

'Morning, miss, how are you this morning?' he asked her as he handed her the post. 'You seem right chirpy, if I may say so. Good weekend, was it?' He gave her a very theatrical wink and tapped the side of his nose. He looked so ridiculous Sally could not help bursting into laughter.

'Oh, Geordie, you really are the pits. You have such a dirty mind!'

Geordie feigned offence. 'Now, miss, please – how can you say that to me? I mean no harm, just trying to be friendly-like, that's all.' He turned and disappeared into the gloom on his way back to the kitchen to put the kettle on, for the first of the many cups of tea and coffee, consumed throughout the day by the inhabitants of number 9, Fitzroy Square.

Sally unlocked her tiny cubicle and found herself feeling quite nostalgic. No more early mornings on the number 13 bus to work. No more Geordie and his nudge nudge, wink wink greetings; from next month she would be a professional actress, working in repertory. She sat in front of her switchboard with her chin resting in her hands and dreamed of applause, and footlights, and bells ringing ... ringing bells meant ... oh Lord! She grabbed a plug and pushed it into the blinking light on the board in front of her.

'British Drama League, good morning, how may I help you?' The answer came rapidly and impatiently. 'Yes, of course. I am putting you through now.' Sally pulled out the plug and placed it in the appropriate connection. She breathed a sigh of relief as the connection was made and she could hear the recipients talking through her headphones on the desk. She had not even had time to put them on. It was going to be one of those Monday mornings, she could tell, but she did not give a hoot because life had turned a corner, and she was on her way up !

Chapter 3

Sally arrived home with her assorted bags and boxes – and promptly burst into tears in the kitchen! Her mother, Patricia, swept her into her arms, plonked her down at the table and handed her a clean white cotton hankie. No tissues for her!

'Whatever is the matter, my darling girl?' she asked.

'Oh nothing, Mum. I am just being stupid and dramatic.' Sally hesitated before blowing her nose on the virgin square of crisp cotton. 'It's just, everything is going to change and I am scared and excited all at the same time, and coming home just makes me realize how much I will miss you all.'

Sally's parents lived in Cheltenham in an old Victorian terraced house. Patricia Thomas had always yearned for one of the Georgian houses in the city, but knew it would have to remain a pipe dream. Her husband, Douglas, was a teacher and part-time collector of antiques, and unless he suddenly discovered a masterpiece in an attic somewhere, they were never going to be able to afford such a property. Patricia had studied at the Slade School of Art in Bloomsbury in the 1950s, and had actually been rather good. When she married

Douglas Thomas in 1950, she was still studying in her final year at the Slade. She had met him at one of the notorious Chelsea Art Club balls. Douglas was taking his finals in History at Oxford, but hoping to become an art teacher in one of the big public schools. He was a very confident young man veering on the arrogant, and saw teaching as a means to express himself in ways he could never have achieved as an artist, firstly because he did not have the talent, and secondly because his parents had refused to let him go to art school. Patricia thought him the handsomest man she had ever set eyes on, and as they danced the night away she fell madly, wonderfully, completely in love with him. Douglas was pleased and flattered. After all, she was very beautiful, and someone who would complement his image perfectly. The pair had spent the summer in passionate embraces, with wild parties at the Arts Club by night and picnics beside the Serpentine by day. Douglas took his young love to Oxford and showed her off to all and sundry. By the end of the summer they had announced their engagement, and life changed very dramatically for the young couple.

Douglas had secured a teaching post at Stowe – a very prestigious public school in Buckinghamshire. He had been offered a small cottage in the grounds, and the newlywed couple set up home. All hopes Patricia may have had of a life as a carefree artist floated out of the tiny latticed window of the damp cottage in which she was now a prisoner. She was alone for long hours of the day while her husband taught privileged, but mostly untalented, boys how to wield a paintbrush. For most of the class it was a period when they could play up, chat and tell dirty jokes. Douglas very soon became disenchanted with the notion of his special calling as a teacher. His power was almost non-existent, and he soon turned his frustration onto his wife. Oh, they were still madly in love, and Patricia did everything in her power to make life easy and smooth for her darling husband, but he would often be quite patronizing and cold towards her.

Slowly, over the coming years she learned to ignore his jibes about her intellect and abilities. She would laugh delightedly in front of guests as he berated her for some tiny misdemeanour or other, and he would eventually step down from his high horse and wallow in her adoration. It was a strange marriage but it somehow worked. They spent the school holidays travelling round Europe, and Patricia was in her element then, giving Douglas endless sermons on the History of Art. She became his part-time researcher, doing most of his homework for him. He would always return from one of their trips abroad full of information for his classes, and presenting the students with reams of slides and photos. He became quite renowned for his 'out of hours devotion' to duty. Obviously, Patricia had no idea just how useful she was to her husband. It was a mutually agreeable arrangement though, because Patricia loved feeling superior in some small way to her gorgeous lovely husband, who was so bright and witty. In turn, Douglas was more than happy to praise his eager young wife and accept all the teachings she threw at him while enjoying the respect and attention from his pupils and peers.

The couple had a good life in many ways, and it was a few years before the idea of children entered their togetherness. Patricia was almost ambivalent to the idea. She was quite happy playing muse, mistress and even mother to her darling husband. Douglas, however, decided the time was approaching when they should try for a family. Two years later, in 1962, Sally was born – and two years after that, her sister Dora arrived. They were both dear little girls and Douglas loved them. In fact, he thrived, surrounded by all the female adoration. He gained a good reputation at Stowe, and was eventually head-hunted and moved to Cheltenham Ladies College as Head of Department. He loved his job and revelled in the attention from his young female students, feeling god-like as he strode down the corridors acknowledging the admiring looks from the girls. He also had more time to spare, and began to collect and deal in Fine Art.

Patricia surprised herself and the family by completely falling in love with her babies. They filled every minute of her life; she gloried in their growth, and grasped every tiny morsel of her daughters' love. She was a wonderful mother, and worked tire-lessly to make their home a warm and welcoming place. However, as the girls grew up and their need of her grew less, so Patricia's own need for self-esteem returned. Douglas was, as ever, completely self-absorbed, and although he appreciated how lucky he was to have such a seemingly perfect family, it never occurred to him that he should contribute anything more to the general well-being of his wife and daughters.

Patricia yearned for another kind of self-fulfilment. There was a part of her that felt empty and unused. She would some-times creep away when the children were asleep, taking her paints and easel outside, weather permitting, and she would sit and paint her frustrations away. Other times she grabbed a sketchbook and pencils, or charcoal, and as she watched her girls in the garden, or playing in their front room, she would draw them quickly and deftly, capturing precious moments. She loved her family with all her heart, but her soul was in her art. Very rarely did she dare to imagine what life might have been like if she hadn't married so young and devoted her energies to her family. She sometimes thought that Douglas was so much luck-ier to have been born a man. He had another life outside the family. She knew he thrived on female attention, and she sometimes allowed a moment of doubt to creep into her thoughts when he did not come home till very late. She never questioned him – that would have been asking for trouble – and anyway, she didn't want to know the answer. As long as he came home to her, and still made love to her, she was able to cope. She had known only her husband sexually, having been a virgin when they met. He had been a very good and practised lover. Well, that was how it should be, in her view. Men were very different animals – and boys would be boys, wouldn't they?

As the girls matured and Patricia had more time of her own, she decided to look for a part-time job as a teacher. Douglas found this highly amusing.

'Dear God, Patricia darling! What could you possibly teach anyone? You haven't painted for fifteen years. Who would have you, my sweet?'

Much to Patricia's delight, and Douglas's amazement, the local council took her on to teach adult art classes. She proved a great success, and the job gave her a whole new take on life. She started to make new friends, and while Douglas was busy at the college Patricia now had a social life of her own. She ignored her husband's little digs and put-downs, and filled her days with laughter and colour. She had hoped one of daughters might have inherited her artistic talents, but it was not to be, although when Sally announced she was going to be an actress Patricia felt a tingle of excitement. Dora, who was two years younger and had just left school, was much more practical and had applied to do Business Studies at uni. Both girls had the security of a stable home background which gave them a certain amount of confidence with which to face life. Sally was sometimes critical of her father's rather patronizing attitude to his wife, and would encourage her mother to answer back.

'Oh, Sally dear, that is just his way. He doesn't mean anything by it. I just ignore it.'

'But, Mum, he has no right to put you down like he does. Where would he be without you?'

Patricia would laugh her girlish laugh, toss her hair and gaily announce: 'Oh, probably with some gorgeous woman with lots of money!' She always tried to sound nonchalant, but deep in her heart she had always feared the day Douglas would announce he was leaving. Once the girls no longer needed her attention fulltime, her sole concern was keeping her husband happy. As she had grown older she knew that he wanted her to be the gay young thing he had danced with all those years ago. She kept her hair long and dyed it regularly to keep the grey at bay. She had retained her figure and knew she was attractive. Sometimes one of her pupils would make an advance towards her and she would laugh it off with a rebuke: 'Don't be so silly! I am very happily married to the man of my dreams!' Patricia really did think that, and Douglas had no idea just how fortunate he was to have her.

Sally always felt she was a bit of a disappointment to her parents. Her mother was very glamorous in her way, but a bit too girly for her liking, and certainly Sally had inherited none of that coquettishness. She was a good cross of her mother and father, and had strong attractive features, but she could not be described as beautiful. Her tutors at drama school had told her she would never play the young heroines as she was just not pretty enough. She had initially been upset, but commonsense had soon taken over, and Sally knew that especially onstage, a good actress could convince an audience that she was beautiful. It almost made her feel more confident, knowing she did not have to rely on her looks and would never have to worry about getting old. She would always be able to play the interesting characters until she fell off the twig. Dora was probably better-looking than her, but that was fine. There was no jealousy between the girls, and they had always been very close. Dora managed their father brilliantly, and could put him in a good mood with a click of her fingers. While she was still living at home Dora was a good foil for him, and their mother did not have to worry about his dark moods.

Sally had been looking forward to spending time with them all over the month of August. Now here she was, feeling sorry for herself. She got up and gave her mother a hug, saying, 'I am so stupid, really. I'm just so happy to be home. Come on, let's get these boxes sorted out and then we can go and have a large glass of wine with Dad.'

The two women attacked the bags, sorting the rubbish from the washing and from the 'keep forever' memorabilia that gathers through three years of college. It was a gorgeous summer's day and all the windows were open. The sweet perfume of honeysuckle and mown grass wafted through the house, along with the call of a blackbird above the constant hum of buzzing bees. Sally was always caught unawares by the clarity of these sounds compared to London, where everything was lost in the general drumming of city noise, sliced through with the occasional siren. Here in her parents' loving home, surrounded by trees and blue sky, she revelled in a sense of complete well-being. It gave her strength.

'Come on, darling, stop daydreaming and get a move on,' her mother urged. 'It's nearly lunchtime and your dad will be expecting a visit.' She gathered all the bags ready to go and went to fetch the car keys, adding, 'We can celebrate having our daughters home for the summer.'

Chapter 4

There was a letter from Crewe Theatre waiting for Sally the next morning. It contained a digs list and a reminder that under the Esher Standard Contract issued by Equity, the actors' union, the artiste (Sally in this case) was obliged to provide an evening dress for the season, and to use her own clothes as and when required. The management was only obliged to provide period costumes.

'Oh my God!' she gasped over her boiled egg and soldiers. 'I have to wear my own clothes!'

'What do you mean?' asked Dora. 'What does the letter say?' She grabbed it from her sister and read the instructions issued therein. Then: 'My God, Sally, there isn't a play written that could possibly include your wardrobe,' she said, and burst out laughing.

'Shut up, Dora! What do you mean by that? There is nothing wrong with the way I dress, is there?'

Dora laughed even louder and Patricia came into the kitchen to find out what all the fuss was about.

'Mum, tell Sally what is wrong with her dress sense,

please. Can one even begin to describe the lack of sartorial savvy?'

'Dora, please stop cackling, it is very unbecoming. What is the problem here?'

'I have had a letter from the theatre,' explained Sally, 'telling me I have to provide my own clothes, except where period costume is required – *and* I have to take an evening dress. I don't own a dress, never mind an evening one!' she wailed.

'Oh dear,' sympathized her mother. 'I do see your problem. Dora, will you stop giggling! Sally dresses very individually, I will grant you, but she is not completely without taste.' This response drew further sniggers from Dora.

'Oh, do shut up, Dora!' snapped Sally. 'The joke wears thin, methinks. So what am I going to do?'

'Well, we will have to sort you out. There is a fantastic vintage clothes shop in Cheltenham, and lots of jumble sales we can rummage through. If the worst comes to the worst, Dora can make you an evening dress, can't you, dear?' Patricia turned to her youngest daughter. 'Let's make a list of useful clothes you might need in a season. Do you have any idea what plays they are going to do? That would help enormously.'

Dora jumped up from the table, saying, 'Listen, sis, we can have a great time putting your wardrobe together. We will turn you into a style icon, don't you worry.'

'I don't want to be a style icon, thank you very much,' responded Sally rather grumpily. 'I am an actress.'

'We know, but there is no reason why you can't be a smartly dressed actress. Come on, let's get down the town and do a bit of shopping.'

Dora was practically out of the front door. Patricia stopped her with, 'Hold on, darling, just a moment.' She went out of the kitchen and across the hall to the study, and came back two minutes later with her purse. 'I want to give you both a little something to spend.' She handed them both some cash.

The girls protested but she went on, 'I don't often get the chance to spoil you, and now seems as good a time as ever. I actually sold a painting last month and I have another commission, so please let me share my good fortune with my beautiful daughters. And listen, if you can't find an evening dress, Sally, get a pattern and Dora and I will make it for you. Dora knows where to buy gorgeous material, don't you, darling?'

'Oh yes, absolutely. Thank you so much, Mum, this is fantastic of you. Oh my God, I am so excited. Shopping – and with some money for a change.' And she was off once more towards the front door.

Sally picked up her bag and started to follow, then stopped and gave her mother a big hug. 'Thank you so much for this. I will make you proud.'

'Go on, you have made me proud already.' Patricia kissed her and shooed her off, 'Now get going or your sister will grab all the best buys first.'

The girls made straight for the vintage clothes shop. Dora knew the owner, Jackie, who was the mother of a girl she had been at school with. Jackie was very interested to hear all about Sally's job and the theatre.

'Please take my number in case you need anything later in the season,' she said to Sally. 'Maybe the wardrobe department at Crewe will be interested in some of my stock. Do you know what plays you are doing yet?'

'No, not yet, but I can certainly let you know,' said Sally.

Dora was already going through the rail of dresses. 'Ooh, look. This is beautiful, Sal, and would really suit you. Come on, try it on.'

The girls spent the best part of half an hour trying on dresses until poor Sally was bug-eyed.

'I can't remember what I have tried on!' she cried. 'It is exhausting.'

Dora had narrowed the choice down to two dresses. One was a 1950s satin dress, very fitted at the waist with a low neckline and off the shoulder. The other was a simple satin dress cut on the bias, so very flattering for the figure, and rather sexy. It was black.

'This one needs some sparkly jewellery to set it off,' announced Dora, holding the black satin up.

'I have no idea which one to choose,' sighed Sally, who had really had enough and was thinking about a glass of wine and some shepherd's pie in the pub.

Jackie suggested they took both.

Well,' agreed Dora, 'that is the obvious answer, but I don't think the budget will stretch that far.'

Jackie checked the tickets on both dresses and said, 'Look, why don't you buy the satin one and I will give you a twenty-five per cent discount? And I will let you have the other dress on loan, so take it up to Crewe with you, and if you decide you can use it, we will re-negotiate.'

'Oh, that would be fantastic,' said Sally. 'If you are really sure?' And when Jackie nodded her assent: 'Thank you *so* much. Actually, it could be very useful for Crewe because we might well need some period stuff and we could liaise with you. That is brilliant, Jackie.'

The girls were on a high as they left the shop and danced down the street.

'How amazing is that?' said Dora. 'Come on, we will celebrate with a quick glass of wine in the wine bar, then onto more mundane attire like trousers and tops. I want to take you to this terrific boutique that has opened recently. They have really unusual stuff and it is cheap.' With that she was off across the street, skipping towards the wine bar, followed by an equally excited Sally clutching her bag of goodies in her hands.

By the end of the day, the sisters returned home worn out. They flopped down on the sofa surrounded by bags. Patricia made them a cup of tea and then sat down and waited for the fashion parade to begin.

Dora took charge and explained about the two evening dresses. Much against her will, Sally made one last effort and modelled them for her mother.

'Oh yes, girls, you have done well. They are both beautiful and so different. I remember having a dress like this for one of the Chelsea Arts balls,' Patricia said softly, remembering the joy of dancing all night and feeling so beautiful in her dress. 'The fifties one is gorgeous, Sally, and has a very flattering neckline because it shows off one's shoulders as well as a bit of bosom.'

Sally laughed at her mother's rather coy choice of word for the old cleavage.

'Bosom? Oh, Mother, that is so ladylike!' she chortled.

'Well, I suppose it is, but it was what we called it in my day. Now the black dress is very sexy, isn't it? Let's hope the theatre does some Noël Coward and then you will have the perfect outfit. It needs some jewellery though, doesn't it?'

Dora chipped in, 'Exactly what I said, so we should go jumble-sale hunting on Saturday and pick up a bit of sparkle.'

'Good idea,' agreed Patricia. 'Now show me what else you have bought, please.'

Sally was secretly thrilled that her sister had sorted out her wardrobe for her. She knew she had no real flair and was not at all interested in fashion. She lived in a couple of pairs of trousers, a few shirts and jumpers, and a standard navy jacket for every occasion. Dora had found her some great-fitting jeans, and some lovely suede boots to go with them. 'But also handy when it gets cold with some thick tights and a short skirt,' Dora had suggested.

There was a very useful three-quarter-length wool jacket which looked great over T-shirts, and also a couple of long tops which just covered the bum, and were simple yet attractive. Dora was able to mix and match and put several outfits together for Sally with ease.

'I don't know how you are able to see these things so easily,' remarked Sally. 'Thank you, Dora, you really have been an enormous help.'

Dora turned to face her, and said in a deliberately casual tone: 'Sally, I was thinking that maybe I could see if there was a job going in the wardrobe at Crewe. I would really love to come and learn all about costumes and design. I have already applied for uni next autumn to do Business Studies, and rather than take a gap year it would be great to actually earn some money and learn other stuff, you know? Who can tell: I may even decide to be a designer instead of an entrepreneur. Shall I telephone and see what the state of play is, do you think?' Dora sighed happily. 'It would just be so great if we could work together, and get a flat or something, wouldn't it?'

Sally felt a flicker of guilt. It *would* be lovely to have Dora with her – but then again, there was a part of her that wanted to have this adventure by herself. It was her first real job and there would be so much to learn. She wanted it to be her experience, her own personal journey. Dora was so different from her. She was extrovert and outgoing and up for anything. Sally sometimes felt outshone by her sister's joie de vivre. But that was so selfish of her. How mealy-mouthed can I be? she rebuked herself.

'Yes,' she replied aloud. 'Why not ring them and see what they say.'

As it happened, things worked out rather well. Giles Longfellow's PA, Susan Chambers, explained to Dora that there was a resident wardrobe mistress called Mrs Enid Weaver who lived locally in Crewe. However, Giles had decided that he needed someone younger for this season, so he had hired a lady called Gwendoline Stewart who would do most of the work while Enid would come in twice a week to supervise. It would have been very difficult for Giles to sack Enid as she was a stalwart of the theatre, so he was treading very softly. It had been suggested that for the beginning of the season, things should be left to Enid and Gwendoline to organize, and then perhaps a few weeks later there might be a vacancy for an assistant. Would it be possible for Dora to hang on and join later?

Dora was thrilled, and as far as Sally was concerned, it was perfect because it gave her a chance to establish herself in the company and find her feet. She would be able to sort out her living arrangements with an eye to being able to offer Dora a home there eventually. But it would be *her* place. She needed to feel secure in herself, and her work, before her sister came and joined her. This way it was her territory.

Sally had thought hard about all this, and decided it was natural to feel territorial. She and Dora were very close and rarely argued, but they had never lived together since school, and certainly never worked together in such a closed environment. Sally knew from her drama-school days just how insular actors could be. They were very cliquey, and could make outsiders feel very uncomfortable. She would obviously ensure that Dora did *not* feel like an outsider – but she could only do that successfully if she was in control of her own surroundings. By the time Dora arrived, Sally hoped, she would be Queen of all she surveyed ...

Chapter 5

Sally was determined to catch up with her best friend from school while she was at home. Muriel McKinney was a teacher in a school for handicapped children, and Sally admired her enormously. She was a rare and special person. The response to her telephone call was immediate and excited.

'Sally! How fantastic to hear your voice. Where are you? How are you?' Muriel screamed down the phone.

Sally couldn't help laughing. 'God, Muriel, that voice could launch a thousand tugs! I am home for two or three weeks so we have to have a catch-up. When is a good time for you?'

'Oh, there is so much to talk about. I am getting married in December,' her friend announced out of the blue.

'Well, that has shut me up for a start. Married? How long have you known the guy? You haven't mentioned him to me.' Sally was taken aback. It only seemed like a few weeks ago that she had been talking to Muriel and discussing a girls' night out.

'Sally, you are hopeless! We have not spoken for months. I feel terrible that I have not been in touch to keep you posted, but you know what it's like with work and everything. His name is Dave and he is a folk singer with a band. In fact, he is doing a gig on Saturday night at the Hen and Chickens – remember where we always used to go? Well, he will be there doing his bit, so why not come with me and Mack. You remember Mack, don't you?' she teased.

'Oh please, come on. How *is* your hunky brother?' Sally recalled how she had always been a little flustered around her friend's big brother. Mack had seemed very moody and mysterious to a young girl like Sally. She could picture him now with his incredibly blue eyes smiling down at her.

'Doing really well. He is a successful photographer and sculptor. I know he would love to see you, Sal. Shall we meet up at the pub at seven on Saturday then, and you can vet my beloved. Not that I will listen to a bad word against him!' Muriel said happily.

'Great. I will see you there. It is so lovely to hear your voice, my dear friend. Bye!' Sally replaced the receiver, beaming with well-being. Life was good.

The rest of the week passed all too quickly as Sally put her house in order. She arranged with Douglas to drive up to Crewe on Sunday morning.

'Is that a good idea?' ventured Dora. 'We are all going out on Saturday night, don't forget. Do you want to be looking for digs with a hangover?'

'Mmmm. You have a point, sister dear. But I don't think I will have any choice. Dad won't want to spend a weekday up there, will he? I will just have to practise self-control.'

In fact, Saturday night proved very jolly, and not at all as raucous as it might have been. Dora didn't join them at the pub in the end as she decided to go to the movies with an old friend. (Or a new beau, if the truth be known!) So Sally met

Muriel and Dave and the lovely Mack in the Hen and Chickens by herself. It was strange to be back on her old turf having a night out like normal folk. Sally always distinguished people who were not in the acting profession as normal. Actors were a breed apart, and a group of them together was like a flock of starlings continually screeching and pecking and jostling for position. Sitting in the pub that Saturday night was pleasantly soothing, and Sally felt very relaxed. Mack was good fun and very attentive. It almost felt like a date.

'So, what do you think of Dave?' Mack asked when Muriel had gone to the cloakroom.

'He seems very nice,' Sally replied truthfully. 'Why do you ask? And Muriel seems very happy.'

'Well, he *is* my future brother-in-law, so I have a vested interest in the success of the romance.' Mack got up to go to the bar. 'Another cider?'

'Yes, please.' Sally passed him her glass and watched him lope off to get the drinks. He really was very attractive – and such a lovely man, she thought to herself. How good would it be to find someone like him to share things with? But she knew it was pointless even considering a relationship while she was pursuing her goals in the theatre. She was going to need every ounce of concentration to do a play every two weeks, and work on the stage management team. At drama school they had had a few classes on stage management, but nothing much. The biggest challenge had been to build a set to scale with all the scenery and furniture. It was fun, but no one took it very seriously. Certainly Sally herself had never expected in a million years that she would be employed as an Assistant Stage Manager, for goodness sake! Like most actors her ego was sufficiently healthy that she had assumed she would be playing roles, not making props.

'Penny for them?' Mack startled her as he sat down and put the drinks on the table.

'Oh blimey, you gave me a fright. I was miles away,' Sally told him.

'In sunny Crewe, by any chance?' he asked.

'Yes, as a matter of fact. How did you guess?' Sally asked, taking a sip of her cider.

'Well, I do know you a little bit, Miss Thomas, and as I recall you are a very committed young lady. Therefore I would imagine that you are already trying to work out what it is all going to be like up there.'

Sally grinned sheepishly. 'Well, yes, I am a bit distracted. Sorry, but it is all rather scary.'

'Of course it is, but you will be great. By the way, have you got a spare hour next week for me to do a photo and a piece about you? The local rag is very keen to support their first true celebrity.'

'Oh, please don't embarrass me!' laughed Sally. 'I am hardly anything near that status. But I would love to do the article with you. Thank you for putting it together.'

Their conversation was halted by the opening number of the band and Dave's voice filling the room. He was rather good actually, and Sally looked round to see where Muriel had got to. She spotted her at the front of the stage, joining in the chorus with great gusto.

By the end of the evening, Sally was singing along to 'Come On, Irene' the big hit by Dexy's Midnight Runners. It was the perfect end to a great night. They all ended up in the local Indian and then Mack offered to walk her home.

'Shall I ring you Monday, to set up our photo opportunity?' he asked as they reached Sally's front door.

'Yes, that's fine, but could you make it at the end of the afternoon because we might not be back from Crewe?'

'Sure thing. Maybe we could go and get something to eat afterwards if you fancied it?'

Sally was suddenly very aware of Mack's lips. They seemed very kissable. How much did she want him to kiss her? Before she could answer that question, Mack had pulled her to him and was giving her the answer. He tasted so good despite the curry and beer.

She returned his kiss with more passion than she had intended. Finally they broke apart.

'That was very unexpected,' said Sally breathlessly.

'Not for me. I have been longing to do that all night, Miss Thomas. However, I know you have to get up early so I won't detain you. I look forward to Monday.' He winked, then turned and walked away, leaving Sally in a bit of a tizz.

She let herself into the house, went to the kitchen to make a cup of tea and sat at the table there to gather her thoughts. Why did this have to happen now, on the eve of her big adventure? Here she was, going off into the unknown to seek her fortune – and all she could think about was her next date with Mack. Maybe it was because he seemed so solid and secure and she was feeling the exact opposite. Sitting here now in the family kitchen, surrounded by all the familiar objects from her childhood, the girl was aware of just how much her life was about to change – and she had little choice in which way it would turn.

'What will be will be,' she sighed, as she switched off the lights and tiptoed up to bed. Roll on tomorrow – and let the play begin!

Sally was up early on Sunday morning and doing breakfast for everyone when her father appeared in the kitchen doorway.

'That's what I like to see,' he said, 'enthusiasm. Good on

you, girl. We will get you sorted you out in no time.' He sat down and tucked into the eggs and bacon Sally had placed in front of him.

'Is Dora awake?' she asked. 'I wasn't sure whether she was going to come with us or not today.'

Before Douglas could answer, Dora herself came bounding down the stairs, saying, 'Course I am coming with you. I wouldn't miss it for the world. Ooh, breakfast! Did you make me some, Sally?'

Sally smiled and presented her sister with a plate of eggs and bacon.

'Oh, great! You really do cook the best "full English" in the world. If you don't make it as an actress you could always open a café.'

'Hmm, it's good to know I have a talent for something,' replied Sally, finishing her mug of tea and clearing up the pans. 'Where's Mother this morning? Is she still in bed?'

'Good Lord no,' snorted Douglas. 'She has gone off to teach a water-colour class. She sent her love, wishes us luck and says she will see us back at the ranch. Come on then, girls, we had better get a move on or we won't make it up to Crewe before lunch.' He swiped his plate with a piece of bread, devoured it hungrily and then placed the plate in the sink. 'Delicious. Thanks, Sally. See you outside.'

The girls rushed round doing the final clear-up in the kitchen, and Sally made sure she had all her addresses and phone numbers, and the maps and sheets of theatrical info she had been sent, and then they were off.

It was still early so the roads were clear, and by ten o'clock they were bowling up the M6 making good headway. It only took them about two and half hours and by ten thirty they found themselves outside the theatre.

Thank God the sun is shining, thought Sally because Crewe was certainly not the most welcoming town on a Sunday morning. The street was deserted and the theatre looked very shut, although Susan had assured her when she had rung that the stage door was always open from 10 a.m. until 5 p.m. every day.

'Let's go round to the stage door,' Sally suggested. 'You can leave the car here, Dad. Come on.'

Dora and Douglas followed Sally down the alleyway at the side of the theatre. The big red sign was still there, pointing into the doorway, and Sally pulled on the handle, relieved as it opened.

'Hello! Anybody around?' she called out.

'Hello, dearie, you must be Sally Thomas. Susan said you were coming today. Welcome.' The greeting came from a cheery, round-faced lady who filled the entire cubicle that was the stage-door entrance. 'Lovely to meet you, pet. I am Mrs Edge – Gladys – and I am mostly front of house but I fill in – you know, when needed. We all muck in here.'

Sally took her hand and shook it, saying, 'Lovely to meet you too, Gladys. This is my sister Dora and my father Douglas.'

There was no room to shake hands so Sally backed up to the outside door and let Gladys come out to them.

'Now, dearie, have you got a list?' Gladys went on. 'I can give you some recommendations if you like, but the trouble is, most of the good stuff has gone. We have a couple of leading actors who come back every year, you see, and obviously they take the same places each time. Let's look at your list.'

Sally handed her the digs list which she had marked up herself with possible addresses near the theatre. Gladys peered at it.

'Well now, I can tell you straight away, luv, none of these are

any good because they are either taken or no longer available.'
She looked up and saw Sally's face drop. 'No, don't despair.
'Cos I knew you was coming, I have had a ring round, and
there are a couple of "possibles". Would you like a flat eventually, do you think? Because there is a very nice
two-bedroom up near the station. It's only fifteen minutes'
walk away, and the lady who owns it is very decent and won't
overcharge, and she prefers females. She has got someone until
October, but if we can get you in a room until then that
would suit, wouldn't it, dearie?'

'That would suit perfectly, Gladys. You see, my sister Dora
here is hoping to come and join me in October, so it couldn't
be better.'

'Can we go and see it now though, do you think?' chimed
in Dora, who was hovering excitedly.

'Well, I can ring her and see,' said Gladys. 'I have also got
the number for a room in a house in the next road. I don't
know the people, but you could go and see it now while I sort
out the flat.'

'Sounds like a plan,' joined in Douglas. 'But before we set
off, do you think I could use a toilet, Gladys? It has been a
long drive this morning.'

'Of course, dearie. Silly me, I should have offered you the
convenience sooner. Go in and follow the passage down and
round the corner. Do you girls want the Ladies?' Sally decided
she had better go in case the opportunity did not arise again,
and left Dora to Mrs Edge's administrations. By the time she
returned, Dora seemed to have the whole plan down pat.

'Right. The landlady of the flat can see us this afternoon
about two, and the room round the corner is available to see
now – so shall we do that, and then go and have a coffee or
something and look round the town?'

'Absolutely. Thanks so much, Gladys, for your help. What is the address again?'

'Number 2, Stanley Terrace – it's the next road on the left and the lady's name is Mrs Blacklock. I have no idea what it's like, mind. But if it doesn't suit, come back here. I have got one more suggestion up me sleeve.' She winked and went back to her guard duty.

The Thomases set off for Stanley Terrace.

'You can see this used to be a miners' town, can't you?' remarked Douglas. 'Rows and rows of back-to-backs. It is a unique landscape to Britain and completely different from the south, eh?'

Sally was feeling a little apprehensive. These houses were so tiny. They could only be two up two down, and the thought of sharing with complete strangers was daunting.

They found number 2 and knocked on the front door.

A dog barked, and a second later the door opened and a short bald man stood filling the narrow doorway.

'Aye?' was all he said.

'Oh hi, I am Sally Thomas. I believe Gladys at the theatre called you about me coming to look at a room here? I hope this is not an inconvenient time or anything. I mean, we can come back later if . . . ' Sally was rapidly running out of steam as she met the relentless grimace of the man, and now behind him a huge Alsatian dog was panting eagerly. Sally was not awfully sure if it was panting with delight or hunger!

'Oh, right. Aye, the wife said. She deals with all that. Come in, luv. Get back, Fred, out the road. Nora, come here.' He stood back to let Sally in, and she tentatively squeezed between the doorjamb, and Fred's dribbling jaws, into the front parlour. Dora followed with no qualms at all, and Douglas was left on the doorstep neither in nor out.

'How do you do. I am Douglas Thomas – Sally is my daughter.' Douglas held out his hand and the bald-headed man looked confused.

'Eh, we don't stand on ceremony here. Come in and sit thissen down. I am Arthur Blacklock. Fred – out to the back wi' thee.' He shoved the drooling dog through the parlour and out of a door on the other side of the room. Douglas inched his way into the room and joined his daughters on the hearth-rug. They could just about all fit in the room. There was an open fire made up ready to go, and two huge chairs either side covered in an array of antimacassars. In the far corner under a 1950s standard lamp was a folding table with two chairs and a bowl of plastic flowers on top. The door leading to the kitchen was shut to keep Fred out, so it was very dark in the room, and the three of them could hardly make out Nora as she appeared at the bottom of the stairs to greet them.

'Goodness, what a crowd! We have not seen the like of so many people in here since me mam's wake.' She laughed. 'I shall put the kettle on and we can have a chat. Which one of you is the young lady who wants the room?'

'Oh, that's me,' said Sally, holding out her hand. 'Pleased to meet you, Mrs Blacklock. This is my father Douglas Thomas, and this is my sister Dora. I am sorry, we didn't mean to invade you like this on a Sunday morning, but I am very keen to find somewhere to stay before the season starts.'

'No worries at all. Why don't you sit down where you can and I will get some tea. Arthur, where have you got to? Get the kettle on, will you?' She opened the door to the kitchen and Sally could see through to a back yard, where Arthur was sitting with Fred smoking a cigarette.

'Oh, you are useless! Stay out the road then and let me get on with it.' Nora went to the sink and filled a kettle. There was an old-fashioned range affair for the cooker, red tiles on the floor and a fine example of a Victorian kitchen sink. Sally felt as if she was in a chapter of a D.H. Lawrence novel. Any minute now, a swarthy miner would appear and start to wash himself at the window. She should be so lucky! Thinking about baths though, where the hell was the bathroom here? And indeed, was there even one?

'Um, Mrs Blacklock, before you go to all the trouble of making tea, would you like to show me the room? I don't have much time today as my father has to get back to Cheltenham, so if we could see the room that would be great,' she said politely.

'Oh yes, of course, my dear. How stupid of me. Well, follow me then. It is not much, I grant you, but it is clean, and I am happy to cook you an evening meal as well as breakfast.' The kindly woman made her way back to the stairs and up they went to a tiny landing, off which were three doors.

Mrs Blacklock threw open the far door with a flourish to reveal what could only be described as a large cupboard. There was the tiniest of windows, letting in a glimmer of hope for the inhabitant who would be sat literally under the window-ledge on the single bed pushed up against the wall. On the other side there was just room to squeeze between a pine wardrobe with no handle, and a bedside table only big enough to hold a single lamp. Sally's heart sank. It was everything she had dreaded and more.

'Is there a bathroom?' she whispered.

'Oh yes, though we would have to organize when you had a bath because of the water-heater. Would twice a week suit, do you think?' The lady of the house was now standing in the middle of a piece of cracked lino beside a free-standing tin bath wedged against a basin, barely clinging to the brackets that held it to the wall. 'The toilet is downstairs in the back yard. We keep meaning to get round to doing something about bringing it in, but it is what we are used to really.'

Sally caught Dora's eye and had to cough to cover her near-outburst of the giggles. Could this be real?

'Um, right. Well, thank you very much, Mrs Blacklock, for showing me round. I think the best thing is for me and my family to go away and have a think, and we will get back to you this afternoon. Is that OK?'

'Yes, if you like, love.' Nora did not seemed bothered one way or the other. Dora was already out of the door, and Douglas was steering his eldest eagerly towards the light.

'Come along, Sally, we must get on,' he was waffling. 'Goodbye, Mrs Blacklock, regards to Mr Blacklock.'

As the door of number 2 closed behind them, the three of them were almost bent double with laughter, trying to put as much distance as possible between them and the house of horrors.

'Oh dear, I cannot believe what I have just witnessed,' groaned Douglas. 'What in hell's teeth was that all about, Sally? Are you seriously telling me that you actors live in these places?'

Sally and Dora were holding onto each other for support. In fact, their hysterical laughter was very nearly tears as far as Sally was concerned. Was this going to be her fate?

'Oh Dad, please don't! I don't know, do I? What on earth am I going to do?'

Chapter 6

The trio found Gladys back in the alleyway, now ensconced in her chair outside. The morning had blossomed into a perfect summer's day, with a clear blue sky and a slight breeze gently moving the August heat across the rooftops. Gladys had her skirt rolled up and was exposing quite a large amount of very white leg to the sun's rays, while negotiating a bottle of stout in one hand and a folded *Sunday People* on her lap. A small table stood to one side on which was a large plate of pie and chips.

'Back again, luvs? How was it then?' she asked.

'Not really big enough, I am afraid,' replied Sally. 'They were very nice and everything, but I wouldn't have felt comfortable sharing their home at such close quarters.'

'I understand, dearie. Those terraces can be really poky, I know. Not like down south, is it?' she added. 'When I first come up here I couldn't get me head round it either. It was like being in *Coronation Street*. I'm from Dagenham, see? Cars to coal. Met my old man on a day trip to Blackpool and ended up here. Anyway, enough about me, you'll be needing another plan.'

'We don't want to ruin your Sunday morning completely,' said Douglas, 'but if you have any other suggestions we would be very grateful.' The three of them stood in front of Gladys expectantly. She hauled herself out of the chair and waddled in through the stage door, returning almost immediately with a number on a piece of paper.

'Here you go. Ring this number and see if they can help. You know Susan, Mr Longfellow's PA?' Sally nodded her head in acknowledgement. 'Well, her niece Janie is coming to work at the theatre this season front of house, because her boyfriend is an actor, and he has got a job in the company. Can't remember his name but he seems like a nice enough lad. So anyway, Susan has got them a little house up the hill behind here. I believe it has two bedrooms, and she did say to me that they would have to rent out the other room to help with the rent. If you ring this number, it is the niece's home and you could have a word. She doesn't live in Crewe but I know they are coming down next week to move stuff in ready to start at the beginning of September. Go in and use the theatre phone now – see if you get any joy. I will eat me pie, if you don't mind, duck, before it gets cold.'

She sat down again and lifted the plate off the side table and proceeded to devour the contents.

'Oh yes, please, do carry on. Thank you so much.' Sally turned to the others. 'Shall we go and find somewhere to sit and have a drink or something and ring this number?'

'Well, you might as well do that here first, as the phone is right there,' Dora reminded her. 'Come on, give me the piece of paper.' She took it from her sister and disappeared into the gloom.

'I'll wait here,' Douglas said. 'Go on, dear.'

Dora had already dialled the number as Sally joined her.

'Give it to me,' said Sally, leaning across and grabbing the phone.

'Patience!' admonished Dora, annoyingly.

Before they could start bickering, a voice at the other end of the line answered, 'Hello? Nantwich 7451.'

'Oh hi, sorry to bother you on a Sunday morning but I have been given your number by Gladys, at the stage door of the theatre in Crewe. Are you Susan's niece, Janie, by any chance? I am so sorry – you must think me very rude.' Sally was trying to squeeze closer to the telephone while Dora was enjoying being obstructive. A small shove and Sally gained the advantage, leaving Dora no option but to get out of the way. She disguised her defeat by pretending to show enormous interest in the faded black and white photos pinned all over the back wall of the cubicle.

'No, not at all, that is fine. Yes, I am Janie Bell, Susan's niece. How may I help you, Miss . . . ?'

'Thomas – Sally Thomas. Well, I am an actress and I am starting the new season at Crewe in two weeks' time and my father has driven me up here today to try and find digs. So far it has been a bit of a disaster, but Gladys on the stage door has just suggested I might try to talk to you, as I believe you and your boyfriend are coming to join also, and have a house with a possible spare room. I would be so grateful if you might consider letting it to me.'

'Well, we haven't really got that far yet but I could talk to my bloke and my aunt, and call you back. Have you got a number?'

Sally tried not to sound too pushy. 'Well actually, I was wondering if there was any way I could see your place today, while I am here in Crewe, because we have to drive back to Cheltenham later today, and then I won't be back until we start. I am just so worried about having somewhere to stay, if you can see what I mean. It is my first job and I am a bit nervous.' Sally caught her sister making boo hoo signs and pretending to cry.

'Go away!' mouthed Sally.

There was a pause the other end of the line and then the sound of a hand being placed over the receiver. Sally held her breath. Eventually the line cleared and a new voice came on the receiving end.

'Hello, Sally? This is Susan Chambers here. I know we have talked on the phone, and corresponded, and I hope you are not having too difficult a day. Janie has just explained the situation to me and I have assured her that I think it would be quite all right for you to go and see the house. Gladys has a set of keys. Are you with anyone?' she asked.

'Yes,' replied Sally, 'my father and my sister Dora. That would be brilliant if we could. I mean, we can ring you later to discuss rent, et cetera, but if I could at least get an idea of the place it would help so much.'

'I quite understand,' the woman replied. 'Call us when you have been to see the house. Good luck.' The line went dead and Sally breathed a sigh of relief.

She then turned to Dora with, 'Why do you have to be such a pain! This is important to me. You are always so quick to take the mickey.'

'Oh, keep your hair on, sis,' retorted Dora, unbothered. 'Come on, let's get on, I am bloody starving.' They got the keys from Gladys, and the address, and set off up the hill towards the station. It was not far, and Sally's spirits rose as they turned into a well-maintained street with a row of Victorian houses. The latter were noticeably larger than the previous terrace, though not huge by any means.

'This looks more like it,' commented their father as he turned the key in the lock. They all stepped gingerly over the threshold, feeling like intruders.

'Hope there are no squatters lurking,' whispered Dora.

'Trust you to think the worst,' Sally whispered back.

'Why are you whispering, girls?' Their father's voice resounded round the room and made them both jump.

'Oh, Dad!' they shouted in unison.

He laughed and turned on the light, revealing a delightful room, simple and welcoming, with a small sofa and dining table and chairs in the corner. There was a gas fire with a new rug in front of it. Someone had cleaned it all and painted it very recently. A door led into the kitchen, which was bright and airy, containing a cooker, sink and kitchen table and chairs. Unlike the last house they had visited, this was clean and light and more spacious. In the back yard was a tub of flowers which had recently been watered.

They moved back into the living room and went up the stairs to the landing. It was similar again to the other house but this time, thank God, the door to the bathroom revealed a reasonable-sized room with bath, basin and toilet – maybe not exactly Habitat, but perfectly decent. They examined the two bedrooms and it was obvious which one was for the lodger, although it was still larger than the last disaster, and so much more pleasant.

'Oh, I could make this lovely!' exclaimed Sally. 'And there is more than enough room to sit in here at night. It would be great if I could get an old telly though.' She threw a sideways glance at her father.

'We will see what we can do,' he muttered.

'It's perfect,' agreed Dora. 'And anyway, it's only until I get here, then we will have our own flat.'

'Oh yes, of course,' said Sally. 'Once *you* arrive, everything will be just fine and dandy, won't it?'

'Stop it, you two,' ordered Douglas. 'Come on, let's go and get some lunch. It might improve your tempers.'

'So what's the plan then?' asked Dora as they made their way down to the city centre. 'We go and see our flat after lunch, and then go back to the stage door and ring Susan?'

'"Our flat"' – what are you like?' said Sally. 'Well, yes, OK, let's do that. Agreed, Dad?'

'Absolutely,' responded Douglas. 'Now for heaven's sake, let's get something to eat!'

The town centre offered them very little. There was a market square around which clung the usual suspects – Woolworths, Smiths and Boots. There was hardly a soul in sight, and not a café or restaurant to be seen. They finally found a pub up a narrow alley which boasted Sunday lunch for £1.50. Douglas went to the bar while the girls found a table. It was quite busy, and there was a darts match going on in the corner which was attracting great speculation from the regulars. A few gave the threesome a sideways glance, and a nod and a smile.

'Natives seem friendly enough,' commented Dora as she smiled back.

They ordered roast beef and Yorkshire pudding and settled back to watch the action. The landlady arrived a few minutes later with their order.

'Hey up, chuck, here's yer dinners.' They were confronted with the biggest Yorkshire puddings they had ever seen in their lives.

'Oh my goodness, that is *huge*!' gasped Sally. 'How on earth am I going to eat all that?'

'Aye, we like 'em big up here,' said the landlady proudly.

'That's fuel, that is. You get that little lot down yer, and you'll keep goin' all day. Enjoy.'

Dora was in fits of laughter as she tried to tackle the basin of batter atop her pile of beef.

'It's a like a Desperate Dan cowpat!' she squealed, as gravy oozed over the side of her plate. 'Oh help! It's going everywhere.' She managed to shove a forkful into her mouth, and was rendered speechless for the next five minutes as she worked her way through her plateful. All three of them had to concentrate hard to achieve inroads into their meals.

Finally Douglas wiped his chin and said, 'Well, I have to say that was delicious. I have never tasted Yorkshire pudding like that in my life, and the beef just melts in your mouth.'

'Absolutely,' agreed Sally. 'I won't go hungry up here, will I? Even if I can only afford one meal a week, this is all I need.'

They finished their food, complimented the chef and promised to come again. They had instructions from the landlady on how to reach the flat and set off. It was now two o'clock and Douglas was hoping to get away by four. They walked back up the hill, passing their car and the theatre. There was no sign of Gladys.

'Maybe she is having a nap inside,' said Sally. 'Let's hope she doesn't shut up shop before we get back.'

As they approached the road to the station there were a few more signs of life. A couple with a push-chair were wending their way towards the park to the right of the station entrance. A group of kids were kicking a football around, and there was a family eating hamburgers on a bench. The sounds of the station came wafting across on the breeze and Sally remembered her arrival, that hot day in July, for her audition.

'The station is enormous, you know,' she remarked to no

one in particular. 'It is very beautiful in an iron kind of way.'

Dora snorted. 'What does that mean, an iron kind of way?'

'Well, it is an amazing building almost like a cathedral, with huge iron girders like arches above the lines. It is quite famous, isn't it, Dad?' Sally turned to her father.

'Oh yes. It is a famous Victorian construction and when the railways were being built, Crewe was very much at the centre of it all. Everybody changed trains at Crewe. Now come on, girls, let's get a move on. I reckon it is this road on the left.' Douglas strode off towards a block of shops on the corner of a square at the side of the station.

Sure enough, they arrived at the door of number 7, Ridgeway Road. Next door was a shop selling all things to do with needlework.

'Oh, this could be handy for you, Dora,' said Sally.

'What do you mean?'

'Well, you will be needing supplies for your job in the wardrobe, won't you?'

Dora didn't look very convinced. 'I suppose so,' she said.

There were half a dozen shops in the parade – a newsagent's, a little tearoom at the end, an insurance office and what looked like a travel agent, and a shop selling second-hand clothes.

The door opened to the turn of the key and they made their way to the upstairs flat, having picked up the usual pile of junk mail from inside the door.

'Is someone living here at the moment?' asked Dora.

'Yes, I think so, but Gladys said they are away for the week-end so hopefully we won't find anyone at home. That would be embarrassing, wouldn't it?'

At the top of the stairs was another door which had a Yale lock. Douglas started to open it.

'Maybe we had better knock first, just to be sure there is no one here?' Sally said anxiously.

'Good idea,' answered her father and he knocked briskly. After a couple of minutes he opened the door and popped his head in, calling out, 'Is there anyone at home?'

Dora had a fit of the giggles and Sally sighed with impatience.

'Oh, do come on, Dora, you are being pathetic. What's the matter with you?'

'It's like *Goldilocks and the Three Bears*,' the girl laughed. 'We three bears are back from the picnic and someone's been sleeping in our beds!' This set her off again. Sighing, Sally left her to it and followed her father along a corridor to the end where he was already opening doors and examining cupboards.

The room at the end was the living room – a huge room with one side all windows. The view left a bit to be desired though, as it overlooked the shunting yards at the back of the station, however, it held a certain quaint interest. The furniture was old and a bit shabby, but clean. There was carpet on the floor which could do with a bit of Shake n' Vac, and some new curtains wouldn't go amiss, thought Sally. However, in the main, there was a nice atmosphere, and it was lovely and light and airy.

Dora had arrived in the room and announced, 'This is lovely, sis! We can do things with this.'

The girls left their father investigating the meter in the corner of the room and went to find the bedrooms, which were in a row off the long corridor. The first bedroom was like the front room, a large, airy space with a huge double bed and big walnut wardrobe. The curtains were in need of attention and the rug at the bottom of the bed was faded and bedraggled, but there was nothing that couldn't be fixed. The second room was only slightly smaller; it too had a double bed and a wardrobe and chest of drawers. Both rooms overlooked small gardens leading to the next row of houses in the road beyond. It was very quiet.

'This is great, isn't it, Dora?' said Sally. 'It will suit us perfectly.'

Their father joined them and agreed it was a find. 'We need to make sure you can afford it though, Sally,' he warned. 'Come and see the kitchen and bathroom and then we must go.'

The bathroom was a big room as well, functional rather than fashionable, but so what? The kitchen was very 1960s, with lots of Formica-topped cupboards and plastic handles, but all perfectly clean. There was a cooker and even a washing machine!

They locked up and set off back to the theatre, Sally desperately trying to work out how much it would all cost.

'Listen, don't fret, we will sort it all out,' Douglas reassured her.

They arrived back at the stage door just before four o'clock, and were relieved to find Gladys back in her corner, no doubt refreshed from her nap.

'Any luck?' she enquired as Sally handed her back the keys.

'Oh, Gladys, the flat was perfect. I love it. I just wish I could move in straight away. But the other little house is lovely too, and I would definitely like to rent a room there with Janie. Is it OK to use your phone again and call Susan so I can confirm things before I leave?'

'Course you can, dearie. There you go. Have you still got the number? That's it then, get to it. Now would you two like a cuppa while you wait?' She turned to Douglas and Dora in the doorway.

'Ooh, yes please,' said Dora. 'I could really do with a cuppa. Thank you, Gladys.'

Sally dialled the number and waited, crossing her fingers.

'Hello, Nantwich 7451.'

Sally recognized Susan's voice. 'Susan? It's Sally Thomas here, from the theatre.'

'Oh yes, hello again. How did it go?' Susan asked.

'Oh, it's perfect,' said Sally. 'I would so love to take a room if it's possible. Is Janie still up for it?'

'Yes, I know they both decided they would have to have an extra person to share the rent. Now do you know the terms?'

'No, I know nothing at all.' Sally held her breath for the umpteenth time that day.

Giles's PA gave Sally all the details.

Sally signalled to her father to come and see what she was writing down. He did a few calculations and nodded his approval. Sally turned back to the phone.

'Hello, Susan? Are you still there? That would be fine. Do you want a deposit? I can send you a cheque if you like.'

'Yes, that's a good idea. Send a month's rent in advance, and address it to me at the theatre, and I will post you a receipt. You have got my number, and if you need to ask any further questions you can ring me. I know you and Janie will get on well, and Pete is very easygoing. I am so pleased things have worked out and I look forward to meeting you on the twelfth of September.'

Sally put the phone down and did a little dance for joy. 'Oh, that is great! I am so relieved I have found somewhere. Thanks so much, Dad. You are a star!' She hugged her father and they went into the alleyway to find Dora and Gladys demolishing a large packet of chocolate digestives.

'We're so grateful, Gladys, for all your help. Just one last thing and we will leave you in peace. How do I secure the other flat for October?'

'Oh, you can leave all that with me, dearie,' said Gladys comfortably. 'Miss Morris is an old friend. I will talk to her and explain everything, and she'll be in touch.'

'How do you know she'll approve of me?' asked Sally.

'Oh, she'd love you, dearie. Well brought-up girl like you.' This last comment elicited a snort of derision from Dora, who was stilled by a black look from her sister.

'Well, if you are sure, that would be fantastic. I can't thank you enough. I will make it up to you, I promise,' Sally added.

'And *I* will be here in October to help you as well,' added Dora self-importantly. 'I will make sure you and me eat cake all day long, Gladys.'

'Goodness me, pet, that won't do me any good at all. But bless you for thinking of me. So you had better all get going now. I have to shut up shop and get home to cook my Ronnie's tea.'

'Yes, of course. We are so sorry to keep you. Take care, and we will see you in a couple of weeks.' Sally gave the large woman a big hug and they left her at the stage door waving the biscuits at them by way of farewell.

They climbed into the car as the sun was beginning to dip behind the rooftops, casting long shadows on the cobbled street.

'I like it up here,' announced Dora from the back seat. 'What it lacks in boutiques it makes up for in heart, don't you think?'

'Oh yes,' agreed Sally. 'It seems so friendly that I'm really looking forward to moving here. And quite frankly I won't have any time or money for boutiques. It's going to be really tough doing a new play every two weeks, as well as learning the lines and doing all the stage management stuff they are going to throw at me.'

'Well, it is what you wanted,' said Douglas, 'and you will give it your best shot, Sally, you always do. Now let's get home to your mother and a second Sunday dinner!'

Chapter 7

The days flew by as Sally gathered herself and her belongings together. Dora was fantastic and made it her mission to provide her sister with even more clothes, to create the most comprehensive wardrobe she could find. Sally gained several more pairs of trousers, one pair of which was velvet, two jackets, three shirts and two pairs of court shoes.

'God, I will never wear these!' Sally shrieked as she wobbled round the shoe shop.

'You may not, but lots of characters in your plays will, dopey,' replied Dora. 'Just think of all those young ladies who need rescuing in those Agatha Christie dramas.'

'You are so right,' Sally said. 'I suppose I was thinking more along the lines of Shakespeare and Chekov. But of course, we will be doing farces and thrillers, won't we?' She sighed and handed the shoes to the assistant, saying, 'Thank you, I'll take these.'

Dora also excelled in the sewing department and she made Sally two beautiful evening dresses using patterns similar to the dresses they had seen in the vintage shop. The girls had decided to go back to Jackie and return the dresses they had originally bought, and use the money to buy some costume jewellery. Dora had promised that she would liaise with Jackie once she was working at Crewe and knew a bit more about the budgets and what might be required. Sally ended up with a black satin sheath dress that made her look really slim and very sexy!

'Oh my, look at you,' said her mother admiringly. 'This is a new Sally I am seeing here.'

'Oh Mum – don't, please, it is embarrassing and not me at all.' Sally wriggled uncomfortably and got a slap on the leg from Dora.

'Keep still or you will get a pin in your bum. Don't be so daft, Sally – you are an actress. This is half the fun, being able to dress up and be something you are not. So just shut up!'

Dora had made the second dress much more demure. Like the one in Jackie's shop, it was a 1950s-style, with a full skirt and petticoats in a gorgeous peacock blue.

'Dora, you are amazing! Thank you so much. I could never have done this by myself.' Sally beamed at her sister.

'Well, I am pleased you appreciate me. In return, you must make sure the wardrobe department see what I can do, so they realize they can't possibly manage without me. Now give me one of those pairs of shoes we bought because I am going to dye them to match this dress.'

Sally sat down one evening with her father and they went through her finances. Her salary was modest, but there'd be enough to live on. There was only one more favour to be asked. A TV!

'Well now, young lady, this is a bit of a luxury, but your mother has persuaded me that you might need the company at first, and it is cheaper than going to the pub every night. So I have invested in a new portable TV for your room.' Douglas lifted a huge box up from behind his desk.

'Oh Dad, you are generous – thank you so much. I promise it will all be worth it in the end. I will make it up to you and Mother, just wait and see.' Sally hugged her father and went in search of Patricia.

'Thank you, Mum,' she said, throwing her arms around her mother's waist.

'Whatever for?' Then light dawned. 'Ah, the TV, I am guessing. Well, it is important you keep up with what is on telly, isn't it?' Patricia said gaily.

'Quite right, Mum, you are a wise old bird and no mistake.'

'Less of the old, thank you,' scolded Patricia. 'Now let's go and find you a suitcase and start putting things in piles. You know how much I like a nice neat pile.' They both laughed and went in search of bags.

Despite her days being full-on, Sally did manage to arrange a photo-shoot with Mack. She went to his studio and they spent a couple of hours taking different shots in different locations. Mack was easygoing and made her feel very comfortable.

'I usually hate having my photo taken,' she ventured as she sat on a chair in the middle of several unfinished sculptures in Mack's studio. Everything was white, even the floors, but whatever Mack had done with the lighting had suffused the whole room in a soft haze. It was very restful, and when Sally saw the Polaroids he had taken as tests, she was pleasantly surprised by how pretty she looked.

'Lighting is the most important factor in photography, I think,' Mack was saying as he snapped away. 'And not just in photography. It obviously makes a huge difference when I am painting or sculpting. I love being in this space and it changes all the time depending on the seasons.' He grinned. 'I get completely carried away in here some days, and Muriel has to come and remind me that there is a world out there.'

'I envy you your solitude,' said Sally. 'It must be wonderful to practise your art without having to rely on other people. As an actor, I need an audience for a reaction. Spouting Shakespeare in my lonely attic is not going to get me a job. I have to be out there in front of people.'

'Yes, I suppose you are right,' replied Mack. 'I have never thought about it from that perspective, although ultimately I am also reliant on someone commissioning and the public buying my work.'

'Yes, but you can create it first without a reaction from anyone. Acting requires a response – especially comedy. As an actor I also need someone objective watching over me. It is all about the director at the end of the day, especially in TV and films. Although at the theatre, the actor is the master onstage. He can rehearse for weeks and the director can give notes all day long – but once that curtain goes up, it is his domain. For those two hours he is in control. What a great feeling that is!'

Sally had risen to her feet with excitement, then realized she had ruined the pose. 'Oh, I am so sorry, but surely you have enough photos by now, Mack? Please let's go and have a drink.'

'OK, you are right. Come on, let's go and have a slap-up dinner. The paper is paying.'

Mack took her to a French bistro near the river. It was very exclusive and Sally guessed that it was also very expensive.

'I told you the local rag is paying for this,' said Mack when Sally raised an eyebrow at the prices. 'You are worth it, Miss Thomas, a potential star in the making!'

They both laughed then got down to the serious business of

eating and drinking. It was a lovely evening. Mack was so easy to talk to, and funny as well. With the rosy glow of a bottle of Beaujolais inside her, Sally was brave enough to suggest that he might like to come and visit her in Crewe.

'You could bring Muriel and Dave and make a weekend of it. See me perform even!' She giggled, thinking to herself, I can't believe I am doing this.

'I would love that,' replied Mack. 'Would it matter if I came on my own?' He was looking at her very intensely now and Sally began to feel a little warm.

'Not at all,' she said shyly.

Mack got the bill and they left, finding each other's hands as they walked home. It felt so good and so right to be there with Mack. Sally was in a state of shock. What was this all about? They stopped at the bottom of the street near her house and Mack kissed her deeply, drawing her into him. He then stepped back and held her face in his hands.

'I am going to miss you, Sally Thomas. I want to come and see you very soon, if that is OK with you?'

'Yes, please,' whispered Sally and kissed him again. She had never felt so alive. She wanted to make love to Mack so badly, but this was just not the right time. She was leaving in a couple of days and he would think badly of her, surely?'

'Mack, I want to say . . .' she began, but he put a finger to her lips.

'You don't have to say anything, Sally. I understand this is not the right time for you to start a love affair with me or anybody. But believe me, I would love to see you again and I don't want to lose this moment however fragile it may be. Let us just try to meet as soon as we can, and see what develops. You are a very special lady, Sally Thomas. I need you but your public needs you more.'

'Oh thank you, Mack!' Sally hugged him hard. 'I can't wait to show you my new life when you come up.'

Mack leaned down and planted a chaste kiss on her cheek, then turned and walked away. As Sally watched him go he turned round briefly, with a wave, and was gone.

Sally began to feel tears welling up and chided herself yet again on being foolish. She was doing what she had always wanted to do. She must not get sidelined.

'Get a grip, girl!' she told herself. 'This is what you want and you are going to make the most of it.'

By Saturday night Sally was ready to go. She had decided to catch an early train on Sunday morning even though her parents had offered to drive her. It seemed important that she made the break this end and showed some spirit.

Now as the train shuddered to a halt and a whistle pierced her dreams, Sally awoke with a start and realized she had arrived at Platform One, Crewe station. Giving a little yawn, she stood up and began to collect her bags. Excitement surged through her.

Let the adventure begin!

Act 2

Take centre stage

Chapter 8

My old man said, 'Foller the van,
And don't dilly dally on the way.'
Off went the van wiv me 'ome packed in it,
I followed on wiv me old cock linnet.
But I dillied and dallied, dallied and I dillied
Lorst me way and don't know where to roam.
Well, you can't trust a Special like the old time coppers
When you can't find your way 'ome.

'Good morning, everyone, and welcome to my wonderful world of theatre!' Giles Longfellow's voice reverberated around the theatre and bounced off the chandelier to land smack bang in the centre of the stage. Sally was reminded of her first visit to Crewe and her gaze immediately flew to the Royal Box. Sure enough, she could see the shadowy figure of their employer hovering behind a gilded pillar. He appeared like a conjuror at the finale of his act and looked down upon the assembled cast.

'Forgive my theatricality, folks, but I love this theatre, and I am determined that this season will be the best ever. I have gathered a great cast and some wonderful entertainment for the next nine months, and together we will ensure that live theatre lives on in the provinces despite the government's best efforts to curb our budget. Heather, please hand out the schedule of works while I come down and join you.' He disappeared through the curtain at the back of the box, and the company turned expectantly to Heather, the stage manager.

Sally had met her at nine o'clock that morning as she arrived at the stage door.

'Hi. I am Sally Thomas – ASM, small parts and understudy,' she had announced rather nervously. 'I am not quite sure what to do first, or who to ask for . . .'

Heather had slapped her on the back and steered her towards the stage, saying, 'Oh, well done for getting here early. That bodes well for the first day. I am Heather Rollings, and I am the stage manager here. It's my third year so I pretty much know how it all works. Come and have a cup of tea in the office and I will fill you in.'

Sally followed her down to the basement and along a narrow corridor lined with huge heating pipes. There was a door at the end and Heather ushered her into a musty room with a light bulb swinging from the ceiling and a desk with a lamp and piles of paperwork on it. A broken armchair stood in the corner next to a side table, on which was a kettle and some cracked mugs, and containers of tea and coffee. There was a half-full bottle of milk that Heather quickly emptied into a tiny basin in the corner. She left the bottle on the floor by a bin as she produced a fresh one from her rucksack.

'We waste so much milk here, but without a fridge what can I do? Tea or coffee?' she asked, filling the kettle.

'Oh, tea please,' said Sally, looking round.

'Not exactly the Theatre Royal, Haymarket, is it?' remarked Heather. 'To be honest I am hardly ever in here, as I'm too busy running round like a blue-arsed fly. Have you done any stage management at all?' She posed the question as if she already knew the answer.

'Well, I did a bit at drama school, but this is my first professional job actually and—'

'Oh crap, I thought so.' Heather cut her off. 'Sorry, Sally, but Giles does this to me every year. Hires would-be actresses to do stage management. You are not in the least bit interested in lighting or props, you just want to perform!' She threw a tea bag into a mug and banged it down in front of Sally. 'It drives me mad. There is another girl in the cast down as ASM as well – Sarah something. I just hope she is the genuine article.'

'I am so s-sorry,' stammered Sally. 'I really am. But please don't think I am not going to pull my weight. I fully expect to do my share, and I am eager to learn, honestly.'

Heather sat down at her desk and studied her for a few minutes. Sally waited for her assessment.

'Fair enough,' came the sighed response. 'At least you tipped up on time today. Let's see how we get on. Now today can go as smooth as treacle, or turn into bedlam. First thing you need to know, my girl, is all about the pecking order. But first, I'll do the tea.' She got up and poured boiling water into the mugs.

'Pecking order?' repeated Sally. 'How do you mean?'

Heather came back and took a list from her bag; she placed it between them. 'This is the cast, and it's important that you learn who is at the top of the list, and who is at the bottom. And let me tell you that very often, some of these buggers shouldn't be on any list at all!' Her good humour restored, over the next half an hour Heather took Sally through the cast, and then led her up to the stage to lay out chairs ready for the 'Meet and Greet'. Two large chairs stood in the centre, and then the smaller fold-away chairs fanned out on each side into a semi-circle.

Heather laid a cast list on the two main chairs, saying, 'These are for Peggy and Percy, our leading artistes – a couple off stage as well as on, known behind their backs as Pinky and Perky.' She snorted. 'They rule the roost, so watch out. Don't tell Peggy anything she can use against you, and keep out of Percy's way unless you are prepared to be a slave to his demands.'

'How many of the cast have been here before?' Sally asked as she put a typed list on each chair.

'Let's see … well, Geoffrey Challis has done a few seasons here. He is lovely, by the way. He has a wife and three kids and I really don't know how he makes ends meet, but I suspect his missus has money. Charmaine Lloyd was here last year. She's OK most of the time, but I get the impression she feels she should be leading the Royal Shakespeare Company. As far as I know, everyone else is a newcomer.'

'I am staying with Peter and Janie at the moment. I met them last night and they seem very pleasant.' Sally followed Heather across the stage to the pass door. Heather held it open for her, and then they both climbed the stairs to the Green Room, which was inevitably at the top of the building.

'This will keep you fit,' puffed Heather. 'I keep trying to give up the fags but it's hopeless.'

The Green Room was the heart of any theatrical company. So-called because it was invariably painted green, it was the communal dumping ground and meeting place for the actors and stage management. Here, there was tea and coffee, a kettle, a fridge and a microwave. The fridge, Heather said, was usually crammed with every type of food imaginable, from salad to Pot Noodles, to mouldy cheese. The room always had that faint aura of curry and burnt toast. This morning was no exception.

Heather went straight to the little window in the corner and opened it, saying, 'Oh God, it always stinks in here. Look at the sink! No one ever washes up the plates or anything. I am going to put up a notice for the new company, and let's try to get them to at least clear up their own mess. We have enough to do without taking that on as well. Now as you will discover, the tea and coffee need constant replenishing – it goes so fast. The management pays for that, and milk, and sometimes biscuits for special occasions, like today. First day we always have biscuits, which I have brought with me, so if you could find a clean plate and put them out, I will make a start on washing up mugs. We are about twenty today.'

'Blimey, as many as that,' said Sally, hunting for plates.

'Yes. The lighting designer comes and the designer, the wardrobe and the carpenter, et cetera. Plus we are quite a big cast, you know,' added Heather. 'Twelve, I think, and more to come later.'

By the time they had sorted out the refreshments and carried them back to the stage, the first arrivals were standing around looking lost.

'Morning, all. There is tea and coffee on the way, so please find a seat and read your production notes and call sheets,' announced Heather authoritatively. 'Sally, let's set up a table in the prompt corner – there is a socket there for the kettle.'

Sally followed her over to the corner and dumped her load, then turned back to the stage to watch the arrivals. Janie and Peter had just come in and waved in her direction. Sally went to join them.

'Morning, you two. Sorry I was in such a state last night but it was such a nightmare journey. I never thought I would make it.' Sally had, indeed, had a terrible time yesterday. Having fallen asleep as the train sped through the Cotswolds, she was rudely awakened by a very loud announcement that due to works on the line, the train was delayed. Sally was not particularly bothered as she had all day, so she decided to find the buffet car and get herself some supplies. To her horror there was a queue right down the train! Thirty minutes later she arrived at the counter only to find there was nothing left except crisps and water or wine.

'I'll have a white wine and a packet of plain crisps, please.' She took her meagre purchases back to her seat and gazed out of the window. It had started to drizzle, and the landscape was definitely no longer as pleasant. She could see two huge concrete silos in the distance, and smoke was billowing from giant chimney-stacks on the other side of the tracks, sending great white fluffy clouds into the grey mass of sky above. Like daubs of paint on a palette, she thought. Further announcements came and went, until two and a half hours later the train squealed to life and shuddered forward slowly, finally gathering speed – but not for long. Thirty minutes later the voice of doom announced from the Tannoy in a fine Black Country burr that, 'This train will shortly be stopping at Rugby. Would passengers please alight and wait on Platform Three for the next train to Crewe.'

By the time the train had spat them all out, the passengers were mutinous, but there was no one to complain to, so they fell back on each other. Sally escaped to the waiting room and found a corner seat. It was now mid-afternoon and she could see her whole day disappearing fast. She wondered if there was any way she could warn Janie and Peter that she would be late.

If they decided to go out she was completely snookered, as she had no keys. But they had no phone in the digs, as she remembered. Maybe she could ring Gladys at the stage door – but then what could *she* do? No, Sally did not want to cause trouble so early in the day; she would just trust to luck. Hearing a commotion, she looked out to see a group of irate passengers accosting a guard. She went to the door of the waiting room and opened it to listen to his excuses.

'Ladies and gentlemen, *please* let's have some calm. We are doing our best to make alternative arrangements for your onward journey. Would you kindly make your way to the ticket office where my colleague will give you details of your onward transport.'

This sounds ominous, thought Sally. She gathered up her things and joined the crowd as they crossed the platform over the bridge to the ticket office. After waiting in the queue, she finally made it to the grille where a very harassed-looking lady was taking down information.

'Destination?' she enquired curtly.

'Crewe, please,' replied Sally.

'Right, there will be a coach outside here in forty-five min- utes to take you to Crewe. Sorry for any inconvenience.'

'How long will the journey take, do you think? I am not from round here, and I have no idea where I am really.' Sally tried to smile her way into the woman's affections.

'Oh dear, well, this is Rugby so if the traffic is OK on the motorway you should be there in an hour and a half. Here's your ticket. Good luck, love.' Her parting shot to Sally came with an attempt at a smile.

Great, thought Sally. I am not going to get to my digs much before eight o'clock tonight.

In fact, she arrived on the doorstep of her new home at

seven thirty, and almost burst into tears of relief when her knock was answered, and Janie was standing there.

'Goodness – we thought you must have got lost!' the other girl cried.

'I am so sorry, but I couldn't ring you, could I?' replied Sally as she practically fell through the door with her bags. 'I have been on a train or a coach since ten o'clock this morning. Great British Rail, how do they manage it?'

'You poor girl. Here, let me take your bags and you go and sit by the fire with Pete. I expect you're starving. We have only got the basics in so far, but I can make you some cheese on toast and a cup of tea or a hot chocolate.'

'Oh, that sounds like heaven,' sighed Sally. 'Thank you so much. Hello, Pete, nice to meet you.' She leaned down to take Peter's hand but he politely jumped up.

'Sally, welcome. It is lovely to meet you too. What a bummer, eh? Still, you are here now, and Janie will have you settled in before you know it. She is a real mother hen, and I can't believe I have been so lucky to find her. She rules my life!' They sat down and let Janie fuss around them. Sally felt instantly at home, and the day's woes faded fast as she ate her cheese on toast and wrapped her hands around a steaming mug of hot chocolate.

'Have you got any idea what happens tomorrow morning?' she asked Peter. 'I am actually ASM, small parts and understudy so I am expecting to be in early doing chores, unfortunately.' She grinned. 'Not like you, Pete – a proper actor.'

'Now, we are not having any distinctions between stage management and artistes in our company. We are all in it together, aren't we, sweetheart?' Peter grabbed Janie's hand as she stood beside him and pulled her onto his lap. She let out a squeal of delight.

'Oh yes definitely, we are all in it together.' She giggled and wrapped her boyfriend's hands around her. 'I have every intention of getting myself a small part in some of the plays as well as making the costumes,' she announced. Then: 'Stop that, you wicked boy! Sorry, Sally, but he is very naughty.' She turned on his lap and kissed him full on the lips.

Sally took this as her cue to go to bed. 'Good night, guys. I will leave you to it. I need to get to the theatre tomorrow for nine, so I will creep out and see you there later. Thanks for the lovely welcome.' She made her way upstairs and left the love-birds clasped in each other's arms. They hardly seemed to notice Sally's exit.

Her little room looked so cosy as she opened the door. Dear Janie had made up her bed and put a bulb in the lamp for her. The curtains only just made it across the window but it was only a temporary home, so it didn't matter for now. She found her wash-bag and made her way to the bathroom. There was a gorgeous smell of lavender from a candle burning in a saucer on the edge of the bath. Sally would have loved a long soak but decided to wait until she had got the feel of the place and how everything worked. She cleaned her teeth and had a quick wash, then fell into her little bed and was asleep in moments.

'Sally, are you there? Come in, Houston?' Heather broke through Sally's reverie. 'Can you make some drinks, please. Our leading actors have arrived.'

'Sorry, Heather, I was miles away. No problem – I am on it.' Sally crossed the stage and took note of two larger-than-life people standing centre stage.

'Percy, my darling boy, take my bag.' The voice belonged to a large-bosomed lady with lots of jewellery swathing her ample chest. Her head was decked with a turban of exotic material. The make-up was thick but immaculately applied, and the nails were long and scarlet.

'Miss Delamaine?' enquired Sally. 'Can I get you a tea or coffee? I am Sally Thomas, one of the ASMs this season.'

'Oh hello, dear, how kind of you to ask. Yes, a white coffee with a sweetener, if possible. There should be some around from last season. If not, I have some in my bag. And do we have biscuits, or have there been cut-backs already?' She laughed and looked around for a response from her audience. Sally obliged with a chuckle and Percy let out a snort.

'Peggy, you are a card! How do you do, dear? I am Percival Hackett, leading man to Miss Delamaine's leading lady. I would like a strong white tea, please, and a glass of water for the meeting.' With that he turned with a flourish and made his way to the centre seats.

Sally went to the wings and prepared the refreshments as requested. She couldn't find any sweeteners but she put a selection of the biscuits onto a separate plate for her 'leading actors' and took them over.

'Thank you, dear girl. Put them on the floor here, would you?' Percy pointed to a spot and Sally obliged, thinking to herself that this could all end in tears. But time enough for all that. First day, just be lovely and get through it, Sally.

There was a clap of hands and all went quiet. Giles Longfellow had taken centre stage and was preparing to address his company. Sally quickly crossed to the wings and fetched him a chair which she placed to the side of him. He acknowledged the gesture with a quick smile then waved her away.

'So, ladies and gentlemen – welcome, and let us begin.'

Chapter 9

While Giles explained his plan of action, Sally sat at the edge of the semi-circle with pen and paper and, while taking the odd note, mostly concentrated on sizing up the cast. Jeremy had seemed pleased to see her, although when Giles arrived he quickly made his excuses and went off to join him. Giles was deep in conversation with a rather handsome young man called Robert, she discovered from Heather, the font of all knowledge.

'That is Robert Johnson, an actor; he has been around a couple of years and done a bit of telly. I think he is a personal friend of Giles Longfellow's as he came to work here last season and then left. I think he was having a bit of a fling with Giles – don't know much about him though.'

Sally watched as Jeremy was introduced to Robert by Giles, and the three of them had an earnest chat about something. Jeremy certainly looked the part of the young actor. He was wearing flared coral-coloured jeans and a floral shirt, and had grown his hair so he could flick it provocatively. His orientation seemed in no doubt whatsoever now to Sally, and by the way that Robert was touching his arm and leaning towards him as they spoke, she guessed it would not be long before they were very good friends. A loud burst of laughter drew her attention towards Peter, her landlord, who was joking with Simon Day and Geoffrey Challis. Simon was a real Jack the lad and seemed full of fun. He had already winked several times at Sally during the course of the morning. Geoffrey was charming, just as Heather had told her, and seemed to fit in with everyone. She did not have a chance to talk to Charmaine or Sarah until they broke for coffee, when Sarah came over to the prompt corner and introduced herself.

'Hi, I am Sarah Kelly the ASM. Can I do anything to help?' she offered.

Heather gave her two mugs of coffee and said, 'Hi, Sarah. Take these to Giles, please. This is Sally, by the way. She is also an ASM and small parts, I believe.'

'Nice to meet you,' said Sarah and went off with the coffees.

Sally took the next two mugs and asked, 'Pinky and Perky, I presume?'

Heather burst into a fit of giggles. 'Ssh! For God's sake don't let anyone hear you say that! But yes – spot on, Sally, you learn fast. I think we are going to get along. Better take some more biscuits, by the look of it. They are probably stocking up for later, or eating them now so they don't have to buy any lunch.'

As Sally was coming back for another mug or two, Charmaine Lloyd approached her.

'Hello, and what is your title in our esteemed little band? I am Charmaine, by the way,' she drawled rather theatrically.

'Yes, I realized,' replied Sally. 'I am Sally Thomas, ASM and small parts – lovely to meet you. Would you like a coffee or tea?'

'No, thanks. I don't suppose there is any Perrier water, is there? No, of course not, how silly of me. I suggested to Giles last year that he get a water-cooler thing, like the Americans have. Don't suppose that has materialized though. God, I feel depressed already ...' She wandered off across the room trailing her coat behind her like a catwalk model.

Interesting, thought Sally. Wonder if she is any good?

Giles had announced the first three productions by the end of the morning, and there was great excitement because the opening show was going to be Joan Littlewood's *Oh, What a Lovely War!* and everybody had to sing. Much to Sally's amazement she was in the production as a Pierrot and had two solo songs!

Heather slapped her on the back and feigned a disgruntled voice. 'Well, that's you out of service as far as my management is concerned. You will be faffing around singing and dancing instead of chasing up props for me.'

'Oh no, I promise I will do all my stage-management stuff as well. Please don't think you can't rely on me,' Sally assured her.

'I am only joking,' said Heather more gently. 'Don't worry, we will manage, and I think it is great you have got the songs. You must have a good voice.'

'Not bad,' said Sally modestly. She hid her true excitement for the time being. But boy, wait till she rang home and told them!

The other two productions were to be *A Man for All Seasons* by Robert Bolt, starring Percy Hackett as Sir Thomas More and Peggy Delamaine as his wife. Percy was in his element, and had already cornered the poor wardrobe mistress to discuss his many and varied outfits. Charmaine was to play the daughter, and Jeremy had the role of More's betrayer, Richard Rich.

The third production in the line-up was to be a musical version of the famous Aristophanes' play *Lysistrata*.

'This will be, in essence, a world première, ladies and gen-tlemen, so it will attract great interest, we hope. It will also be the production to launch a three-day conference that this theatre will be hosting, for the Association of Repertory Theatres throughout the UK; so an important time for us all. Now the lead in this production will be our own, very lovely Charmaine Lloyd. I would like Sally Thomas to understudy you and play one of the neighbours in the town. So you will be very busy, Sally, combining all your posts. Heather, I am sure, will give you as much help as she can, although it will be a tough one for you, Heather, as all the girls will be in the show in some form or other. Sarah, that includes you.'

Giles turned his gaze upon the young ASM who perked up considerably and said, 'Oh, that's great. I will really enjoy being part of the company. Thank you, sir.'

'So now you all have your work cut out, we will break for a quick lunch and then everyone back here for two o'clock. I will start with a musical rehearsal taken by our musical direc-tor Mr Timothy Townsend. Take a bow, Tim.' The musical director stood for his applause. He was a very unprepossessing little man with a bald head and ample paunch, which must get in the way of him playing the piano, thought Sally.

The company broke, and Sally was about to suggest a bag of chips when Heather took her arm and led her towards the cluster of folk in the corner who had not been part of the cast list as such, but consisted of the designer and lighting crew and the chief carpenter.

'There's no time to stop. You have to join the production meeting now, my girl. Though I suspect it will be held in the pub?' Heather addressed this last word to a huge man in overalls with shoulder-length hair and a fine beard and very twinkly eyes.

'Pub is right on, Heather my lass, and is this fine-looking young lady my dinner for today?' He peered down at Sally, who fleetingly felt a shiver of panic before the giant burst into a huge guffaw and introduced himself. 'Will Black at your service, chief carpenter and maker of magic. You are Sally, are you not? ASM and not so small parts, I gather. You will be a busy little bee. Come on, let's get to the pub so we can start our very important production meeting.' He gave her a big wink and turned away to the rest of the group to chivvy them up. Sally followed on feeling like Alice in Wonderland. Nothing seemed real any more.

The pub was opposite the theatre and a world away from the picturesque Cheltenham scene. This was a drinking pub and nothing else. The tables were stained and chipped, and the chairs hard and uncomfortable. There was scarcely a female in sight, as men stood shoulder-to-shoulder at the bar, their arms lifting their pints almost in unison, like some sort of tribal dance. Will caused a parting of the ways and they all followed him through to a back room.

'Fetch a few more chairs and I'll get the drinks in. Pints all round, is it?' He paused when he caught Sally's eye. 'Ah well, maybe not quite. What are you having, my dear, gin and tonic?' Sally would have given her right arm for a gin and tonic but had the good sense not to rise to the taunt.

'Pint of cider, please,' she said. 'Draught if they have it.'

Will gave one of his guffaws and disappeared into the bar. Once everyone was settled, the plans came out on the table and design took over while Sally and Heather, notepads at the ready, awaited instructions. Sally was in a complete state of giddy excitement about her roles in *Oh, What a Lovely War!* and trying to fathom out just what her duties were going to be backstage. Because they did a new production every two weeks the sets all had to be very adaptable, and Will had his work cut out to keep new ideas coming. The lighting designer had a standard rig, but subject to finance would try and give each production a little extra something. What struck Sally very clearly was just how passionate everyone was about their jobs. She began to feel a sense of pride in being part of the team. But then suddenly it was five to two and Sally had to put her actress's hat on and get back for the music call.

'I am sorry but I have to go,' she whispered to Heather.

'Yes, go on. Don't worry, we are nearly done here anyway, and when the pub shuts that is definitely the end of the meeting,' the other girl laughed. 'Go! Or you will be late and that will not look good.'

'Tell Will I shall get the next round in when I see him.' Sally rose and nipped out before anyone could pass comment. She just made it to the stage as Timothy was handing round the music sheets.

'Now I think the best way to go about this is to start with an ensemble number so we can all warm up our voices, and then I am going to listen to each one of you in turn, and put you in the correct place for your range. So please all look at the title song "Oh, What a Lovely War!"'

The company spent the next half an hour belting out the tune and feeling very uplifted.

'There is nothing like a good singsong to lift the spirits, is there?' a voice whispered in Sally's ear. It was Simon and she laughed and nodded.

Timothy was a wonderful pianist despite his paunch and was soon putting people in different spots next to each other.

'We are going to have to learn harmonies. Have any of you got tape machines? If so, I can play your harmonies for you and you can record them and learn them at your leisure.'

Robert and Jeremy put their hands up, and surprisingly, Sarah did too. The rest of them all looked a bit pathetic. Percy and Peggy laughed it off, announcing that they would pick up the tunes soon enough. Charmaine looked pained and said, 'I don't really *do* singing. Can't I just stick with the tune?'

Timothy looked a little taken aback. 'Well, that is not quite the spirit, Charmaine, but we will see how we get on. Sally, what are you going to do, especially about your solos? I won't have much time to spend with you on your own. Would you be able to get hold of a cassette, do you think?'

Sally was already thinking what to do. 'Um, yes, of course – I will see what I can do. Sorry I am not prepared. I had no idea I would be used so soon.' She looked round the room, embarrassed, feeling very unprofessional.

'Well, I understand you have a beautiful voice,' encouraged Timothy, 'so we must make use of it. Now I want us to have one more go at all the company stuff then we can call it a day, because some of you have to go to Wardrobe now, I understand.'

After the rehearsal was finished Sally went to find Heather for further instructions. It was already five thirty and she was exhausted. All she wanted to do was go back to the digs, have a hot bath followed by some baked beans on toast and go to bed – which reminded her: she would have to do some shopping on the way home, because she had bought no supplies, and could not expect Janie to cater for her again.

Heather was in her office printing out the next day's calls.

'Listen, love, you have had a long day so I won't go through all this now. Let's meet tomorrow at nine and I'll show you the schedule, et cetera. But if you wouldn't mind just handing these out to those still left in Wardrobe and pinning one on the noticeboard at the stage door when you leave, that would be great.'

'Oh thank you, Heather, so much. I must say I am knackered. I will get the milk and biscuits for tomorrow so you don't have to worry.'

'OK, but remember – no more biscuits now until the next special event. Don't spoil them. If this lot have them every day they will never appreciate the treat. Plus it will cost you an arm and a leg, and believe me you will find your wages go quick enough without feeding the five thousand.'

'OK thanks, point taken. Just milk then. See you in the morning,' Sally called back over her shoulder. She found Janie in a tiny room off the wardrobe going through baskets of costumes and said, 'You still at it, you poor thing? What time are you going to finish?'

'Oh, I am just filling in time while Pete has his fitting. He is nearly done. Shall we walk back together? I have made a stew for tonight. It only needs heating up, and we can get a loaf on the way home from the corner shop. Thank God it stays open late because we have discovered nothing much stays open in Crewe after five.' Janie closed the lid of a trunk and stretched her back.

'Oh Janie, I can't eat your food,' replied Sally. 'You can't cook for me all the time.'

'I won't, don't worry. You can cook sometimes, and Pete is pretty good at certain things. Curry, curry and curry,' the other girl laughed.

'OK, that's great. We can set up a rota. I have to buy milk for tomorrow, so I will get the bread at the same time – and how about a bottle of wine to celebrate our first day?' Sally suggested, warming to the plan.

'Good idea. Oh, here he comes, my little Pierrot. Sally, you will have to be fitted for your Pierrot costume, as we are hiring them. Do you want me to do it now while you are here?'

Sally sighed. It was the last thing she wanted to do, but needs must. 'I suppose it is a good idea to get it over with,' she agreed.

'Pete, why don't you go to the pub and we will pick you up on the way out?' Janie gave him a kiss and sent him on his way.

They went into the wardrobe and Sally was properly introduced to the wardrobe mistress Gwendoline Stewart. She looked very proper, and had big black glasses and her hair in a bun, of all things. Sally had an instant image of some man removing her glasses and taking down her hair, then ravaging her over the sewing machine. It made her giggle, which caused Gwendoline to give her a straight look.

'Something funny?' she asked crisply.

'No, sorry, I am just hysterical with tiredness. It has been a long day.'

'Huh, you think this is long, just you wait until the dress rehearsal and technical days. They are flipping murder.' Gwendoline seemed to enjoy imparting this piece of information. She took her tape measure from around her neck and started to measure Sally's waist, saying, 'Right, Janie, take down these measurements, please, then we can all go home.'

Once they were finally out of the building and making their way to the pub, Sally ventured to ask Janie about Gwendoline.

'Oh, she's OK when you get to know her. She is a bit of a goer by all accounts – at the Christmas party last year she came dressed as a Moulin Rouge dancer. I think though that normally she is just a bit shy and finds actors intimidating. I get on with her fine and am even allowed to call her Gwen. She is supposed to be second-in-command to Enid, but I think Giles feels that Enid is past it now, so he is easing Gwen in, hoping Enid won't notice!'

Sally laughed and decided she would work on Gwendoline, if nothing else than for Dora's sake, because it could be awkward for her sister if they didn't get on.

The two girls dragged Pete away from Simon, Robert and Jeremy, and trudged up the hill to their little house. The corner shop was just closing, but Sally managed to get her milk and a white sliced, and a bottle of white wine, though God knows what it would taste like. At home, Janie got the stew on and Pete helped her while Sally went and had her bath. It was heaven and she vowed to make sure there were always candles and bath goodies for them all.

They ate the stew at their little dining table by candlelight.

'Well, saves on electricity, doesn't it?' remarked Janie. 'And we all look so much prettier. This wine is hitting the spot, Sally, thank you.'

They all washed up and then made a beeline for their beds.

'So much for the sex, drugs and rock 'n' roll life of a wandering actor,' called out Peter as he switched off the landing light. 'Night night, everyone. Sweet dreams.'

But there was only silence!

Chapter 10

'Again, please, everyone.'

'Oh! Oh! Oh! It's a lovely war!'

The piano was jumping off the boards as Timothy banged out the rhythm. For three days the music rehearsals had taken over everyone's lives. Wherever one went inside the theatre someone could be found hunched in a dark corner singing to themselves, or tapping out the tune on the kettle in the Green Room. Two or three of the actors would break off in the middle of a hasty bite of a sandwich and burst into their harmonies, then fall back against the battered old sofa exhausted.

'This is ridiculous,' announced Charmaine. 'I am *not* going to be bullied like this. I am an actress, not a music-hall turn!'

Peggy, who was standing in the doorway, stopped her in her tracks with: 'Charmaine, my dear, shut up. You only have to sing the tune once. God only knows, it is obvious you are not a singer, but be grateful for small mercies and *just get on with it.*'

Sally wanted to giggle out of sheer nerves: the whole thing had become a nightmare. She had never worked so hard in her life. Not only was she trying to learn her two solos, but she was running all the errands for Heather on the props side with Sarah. The girls took it in turns to go round the town begging and borrowing whatever was needed. In fact, the props on this production were not too bad as the set was minimal. It was more a question of the actors setting the scene. The lighting was going to be important in giving each scene its own atmosphere. Sally had managed to buy a second-hand cassette machine in a charity shop, and every minute she was not working on set she was playing back her songs. Sarah had proved quite a dark horse. She seemed to know every song backwards – and all the harmonies. For a girl who professed to be committed to stage management, she was showing an uncanny interest in the show. Sally made a little note to keep an eye on her.

The whole theatre had come alive in this first week. Even the front-of-house staff seemed to appear out of nowhere. Posters went up in the foyer, and Evie in the Box Office was like the fairy on the Christmas tree. She was always immaculately dressed in something bright and sparkly, her make-up in perfect order, and her hair coiffed to within an inch of each sprayed peak, like a lemon meringue pie. People daring to pass the front doors of the theatre were somehow drawn into her web, like insects into a Venus fly trap.

In the wardrobe department, Gwendoline, Enid and Janie were lost behind lines of clothes and piles of shoes, and great mountains of black velvet used as curtains to hide the wings at the side of the stage. Huge baskets called skips filled the corridors outside.

Poor Heather was not only having to deal with the set designer, lighting rig and carpentry demands, but also the constant demands of the cast. Pinky and Perky were up in arms because their dressing rooms were not ready. Percy's over-trained vowels could be heard echoing down the stairs, 'Heather dear, I need a light in here!'

Peggy would grab Sarah and force her to drop whatever important job she was doing on the production so that she could bring the mistress a small armchair from the store.

'I have to get my feet up, darling, when I can,' she would wheedle. 'See if you can't find me a little velvet cushion to go on top, there's a dear.'

Charmaine was in Dressing Room 3 and wanted Sally to clean it from top to bottom before she would unpack.

'Honest to God, it is *filthy*, Sally. I will contract some dreadful disease if I set foot in there now. Please, can't you just spare me an hour or so and give it a good wash-down?'

Sally had sought Heather's advice on this and received a very concise answer: 'Tell Madam to Foxtrot Charlie off!'

The boys, Simon, Peter and Jeremy, were having a ball. Sally envied them their carefree camaraderie. They were up and down the stairs all day long, singing their soldier chorus. Jeremy had to be reminded every so often that he too was an ASM, and Sally would suddenly have to go and pull him out of the pub to help with the prop-building. Robert and Geoffrey stayed on the sidelines. Robert was never far away from Giles Longfellow, who would appear in the Royal Box from time to time and check that all was moving in the right direction. He had announced to the cast that first day, that he would rehearse the scenes only once the actors had mastered the songs. Timothy was on a mission for sure, and suddenly by Thursday the light seemed to dawn and the whole thing came together. It was so exhilarating to stand there and sing out in joyful harmony. Everyone clapped and hugged each other at the end of the run-through. Even Charmaine's solo sounded all right, as she had a sort of warble to her voice that was very much of the period of the First World War.

'You'd think she had created it especially,' whispered Peggy to Percy. 'Bloody woman has the luck of the devil.'

Sally had performed her two songs well, if somewhat tentatively. Timothy took her aside afterwards and gave her some suggestions.

'You have a beautiful voice, Sally – now you must add some emotion. *Act* the songs. When you sing "Keep the Home Fires Burning" we want to feel your pain, your loss. I want them to be sobbing in the stalls. With the other number, "I'll make a Man of You", I want you to be saucy and seductive. You need to twinkle more. You know the songs perfectly, so forget about the mechanics and just enjoy. Speak to Wardrobe about getting you some kinky boots or something for that second number.'

Sally was slightly miffed that somehow she was not sexy enough, and decided to have a word with Janie. She found her as usual with her head in a skip.

'Honestly, Sally, I stink of mothballs! It's my new perfume. What can I do for you?'

'Timothy has basically just told me I am not sexy enough in my number. I need some help with my costume, Janie. I know you are up to your eyes, but can you give me an idea of what I am going to be wearing?'

'Oh God, Sally, I haven't a clue. But Gwen is in the other room – we can ask her.' Frankly, Sally would rather have avoided the issue and not bothered Gwendoline, who was still a bit stand-offish as far as Sally was concerned. However, needs must.

'Hi, Gwendoline, we have a small problem with our artiste here,' breezed Janie. 'Timothy wants her sexier, and as we don't have a costume as yet, this could be a problem – though I suppose you could go on naked, Sally, and that would do the trick!'

Janie laughed throatily, and Sally felt sick at the thought. 'I am really sorry to be a pain, Gwendoline, but if there is anything I can do to help, I will. I could go and see if I could get some black boots – long ones, you know – to glam up a bit.'

Gwendoline studied Sally for a few moments and then decided. 'Yes – good idea, Sally. That would be a great help, then I will make you a sort of drum majorette-type outfit with a little soldier hat, and we will give you a cane to play with – and away you go! Oh, and get some fishnet tights as well. Can you afford all this, because I am not sure the budget will stretch?'

Sally's heart sank. More expense, but if it helped get her in with Gwendoline it could all be worthwhile, especially when Dora arrived. At least then she would have back-up and her own personal dressmaker!

'OK then, I will go out right now, and find those boots,' Sally declared. 'Tell Heather I have gone on an emergency mission.'

It was a relief to get out into the fresh air. Sally had been coming in to work every day at eight thirty and leaving after dark. The theatre was dirty and full of dust, only made worse by all the scenery-building going on. Suddenly she was walking in September sunshine, the light playing on the autumn leaves rustling above her. She could almost pretend she was out on a day's shopping spree without a care in the world. Almost. She was plonked back into reality by a shout from behind.

'Fancy a good time then, girlie?' Simon and Jeremy were descending on her with a huge plant between them. She burst out laughing.

'What is that? You idiots!'

'Please don't mock, it is very unbecoming,' pouted Jeremy. 'This is our palm tree for the camel scene.'

'But it's an aspidistra,' hooted Sally.

'It may well be, but it is all we could find at the market so bog off, Miss Noddy Know-it-all!' replied Simon. 'Look, it's green, and it will wave in the breeze so it will be fine. Just have to use your imagination. Where are you skiving off to anyway?'

'I have got to find a pair of boots for my costume as the drum majorette,' said Sally.

'Ooh, lovely! Kinky boots,' growled Simon. 'I knew you'd got it in you, Sally Thomas.'

'Oh please, give me a break,' she retorted. 'Jeremy, keep your friend under control, and don't forget, by the way, we have to pick up that chaise longue from the junk shop later. Did you manage to get a trolley from the scene dock?'

Jeremy looked crestfallen. 'Oh shit, I forgot all about it. I am so sorry, Sal. I know, I'll ask Robert if he can help me pick it up in his car. We could tie it on the roof.'

'OK, but please get it done.' She turned and left them to it.

Sally decided to make for Freeman Hardy & Willis round behind the market. She vaguely remembered seeing some boots in there in the course of her travels. This was the thing about looking for props all day long – one passed so many windows and stores, it was hard to remember what was what. She arrived at her destination and peered into the shop window. It all looked rather dismal, but nothing ventured . . .

Through the gloom inside Sally detected a young girl sitting on a bench below shelves of shoeboxes, filing her nails.

'Hi. I am looking for some black knee-high boots. Can you help me at all?' she asked.

The girl jumped up with a start. 'Sorry, what did you want?'

'Black boots.' Sally repeated the question.

'Oh right. Well, yes, we have got these really nice black-patent-leather ones. What size are you?'

'Six,' said Sally, sitting down on the bench and starting to take her shoes off.

The girl disappeared into the back, leaving Sally to ponder on why some shops put yellow cellophane in the windows to make the shop even darker. The girl returned with a large box and proceeded to unpack the promised boots. They were in fact rather impressive, thought Sally. She slid her leg into the boot and started to zip it up, only to find a gentleman kneeling at her feet, his hands deftly taking over from hers, and moving up her leg with alacrity.

'Oh, sorry – who are you?' stammered Sally, trying to gain back her leg from his grasp.

'Mr Leslie Tibbs at your service, miss. These are our top-of-the-range boot for this winter. Just a penny under thirty pounds, and cheap at the price.'

Oh blimey, thought Sally. That is a fortune.

'Actually, I was wondering if you might be able to help me a bit here,' ventured Sally. Holding her leg as seductively as she could in front of Mr Tibbs's nose, she put on her best, most dazzling smile, and whispered, 'I am an actress here at the Crewe Theatre, and we are doing this wonderful show called *Oh, What a Lovely War!* I am playing a drum majorette, and singing this big number, and it would be so fantastic if you could lend me the boots for the run of the show. The trouble is, we have so little money for costumes but this would just make my outfit perfect.'

Mr Tibbs released her leg and let it drop unceremoniously to the floor.

'Oh, I am not sure we can do that, my dear. These are expensive boots, you know. What if they get damaged?'

'Well, obviously the theatre would have insurance to cover anything like that. But I would take such good care of them, honestly. I could get you and the shop some publicity, probably in the local paper, and we would be able to give you front-row tickets for the first night and the party afterwards. I would be so grateful.' Sally forced herself to lean in close and bat her eyelashes.

'Hmm, I see. Maybe we could come to some arrangement. Local paper, you say? That would be very good for business. Very well, you find out what can be done about publicity, and I will hold these boots for you until the end of the week.'

'Oh, you are so kind. Thank you. I will go right away and sort it out.' Sally nearly kissed him, but thought better of it as she could see the twinkle in his eye at the thought of rewards from 'this actress'. She knew exactly who to contact at the local press office, as Evie in the Box Office had already instructed her on the power of the press at all times.

'Court them at all times, luv, shamelessly. We need every bit of publicity we can get. Make friends with Tommy Nuttall. He is also their photographer and the bloke is a sucker for a pretty face.'

Here I come, Tommy! Sally found him in the Crewe *Chronicle* office, feet up, having a fag.

'Well, well, to what do I owe the honour of a visit from one of the local talent? How is it going up at the dream factory?'

'Fine, thanks, Tommy. Look, I have an idea for a photo opportunity. The manager at Freeman Hardy & Willis has agreed to donate a pair of boots to me for my number in the show if he can have some publicity. So I thought it would make a nice picture if I get my costume on and he fits the boots. Bit of leg, you know?' Sally couldn't believe she was saying this rubbish!

'Well, listen to you, sensible girl. I like someone with a bit of nous about her. Yes, spot on. Can we do it tomorrow morning so I can get it in for next Wednesday's show page?'

'Well, I can try. The costume has got to be made yet. Leave it with me and I will ring you this afternoon. Have you got a number?'

'Here's my card, darling, I await your call.'

Sally practically ran back to the theatre and up to Wardrobe.

'Gwendoline, I think I have cracked it! I have secured a great pair of patent-leather boots on condition I have my photo taken with the manager of the shoe shop tomorrow morning. Can we get a costume together by then?'

Gwendoline gave a huge sigh and leaned dramatically on the door. 'Oh my goodness, to be taken for granted like this. Let me see. Very well – give me half an hour then come back and I may just have something for you, darling.'

Sally forced a smile of thanks and disappeared downstairs, thinking the bloody woman was far more theatrical than any actress in the company!

Heather grabbed her at the stage door and pulled her into the stalls. 'Where have you been? Giles was looking for you to rehearse a scene with the chorus. I lied and said you were out on a job for me.'

'Well, it was not really a lie. I was out on a job for Wardrobe, trying to get myself a costume for the show. I did ask Janie to tell you. Honestly, Heather, it is a nightmare trying to do all these different jobs at once. I am never going to get my bloody act together for the first night,' she wailed.

'Don't fret, hon. You will be fine. I promise you, when that curtain goes up you will be there dazzling the punters. Now get over to the rehearsal room and do your thing. By the way, have you had any lunch? I thought not. Here, take this Kit-Kat to keep you going.' Heather handed it to her and patted her on the back. 'Go on, get going.'

Sally chucked the chocolate gratefully down her throat and sped off to find Giles. The rehearsal room was next door to the theatre and had been a bar once, as part of the original foyer. It had just a few bulbs for lighting and some rickety chairs. The actors were all huddled round a two-bar fire.

'Aah, at last you have deigned to join us, Miss Thomas,' bellowed Giles.

'I am so sorry, Giles, I had to go and get some boots for Wardrobe. I had no idea we were going to rehearse this afternoon,' she stammered.

'Fine, leave it for now. Just get your script and we can run through the first chorus scene. It is going to be tight, luvvies, but we will get there. Now from the beginning, please.'

Sally sat down next to Jeremy, who whispered, 'Don't worry, Sal, it will all come right in the end.' And he squeezed her hand.

Sally felt like bursting into tears. She had never felt so out of control. She hardly knew what day it was, never mind what her first line in the play might be. Still, if she got those boots she had a pretty good chance of pulling off that number and showing the guys a thing or two!

Chapter 11

'Oh wow, it is amazing! Gwendoline, you are brilliant.' Sally stood in front of the cracked old mirror in the wardrobe department, transfixed by her appearance. She was staring at a sparkly, sexy drum majorette, dressed in black fishnets, with patent-leather boots to the knee, short gold hot pants, a sequinned tunic with gold tasselled epaulettes, and all topped off with a peaked helmet with a huge black feather. She turned and gave Gwendoline a hug.

'I can't thank you enough. This has just made everything possible. I will perform to the costume now, don't you see? I can't let you down after all this.'

Gwendoline was still recovering from the hug but managed a weak smile.

'Well, I am certainly glad to be of assistance, and I must say it does make a change to be appreciated. Now if you'll excuse me I must get on as I have to sew pom-poms on twelve Pierrot outfits.'

Sally went in search of Mr Tibbs from Freeman Hardy &

Willis who was waiting in the foyer with Tommy the photographer to have his photo taken for posterity.

'Oh I say!' said the shoe-shop manager, on seeing Sally's outfit. 'That is certainly eye-catching, Miss Thomas. You look splendid, and the boots finish it all off a treat.'

Tommy set up the photo with Sally seated with acres of leg and thigh on display, while Mr Tibbs knelt at her feet adjusting the zipper and smiling at the camera.

'Great shot, great shot. Lift your leg a bit more, Sally.' This last request was met with a black look from Sally who had had enough of being exploited for one day.

'OK OK, no problem,' added Tommy quickly, 'I have got the shot. Thank you very much, Mr Tibbs. This will be in the *Chronicle* on Wednesday and I will try to get it in the *Manchester Evening News* as well.'

'Much appreciated, Mr Nuttall. Thank you, Miss Thomas, for all your help, and my wife and I look forward to the opening night. Give us a wave, won't you?' He winked and was gone.

'Well, there goes a happy customer,' said Tommy, packing up his equipment. 'Well done, girl, that was a result all round. Keep it up, and you and I will make a few bob.'

Sally laughed. 'You mean *you* will. Still, it has been a good result, I must say. The boots really make the outfit. I will certainly keep in touch, Tommy, and thank you. Now I must fly or I will get the sack. See you later.'

Backstage was becoming a 24-hour hive of activity. It was as if the theatre had been asleep for months and now the light had been switched on and every nook and cranny was lit up. Sally imagined it like a doll's house. As she pulled open the front she could see every room in the place, and in each room there was a story unfolding, with each of the characters creating their own dramas within their elected spaces. The cast hardly left the theatre for the next week so they all retreated to their dressing rooms. Heather and Sally had spent a morning allocating dressing rooms, and checking lights, plumbing, radiators and electric fans. There was so much rubbish piled behind curtains and cupboards. Dust and grime curled around every knob and knocker.

'I just can't understand why Giles never spends any money on getting all this sorted,' sighed Heather, trying in vain to apply a spanner to a radiator tap. 'It's classic, isn't it? They spend thousands doing up the front of house, and gilding the lily, but completely abandon the real heart of the place and the people who work here. I can't get this bloody thing to turn. Do us a favour, can you? Go and ask Gladys at the stage door if her Ronnie could come in and repair this, and maybe her daughter Cheryl might like to come and clean for a couple of hours with a mate and earn a few bob. I can probably fiddle it from petty cash and then at least there will be some semblance of organized chaos and Peggy and Percy will shut up for five minutes. Have you been in their rooms lately? It is real home from home.'

Sally went off to find Gladys and then decided to pay Peggy a visit. The door to the dressing room was shut, and as Sally went to knock she noticed the brightly polished brass number 1 nailed in the centre of the door.

'Enter!' Peggy invited the caller in. 'Hello, darling! How is it going? Would you like a cuppa and a biscuit? I bet you haven't had time to spend a penny, never mind drink a cup of tea. That's showbiz, my dear.'

While Peggy got out cups and saucers Sally had a chance to take in the room. It was like a grotto in a circus or a carnival. Every inch of space was filled with 'stuff', from the beaded trim round the ceiling light to the fairy lights around the mirror lights. Everywhere twinkled. Goodness knows what the electrician would have to say about the safety aspect! In front of the dressing-table lights and mirror was an elaborate hand-embroidered mat covering all the tatty and chipped paintwork of the wooden dressing table. Laid out in neat rows were sticks of make-up, all of them in the original gold and black paper carefully folded down as the greasepaint was used. At drama school the students had been given a couple of lessons in stage make-up and Sally had bought the obligatory sticks of five and nine from Fox's of Covent Garden, which was the famous make-up supplier to the theatre. Five and nine were sticks of greasepaint which, when applied together, formed a base for the face. It was thick and glutinous and looked terrible close up, but from a distance and under the lights gave the face a reasonable colour and skin quality. There were hundreds of variations of colour, and depending on the kind of parts one got to play, the quantity of sticks required would vary. However, for the juvenile lead there was really just the basic five and nine plus a carmine stick which doubled as lipstick and rouge – and, as Sally discovered from Peggy, provided the dot in the corner of the eye!

'What is that?' Sally had asked one evening when she was delivering groceries to the dressing room.

'This, dear girl, is called definition. When one is playing to the gods it is vital that they see one's eyes, and this creates a point of reference.' Sally watched transfixed as Peggy applied the bright red dot to each eye. This was followed by a thick black line along the eyelid, finishing in a tick at the edge of the eye. Greens and blues had been applied in sweeping strokes to the eyelid, each brush-stroke reaching for the outer corner of the eyebrow with alarming insistence, and joining the thick black eyebrow in its final quest to hit the hairline! Uplift was an understatement, thought Sally. The result was two huge orbs of multicoloured delight. If they didn't see that in the Upper Circle, they must be blind indeed.

Over the next few months, Sally came to appreciate that in terms of make-up, Peggy's routine was unchanging and resulted in all her performances bearing the same basic look – that of an aging Cleopatra. It worked fine for most of the time, but when she came to play Sir Thomas More's wife in *A Man for All Seasons* it was down to Percy to quietly take her aside and suggest she wipe it off immediately! To her credit she did as she was told – all but for the red dots. Some things would never change.

'Here's your tea, love.' Peggy broke through Sally's thoughts, and she took the cup.

'Gosh, Peggy, this room is miraculous. You've completely transformed it. Do you do this wherever you go?'

'Do what, darling?' asked Peggy, sitting down in front of her mirrors.

'Well, bring all this stuff with you. I mean, you must have so much to haul around with you all the time.'

'Oh, I couldn't travel without my things. This is my life, darling. You will soon come to realize that an actress's dressing room is her real home. This is my sanctuary. As long as I am surrounded by my bits and pieces, I feel safe. Percy is the same. Have you seen his room?' Peggy got up and made towards the door which led to the adjacent dressing room. When Sally had first been going round with Heather sorting rooms, she had commented on the fact that these two rooms were connected.

'Surely Pinky and Perky don't like this arrangement much, do they?' she had questioned.

'Ah well, hereby hangs a tale,' replied Heather. 'These two

rooms were originally just Dressing Room number one. In the old days the leading actor was often also the actual manager of the theatre and the company, so he had the big plush room. Apparently there was one season where the two leading actors both thought they were entitled to Dressing Room number one, and it got so heated that a compromise had to be found. So they split this into two and put the actors' names on the doors rather than numbers. So everyone was happy.'

Sally watched Peggy now as she moved to open the connecting door. What did Percy make of that? she wondered.

'Actually maybe we had better not intrude into his room while he is not there.' Peggy stopped suddenly and turned back to Sally. She looked sheepish. 'I mean, here's me going on about an actor's dressing room being his sanctuary, and I am about to invade the privacy of a fellow artiste. No, you will have to wait and ask Percy yourself to show you his bits.'

Peggy returned and took up her place again in front of the mirror.

'Now where were we? Oh yes, my things. Well, as you can see, I have collected from all over the place. Those little bells hanging over the lampshade came from China, you know. I had a dear friend who sent them to me. All the ornaments have a meaning. Mostly they are First Night presents given to me for luck, so naturally one would never get rid of them. It is a wonderful feeling to come into the theatre of an evening and wipe away the outside world. I am always in at least two hours before a show and will spend my time just pottering, you know? If I have been out during the day, to lunch or the cinema or something, I like to clear my head of all these events and just breathe in the atmosphere in my room – the make-up and the candles and the costumes. It makes me feel secure. Life is so full of insecurities, don't you think? Things we can't control, people we don't understand. Well, here in my world I am secure and safe, and in control.'

Peggy looked through the mirror at Sally sitting behind her and smiled a little sadly. 'Don't mind me, darling, just a silly old actress doing "her thing".'

'Don't be silly,' said Sally, who was genuinely moved. 'I find it all really interesting. I have so much to learn yet. Thanks for the tea, Peggy. I will leave you in peace now and go and find Percy, because Giles wants you both for the last scene. Will you be down in five?'

'Of course, and tell that Sarah to make sure my prop chair is placed stage right. She got it wrong this afternoon and I couldn't find it. Threw my scene completely, and then she had the nerve to give me a note! Bit above herself, that one, I might say – I'll have to make sure she knows her place.'

Sally left before she got embroiled in backstage diplomacy. So far she had managed to keep her nose clean.

Chapter 12

The run-up to the first night was like a roller-coaster gathering pace as it reached the top of the incline and hung there for a few seconds before dramatically plunging down again. The cast ate, drank and slept their allotted parts. Giles finally pulled them all together, casting his magic from the front of the Royal Circle, or whispering from the box. He seemed to feed them all energy. Sally could no longer feel her feet as she stomped out the beat with the rest of the cast for the finale. Every bone in her body was crying out for release from the pain of spending eighteen hours on her feet. On the Sunday night, when the technical rehearsal threatened to go on until the early hours, succour came from an unexpected source. About midnight, Mrs Wong from the Chinese takeaway next door appeared at the side of the stage with a huge box of food. Delicious aromas were wafting across the stage and everyone was transfixed by the thought of sweet and sour pork balls.

'Who dares to interrupt my rehearsal?' bellowed Giles from the auditorium.

But Mrs Wong was not cowed. 'Mister Giles, you terrible

man make all work too hard! Mrs Wong bring food and all will go better. Come, come, everybody, eat now. Mister Giles, you come too and take a break.'

The cast let out a spontaneous cheer and fell upon the food, tearing off the foil and stuffing their mouths.

'Oh my God, this is so good!' mumbled Sally through a spoonful of chicken in black bean sauce. It was the turning point of the night, and Mrs Wong became the heroine of the hour. For the rest of the season the cast would turn to her sweet and sour sauce and chunky chips for inspiration. It became the one constant in their schedule: technical rehearsal and Mrs Wong's takeaway.

They finished the run at around three o'clock in the morning. Janie and Pete and Sally staggered up the hill to the house and fell into bed. Next morning came round in a flash and they all appeared in the kitchen, bleary-eyed but ready for the next onslaught. Pete had cooked them a huge 'full English', since Janie, efficient as ever, had cannily found the time to stock the fridge for such occasions.

'This will probably be the last thing we eat today,' she warned them.

Sally felt guilty that she herself was so behind in organizing things in real life. For the last week all she could think about was the show. How would she ever survive when she moved to her flat? And what on earth would Dora make of it all?

The three of them gathered everything they needed for the rest of the day and set off for the theatre. The dress rehearsal was scheduled to start at two, but Sally had so much to do before she could even start thinking about her own performance.

Heather was waiting for her at the stage door.

'Listen,' she said. 'Before you get stuck in here, can you

whip down to Woolworth's and buy some balloons and those party-popper things? Bloody Giles has decided he wants the cast to set them all off at the end of the show. Here's some petty cash – I hope it's enough.'

Sally dumped her stuff with Gladys and set off. She practised her numbers as she sped along the road, until she caught the eye of some youths hanging out on the corner of the street, pointing at her, and laughing and hollering along with her. Oh well, so they thought she was potty – who cared!

When she got back to the theatre there was a traffic jam at the stage door as the band appeared to have arrived. Frank, George, Terry and Gil – double bass, trumpet, piano and drums all on loan from Crewe's very prestigious brass band.

'Hi, can I help at all?' she asked.

'Frank Masters, at your service,' said a tall jolly man with a fine head of hair, extending his hand from behind his double bass.

'Sally Thomas,' said Sally, taking his hand. 'Pleased to meet you. Shall I show you to the Band Room?'

Frank laughed. 'Oh, I think we know the way there by now, don't we, lads? This is our tenth year playing for this lot.'

'Oh sorry, how stupid of me,' apologized Sally, feeling very foolish. 'I am the new girl, of course. But let me help you at least, and organize some tea or coffee.'

'Don't you mither yourself, my girl, we are fine. You get on and we will see you in the pub later.' Frank managed to make a space for Sally to squeeze past. She went straight to the props corner and presented Heather with her purchases.

'Well done. Now can you make sure that everyone has their opening costumes and that all their props are checked on the prop tables either side, please? I will be calling the half in five minutes, God help us.'

The half was called twenty-five minutes before curtain up and it was legally binding that every member of the cast be in the theatre when it was called. This allowed stage management to keep tags on anything untoward or any latecomers. The biggest problem would be a no show from an actor, so the understudy would have to be informed and dressed and ready to go. If the actor arrived after the half had been called, he would still not be allowed on; it was down to the understudy.

Five minutes! Sally rushed to complete her tasks. She was desperate to get to her dressing room and practise a little with her make-up. She took the stairs to the top of the theatre two at a time. That would have to be her warm-up for the show. She was sharing one of the dressing rooms with Sarah; it was usually reserved for the chorus so it was slightly larger, with several dressing tables and a couple of basins in the corner. The boys were next door in an identical room. Needless to say though, theirs was in a hell of a mess. The boys had hung a makeshift clothes-line across the room, from which hung a huge variety of underwear, some cleaner than others. Odd socks and shoes lay where they'd been chucked in the corner. Smelly trainers and the odd football and soggy towels lay in piles, and books and magazines were scattered all over the floor.

It was horrible to see!

Not my problem, thought Sally as she passed the ever-open door and moved to her own dressing room. There had been no time to personalize it at all, so everything was rather cold and pristine. Sarah had managed to put up a couple of posters her end of the dressing table and laid out her make-up and towel, but poor old Sally's end was decidedly bare. Oh well, time enough for all that later. She had picked up her opening costume on the way up and hung it carefully on the rail then quickly unpacked her bag of goodies. She sat down in front of the mirror and finally drew breath.

The face that stared back at her through the rather grubby glass was wide-eyed and pale. She had bags under her eyes for the first time in her life, and her hair needed washing. Was this an actress in the making? Too bloody right it was! She had fifteen minutes to get ready. She stuck her head under the tap in the basin and pinched some of Sarah's shampoo. The water was cold but did the job. She had actually bought herself a little hairdryer so she attacked her wet locks with vigour for five minutes and then stuck it up in a roll ready for her nifty hat! She then whacked on the five and nine and a good dollop of scarlet on the cheeks, but no time for the red dots this show. She gave her lips a good outline though, with the old lipstick and some awful gloss stuff she had seen on offer in Woolies. It tasted disgusting, and when she smiled she had it smeared all over her front teeth. Not a good look.

She started to haul herself into her black fishnets as the Tannoy over the dressing-room door suddenly crackled into life, making her jump.

'Five minutes to curtain up, ladies and gentlemen. Five minutes, please. Could Miss Thomas come to the prompt corner immediately, please?'

'Oh shit!' Sally swore as she got her boot-zip stuck. 'I am not going to be ready.' But she managed it. Took a quick look in the mirror and was amazed how a bit of theatrical make-up and sparkle had transformed her from tired ASM to cheeky drum majorette, and sped down the stairs.

She made the prompt corner just as Heather was calling beginners.

'Well done, girl, you look great. Now just make sure they

all line up in the right order and stand by to raise the curtain, please.'

Crewe was still waiting for its automated Tabs (curtains) so they had to be raised by hand on pulleys. Sally assumed the position, and was ready to haul away, much to the delight of the boys who were all lined up behind her ready to go on, and had the perfect view of her fishnets. As she raised her arms to pull the curtain, her rather short tunic was beyond the realms of decency.

'Oh shut up, you losers!' she hissed and then got an attack of the giggles.

Suddenly there was only bright lights and the sound of the drums beating out their entrance, and they were off and running. Well, nearly . . .

'Stop! Stop, hold the tabs! We have a problem with the follow spot!' Giles was screaming from the centre of the circle. 'Go back and reset and start again.'

Unfortunately, dress rehearsals are notoriously fraught with danger. The old adage 'Bad dress rehearsal great show' is always there to adhere to, cling to – pray to!

They managed to get through the whole show just about intact, but it was now nearly six thirty and the show was to open at seven thirty! The cast were gathered in the stalls for their notes. Some had managed to grab a cup of tea, or an apple, just to keep them going. Giles gave each actor their notes, ticking them off his pad theatrically with a grand gesture of his pen.

'Well, it is the usual kick bollock and scramble,' he said, 'but the basic show is there, and we are going to get out there tonight and sell it one hundred and fifty per cent. We want our audience to come back again and again. So, I know you are tired and hungry, but this is it, guys! This is why we do it and we are going to do it well. Good luck – and see you upstairs in the bar afterwards for a glass of bubbly.'

They all clapped and hugged each other and suddenly disappeared. Sally was just clearing final pieces of paper from the stage and was aware of the silence in the auditorium. It was as though the theatre had taken a deep breath and was waiting. She could almost hear the walls whispering with all those voices from so many shows over so many years. The air was filled with a hidden energy, waiting for the spark to ignite the show; it was a bit like being in a church. She tiptoed off the stage, not wanting to disturb the setting before it was time.

As she made her way upstairs to the dressing room she was reminded of her impression that the theatre was like a doll's house. If she opened any of the doors now as she passed there would be a slice of life taking place. An action, a word, all in miniature, captured behind these doors. The sounds of laughter, a high note soaring out. Someone gargling, a thumping of feet on the floor followed by a cheer. Every corner of the building was alive and throbbing with anticipation, and then suddenly it was released.

The band played out and Sally felt the thrill of hearing the pure chords of a live trumpet against the beat of a drum. The audience started to clap along with the band. Then as quickly as the crowd was cheering they went quiet, hushed as the lights went down, and the huge embroidered curtain rose above the stage with a swish. Momentary blackness, then white light bursting onto the stage as the cast seemed to spring from the wings in their bright Pierrot costumes, singing, 'Oh! It's a lovely war!'

The two hours went past like a shot and suddenly it was over. The cast were all standing in a row in front of the footlights taking their bows to an ecstatic audience who were on their feet, and the balloons were floating above them, and the poppers were popping!

Sally thought she would burst with happiness. Nothing in her drama training had prepared her for this. She waved at Mr and Mrs Tibbs, and hugged Charmaine who was standing next to her.

'Isn't this fantastic,' she shouted above the cheering to a rather bemused Charmaine.

'Well, it is certainly different from the Royal Shakespeare Company,' replied the actress.

Once the curtain was down, after several encores, the cast tore back to their rooms and whipped off the make-up and costumes and made their way to the bar. They had been promised champagne, which had been a bit misleading on Giles's part, but there was free beer and a glass of warm white wine. No one cared: it was alcoholic, and there were even some sausage rolls and crisps. The cast did their bit and chatted to the local dignitaries. Sally got stuck with Mr and Mrs Tibbs for a while but was then moved on to the Mayor, who was very chatty.

'Wonderful show, Miss Thomas. And your number was a triumph. What a costume, eh?' He almost did a nod nod, wink wink routine, but a pat on the arm from his wife silenced him.

The cast slowly began to withdraw as was usually the way. The actors needed their space to come down from the high. Word spread round the room that it was all back to Janie and Pete's for some of Mrs Wong's chips and sweet and sour sauce, and bring a bottle if you had one. The pub was closing in five minutes so suddenly the theatre bar was empty, save for the few remaining programme-sellers and bar staff. Sally had actually managed to remember to buy a bottle on her way in that day, so she set off home with Simon and Jeremy, who were in charge of the chips.

They sang all the way home and fell into the front room in a pile of hysteria.

The little terraced house shook and shivered for a good two hours until the inhabitants could stay awake no longer. There was not a spare inch on the floor that was not inhabited by a body. Had anyone ventured to open the door they would have been knocked back by the pungent odours of stale beer, sweet and sour sauce and greasepaint. But the floor was covered with smiles!

Chapter 13

Jeremy woke up as an elbow nudged him in the ribs. For a moment he was completely thrown as he slowly sat up and found himself surrounded by bodies. What the hell . . . ? He eased himself out from under a leg or two and made his way gingerly across the room to the kitchen. Slowly the previous evening was coming back to him. He searched the debris scattered across the draining board and decided to risk a half-full pint glass to rinse under the tap. He ran the cold water and splashed his face, then filled the glass and drank like a man returning from the desert. The beginnings of a headache tapped on his forehead but he refused to acknowledge it. He had work to do. Cursing his stupidity, and regretting the last two shots of vodka he had downed the night before, he wiped his hands on his trousers and beat a retreat from the sleeping house, closing the door quietly on gentle snores.

It was still early and the sunrise was just completing a fiery red blaze across the rooftops. Crewe looked almost beautiful. There had been a frost and Jeremy shivered in his thin jacket. He quickened his pace and practically jogged to the theatre.

Not great news for the headache! He arrived at the stage door numb with cold to discover it was locked. Of course it would be. It's eight thirty in the bloody morning, you pillock! Jeremy admonished himself. Now what? His digs were a bus-ride away, and by the time he had gone home and come back again, the morning would be gone and he had to get this script under his belt. He had arranged to meet Robert at the theatre at eleven to go through his part in *A Man for All Seasons*. This was to be his first decent role of the season and Jeremy was determined that Giles would see his potential. There was so little time to rehearse that any help he could get was a bonus, and Robert's offer was a godsend.

Jeremy would just have to wait until nine thirty to get into the building when the cleaners arrived. He had no choice but to hang around outside the theatre. By the time Alice, the cleaner, arrived he was almost frozen on the spot.

'Oh chuck, you poor thing. Come on, pet, get inside and I'll make you a cuppa. Bless your heart.' Alice clucked and fussed as she led Jeremy through the foyer and upstairs to the Green Room where she put the kettle on and produced a bottle of milk from her bag. 'Let's get the fire on and you thaw out a bit. You look terrible – are you going down with summat?' she asked.

'No, but I do have a bit of a hangover,' admitted Jeremy. 'Nothing a paracetamol won't cure.'

Alice laughed. 'Nothing changes, does it? You lot will never learn.' She was busy putting tea bags in mugs. 'There is some bread here, still edible. Do you want me to make you some toast and Marmite? It's just the ticket for a hangover.'

Jeremy nodded a yes, and stuck his bum in front of the two-bar electric fire kindly donated by the management to keep the actors alive in the coldest months. Five minutes later he was finally able to feel his hands again, which were now wrapped round a mug of hot sweet tea. The cleaner brought him a plate of Marmite on toast and he almost felt human again.

'Thanks so much, Alice. I owe you one. Perhaps I can treat you to a Mrs Wong's Special one night. How does that sound?'

'Lovely, pet, anytime. Now I must get on. Clear this up a bit in here when you've finished, will you? It is not my job to wash up after you mucky lot!' With that admonishment she was gone.

Jeremy finished his toast and washed up his plate and mug, and the rest of the mugs strewn around the room. He then wiped down the table, emptied the ashtrays and filled the bin with whatever he could pick up. He then made his way to the boys' dressing room, where his heart sank. From one mess to another! The room was a tip. Costumes from last night were tossed over chairs. Underwear was draped over hooks, and socks scattered like confetti all over the floor.

Christ, what was it with these guys? Why couldn't they just show a modicum of thought for others? Why was it commonly accepted that blokes had to live like pigs? That somehow it was OK – almost manly, in fact? That real men don't bother to tidy up? Jeremy pondered these facts as he automatically went into tidy-up mode. He could not live in chaos, and he certainly would not be able to sit here and work surrounded by his fellow actors' debris. Locating a large black bin bag, he filled it with all the dirty washing, took it down to Wardrobe and filled the two washing machines there. Just great, doing the washing for all those lazy bastards on a Sunday morning! Jeremy then spent an hour cleaning all the dressing tables and the basins, asking himself if this was going to happen

every week. Did his attention to cleanliness make him a figure
of ridicule? Would he become the resident poof because he
was tidy?

All through drama school Jeremy had had to cope with the
jibes and innuendos about his sexuality. He took it all on the
chin and could even laugh about it sometimes, but deep down
it niggled at him. He had never really paid much attention to
his sexuality; it was not a priority for him. Only his career as
an actor mattered; only his development as a performer. He
had never been bothered about 'pulling birds' when his
schoolmates had discovered the joys of the opposite sex. He
would rather go to the theatre and watch one of his heroes
such as Peter O'Toole or David Warner. Most weekends he
went to Stratford upon Avon, to the home of the Royal
Shakespeare Company, where he'd sit in the gods and feed on
the glorious words of the Bard. His parents, who were not
theatrical in any way, were rather puzzled by their son's obses-
sion with the theatre. But to give them their due, they
supported him every step of the way and when he announced
he wanted to go to drama school they did not object.

Jeremy had imagined that when he joined the ranks of the
other drama students they would all be of a like mind. He was
disappointed. Most of them were like every other student –
there for the sex, drugs and alcohol. Acting was a mere sideline
to the main event, which was having a good time. Once again
he found himself the butt of the jokes and everyone assumed
he must be gay, except Sally. It was her interest and dedication
that drew them together as friends. Not that either of them
was particularly mad on socializing, but they did form a pact
and would often rehearse together. Sally possessed a kind of
reserve that Jeremy could identify with; they both seemed to
share the same sense of reserve about their bodies too, which

somehow disappeared when they were acting. They could lose themselves in a character.

When Sally had got her job at the British Drama League she introduced Jeremy to James Langton and he had found a place for Jeremy as well. It was a slightly strained relationship, as Jeremy suspected that James had a soft spot for him, and although he knew James Langton was married, his gut feeling was that he might well have a penchant for young men. This instinct had taken Jeremy by surprise. Why would he think like that? Was he being naïve about his own sexuality? Yet if, and when, he had these thoughts, they did not linger long enough for him to really give them proper consideration. Basically, he was just not interested in anything else except acting. All his physical and emotional energy was geared to honing his skills as a performer. Everything else could take a back seat.

So deep in his own thoughts was Jeremy that he was unaware of Robert standing in the doorway until he heard him comment, 'Well, well, Cinderella, you poor thing. Left to do all the housework and not a fairy godmother in sight! Allow me to wave my wand and take you away from all this drudgery.' Robert had a knack of making everything he said sound bored or insulting. He didn't so much speak as drawl his comments.

'Oh hi, Robert, thanks so much for arranging to meet me. I am sorry about this but I just can't work in a mess. Please, have a seat. Can I make you a coffee?' Jeremy pulled out a chair.

'Oh, don't worry on my account. I have actually just had a coffee, so not a problem. Do you want to work here or on the stage?' Robert asked.

'Oh – well, I hadn't really thought about it. It would be

great to go onstage eventually maybe, but I think for now it would be good to just read through it here, if that is OK?' Jeremy suddenly felt nervous under Robert's scrutiny.

'Sure. No problem. Let's get down to business,' the other man replied, taking off his coat and sitting down.

They spent the next two hours going through all the scenes Jeremy was in as Rich. The character was a very intense young man who was opinionated and a little pompous. Robert talked Jeremy through the obvious pitfalls and pointed out various key moments. Jeremy listened to every word and absorbed all he could, making notes as they went along for future reference.

Finally, Robert sat back and lit a cigarette, saying, 'Well, I think we have covered just about everything you need to bring young Rich to life, don't you?'

'Yes. Thank you so much, Robert. I really appreciate this. There is so little time, as you know. I feel I can go into rehearsals tomorrow with confidence.' Jeremy tidied his notes.

'Don't hesitate to come and ask me anything else that you might discover. I am going to be around quite a lot as I am assisting Giles on this, and we will be working together on *Hamlet*, which as you probably know is his pet project. Now, shall we adjourn to the pub and warm our cockles with a pint?' He rose and started to put on his coat.

'Oh yes, what a good idea,' agreed Jeremy. 'The drinks are on me – it is the least I can do to thank you for this morning. Oh, I just remembered the washing! You go ahead and order while I just pop and empty the machines.'

Robert burst out laughing. 'Oh, the glamour of it all! Showbiz, eh?' He swept out and left Jeremy to his chores.

Later in the pub, Robert regaled Jeremy with stories of fellow actors and various productions he had been in over the years.

'How did you meet Giles?' asked Jeremy.

'Oh, we go back a few years,' replied Robert airily. 'We were lovers for a time – oops, I mustn't be wicked, must I?' He gave Jeremy a wink. 'Has he tried out his charm on you yet?'

Jeremy suddenly felt uncomfortable. 'No, why would he?' he returned.

Robert studied him for several minutes. 'No particular reason, I suppose,' he mused. 'Of course, one should never make assumptions, but I had wondered if you were gay. Is that not the case?'

'No – not that it is anyone's business,' retorted Jeremy. Here we go again, he thought to himself. Why does sex always have to come into everything?

Robert smiled. 'Now, now, there is no need to take umbrage. There is nothing wrong with being gay, you know. There are a lot of us about – doesn't make one a bad person.'

'Sorry,' said Jeremy. 'I didn't mean any offence. It is just I find it so frustrating that everyone in this business wants to know about one's sex-life. What business is it of anyone's? What difference does it make? I want to be judged on my talent, not my sexual orientation.'

Robert clapped his hands slowly. 'Bravo. Well done, young man.'

Jeremy was not awfully sure if the other man was being sarcastic or not. So he changed the subject. 'Would you like another drink?' he asked, rising from his seat.

'Thank you, but no. I must get off to my next appointment. It has been a most enlightening sojourn, dear Jeremy. You are, indeed, a very serious young man and I wish you well in your search for integrity in this fickle profession.'

Robert stood up and leaned across and kissed Jeremy on both cheeks.

'Never say never,' he whispered in Jeremy's ear and was gone.

Jeremy sat down and finished his pint. Bloody poofs! Why did they all assume he was gay? He just wasn't interested in relationships; he was completely content in himself, and with his own company. Falling in love seemed fraught with danger and best left alone. Let others fall in love with *him* – and preferably onstage. He would stay out of all the messy emotional stuff.

But then he met the love of his life – and everything changed.

Chapter 14

The cast quickly learned that they had to pace themselves very carefully in order to survive the schedule. Struggling in on Monday morning after having only a few hours on Sunday to recover from Saturday night's hangover, and trying to do washing and weekly chores, plus prepare their heads for the next play was no easy task. It was a shock to the system, and all the newcomers to the game acknowledged the fact in the pub Monday lunchtime.

'Bloody hell,' announced Simon, taking a swig of his pint. 'I don't know what day it is now, let alone in two months' time. I can't believe I have got to learn another play, and we have only done one night of *Oh, What a Lovely War!* My brain is fried.'

'We will have to curb our drinking,' said Pete. 'Either that or increase it.' He laughed. 'Come on, Si, don't be such a wimp. We can do it. Now let's get the pies in.'

Sally was certainly struggling to get through the day. Like everyone else she had over-indulged on Saturday night, and spent most of Sunday trying to get rid of her hangover. Jeremy had appeared in the afternoon wondering if she would read through the script with him.

'Oh my God, Jeremy, I haven't given it a thought!' she wailed.

'Well, don't worry. It is just I worked with Robert this morning, and it really helped me to go through the words with someone,' he said, feeling a bit of a swot now when confronted by his friend's agonized face.

'No, you are right. Come on, let's do it. But can I make a cup of tea, please?' Sally went and put the kettle on and then they settled down in her room to read the play.

The rest of Sunday was gone in a flash and Monday loomed. The cast had a read-through of the play and various discussions with Costume and Design and suchlike, and then Giles started to block the play. Sally was running round organizing fittings and set-design meetings and making tea for all and sundry. By five o'clock, when they broke for supper, she was exhausted but she still had to prepare all the props for the evening show and sort out her own costumes.

Heather could see that she was having problems. 'Don't worry, pet, you will soon get into a routine and forget how tired you are,' she said kindly. 'It is tough, but you will need to learn to take little naps when you can. Have you finished checking the props?' Sally nodded. 'Then go and get something to eat and try to close your eyes for ten minutes. It will really help you,' she advised.

Sally thought it highly unlikely she would be able to sleep just like that but she was starving so she went next door to Mrs Wong's and got some lunch, then went back to her dressing room. Sarah was there reading the play so there was a pleasant silence. Before she knew it, Sally was asleep and only woke when Sarah shook her awake.

'Sally, wake up! It is nearly the half and you will feel awful if you don't get yourself together.'

'Oh, thank you so much. Gosh, I can't believe I fell asleep so easily,' Sally said drowsily. 'I'd better have a shower to wake me up.'

She was soon back up to speed and dressed in her opening costume, standing in the wings waiting to raise the curtain.

The show was definitely a little subdued on the second night and Giles was less than pleased. Before starting rehearsals the next morning he gave the company a lecture on the danger of second nights, and never letting the standards drop.

'You have to try extra hard the second night,' he pro-nounced. 'The audience have paid their money just the same as the first-night audience: why should they get second-best just because you lot had too much beer and not enough sleep? I will come down hard on you all if I see any more signs of slacking. Understood?'

There were murmurs of 'Yes, sir' and the cast all sat up straighter. It was going to be a tough nine months!

That afternoon, Sally rang home to check on everyone, and Dora came on to inform her that she would be arriving next week.

'Oh my goodness! I haven't even given you a thought,' said Sally.

'Well, that is charming I must say,' replied Dora. 'Aren't you moving into our flat this weekend?'

'I don't know,' said Sally, dismayed that all this information was coming at her. 'What date did we agree? Honestly, I am so sorry, Dora, but you have no idea what it has been like, the last few weeks. I just have not had a minute to do anything else except come to work and sleep. But yes, I guess you are right – we were going to move in the second week of October, weren't we?'

'Yes, exactly, dummy. So is that still the plan?' asked Dora.

Sally tried to think what the schedule was going to be like for this weekend. In fact, if they were going to move it would have to be this weekend, because the following one was the Get-in when they worked all hours.

'Dora, listen. Let me ring the landlady Miss Morris and see what she had in mind. It might not be possible now until the beginning of next month because I am not sure I have the time. I am really sorry to mess you about,' she added, knowing her sister would not be pleased.

'You are hopeless,' came the expected reproach. 'Why do I bother to try and support you? You are so selfish, Sally.'

Sally sighed and waited for a pause in the tirade.

'Look, I have told you, I will ring the landlady right now and do my best to sort it. I am really sorry, Dora, but I can only do my best, so just give it a rest. Can you put Mum on the phone now, please?'

Sally heard a loud snort the other end of the line as the phone was banged down and Dora shouted to their mother to come to the phone.

'Hello, darling, how's it going?' The sound of Patricia's voice made Sally feel desperately homesick.

'Oh Mum, it is so good to hear your voice,' she said, trying not to burst into tears. 'I am so sorry about Dora, but honestly you have no idea how hard I have been working. It is a nightmare.'

'Don't worry, my darling. Dora will calm down. She has just got so over-excited about coming to live with you. It is all she talks about. I am worried about you though, Sally. Are you eating properly? Do you get enough sleep?' she fretted.

'The answer is no, and no – but honestly, Mum, it is fine really. It is just a shock to the system after not doing very much, and it is certainly nothing like drama school. God, we didn't know how lucky we were just playing at acting. But it is great fun, and when I am actually performing, it is completely magical!'

'Well, please look after yourself, dear. Is there anything you need?' asked her mother. 'We can send supplies with Dora. But don't worry about arranging the flat right now if you are so busy. Dora will have to be patient.'

'No, I understand how she feels,' said Sally. 'It is just that I have had so much on my mind it was a shock when she launched into the plan. I will ring her later, tell her, when I have spoken to the landlady. Now I had better get on. Give my love to Dad and of course to you.'

'All right, my dear. Lots of love to you – and ring any time won't you? Bye.' Her mother hung up.

Sally took a deep breath and went to find the number for the landlady of the flat.

As it turned out, Dora was quite right and Miss Morris, the landlady, *was* expecting them the coming weekend. Sally agreed she would pick up the keys during the week from the agent's office, which was only down the road from the theatre, and move in on Sunday.

Sally went to find Janie and break the news of her imminent departure.

'Oh no – I will miss you so much. It is going to be just me and the boys all the time. Promise you will come round some-times and give me some female support,' Janie pleaded.

'Of course I will. And you can come to me to get away from them all. Honestly though, I am not sure I am ready for this at all. I haven't given it a thought since I came up in the summer. I just hope it is all going to be OK – with Dora and everything, I mean. I need to talk to Gwendoline as well, about letting my sister work in Wardrobe. Will she pay her, do you think?'

'Well, we could certainly do with some help, and if she is willing to do some laundry et cetera as well as the sewing, I am sure Gwendoline will find the money from somewhere.'

Sally went to Wardrobe as soon as she got to the theatre that night for the show. As usual Gwendoline was surrounded by washing. Crossing her fingers, Sally reminded her about Dora.

'Yes, I remember Susan mentioning your sister,' Gwendoline said. 'I think she could be just what we need. When would she want to start?'

'Well, we are moving into the new flat on Sunday so she could start Monday if you wanted. We have got a washing machine as well so she could always do stuff for you at our place,' suggested Sally.

Gwendoline laughed. 'Perfect. Not sure your sister will thank you for volunteering that information, but still, it sounds good to me.'

'Thank you so much, Gwendoline. It is very kind of you. I will go and ring her now and tell her she is hired.' Sally went down to the stage door to use the phone.

Gladys was sat in front of her ever-glowing electric fire and greeted her warmly. 'All right, dearie? You coping with it all? I know it is hard the first few weeks adjusting to the long hours. Bless yer heart, you look worn out already. When's that sister of yours turning up then?'

'You must be psychic, Gladys. I am just about to ring her and arrange for her to arrive on Sunday when we move into our new flat.' Sally pressed the button to the tinkle of coins dropping in the box. 'Mum? Can I speak to Dora please? Yes, it is all arranged. No, I'll manage, don't worry.' Sally smiled at Gladys who was pretending to look busy with her knitting, while eavesdropping on Sally's phone call.

'Sally? What's happened? Is it OK for me to come on Sunday?' Dora hardly drew breath.

'Yes, it is all sorted. Miss Morris is expecting us to move in then. Good job you are on the ball, Dora. Listen – are you coming by train or is Dad bringing you?'

'Dad has offered to drive me and I think Mum would like to come as well and see where we are going to be living. Is that OK?' Dora sounded unsure.

'I suppose so, but the trouble is, it will be quite a rush if they want to stay for lunch because we have to move every-thing and unpack and I only have Sunday, plus I will have to work on my lines. It is all a bit overwhelming really,' sighed Sally.

'Don't get your knickers in a twist, sis. Mum and Dad will understand and you will be in need of a free lunch by then. We can go to that place we went to before and have a Sunday roast, then Ma and Pa will go and we'll have all afternoon to sort ourselves out. Then I can make the supper while you do your lines. How's that sound?'

Sally could not help but think it sounded great. 'Perfect,' she replied. 'You are a star, baby sister. I can't wait to see you. So you will be arriving mid-morning, do you reckon?'

'Absolutely. See you then, sis.' And Dora was gone.

Sally had a sneaky feeling her life had been taken over, but at the moment it didn't seem such a bad thing.

The rest of the week was full on, as on Wednesday they had a matinée and an evening show. Thursday, Giles finalized the cast for the next production, the musical version of *Lysistrata*, a Classic Greek comedy about women withholding their

sexual favours from their husbands until the latter agree to stop
going to war. Charmaine was to take the lead of Lysistrata, and
Sally was to understudy and also play one of the other neighbours, plus she had a great solo. Fortunately it was all set on an
empty stage, with few props, so that was something less to
concern her. However, the thought of Greek women and
sexual favours was a lo-o-o-ng way from Sir Thomas More
and his troubles. One thing at a time, please!

Chapter 15

Dora let out a scream of delight and hugged her sister.

'We are here! Isn't this great? Dad is unpacking as we speak. Oh sorry, Mother, here you go. Big hugs all round.' Dora moved aside so Patricia could take her place in Sally's arms.

'Oh darling, you look exhausted. Come on, let's bring everything in and then we can sit and talk. Douglas, don't unpack anything yet, please. We need a plan.'

Sally looked at her family standing there in the road beside a car loaded with stuff. Where to start?

'OK, guys, first things first – let's go to the new flat. Is there room for me in there as well, or shall I walk?' She already had her coat on.

'You can sit on Dora's lap,' suggested Douglas. 'It's only up the road, isn't it?'

'Yes, come on, Sally. We can squeeze in the front and Mum has a little spot in the back between the pillows and the laundry basket.'

They all piled in and set off up the hill. Sally produced the keys to their new home, opened the front door, and she and

Dora jockeyed for position. Both girls managed to reach the inner door at the top of the stairs together. Breathless and flushed with excitement, Sally finally managed to open the door and they practically fell into the hallway. Thank goodness the sun was shining and the flat looked bright and welcoming. As the girls went from room to room, it was clear that someone had taken the time to clean the place very thoroughly.

'Oh, it is fantastic,' said Dora. 'Much nicer than I remember.'

'You are right, sis,' replied Sally. She made her way to the kitchen and found a potted plant and a note. 'Hey, come in here, Dora. Look – the last tenants left us a note and a plant.' Sally read it aloud.

'Dear new tenants,

Hope you will be as happy as we were in the flat. See other note for instructions for hot water, etc.

Miss Morris likes to collect the rent herself and have a poke around. But she is no trouble!

Good luck.

Jean and Trevor

'Oh, that is so sweet of them,' remarked Patricia, making an entrance through the door with a laundry basket full of groceries. 'Now come on, girls, get this unpacked asap, then we can go and have lunch.'

They all got down to work, making beds and unpacking food. The flat very soon looked like a home, especially with the added touches of big cushions made by Patricia, and a secondhand rug or two. The pièce de résistance was finally brought up from the car by Douglas and given pride of place in the lounge.

'Oh Dad, you are a star!' Sally rushed to give him a hug as her father set down the TV.

'Well, I am glad you are appreciative, my girl. But it will be useful for you both on a cold Sunday afternoon.' He fiddled and faffed with the tuning until it all worked perfectly. 'Good job there is an aerial. How did you find out?' he asked.

'I rang Miss Morris, of course. She is such a lovely lady and quite understood the need for a TV. "I wouldn't be without mine," she told me. Listen, everyone, are we nearly finished? Only it is already one thirty and I have got work to do this afternoon. I am sorry to be so boring.'

'No, darling, don't worry,' said her mother, coming into the room with a bowl of pot pourri. Everyone looked at her. 'What? Why not? It might have been awful when we got here and this would just help things smell a bit more pleasant.' She plonked it slap bang in the middle of the rather scratched coffee table and the rest of the family burst into laughter.

'Only you, Patricia,' chuckled Douglas. 'Now come on, get your coats and let's get going.'

Fifteen minutes later the family were sat round a table in the pub, ordering the infamous Yorkshire puddings.

'You wait till you see the size of these suckers, Mum,' announced Dora, already tucking into a packet of pork scratchings.

The meal was a big success and Sally relished the food and the company of her family. She realized how much she had missed them. Still, at least now she had Dora with her which would give her so much support.

'It is lovely to see you, Mum,' she whispered as Douglas was paying the bill. 'I do love you.'

'I know, darling, and we love you. Try not to get too tired and make sure you eat properly. We will come and visit you whenever you want. Which show would you like us to see?' asked Patricia.

'Blimey, Mum, I haven't given it a thought, to be honest,' replied Sally. 'Let me get through the next couple of weeks and then I will have a better idea. I don't know if I am going to get a really good part yet. *Hamlet* should be marvellous, but I am only playing the Queen in the Dumb Show. But I am directing that, by the way, which will be very interesting.'

Her mother gave her arm a squeeze. 'I know you will do your best at whatever is put before you,' she murmured. 'We are so proud of you, Sally. We just want you to be happy.' Then Patricia leaned over and kissed her daughter. Douglas had paid the bill and farewells were exchanged in the pub, and then Sally and Dora were dropped off at their new front door.

The girls waved their parents out of sight and stood on the doorstep. It had turned chilly now the sun was going down, and dusk was spreading its blanket over the rows of terraced houses with their identical red-brick chimneys and their gently curling smoke signals evaporating into the darkening sky.

Sally opened the door and they both stepped inside without a word. They climbed the stairs to the landing, and then walked slowly into their new home. Dora turned on an overhead light which needed a shade, while Sally went and plugged in the electric fire. It was soon glowing like a fairground ride thanks to their father's donation earlier to the meter in the kitchen. Sally switched on a table light with a warm pink shade, again donated by the parents, its rosy light spreading tranquillity through the room.

'Look what Mum has left us,' announced Dora, coming in from the kitchen with a bag of crumpets and a plate of cream cakes.

Sally sank into the battered armchair and let out a sigh of contentment. 'Dora, this is perfect, our very own space. It is so cosy already. I love it. Would you be an angel and put the kettle on while I start to attack this script?' she asked.

Dora looked slightly miffed. 'Well, I suppose so, just this once. But don't think I am going to wait on you hand and foot, once I start working, sister dear.'

Sally looked up at her, checking for signs of real bad temper and found none. She grinned.

'No, of course not, silly – just today. I am so behind, and it has all been a hell of a learning curve. You wait till tomorrow, Dora – you won't believe the hours!'

Dora went into the kitchen to fill the kettle.

'I can't wait,' she said to herself with a big grin on her face. 'I simply cannot wait.'

Chapter 16

The inhabitants of the upstairs flat at number 7, Ridgeway Road were a little stressed the next morning. Sally was up bright and early, but her sister proved more of a problem. The coffee failed to raise her, so did the radio on full blast, so finally Sally was forced to resort to pulling the covers off, hardening her heart to the moans and groans of protest.

'Dora, I am sorry, but this is the reality. We have to be at the theatre by nine, so come on, move your arse, please. You've got fifteen minutes.'

Dora let out a scream and leaped from the bed. She made a dash to the bathroom, wailing, 'It's *sooo* cold!'

Sally couldn't agree with her more, but there was no central heating, and the idea of getting up even half an hour earlier to put the electric fire on was too much, not to mention the electricity bill. So Sally had got used to the morning dash to the ablutions, and often didn't bother until she got to the warmth of the theatre.

She made Dora another coffee and a piece of toast to make amends, and when Dora appeared at the bathroom door wrapped in her huge fluffy dressing gown, Sally explained the problems, and suggested that her sister do the same and just make sure there were lots of woollies to hand each morning to slide into at speed. Dora's answer was a bleary-eyed nod.

They managed to leave on time and jogged down the hill to the theatre which warmed them up a little. They arrived just after nine, in fact, so the wonderful Gladys was there to greet the new recruit.

'Morning, Sally, and good morning to you, Miss Dora. We have been expecting you. It is a pleasure to have your lovely face gracing my stage door, and I wish you every success with the season. Anything you need or any problems, come to Gladys.'

Dora puffed up with pride and plonked a big kiss on Gladys's cheek. 'Thank you, darling, I will.' And with that she flounced off down the stairs.

'Quite the actress, eh?' said Gladys with a wink. 'You wanna watch yourself, duckie. She will be after your job next.' She laughed so hard she had a coughing fit. Sally left her to it and hurried after Dora. She found her talking to Heather outside the wardrobe department.

Heather was already doing her recruiting speech but Sally interrupted her with; 'Hang about, Heather. Gwendoline has first refusal, you know.'

Heather sighed. 'I know, I know, but it would be great if Dora can spare me a bit of time to get some props when you are doing your acting. You know what it's like now, Sally – every bit of help is needed.'

Sally nodded in sympathy, but added, 'Yes, you are right – but can we just start Dora where she was supposed to be and then take it from there?'

Heather laughed. 'Yeah, of course. Good luck, Dora – but

remember me, please.' And the stage manager was off up to the stage to begin the day.

Gwendoline was inside the wardrobe department with her head in the washing machine as usual.

'Hi guys, be with you in five minutes,' she said. 'Why don't you make us all a coffee? I even brought some buns in this morning as a special treat to welcome Dora.'

'Oh thank you so much, Gwendoline,' gushed Dora, ignoring the signs from her sister indicating that she should lay off the creeping.

Sally said, 'That is lovely of you and we will get started. Come on, Dora, take at least one of those cardigans off and let's get to work. I will make coffee while you acquaint yourself with where everything is.' Dora took the hint, and slipped off her coat and top cardigan then went to join Gwendoline.

Sally made coffee and put the buns on a plate, not before stuffing one in her mouth. Then she called out to the others: 'Coffee's ready. I am off to set up with Heather. Come and find me later, Dora, when Gwendoline has finished with you – if she finishes with you at all!'

Up onstage the actors were all gathering for the first scenes. Sally found Jeremy in a corner as usual.

'I am so sorry I was not around yesterday,' she told him, 'but my family arrived with my sister Dora, and we moved into our new flat. Do you want me to read a couple of scenes with you now, before we start? Is there time?'

Jeremy looked relieved. 'Yes, come on, let's whip up to the Green Room and you can take me through these two scenes.'

Sally told Heather where she was going, and Heather waved her off, saying, 'See you in half an hour.'

The two friends left the stage and went upstairs. After they had finished and were on their way back down, they passed

Geoffrey Challis's dressing room and Gwendoline came out, looking a little ruffled. Just before she managed to shut the door, Sally caught a glimpse of Geoffrey very much in a state of undress.

Her surprise must have registered on her face enough for Gwendoline to feel the need to stammer: 'Just sorting Geoffrey out with a costume that needs adjusting. The poor man is hardly awake.' And she scuttled off.

Sally looked at Jeremy and said, 'Well, that was a bit odd at this time of day, don't you think?'

He looked perplexed. 'What do you mean exactly?'

Sally laughed. 'Oh Jeremy, you are useless. You miss everything. The wardrobe mistress coming out of an actor's dressing room, before nine thirty in the morning, looking a little flustered. And the actor with only his pants on. One could be forgiven for suspecting a bit of hanky panky!'

Jeremy eyed his friend a little crossly. 'Oh, for goodness sake – not you as well, Sally. Why does everyone have to bring sex into everything? Maybe she was just fitting him.' He marched on down the corridor followed by a giggling Sally. Fitting him for what though? she thought to herself, and made a mental note to find out what was bugging her friend about sex.

On stage, Giles was clapping his hands and calling for quiet.

'I need to tell you all a couple of things about the next two productions. Is everyone here? Where are Sally and Jeremy and Geoffrey? Heather, can you give them a call over the Tannoy, please. In the meantime, I will start with Act Two this morning so if everybody would be kind enough to hang around the theatre or at least keep close by – preferably *not* in the pub, Percy.'

This drew a groan from Percy and a snort from Peggy, who said, 'He will be in my dressing room with me, sir, doing his lines.'

Sally and co arrived with apologies and the cast was complete.

Giles took the floor.

'There are a couple of problems with *Lysistrata* and the chorus. We have some wonderfully strong voices already but we need to swell the numbers. I have two thoughts. First, is to engage a couple more actresses from local sources if possible, and second, we pre-record the songs and then play the choral numbers on speakers from the wings to increase the volume. I would appreciate any suggestions for the actresses and I have, in fact, already contacted the stage school to see if any of the teachers fancy a go.

'The second point is to give you all a heads-up on the casting for *Hamlet*. We are very excited to be able to announce the arrival of Rupert Hallam who is making a name for himself on the small screen in the very popular *Up at the Big House* which is in its second series, and I know he is going to do a wonderful job as Hamlet. Opposite him I have engaged another rising star, Isabelle James, fresh from her first film, playing a part in a new Woody Allen movie, as yet untitled. I hope you will all make them most welcome. With regards to the rest of the casting, I would like to see Jeremy, Simon and Peter tomorrow lunchtime, and can you all be prepared to read different scenes and different parts for me, please? Right, that is housekeeping over, now let's get back to good old Sir Thomas, shall we?'

The boys all went off to a corner to discuss their chances, and Jeremy found his way to Robert who had been standing behind Giles throughout, as usual.

'Could I have a word please, Robert?' Jeremy asked a little tentatively.

'Of course you can, my dear. Fire away.' Robert turned and fixed Jeremy with his very blue eyes which seemed to bore into him like a laser.

Jeremy took a deep breath and said, 'I would very much like to have a stab at Laertes, and if you think I am in any way suitable for the part, would you put in a good word for me with Giles?'

Robert looked at Jeremy, appraised him, and took his time. Jeremy held his ground and waited.

It seemed an age before Robert finally gave his response. 'Yes, of course I will. Leave it with me.'

'Thank you very much,' replied Jeremy and left Robert watching him depart to join the boys.

Sally in the meantime had dashed up to Wardrobe to grab Dora.

'Listen, sis, I think there may be a job for you in the next production, singing in the chorus. Maybe even a couple of lines. What do you think?'

Dora was on her sewing machine already and had to stop production to take all this in.

'Oh my God, you really think so? But can I do it, Sally? I am not an actress.'

'Oh, don't be ridiculous,' scoffed Sally. 'You have an amazing singing voice – nearly as good as mine. That's a joke, by the way. You can do it standing on your head and you have got me to help. Giles wants suggestions and then he will audition you.'

'Audition me?' yelped Dora. 'I will be so nervous though. What will I sing?'

'Anything you like. A Beatles song, a folk song – you know

loads of them – and I can always take you through some of the actual chorus from the play. You must have a go, Dora – please!'

'OK, OK I will do it. Now let me get on with this, or I will get the sack before the end of my first day!'

Sally went to find Giles and talk to him about her sister. He seemed pleased and impressed by the Thomas family's talent.

'That is good news, Sally. Tell your Dora that I will see her next Saturday morning at ten o'clock onstage.'

Thrilled to bits, Sally spent the rest of the morning working her way through the props. Simon, Peter and Jeremy had gone off to Wardrobe to check out the new girl, and were all very happy: there was a sudden rush to be measured for their costumes. Gwendoline came to Dora's rescue by informing them that the costumes were all hired, and if there were any alterations, she and Janie would be doing them, as Dora was assigned to making the girls' costumes for *Lysistrata*. Knowing they were going to be very flimsy, this only increased the boys' interest in design, and Dora was invited to the pub at lunchtime for a chat.

'Oh, go away, you horrible lot and let me get on,' scolded Dora. 'But I shall expect the drinks to be on you later, or my mouth is sealed.'

Sally laughed and made a mental note not to worry too much about her sister; she could obviously take care of herself. There were far more important things to concentrate on, like finding a throne for the play and doing another performance of *Oh, What a Lovely War!* tonight. As the actors all traipsed downstairs Sally felt obliged to remind them of this and suggested they rest between the rehearsal and the show. Fat lot of good it would do.

Heather was coming towards her brandishing a notepad.

'Oh, this looks like bad news,' sighed Sally. 'Where do you want me to go?'

Heather was apologetic. 'We need to nail this throne as it is the main prop really. Lord Edward Graham has offered to lend us one. Amazing, eh? He is a great friend of Giles's, apparently. Anyway, if you could go with Peter in the van and pick it up this lunchtime, it would be perfect. I know you will probably miss lunch but I will treat you both to a McDonald's on the way back.' She handed Sally some cash. 'Is that a fair deal?'

Sally knew she had no choice but that was OK – all part of the job. 'Your wish is my command,' she said brightly. 'Just one favour, will you keep an eye on Dora in the pub? You might have to remind her that she has to come back at two and work.'

'Will do,' replied Heather, hurrying off to her next assignment.

Sally stood in the corridor for a minute trying to remember what she was going to do next. Oh, yes of course – she needed a pee!

Chapter 17

Sally and Peter drove through massive black wrought-iron gates, topped with a crest and a motto in Latin. Before them stretched a road winding its way between two lines of beautiful conifers; spreading back across the adjacent lawns were huge oaks and chestnut trees which had obviously been planted hundreds of years ago. The road twisted for at least a mile and a half and then suddenly, over the brow of a little hill, Crewe Hall came into view.

'Wow!' breathed Peter.

'Yes, indeed,' Sally managed to stutter. 'Golly, this is stunning and it must be very old. All that half-timbering is fifteenth-century Tudor, isn't it?'

They drove round the sweeping courtyard past an impressive fountain which, despite the winter frosts, was spouting happily. While they were wondering if they could leave their rather tatty van outside the front entrance, a man in a pin-striped suit appeared.

'Good morning, folks,' he said pleasantly. 'I am Chester, the butler. You must be from the theatre. You can leave the van here and we can go and fetch the throne. It is quite heavy, I should warn you, young man.'

Sally made the introductions and then they followed Chester inside the enormous pile. She wished her father could be here to see this magnificent entrance hall, with its high vaulted ceiling soaring over a huge oak staircase that wound its way down from heaven above to the ground floor. All the wood was in such good nick and polished to perfection that Sally couldn't help but comment, 'Gosh, you must have quite a staff working here to keep this in such good condition.'

Chester answered quite naturally, 'Oh yes indeed, we have a team of cleaners on a rotation scheme. Crewe Hall is like the Forth Bridge: by the time you get to the other end you have to start again. I am sure His Lordship would be happy for you to have a tour at some point. We do official tours in the summer, but yours would be private. I will mention it to him at the next Housekeeping meeting. Now here is the throne. We brought it down from the throne room for you to save time. Can you hold the cushions, Sally? And, Peter, if you take the other arm, hopefully we can lift the chair or drag it outside.'

The two men managed to make it to the front of the house, but then hit the problem of the gravel driveway.

Peter had a suggestion. 'I will back the van up so we can lift it in without damage.'

This accomplished, the three of them managed, with the help of a rope or two, to get the throne into the van, laid carefully on its side on top of a rug.

'Well done,' said Chester rather breathlessly. 'I can see you both have some commonsense. I would just remind you again, and please pass this on to your colleagues, that this throne is very old and very valuable.'

'Absolutely understood, sir,' replied Sally. 'Is His Lordship coming to watch the play?' she added.

'Yes, I believe he will be attending with his son and daughter. He is very keen on history, as you can imagine, and likes to encourage that interest in his children. After all, they will inherit all this eventually, so it is important they understand the historical background of Crewe Hall and where they come from.'

Sally and Peter thanked the friendly butler and set off down the beautiful drive once more. They drove much more slowly on the way home, aware of the priceless item that was on board. When they queued at the drive-in for their McDonald's, they both giggled at the thought of what they carried in the back of the van. It was a long jump from Tudor lords to travelling players like themselves, partaking of an American hamburger!

Heather was waiting back at the theatre worrying about her most precious prop. She had the scene dock open for easy access and Peter drove the van straight in. They managed to unload the throne with no difficulty, and placed it, wrapped in its blankets, in a safe corner.

Heather announced: 'This is now my responsibility for the whole of the run. Giles has informed me that the throne is insured for thousands of pounds. So if it goes missing or gets damaged, I am in deep doo-doos!'

During the tea break, Sally went to find Percy to suggest he come and take a look at his magnificent throne – maybe sit in it and get the feel of it. She also thought it might be a good idea to make sure he understood how valuable it was before he had his mid-morning coffee and biscuits while seated in it! She knocked on Percy's dressing-room door but, as was often the case, it was Peggy's lilting voice that called out, 'Come in! Oh Sally my dear, how lovely of you to come and see us. The kettle has just boiled, and I am making a pot for Percy and me, but we can add another cup.' She rose from her chair and went to the cabinet of crockery to find another china cup and saucer. It was always china cups for tea, with Peggy.

'I don't want to be a bother,' said Sally. 'Is Percy OK? He has such a mammoth part in this play, he must be working all the hours God sends.' She took the cup and saucer from Peggy and laid it on the tray with the others next to the matching milk and sugar bowl. There was also a china stand with some rather delicious-looking biscuits laid out. Definitely the place to come for tea, thought Sally to herself.

Peggy had warmed the teapot and was now measuring heaped teaspoons of tea leaves into the pot and adding boiling water. 'This will put hairs on your chest,' she teased. 'Mind you, it hasn't done a lot for Percy. Talking about Percy,' Peggy lowered her voice, 'I am a bit concerned about him, to be honest with you. He has taken to staying late in his dressing room, saying he is doing his lines. Now that is all well and good, as long as he stays off the sauce, but he can't always do that on his own. So I offered to stay with him but got short shrift. He said he was fine, thank you, and didn't need me spying on him. Well, I must admit that hurt me somewhat, but then again I am used to the other side of his tongue. Anyway, the other night I stayed in my room catching up on some let- ters, et cetera, and time went on. Then I heard voices next door. This was now about midnight. Well, I was curious, to say the least, and knocked on the door. Percy called out, "Hold on a minute!" so I assumed he was in the toilet. But when he finally unlocked our dividing door he looked very dishevelled, and sitting in his armchair as happy as Larry was Sarah, with a copy of the play conveniently placed on her lap.

'"What's all this," I asked,' continued Peggy, pouring out their tea.

'"Nothing, my sweet, just a bit of work on my lines and young Sarah is very kindly taking me through them."

'So I said, "Well, when I offered, you refused. But I can see the attraction of going through lines with a pretty young thing like Sarah and not a raddled old bag like me."

'"Oh come on now, my girl, you are being daft. I just wanted to save you having to stay up late. I know how much your beauty sleep means to you. So when Sarah offered I took the opportunity. I was only thinking of you, my love."

'What could I do but leave them to it?' Peggy asked Sally. 'So I said something like: "Well, you need your beauty sleep as well, Prince Percy, preferably on your own. I will see you back at the digs in an hour."'

Peggy passed Sally her cup of tea and proffered one of the delicious biscuits.

'What do you make of Sarah?' she enquired, watching Sally very closely.

'I'm really not quite sure what to make of her, to be honest. She doesn't really muck in with the rest of us, and I do get the feeling sometimes that she thinks she is above us. I suspect she is quite ambitious too, but with all due respect to Percy, can he really help further her career?'

Just as Peggy was about to reply, the dividing door opened and there was the man himself.

'Ah, we have company – and beautiful it is too. Hello, Sally. To what do we owe the honour of this visit?'

Peggy had jumped up to allow Percy to seat himself in his own armchair and wait for his tea and biscuits to be placed on the little table beside him. Peggy did the honours, then went and sat back at her dressing table, occasionally turning to the mirror and checking her hair. Occupational hazard with actors, thought Sally. They cannot resist a mirror!

'Oh, I was just passing, and thought you might be having a heavy week with all your lines and wondered if you needed anything done,' she said. 'Also, I wanted to let you know that Peter and I just went to pick up your throne from Crewe Hall. What an impressive place, and what a magnificent throne you will be having, Percy. It is insured for many thousands of pounds. So do sit carefully.'

'Blimey, that is some responsibility, isn't it, my little flower?' Percy smiled at Peggy. 'I have never had to deal with an expensive antique on stage. Children and animals are one thing, but furniture? What do you say, old girl?' he chuckled.

'Oh indeed my dear, we really don't like animals or children. Not onstage anyway,' Peggy added with a sad little smile through the mirror to Sally.

'Well, that was the perfect cup of tea. Thank you so much, Peggy, and I am glad that you both seem to have the script well and truly under your belts. I think it is going to be a really super show, and you will hold it all together as the leading man you are, Percy.'

'Don't flatter him any more, dear, or he will be impossible to manage. Now get off and have a sit-down before tonight, love.'

Sally left them to it, feeling a stab of apprehension for poor old Peggy. What on earth was Sarah up to? For the second time in the season so far, Sally was wondering the same thing and she resolved to pay more attention. As for Gwendoline and Geoffrey – that also required some serious investigating.

*

Sally now had the setting up for the evening show and was wondering where Dora might be and whether she might be in the mood to help her rather hard-pressed sister. Sally found her in the boys' dressing room holding court with a variety of the rather filthy jokes that she liked to tell – usually in the pub after a few drinks, but they were going down very well this afternoon, it would seem.

'Sorry to interrupt, but can you come and give me a hand if you have finished your sewing for the day, sis?' Sally ventured.

'Oh, must I? Sally, I am exhausted, and it has been my first day. I wanted to go home and get a couple of songs sorted. I will cook something for when you get back tonight though.' This raised a cheer from the boys, who all wanted to come back for supper. 'You have to ask the boss,' Dora told them, smiling sweetly at Sally. 'She has a lot more to do than me.'

Sally felt a bit miffed. 'I really don't know what state I will be in tonight, so can we take a raincheck, everyone? If you are not coming to help me now, Dora, I need to get on, so see you some time later.' Sally nodded to the room and left wondering why she felt so annoyed.

Can't worry about it now though, I've got too much to do, she thought to herself, and disappeared into the Props Room to find the rifles for a very lovely war.

Chapter 18

The rest of the week was the usual stressed mix of rehearsing all day in one play, then clearing one's head ready for performing the evening show – then if one was really stupid, clearing one's head the next morning from the pub the night before! Sally succumbed to Dora's invitation to the boys to come to supper after all. The trouble was, once they had all performed together at night, and the show had gone well, one quick drink in the pub before closing was not enough to bring them all down to a normal level where they could go home and go to sleep.

It turned out to be a fun evening. Simon was on very good form, as was Peter, and even Geoffrey came – followed discreetly half an hour later by Gwendoline.

'Not too late, am I?' she asked at the door, carrying a bottle of wine. 'Had to wait for the dryer to finish, as usual.'

Sally led her upstairs. 'Not at all, it is lovely to see you.' She watched Gwendoline look around the room until she found Geoffrey sat in a corner talking to Janie, and with no further comment she was off like a greyhound from the traps. Well, thought Sally, we know where *that* is going.

Dora was holding court in the kitchen where she was dishing up her famous chilli con carne.

'It is actually the only thing I can cook so you may get a little bored after nine months,' she giggled. Simon was in her thrall and helping pass bowls.

'Well, it must be love if Simon has anything in his hand other than a bottle of beer,' remarked Sally.

'Oh now come on, that is a bit unfair, Sal. I do my share of clearing up when needs be.'

This last remark brought a howl from Jeremy, who was busy at the sink washing up cutlery to be used again.

'Jesus, Simon, you talk absolute bullshit sometimes. You don't pick up anything in the dressing room, not even your pants, which I wash for you!'

'Ooh, now come on, girls, put your claws away!' laughed Dora. 'People will talk.'

'They talk anyway,' replied Jeremy disconsolately. 'Story of my life.'

'Tell me, I am all ears,' said a voice from the kitchen door, and they all looked up to see Robert standing there with one of his sardonic looks and a huge box of wine in his arms. 'I thought tonight I would get down and dirty with the artistes. Here, someone take this. I will exchange this box of wine for some of Dora's wonderful chilli, and, Jeremy, you can come and tell me your life story while I eat.'

It almost sounded like an order, and everyone hesitated slightly, but Jeremy nobly faced up to the challenge. He opened the box of wine and poured two large glasses, then collected a bowl of Dora's chilli and swept out of the kitchen, passing Robert in the door, with a, 'Follow me.' And then they were gone, leaving everyone in the kitchen to carry on.

Simon turned to Sally with the question on everyone's lips. 'Is Jeremy gay?'

Sally felt cornered. She didn't want to be put in a position where she had to comment on her friend, but could not see a way out.

'I honestly don't know, and that is the truth, guys. But if he is, does it matter? He is one of the kindest people I know and a bloody good actor. I'm aware that he gets really pissed off because he feels there is too much emphasis on someone's sexual orientation and not enough on their talent.'

'Well, I agree with him there.' Geoffrey had come into the room and joined in the discussion. 'In the end it is about talent, not your sex-life, isn't it?' The room went silent while they all looked at Geoffrey, who was a bit the worse for wear.

'How's your wife and family?' asked Peter suddenly.

'None of your business,' shot back Geoffrey. 'Have *you* learned your lines properly for that last scene? And don't say it is none of my business, because it is; you cock up on the night, we all suffer. So I suggest you make bloody sure you are line-perfect, young man. Good night, everyone.' And with that, Geoffrey turned on his heel and was gone, wending his way across the sitting room to their front door where Gwendoline was conveniently waiting with his coat over her arm.

The kitchen brigade quickly dispersed into the other room, leaving Sally and Dora alone.

'Wow – is it like this every time you have a party?' asked Dora, pouring herself a glass of the boxed wine.

'God, no, it would be a nightmare. No, I think though that as time goes on one has to be very careful not to get caught up in all the dramas. Are you listening to me, Dora? Seriously, anything you might get involved with – or anyone, for that matter – you need to make sure that it doesn't come back to haunt you. That goes for me too,' she added almost to herself.

'The trouble is,' she went on, 'we all live in each other's pockets and people need to feel secure in the environment they are living in. Actors especially get far too close to each other, far too quickly, and create these false relationships. I mean, look at us now. We have only been here a month and suddenly it is all kicking off.'

Dora came over and gave her big sister a hug. 'Listen, don't get your knickers in a twist, Sally dear. We are here to have a good time and help you up the ladder of success, and for me to discover what I really want. Speaking of which, I must confess I am really keen to pass my audition for *Lysistrata*, so you will help me, won't you?'

'Of course I will, you daft girl, but don't take things too fast. Establish your usefulness first, and you can do that by helping me more.'

'Agreed,' said Dora. 'Now come on, let's finish the chilli. I am absolutely famished!'

The party turned out to be lovely. Everyone mellowed and relaxed, and the talk ended up on Rupert Hallam and Isabelle James, the two newcomers, and how their arrival would affect the rest of them.

'Do we have any idea how the casting will go?' asked Peter. 'I mean, there are obvious choices for characters like Polonius and the King and Gertrude, aren't there?'

Robert was sitting on the sofa with Jeremy and Janie, who piped up: 'Not necessarily, Peter. What do you think, Robert? You are assisting Giles, after all – you should have some ideas?'

Robert looked round the room and realized it was time to

go. Speculation could often become very negative, and he didn't want to lose his credibility.

'Ah, now I think it is my bedtime.' He rose and gave them all his best, most reassuring smile. 'All will be revealed in good time – and never forget, there are several plays in the offing this season. It is not all about *Hamlet*, you know.' The room let out a communal sigh.

Sally decided to move things along. 'Come on, guys, it's late and never mind the Dane – Sir Thomas More has to be sorted out first. Jeremy, do you want the sofa tonight?' Sally was giving her friend a way out of a walk home with Robert. She could see the gratitude in his eyes.

'Yes, that would be great. Thanks, Sal. And you can take me through my lines first thing, can't you?' This elicited a sigh from Sally and a groan from the rest of the room.

'OK, coats on – it's bedtime, everyone. We have still got three more days of *Oh, What a Lovely War!* and then our leap back in time to Henry the Eighth. Then we have sex, drugs and rock 'n' roll from the Greek girls!' This sent up a huge cheer and moved everyone out of the door. Sally, Dora and Jeremy cleared up and then made some hot chocolate.

'We will survive, you know,' remarked Jeremy. 'Your sister and I have a lot in common, Dora. We want to succeed on our merits and we are in it for the long game.'

'I can see that,' said Dora, 'and I think you will succeed. I have only just arrived, but from the outside you both seem so much more focused than most of the cast. I have to confess I have been bitten by the bug though. If I can get that part in the chorus, who knows where it may lead next? Can't I play Ophelia in your Dumb Show, Sally? I mean, you are directing it, and I am your sister. Nepotism is acceptable, isn't it? I just have to make sure I am one hundred per cent more talented than anyone else.'

Sally laughed. 'You are incorrigible, sister dear. There is no Ophelia in the Dumb Show, but let's wait and see.'

She looked across at Jeremy, who was busying himself making up the sofa, and caught his eye. He tapped his nose and mouthed, 'Watch out!'

Lying in bed later, Sally tried to gather her thoughts. There suddenly seemed to be a great deal going on behind the scenes. She thought back to Peggy and Percy and their situation. Then there was Geoffrey and Gwendoline – what was going on there? Geoffrey had seemed the most stable of all the company, with a happy marriage and a loving wife and three beautiful children. Not that anyone had seen them so far this season. Even Jeremy seemed unsettled, and Sally was suspicious of Robert's motivation for helping him with his script. She tried to work out what she was doing in all this. Just getting on with the job, she hoped.

But was this enough? Even her sister was making plans already. Was this how it was going to be? Nine months of people vying for position. She thought about Charmaine, who so far had kept her distance from the rest of the cast. Did she learn to do this during her two years spent at the Royal Shakespeare? Sally had heard many actors moan about the politics of the company and how unfair it was. You joined the chorus, fully intending to work your way up through the ranks, only to discover that the powers-that-be could bring in whoever they wanted along the way to play the leads, and even the smaller roles. So what was the point of dedicating your early career to a company that showed no loyalty?

Well, it was still early days, and Sally had every intention of making her stage presence well and truly felt. Dora might have her own agenda, and as long as it did not cross Sally's path, they would be fine.

She finally fell asleep wondering what Rupert was going to be like and whether his Hamlet would achieve the notoriety that Giles so craved for his theatre.

Chapter 19

By midnight on Saturday night *Oh, What a Lovely War!* was but a distant memory, and as the set of *A Man for All Seasons* sprang up around them, and the speakers played a harmonious selection from the Franciscan Monks collection, the crew and cast seemed to become quieter and more serious. Well, they did for about half an hour, until Mrs Wong's sweet and sour chips arrived, and the carpenter opened the beer! Then it was all hands to the deck as usual, and a race to get through it all before dawn.

Sally and Dora and Janie finished the washing and then went back to Janie and Peter's house for a quiet bottle of wine and a bit of a gossip.

'So come on then, Janie, what's with Gwendoline and Geoffrey?' asked Sally, hunkering down in a comfy chair with her glass of red and a packet of crisps.

'How did you find out, you wicked girl? It is supposed to be the secret of the century.' Janie looked at Sally's surprised face and groaned. 'Oh God, you don't really know, do you? You guessed and I fell for it. I am such a klutz! Please don't say anything to anybody as I could get the sack. Gwendoline has sworn me to secrecy, Sally. Please—'

'Oh blimey, Janie, stop panicking – of course we won't say anything,' Dora interrupted. 'Calm down and enjoy your drink. Listen, it is just interesting though, isn't it, those two? I thought Geoffrey was happily married – or so you said, Sally.'

'Well, I thought he was, wasn't he, Janie?' Sally and Dora turned and waited for their friend to fill in the gaps.

'Yes, he was. Certainly, last season things seemed fine – but Gwendoline has been hanging around on the edge of his marriage for quite a while, I am beginning to suspect. She tells me that she and Geoffrey were an item at college years ago and then, when he went off to be an actor, they lost touch for a couple of years. She had no idea he had even become an actor; she thought he had gone to teach drama at some school up north. Anyway, they bumped into each other at a school reunion, and it was as if they had never parted, except he announced that he had a wife and three small children – these daughters who are the apple of his eye. Gwendoline is completely obsessed with Geoffrey and decided to get him into the cast last year so she could "work on him" – her words, by the way. I have no idea what went on last year, but this year, so far, there is no sign of the wife and kids, and Gwendoline is on a mission. Believe me, it is embarrassing for me because they are always touching each other up and disappearing into the laundry room, and I dread going to his dressing room in case I catch them at it.' Janie stopped and looked at the other two girls, who were helpless with laughter.

'What is so funny, may I ask? It is not funny if you are involved even if you don't want to be. Stop laughing!' she ordered.

'Sorry, Janie, really but I have got this mental image of

tight-arsed Gwendoline whipping off her glasses and her Alice band and grabbing Geoffrey in his Pierrot costume and breathing into his ear "Take me, Geoffrey darling" and Geoffrey peering at her and saying those immortal words: "God but you are beautiful behind your glasses. Come to me, Gwendoline!"' This resulted in more squeals of laughter from Dora and Sally, while poor Janie looked on aghast.

'Please stop it, guys. What am I going to do?' she pleaded.

The two sisters finally calmed down and tried to offer helpful suggestions.

'Just try and stay out of their way,' advised Sally. 'I was only talking about this the other day to Dora, explaining that it's fatal to get involved with all the goings-on. Why can't we all just muddle along like the boys do? Go to the pub, have a few drinks and don't ask any questions. Classic male behaviour. Sorry, didn't mean to be quite so sexist.'

'Do we think Charmaine is gay?' asked Dora, completely changing the subject.

'Gay? No, why do you ask that?' said Janie, pouring more wine for them all.

'I don't know really,' replied Dora. 'It's just a feeling I have and she came on to me yesterday.'

Sally looked quite shocked. 'Came on to you how? And anyway, how would you know what coming on from a woman was like, Dora?'

'Oh please, Sally, give me a break! I am not a child. We had gay relationships at school. Didn't you?' retorted Dora.

There was silence while Sally took this all in. 'Um, no actually, I wasn't aware of anything like that at school. I just never noticed, I suppose.'

Dora sighed and said to Janie, 'That is so typical of my sister. She lives in a little world of her own. I think that's why she and Jeremy get on so well. They just never notice anything except maybe their acting roles.'

Sally felt rather foolish. 'Maybe Charmaine just likes to keep things close to her chest,' she suggested, 'as does Sarah. What do we think about Miss Kelly then?' To her relief this brought all manner of speculation from the other two girls.

'She is quite hard, I think,' said Janie. 'And she uses people. I have noticed she is all over Percy Pig, helping him with his lines. Mind you, I am not sure Percy can pull any strings for her.'

'Except,' said Sally, 'Giles does listen to him quite a lot about casting, and they have worked together for many years. If Sarah can get to Giles through Percy and land herself a good juicy role this season, she can get agents to come and see her. God, listen to us! The poor girl is probably just lonely and shy, and it is easier to make friends with Percy and Peggy than us lot of witches.'

'Actually, I think you were right the first time, Sally. You have always been a good judge of character and having come into all this after you and Janie, I think I can say I have noticed things as a bystander. Sarah is not to be trusted and I suspect she is after taking parts away from you, Sal. She is always sidling up to Robert and asking about characters. She has learned all the songs for *Lysistrata* and I wouldn't be surprised if she angles for the part you are lined up for – and to under-study the lead. Just keep an eye on her, sister dear.'

'Well, you're a dark horse, Dora,' commented Janie, gathering up their glasses. 'Did you know you had such an observant sibling, and with such a cynical heart, Sally? I think you should go home and sleep on these things, girls. But please, can I remind you that these dark thoughts are a secret between us.'

Sally got her coat and bag and Dora said to Janie: 'Thank you for the wine. I am really sleepy now and my little bed is calling. Come on, Sally, it is Sunday tomorrow – how cool is that? A lie-in!'

As they walked home, arm-in-arm, the sisters did not speak, each deep in their own thoughts.

The next morning, Sally woke to a grey blustery November day, and decided that it was the perfect Sunday to stay in and watch telly and eat toast. Dora, however, had other ideas, and came bouncing into the kitchen humming a song from *Lysistrata*.

'Can we go through some songs for my audition today?' she asked through a mouthful of cereal. 'I thought I could sing the main one that old Charmaine sings to gather all you ladies together. It is quite funky and I know I could sing it well.' She proceeded to demonstrate her point.

'Oh please, Dora, not just yet. Let me wake up first,' shouted Sally, putting her hands over her ears.

'Sorry,' said Dora, looking rather forlorn. 'Just want to get on with it.'

Sally looked at her sister across the table for a good few minutes, wondering where this sudden desire to act had come from. Dora had never shown any interest in acting while Sally was at college, and certainly did not pursue it through school plays or anything as Sally had done. Why now?

'I hope you don't mind me asking, Dora, but why all this sudden wish to be an actress? I thought you had come up here to Crewe to help with the wardrobe department and learn a bit about design? Now all of a sudden you want to perform.'

Dora didn't reply immediately. She finished her cereal in silence, then got up and rinsed the bowl in the sink and left it on the draining board. Wiping her hands on the tea towel, she turned round and leaned against the sink.

'To be honest, I really don't know. But watching you all these last two weeks has awoken something in me, sis. I just feel so alive and I want to join in. Listen, I may be hopeless, and it will all come to nothing, but I need to have a go at least. Do you mind?' she asked Sally, holding her gaze.

'Why should I mind?' her sister answered, a little too quickly. 'You can do what you like, but don't expect too much, will you? I mean, Giles is no pushover and he has his cast already.'

'Oh, I know that, of course. But there is this opportunity in *Lysistrata*, isn't there? Why not go for it?' Dora's eyes were bright with excitement. 'Can we just run through the song a couple of times, please? *Please?*'

Sally laughed. 'Come on then, let's get it out of the way then I can relax for the rest of the afternoon.'

The girls worked on the song and Sally had to admit that her sister was pretty impressive. It was very strange to be in this situation, and she felt a niggle of uncertainty. After the conversation last night about the other actresses and their ambitions, Sally wondered if she was taking things too much for granted. She just assumed she had her place in the company. Giles had promised her some decent roles and he seemed pleased with her work so far. But maybe she should be more pushy. She decided to talk to Jeremy and find out what he knew about future casting from Robert.

The sisters spent the rest of the day lying on the sofa and listening to the wind and the rain lashing against the windows. They had ham sandwiches for tea and were in bed by nine. Fast asleep by five past . . .

Chapter 20

The opening night of *A Man for All Seasons* was a great success. To give him his due Percy Hackett turned in a more than adequate Thomas More. Sally watched from the wings for most of the performance as she did not have too many props to deal with, and Heather had wanted her to learn the book and be able to prompt and give cues to the actors and crew. It was a scary job initially, as everyone relies on the prompt corner and basically the buck stops there. However, Sally soon managed to deal with six different things at once and actually enjoyed the power she had in her hands during a show. Tonight had gone without a hitch, and Sally was smiling as the cast took their bows.

There had been great excitement at the opening of the play as Lord Graham had arrived with his son and daughter. They took their places in the Royal Box just as the lights were going down. Giles was faffing around in the interval organizing champagne for the guests.

'Lord Graham is a very dear friend,' he explained to Sally. 'He does so much for this theatre, and I don't know what we would do without him.'

After the play, the cast were invited to meet His Lordship in the bar.

'Is there a free pint in it?' asked Simon as they came offstage.

'Absolutely,' said Sally, who was in charge of passing on the invitation. 'Glad to see you have got your priorities right as usual, Simon.' She grabbed Jeremy by the arm as he was leaving and asked: 'Are you going up to the bar?'

'Wouldn't miss it for the world, my dear. Nothing like a bit of landed gentry, is there?' He winked at her. 'I'll see you in the bar.'

Jeremy was feeling terrific. He had nailed the role and knew he had given a good performance. As he was changing, Robert had come in and slapped him on the back, saying, 'Congratulations! You managed to make that character watchable for a change. He is written as such a prig but you made him human – even gave him some charisma, dare I say it?'

Jeremy glowed with pride. This was what he wanted. This was what he lived for. He was going to show the world what a great actor he could be. He arrived in the bar feeling fantastic and in control of his destiny – and then he saw the boy, and everything fell away. There was only silence and the space between him and the young man standing at the bar smiling at him.

'Hi, I loved your performance. Can I get you a drink?' The young man shook Jeremy's hand and then placed an arm round his shoulders and steered him towards the drinks. It seemed the most natural gesture in the world, yet so intimate that Jeremy could hardly get his breath.

'I am Eddie Graham, by the way, son of the Lord.' The boy made a face and laughed. 'It is always embarrassing at first. Hopefully you won't hold it against me. Here, have a glass of champagne. You look done in.'

Jeremy took the glass and desperately tried to pull himself together. What was the matter with him? He was trembling.

'Um, thanks very much,' he said, taking the glass and throwing the contents back in one gulp. 'Yes, I am sorry to be so slow but it has been a long day. Could you pass me another drink, do you think?' Jeremy handed Eddie the empty glass and waited for the replacement. He couldn't move from the spot. Eddie laughed and his whole face lit up. It was such an open, beautiful face, thought Jeremy, losing himself once again in the moment, only to come back down to earth with a bump as he felt a hand on his arm moving him away from the bar – and there was Giles, beaming down at him.

'Well done, Jeremy. Fantastic performance! You've met Eddie? Good, lovely, well let me introduce you to his father, Lord Graham.' Giles spun Jeremy round to face a tall handsome man, who rather spookily resembled an older version of Eddie. Well, he would, wouldn't he? *Pull yourself together, Jeremy, for God's sake.*

'How do you do, sir,' he managed to mumble and shook the proffered hand.

'Pleased to meet you, my boy. Thoroughly enjoyed the evening. This is my daughter Tilly, by the way.' His Lordship stepped aside to reveal a strikingly pretty girl with the same open face as her brother, and mountains of golden hair.

'Hi,' she said. 'Congratulations on the play – it was fab.'

Jeremy was now completely at a loss as to where to go with any of this. The bar was so crowded and the noise level had reached epic proportions, and he felt a bit dizzy.

'Do you mind if I just sit down for a moment?' he asked no one in particular and Eddie jumped to attention.

'Of course, sorry. There is a chair. I'll get it.' And he had gone off before Jeremy could stop him.

Jeremy turned to the girl and tried to explain: 'You must think me very odd just standing here, but the thing is, it is always rather overwhelming coming up to all these people after just finishing a show. It is like coming out of one world and into another.'

'Oh, please don't apologize. I think it's great you even bothered to come. I am not sure I would.' Tilly smiled at him and he basked in the glow.

Eddie was suddenly at his side, saying, 'Here you go. Please sit and relax. We rather bombarded you, didn't we? Sorry, but it is so exciting being here and seeing all the actors and everything.'

The two siblings spent the next few minutes chatting and generally being very pleasant. Jeremy still couldn't quite bring himself up to speed and was desperate for some help to get him out of his coma.

'There you are – I have been looking everywhere for you. Oh, sorry, didn't mean to interrupt.'

It was Sally.

She stopped and acknowledged the two guests.

Jeremy finally found his tongue. 'Sally, this is Eddie and Tilly Graham. They have been to see the show tonight with their father Lord Graham.'

'But don't let that put you off,' laughed Eddie. 'We are quite nice really, aren't we, Tilly?'

Sally smiled and shook their hands.

'How lovely to meet you. I am sorry I barged in, but when my best friend goes missing I am always a bit concerned. He is not safe out on his own!' They all laughed and Jeremy started to relax for the first time in the evening. Thank goodness Sally was here to rescue him. But rescue him from what, exactly?

The bar was finally emptying out as the audience left. As

usual the cast and crew had their eye on the pub and most of them had already left. Giles and Lord Graham were deep in conversation at the other end of the bar so Jeremy ventured to invite their new friends for a drink with them.

'Oh, that would be terrific, but I think Dad is on a bit of a mission to get back tonight as he has to be in London tomorrow,' replied Eddie. 'But it would be great if we could meet up sometime. I would love to see backstage – but I don't want to be a nuisance.'

'No, no, of course you wouldn't be a nuisance. We work every day until about five so if you wanted to turn up then we could show you round. It would be a pleasure,' said Jeremy, turning to Sally for confirmation.

'Oh yes, absolutely,' she agreed. 'Listen, I hate to be a partypooper but we need to get going, Jeremy.'

'Oh yes, please don't let us keep you. It has been a pleasure meeting you and I look forward to my guided tour.'

This little speech from Eddie was directed solely at Jeremy and it was picked up by Sally, who made a mental note to ask Jeremy all about it later. In the meantime she grabbed his arm and joked, 'Don't you know that a clean exit is always best? Stop dithering and say goodbye.'

'Goodbye,' Jeremy said obediently, watching the two beautiful young things cross the bar towards their father.

He felt the butterflies in his stomach again and turned guiltily to see if Sally was watching him. Fortunately she had her head down and was concentrating on dragging him across to the door. He swallowed hard and tried to pull himself together. He needed to be alone to examine what had happened to him tonight. One thing he knew for sure: it had nothing to do with acting or his performance.

Act 3

Exit stage left

Chapter 21

The boy I love is up in the gallery,
The boy I love is looking now at me.
There he is, can't you see, waving his handkerchief
As merry as a robin that sings on a tree.

Jeremy arrived at the stage door the next day to be greeted by a very excited Gladys, who handed him an envelope. The woman was desperately hoping he would open it there and then, and put her out of her misery. Needless to say she had examined the envelope extensively, but it had given her no clues, except that it was expensive stationery. She watched Jeremy disappear upstairs with a frustrated sigh. Oh well, you couldn't win 'em all.

Once in the dressing room, which mercifully he had to himself, Jeremy tore open the missive. The card was also expensive and matched the envelope. The handwriting was smooth and flowing.

Dear Jeremy,

*It was so wonderful to meet you last night and be a small
part of your celebrations.*

I was so disappointed when we had to leave.

*You very kindly suggested you might meet with me one
day soon and show me round the theatre.*

*I just wanted to make sure that you understood how
much I would appreciate your offer. Here is my telephone
number and you can leave a message if I am not around. I
am working on my father's estate at the moment so am out
most of the day, but you will always find me in after
5 p.m.*

I do so hope you will call.

Kind regards,

Eddie Graham
01270 998662

Jeremy could feel his heart pounding, and realized that he was
holding his breath. He let it go with a big sigh, wondering
what this was all about. Did Eddie feel the same way, or was
this just a polite note showing a mild interest in the theatre?
Surely it was more than that. Deep down inside him a little
voice was telling him that there *had* been a connection last
night – he was not imagining it. What should he do now? He
put the card back in the envelope and pushed it down inside
his bag. He would go and ask Sally.

He found his friend folding clean washing in the wardrobe
department with Dora and Gwendoline and Janie. Now was
obviously not a good time to discuss his life.

'Hi, Jeremy,' said Dora gaily. 'You are looking a bit stressed.'

Sally crossed to Jeremy and took his arm. 'Is something wrong?' she whispered. 'Come outside.' She pushed him through the door into the corridor.

'I have had a card from Eddie,' replied Jeremy. 'He wants a guided tour of the theatre.'

'Well, that's great. Say yes, you numpty, and get him here and then you can see how the land lies.' Sally gave him a hug and said, 'I have to work, let's talk about it later.'

Jeremy went back to the dressing room and reread the note, then lay on folded arms at his dressing table, trying to control the swirling thoughts going round in his head. Finally he fell asleep, and was awoken an hour later by the lads arriving for the evening show.

Sally meanwhile had finished the laundry and had gone off to set the stage and check props. Dora called after her, 'Hey, wait for me, sis! I need a favour. Giles has asked to see me tomorrow during the lunch-hour to audition for the chorus, so will you just listen to my song a couple of times?'

'Sure,' replied Sally, making her way onto the stage. 'Why don't you sing for me now, onstage, while no one is around?'

Dora stopped in her tracks and looked around. 'OK then, if you think it is all right.'

'Yes – go on, go for it. I will whip up to the box - just give me a minute.' And she disappeared out of sight.

Left on her own in the middle of the stage, Dora was suddenly very aware of the whole theatre. The auditorium in front of her, with the rows of red velvet seats creating a crimson sea, calm now, but which would soon be rippling with life. She gazed upwards to the balcony, a distant land, and let out a small sound, aiming for the back of the theatre. Her tiny note floated away and was lost in the crimson velvet tiers above her.

'You will have to do better than that,' came Sally's voice from the semi-darkness. She sounded so close but when Dora looked up she could see her sister away in the box. It was deceptive.

'Sorry, I was just suddenly overwhelmed by the whole building. It really is so beautiful, isn't it?' murmured Dora as she moved to the front of the stage and peered over the edge into the pit.

'Come on, Dora, stop messing about and give me a blast,' ordered her sister, and her voice chased the shadows round the theatre.

Dora cleared her throat and launched into a gutsy rendition of the opening number from the new musical *Lysistrata*. Her voice was strong and clear, and she really gave the high notes a blasting. It was very rousing and just right emotionally for the scene, in Sally's opinion. She was just about to say as much when she was stopped in her tracks by the sound of clapping. The hands were very slowly coming together and each clap reverberated round the auditorium.

'Encore! Bravo! You are hired, my girl, is she not, Timothy?'

The two sisters were trying to gauge where the voice was coming from. Sally left the box and came down to join Dora on the stage, by which time Giles and Timothy Townsend, the musical director, were leaning on the edge of the pit in the stalls looking up at them.

'Are you serious?' asked Dora, unable to keep the excitement out of her voice.

'Absolutely, my dear,' replied Giles. 'We have two talented sisters in our midst. Marvellous! Sally, I have been looking for you, because I want you to talk to Timothy here about taking a solo number in the next show. At the moment it belongs to the leading character, but Tim and I agree you have a wonderful soprano voice and it would be a shame not to use it. So if you are game, he can give you the song now so you have time to get it under your belt for rehearsals tomorrow. As for you, Dora – that is your name, I believe?'

Dora nodded her head so hard Sally thought it would drop off!

'Well, if you could come with us now,' Giles continued, 'we will take you through the role and Timothy can check out your range, et cetera. See you in the rehearsal room in five.'

The two girls were left standing staring into an empty theatre and silence prevailed. For a few seconds!

Then: 'Oh my God!' screamed Dora. 'I am going to be in the show. I am going to be an actress. Oh my God!' She grabbed her sister and proceeded to waltz her round the stage.

'Well done,' said Sally, trying to catch her breath and at the same time work out what exactly had just happened and where she herself fitted into all this. A solo in the next show, that was great – but how would Charmaine feel about losing a number to Dora, of all people? What would she have to say about that?

'Hang on, can we stop, please? I need to think.' Sally escaped from Dora's arms and went across to the prompt corner to find a script of *Lysistrata*. 'I just want to check how all this fits together,' she explained to Dora.

'Does it matter?' the other girl asked. 'All we need to do is wait to be given our new roles – and away we go. I can't believe I am going to be in *Lysistrata*. Come on, let's go and tell everyone.'

'*No*. Hang on, Dora, that is *not* a good idea. People are very sensitive about their roles and it is not your place to announce cast changes. Leave it to Giles to tell everyone tomorrow morning. Please trust me on this.' Sally took hold of Dora's arm and looked her straight in the eye. 'Do you understand? You do not want to start out at the beginning of the rehearsals on the wrong foot, believe me. Promise me you will not say a word?'

Dora made a zip movement across her mouth with her fingers.

'Mum's the word, sis!'

Chapter 22

The next morning at ten o'clock sharp the company was assembled in the rehearsal room waiting with anticipation for their next roles. It was freezing, despite the efforts of the two big blow-heaters that had been brought in, and everyone was hidden behind scarves and mufflers and woolly hats. Giles was pacing back and forth as the last stragglers tumbled in, landing in a heap on the floor. Simon and Peter had had a heavy night!

'Thank you, gentlemen, for deigning to grace us with your presence,' boomed Giles sarcastically. 'You can in fact pick yourselves up and go and get coffee for the rest of us as a punishment. You have very little to do in the next production, but I shall expect to see your support in other areas.'

The boys mumbled apologies and scrambled off to make the coffee.

'Now, ladies and gentlemen, before I go through the casting, I want to explain about the conference that is going to be held here the week our production opens, and the part we will be playing as hosts. It is the annual conference of the

Association of Repertory Theatres, and they hold it every year in a different theatre. They also like to open with a bit of a bang, so *Lysistrata* has appealed to them enormously, and they have announced that the conference proceedings will coincide with our first night. There will be a "Do" afterwards, which they fund, I am delighted to say, and all they ask of us is that we stay after the show, and chat to all the dignitaries and such. In my experience, from past events, it can be very handy for you actors, because you get to meet all the directors of almost every theatre in the country, and having given your audition on stage during the evening, you just have to be charming – and your career is in the bag.'

There was a collective groan from the cast. Actors are notoriously bad at schmoozing. Very few learn the art of chatting up producers and securing a job. Same thing with the casting couch: it is never as simple as just being chased round an office by a large amorous producer with a big fat cigar!

Giles clapped his hands and put a stop to any chat that was threatening to bubble up under the scarves. Everyone had a story to tell about some famous actor who had slept their way to the top.

'Now as far as the lead is concerned, Charmaine, you already have your instructions. However, I have made one slight change to the role and given the battle song to a new recruit called Dora Thomas.' There was a murmur amongst the ranks at this, and Charmaine scanned the room until she found Dora. The latter was not difficult to spot, as she was sitting bolt upright in the centre of the actors, looking bright-eyed and bushy-tailed.

'Secondly,' Giles boomed on, 'Sally will be singing a big new number at the top of Act Two, and I have combined the parts of the neighbour and the council member who opposes

Lysistrata into one role, which will be Sally. Peggy, you are the oldest woman in the village.'

This brought much laughter from the cast and a howl of displeasure from Peggy, though she turned it into a superior smile as she explained: 'Listen, you toe rags, it is the best part in the play and I will wipe the floor with you all – wait and see!'

Giles continued to read out the names. Out of the corner of her eye Sally watched Sarah's reaction since she had been given a very minor role as the servant to Percy's senator. Surprisingly, the girl was smiling and was hanging onto Percy like a limpet. Watch this space.

Geoffrey was also a senator and a hard-done-by husband. He winked across the room towards Gwendoline, who blew him a kiss. No discretion there then, observed Sally.

Simon and Peter returned with the coffees just as Giles was announcing that they would be playing general riff-raff and crowd, and everyone burst out laughing again. The maestro raised his hand and the room went quiet.

'I know it is a play for the women, in the main, but guys, that does not mean you must sit back and just let it roll along. I want you all to have real characters. I want to be able to understand how this strike of sexual favours, by your wives and mistresses, affects you and your lives. There is a serious message in the play even though we are doing it as a musical. So I don't want to see any slacking – and remember, you will be on show not just to our audiences but to every repertory director in the country.'

Giles broke up the group and called Timothy Townsend, the musical director, to talk to the actors about the music rehearsals.

Sally was making her way across to the piano when she was joined by Charmaine.

'I am not quite sure how to take these changes,' the other actress challenged Sally. 'Am I not good enough to sing those numbers?'

Cringing inwardly, Sally replied as positively as she could, 'Oh no, I just think Giles needed to spread the music a bit so we all got a go. You have that lovely song to your husband, and I expect Giles thought that as you have so many more lines to learn than the rest of us, you could concentrate on them and not worry about all the numbers. Which let's face it, do take up a great deal of time.'

'I suppose so,' said Charmaine, but she sounded less than convinced.

Fortunately the conversation did not continue as they had reached the piano, and Timothy was very busy handing out sheets of music.

The rest of the morning was spent learning the songs. By the end of the session, coats and scarves had been tossed aside, and everyone was rosy-cheeked and full of *con brio*.

Singing did that to people, thought Sally, who was having the time of her life, as was her sister. Dora had sung her number note-perfectly, and the room had responded with a round of applause. The girl was in her element.

It was only when they broke for lunch that Sally realized that Jeremy had not been in rehearsals. How odd, she thought. She went to the Props Room to find Heather who was the font of all knowledge – after Gladys at the stage door, of course.

'He had a dentist appointment,' announced Heather, 'but he did ask me if he needn't come back until after lunch. As he is not in the play I thought there would be no harm – and he did have a list of props he was going to pick up for me.'

Sally wondered what was going on with her friend. Still,

there was plenty of time to find out later. For the moment, she had work to do, starting with keeping her sister's feet on the ground.

The next few days were full on for the girls. The songs had to be learned before Giles could really tackle the emotional content of the play. The other big challenge was the costumes. Giles and Gwendoline had this idea of flimsy and sexy to enhance the idea of women's femininity while at the same time showing that the women themselves were not flimsy in any way, and as far as sex was concerned, they would use every trick in the book to make their husbands' lives hell until they agreed to stop going to war.

Gwendoline had all the girls round the table in her office while she produced sketches of each character's costume.

'Oh Charmaine, look at yours!' yelped Dora, holding up a drawing of the skimpiest costume they had ever seen. 'It's more of a handkerchief than a dress.'

Charmaine looked a little taken aback but Gwendoline was ready.

'Charmaine, don't look so worried. It will all be very tasteful and I will only work to your requirements. But I do want you to look incredibly sexy. I have also got some gorgeous wigs to show you. Listen up, everyone. We want a feeling of this hot Greek island full of lushness and sensuality, against the horrors of war. These women have had enough of months and months without their husbands, who went away fighting while they had to tend the fields and work hard to make ends meet. They want to be feminine again, and enjoy the fruits of their labours. So by withdrawing their sexual favours from their husbands when the men get back from fighting, they are making a strong statement, not just about peace, but the needs and importance of women on every level. By emphasizing their physical appearance and attractiveness, I want not only the men in the audience to really understand what it must be like for the poor homecoming husbands, but I want women to realize that being attractive is not about being a victim. We do not make ourselves gorgeous just for our men, and we can use our attributes for important issues, not just to please our husbands.' She paused for breath.

'So we will start with Charmaine and then I will fit Sally, then Dora. Sarah has gone on an errand with Percy so I will fit her last. We have got a teacher joining us from the local stage school. Apparently, she used to be an actress years ago, and she is happy to be in the chorus, and I think our very own Janie is going to join you onstage.' She turned to Janie who was busy ironing costumes as usual, and Sally gave a cheer and was joined by the others. Janie did a curtsey and looked very pleased.

'Just don't expect me to sing by myself because I am tone deaf,' she warned them.

'Hmm, that doesn't bode very well for the company numbers,' said Charmaine, looking displeased.

'Oh don't worry, I am only kidding. I can hold a tune OK, I just don't want to sing on my own.' And unruffled, Janie went back to her ironing.

'Right, come on, ladies – let's get down to business. Charmaine, try this, Sally take this one and Dora, you try the red one.'

Dora screamed with delight. 'Oh, how brilliant! I have always wanted to be a redhead.'

Sally and Charmaine took their wigs to the dressing room and sat next to each other in front of the mirrors.

'I must say, I had hoped my debut leading role this season might have been something a little more serious,' lamented

Charmaine, as she pulled the mass of strawberry-blonde curls onto her head. 'When Giles mentioned *Lysistrata* originally to me, I thought he meant the play. He never mentioned music or singing . . . Oh my giddy aunt!'

Charmaine had been stopped in her ramblings by the image staring back at her from the mirror. Sally had to turn away and pretend to be struggling with her wig, so as not to laugh out loud. There was so much hair one could hardly make out Charmaine underneath. She resembled Jane Fonda in *Barbarella*.

'This is ridiculous! Where's Gwendoline?' the actress snorted, and steamed off. Sally recovered herself and adjusted her wig which was actually rather nice. It was several shades of auburn, and although it was full, it did not have the abundance of curls that Charmaine's wig had sported. She turned round to see Charmaine stomping back followed by Gwendoline with an armful of hair.

'There is no need to panic,' Gwendoline was saying, trying to soothe the troubled waters. 'Of course we want you to look beautiful. Now sit down and try this one on.' She presented the actress with a much smoother head of hair though still on the blonde side, this time veering to platinum.

'I just don't see myself as a blonde,' said Charmaine. The wig was better than the last but did not enhance her features. Unfortunately, Charmaine had a long face which could look a little horsey. She did really need a few curls to lift her face.

Sally was sitting in her auburn wig quite happily taking all this in when she felt the hair being removed.

'This could work really well for me, I think,' announced Charmaine, donning the filched wig.

'But that is mine,' began Sally, knowing only too well it would make no difference when push came to shove.

'Here, you try the strawberry blonde,' said Charmaine, passing it across.

Sally put on the blonde abundance of curls and burst out laughing. 'I look like a Shetland pony,' she giggled.

'Well, how appropriate. I myself have always been compared to a thoroughbred racehorse,' stated Charmaine rather grandly.

Everyone in the room looked at each other to check whether this woman was actually serious or not, realized she was, and had to avoid eye-contact in order not to gag.

'Thank you so much for that, Charmaine. It is good to know where I stand in the breeding stakes of horses. I wonder where we are in the acting profession?'

'Now, come on, ladies, please let us try and resolve this because I need to get on,' intervened Gwendoline before things got out of hand. 'I must say the auburn wig is very good on you, Charmaine, and actually, Sally, if we trim that wig, it will be rather fetching. You look very sexy, as a matter of fact,' she added for good measure.

Sally looked at her hard to see if the wardrobe mistress was taking the mickey and decided she was being serious.

'OK, fine, I bend to your taste and you are the designer, after all.'

'Thank heavens for that,' said Gwendoline. 'Now wish me luck, girls. I have to go and break it to Peggy that she is wearing a bald cap.'

Chapter 23

'How does your mouth feel now?'

'OK, except I can't stop dribbling.'

'Yes, I must say it is not a pretty sight. Here, take my napkin.'

Jeremy took the proffered napkin and briefly touched Eddie's fingers. It sent a shiver through him. He wished the dentist had anaesthetized his whole body, he was trembling so much. Could Eddie tell? He could hardly believe he was sitting opposite the cause of his angst, in a tearoom in Nantwich. He had rung Eddie first thing this morning, having written down a message for the answer machine in case he had to speak into it. It had taken him several attempts to get the tone just right. Not too friendly, but warm and inviting at the same time.

Hi, this is Jeremy Sinclair here. We met the other night at the theatre. You said you would like a tour backstage at some time. I have spoken to our general manager who says that is absolutely fine, so any time you and your sister would like to come, just give me a call. The number at the stage door is 01270 377555. I look forward to your call.

He had dialled Eddie's number and tried to do vocal

exercises while he waited to calm himself down. He was totally caught offguard when he heard Eddie's voice answer, 'Hi, Eddie Graham here, how can I help you?'

'Oh, um, hi, is that Eddie? Blimey, I wasn't expecting your voice at all! Sorry, you have completely thrown me.' Jeremy could feel his cheeks burning and was so glad the recipient of this call could not see him at this moment.

'Is that Jeremy, by any chance?' asked Eddie.

'Yes – yes, it is. I am so sorry. Please forgive me for being so pathetic. I just assumed you would be out in the fields some-where, as you told me you were working on the estate.' Jeremy was trying very hard to pull himself together and sound like a grown-up.

'Well, normally I am, but I was waiting for a delivery of animal feed – fascinating life I lead, don't you think?' Eddie laughed and Jeremy had a mental picture of his beautiful face lighting up. 'So what can I do for you?' Eddie continued.

'Well, I was just wondering if you and Tilly still wanted to come and look round the theatre. I am actually free this week, as I am not in the next production so I have plenty of spare time,' explained Jeremy.

'Oh wow, that would be tremendous, thank you so much. I will have to check with Tilly, as she has school. If she can't make it, could I come on my own?' Eddie asked.

Jeremy felt his heart leap into his mouth and he desperately fought to keep control of his tongue which was trying to tie itself in knots.

'Yes, not a problem, just give me a ring at the stage door. Have you got a pen? The number is 01270 377555.'

'Got it, right. Fantastic, thank you,' Eddie said. 'How is it all going? Are you getting good audiences? My father mentioned that you had a good write-up in the local rag this week.'

'Yes, really good, thanks,' replied Jeremy. 'I am just off to the dentist in Nantwich to have a filling done. Not looking forward to that, I can tell you. But it is fortunate I am not working this week so I can get it sorted out.'

'Nantwich? Whereabouts? I have to go into town this lunchtime to pick up some tools. We could meet and have a coffee. What time are you going to be finished with the dreaded dentist?' asked Eddie.

'About noon, I guess,' whispered Jeremy in a fever of excitement. Why couldn't he pull himself together? 'Where shall we meet? I don't know the town at all, but the address of the dentist is 126 Chester Way. Do you know where that is?'

'Oh yes, I know exactly where you are going. I tell you what the best thing to do is: you wait there and I will pick you up and we can find a coffee place somewhere around there. How does that suit you?'

Jeremy agreed. The phones went down and he was left in a state of complete panic. What was he doing? This was madness.

And here they were, three hours later, sitting in a quaint little tearoom, and Jeremy was trying not to dribble on the tablecloth! They found so much to talk about, amazingly. The conversation flowed and they had laughed and joked like old friends.

'I guess I had better make a move or I will get the sack,' Jeremy said finally, remembering he had some shopping to do for Heather for the theatre. 'Can you tell me how to get back to Crewe? I came by train, but I can't remember where the station is now.'

'Don't worry, I will take you. It is only round the corner, and there are loads of trains. Come on.' They both got up and Eddie paid the bill.

'You don't have to do that,' protested Jeremy. 'Let's split it.'

Eddie laughed. 'I think I can afford a teacake or two. You can pay next time, and we will go out to dinner.'

They were standing on the pavement outside the café and Eddie took Jeremy's arm. 'Please say we can meet up soon.' He held onto Jeremy's arm as if his life depended on it, and Jeremy had an overwhelming desire to take Eddie into his arms and hold him.

'Yes, of course we can. Whenever you want.' Jeremy held Eddie's gaze until the boy let go of his arm and they both seemed to relax back into the world around them.

'We'd better get a move on,' mumbled Eddie and strode off to the van he was driving. Jeremy hurried after him. The station was, indeed, just around the corner, and as Jeremy was searching for the door handle he felt Eddie move towards him. He turned slightly and was caught by a kiss from him. He started to respond and then gasped and broke the moment. Eddie pulled back and Jeremy could see fear in his eyes.

'I am so sorry, please forgive me. Please don't say anything. I—' Jeremy took his hand and stopped him. 'You have done nothing wrong, Eddie, but now is not the right time or place. Please, leave me a message at the stage door, or come and meet me after the show one night if you can and we will talk. But we have to be careful.'

He squeezed Eddie's hand and climbed out of the car. He turned and waved, and then walked to the platform. He could hardly put one foot in front of the other, for his legs felt as numb as his mouth – but he couldn't blame the dentist for this. Oh God no, this was completely of his own making, yet he felt out of control. Suddenly his life was about to change forever, and Jeremy really was not sure if this change was for better or worse.

Chapter 24

When Jeremy got back to the theatre it was getting on for four o'clock. He had brought the bits and pieces that Heather had asked for, and was about to go and find her when he was stopped in his tracks by a piercing scream. He ran towards the sound, leaping up the steps to the dressing room two at a time. What the hell was going on? The screams grew louder as he neared the girls' dressing room, and as he flung open the door he was greeted by a terrible sight.

There were several women – well, they seemed to be women, but they were covered in copious amounts of hair of all different colours and in the middle was one horrible grotesque creature with a bald head and wisps of hair straggling down her neck. She was semi-naked, as were the other women, clad only in skimpy veils of transparent silk. As Jeremy ran in they screamed again, and then burst into hysterical laughter.

'What the fuck is going on?' he demanded. He was slowly beginning to realize that these creatures were in fact the girls he knew and loved. 'Sally, what has happened? What is going on here?' He had finally managed to recognize his friend under her mountain of blonde hair.

Sally was laughing so much she could hardly speak.

'Oh, my God, Jeremy, can you believe these wigs and costumes? Gwendoline is having a breakdown. She must be to create this. Look at poor Peggy . . .' Sally turned to point at the bald crone and collapsed into fits of mirth again.

Peggy was indignant. 'Pipe down, Sally! It is bad enough I have to look like this without your mockery. Come on, girls, we have got to see a way through this.'

At this point, Charmaine appeared at the dressing-room door looking stunning in a long diaphanous robe with her auburn locks cascading down her back.

'Hi, everyone – isn't this just wonderful? I am so thrilled with my costume – and look at Sarah.' She turned and let Sarah come forward. She was dressed in a white silk Grecian-style dress which hung from her shoulders in very flattering folds. A hairpiece at the back gave her thick golden-brown tresses, and the false hair had been braided into her own hair at the front. The whole dressing room went quiet.

'Sarah is going to play my maid and the sort of Vestal Virgin of the town,' Charmaine informed them. 'She represents love and purity, and all that was good before the men started going to war and causing grief and famine.'

Sally was the first to find her voice and she half-whispered, 'Sorry, but I don't remember any of this in the script I have been reading from.'

Sarah glided towards her with a triumphant gleam in her eye.

'Oh, I know – it has only just been added,' she said. 'The thing was, Percy had been talking to Giles about the play because he did it years ago, and mentioned a scene that was not in this translation. Well, Giles loved it when he read it, and as I have so little to do in this play, and because Percy has been helping me with audition speeches and knows what I can really do, he persuaded Giles to put me in the scene. Isn't that fantastic?'

Sally sat down slowly and looked at Sarah through the mirror. 'Yes, fantastic,' was all she could muster for fear of giving the girl a real piece of her mind. Clever little minx, she thought. That'll teach us to take our eyes off the ball.

Jeremy could sense that the atmosphere in the room had dropped several degrees; it was feeling positively frosty, so he beat a hasty retreat. 'Sally, I have to go and deliver this stuff to Heather, but can we talk later, please?' He was gone before she answered.

Gwendoline was gathering wigs from the ladies, telling them, 'Look, girls, please don't panic. By the time we have dressed the wigs they will look gorgeous.'

'How can you dress a bald pate?' whined Peggy. 'Do I really have to play this old hag? What have I ever done to Giles to deserve this? I will never work again.'

Dora came to the rescue and put her arm round the distraught actress.

'Now listen to me, Peggy. You are a fantastic actress and you will make this work. In fact, you are the only one who *can* make this work. Think of that scene where you get us all in the square and talk about women, and what we do for society, and how beauty is but a fleeting distraction ... all that stuff anyway. Your voice and strength onstage will be fantastic, and maybe, Gwendoline, Peggy can wear a robe of some sort that has a regal quality to it, to balance the head and the baldness; something in a wonderfully rich colour.'

Gwendoline responded with the perfect answer.

'Absolutely! You are quite right, Dora. Peggy's character should have a regal quality about her. Time has ravaged her looks, but not her mind.'

Everyone waited to see Peggy's reaction. The woman knew how to hold a moment, and she milked it for all it was worth. Slowly she raised her head and wiped away a tear. Slowly she rose from her seat and walked to the door and then turned back to the room. A straggling wisp of hair strayed across her face and she blew it away, declaring, 'Onwards and upwards, girls. I have never been beaten by a role yet. This will be my greatest challenge, and I shall embrace it with all my being. Bald is beautiful!' With that she turned and swished out.

Everyone let out a sigh of relief. Sally turned to Dora and said, 'Come on, sis, let's go and get some tea and take these bits of hankie off. I take it we will be wearing a bit more than this on the night, Gwendoline?'

'Oh yes, of course. I was just trying to get a general feel of the thing. Goodness knows where Sarah got her costume. It certainly didn't come from this wardrobe.'

'I bet she made it herself,' ventured Janie. 'She is always up to something, isn't she?'

'I wonder what Peggy makes of all this?' mused Sally, thinking that she was no doubt fully aware of Sarah's machinations, and watching her progress very closely.

'Well, there is a lesson for all of us,' announced Dora. 'Go for what you want in life.'

No one in the room was cheering.

Chapter 25

Sally found Jeremy in the pub.

'Not drinking before a performance, I hope?' she scolded.

'No, don't be daft. I take my career way too seriously to do that,' replied Jeremy. 'Would you like a drink?'

'Just an orange juice, please,' said Sally. 'So how are things? I have hardly seen you this week. Is it strange not being in the next play? Mind you, the way things are going you should be grateful you are not in it. What about those wigs and costumes, eh? I can't believe Gwendoline is going to get away with her whole concept. And we have got all the bloody repertories coming to watch us make fools of ourselves.'

Sally was in full flood when she suddenly realized she was getting no response from her friend at all. He was staring off into space, fiddling with a card.

'Hey! Hello, earth calling, anyone at home? Jeremy, whatever is the matter with you?' Sally shook his arm and finally Jeremy focused on her.

'I am so sorry, Sally. I have a lot on my mind. There is so much to tell you, but I am not sure we should talk about it now as we have got a show in an hour. Can I come to your place tonight, after the play finishes? I really need to talk to you.'

'Yes, of course you can, silly. We'll get some fish and chips or something on the way home.' Sally gave him a hug, finished her orange juice and went back to work, leaving Jeremy once more gazing into space. At the stage door Sally bumped into Giles and Robert deep in conversation. She nodded as she passed but didn't stop. She was curious as to what their relationship actually was. Were they lovers? She didn't think so, but maybe they had been once. Robert certainly kept close to the man at the top, and played all sorts of political games that Sally could only guess at. She really didn't care, unlike Sarah; the latter, it would seem, was on a mission to make herself the leading lady. She really was something else, and Sally wasn't sure she had much respect for the girl. Success at any cost? Not for Sally anyway. She wanted to be able to face herself at all times, and know she had shown integrity and respect to herself and others. She adored being an actress and just wanted to be able to do the work, knowing she had fulfilled those criteria.

Sally went down to the Props Room to find Heather, who was as usual surrounded by an assortment of props, dirty coffee mugs and always one member of the crew asleep in her chair or eating her biscuits.

'Sally, the very person I do want to see!' exclaimed the stage manager happily. 'Can you be on the book tonight? I need to have a meeting with all the heads of departments about our next offering. I gather you actors or rather actresses are not happy with your costumes?'

Sally chuckled. 'Well yes, that would be an understatement, but to be honest with you, Heather, I don't think anyone much cares what the actresses think. Giles has a vision of sex and Ancient Greece that he is going to parade before the residents of Crewe and the directors of the Repertory Organization, whether we like it or not. We will either be run out of town, or never work again – or both! Yes, I will be on the book tonight, no problem. Is everyone in and on the job who should be?' she added.

'All present and correct. Thanks, Sally, I owe you one.' Heather gave her a smile and set off to find her team.

The evening show went without a hitch until Act Two, when Percy, in his robes as Sir Thomas More, got the edge of the huge coat he wore caught in the great oak door. Obviously the great oak door was only plywood cleverly disguised by the scene builders and painters as solid oak. If one opened or closed it too vigorously, it shook, or was in danger of snapping. Percy was trying very hard to extricate himself while giving a rather moving speech to Mrs More. Peggy was also trying to hide the problem from the audience by standing sideways, and holding out her long dress. Word spread backstage and suddenly the wings were full of actors bent double with laughter. Percy kept looking into the wings towards Sally, desperate for help, but even she was trying hard not to laugh. It was just one of those awful things that happen onstage sometimes. Suddenly there was a ripping sound which Peggy covered with a wrenching cough, as she fell upon Sir Thomas and tried to get him out of the great oak door. But the bloody door was stuck fast. Peggy was now so determined to get them off the stage that all reason and logic left her – and the next thing, she was climbing out of the window, pulling Sir Thomas with her. Bearing in mind they were supposed to be in a castle, even if they were lucky enough to have been on the ground floor, it was still a leap to terra firma. But Peggy could not care less about the reality of the scene, she just wanted out. So Sally brought the curtain down as Sir Thomas More disappeared, arse over tit, out of the castle window. Happy days!

Percy and Peggy came charging into the wings absolutely furious.

'Why didn't you do something, Sally? How could you leave me there struggling?' Percy demanded. 'I have *never* been so humiliated in all my life. Come on, Peggy, let's get changed for the last act, though God knows if anybody has bothered to stay and watch. My performance was *ruined*.'

Percy was off up the stairs followed by a placatory Peggy clutching a packet of digestives that she always kept in the wings for emergencies. The rest of the play passed without incident and the cast took an extra curtain call, so Percy was mollified.

Everyone decided it was definitely a night for the pub.

'You coming, Sally?' asked Simon, giving her bum a squeeze as he passed. Truth be told he rather fancied Sally, but the opportunity had never presented itself yet. Maybe tonight.

'Get off my bum, you pervert,' Sally laughed. 'Sorry, Simon, not tonight. I have got a date with fish and chips and Jeremy.'

'Oh Gawd, more line learning and intellectual discussion about his "Acting",' mocked Simon. The boys often took the mickey out of poor Jeremy now, because he did take his work so seriously. 'Well, more fool you is all I can say,' Simon went on. 'You could have had a fabulous evening with me in the pub. A few pints then a quick trip to Mrs Wong's and back to my place for a shag. What more could you want?'

Sally shook her head as she took a swipe at the incorrigible boy and told him to get lost. She finished clearing up and switching off all the lights, then went upstairs to get her stuff

from the dressing room. As she passed Peggy and Percy's dressing room she heard a stifled giggle. She paused and knocked
on Peggy's door.

'Are you OK, Peggy? Can I get you anything before I go?'

There was the sound of shuffling and someone moving
around and then Percy's voice rang out loud and clear.

'She has gone home already, my dear. Thank you for your
concern. Let us just hope the great oak door opens tomorrow
night, shall we? Good night.'

Sally called back a good night as she climbed the stairs to
her room. Well, what was that all about? No doubt young
Sarah doing some more work on her part . . . Just then, Jeremy
came out of the boys' dressing room and interrupted her
musings.

'Hi. Are you ready to go?' he asked.

'Just getting my bag and stuff,' she replied.

As they went downstairs Sally tried to listen for any sounds
from Percy's room. Jeremy looked at her as if she had gone
mad as she tiptoed past the door.

'What the . . . ?' he started to ask, but she put her finger to
her lips and mouthed, 'Tell you later.'

Outside, Sally took Jeremy's arm and started to explain all
about the incident with Sarah and the dresses and her new
role. Jeremy, however, was only half-listening as he tried to
work out exactly what he was going to tell his friend tonight.
He had spent the whole day trying to get Eddie out of his
mind. All through his preparations for the evening performance, all he could concentrate on was Eddie's kiss. His
mouth. There had been a moment onstage tonight when he
had dried, forgotten his lines. It is every actor's worst nightmare. One minute everything is going swimmingly then
suddenly there is a pause. Jeremy had a vision of Eddie's smile

in front of his eyes, he was leaning in to touch his face and all around was silence, deafening silence. Silence! Christ, who was supposed to be talking? The face in front of Jeremy was Percy's, panic in his eyes, begging Jeremy to come up with his next line. The moment seemed to last for hours though it was only a few seconds, but Jeremy wanted to die. Never had this happened before. He was mortified. He apologized to Percy when they came off stage but the older man just laughed it off.

'Don't worry, mate, happens to the best of us. Doesn't half give you a kick in the bollocks though, eh?'

'Jeremy?' Sally's voice was concerned. 'You keep going off into another place, and I have no idea what you are thinking. Are you worried about work, because if you are, don't be. You are a marvellous actor and I am sure they are going to give you Laertes in *Hamlet*. It will be so exciting and—'

'Sally, please.' Jeremy literally stopped Sally there and then in the street and took both her hands in his as he faced her.

'Please stop. I have to talk to you. I am going mad. Sally, I have fallen in love!'

Chapter 26

When the two friends got back to Sally's flat, she put the fire on, opened a bottle of wine and made poached eggs on hot buttered toast, while Jeremy poured his heart out. Once they were settled in front of the fire Sally offered her opinion.

'Why is it so terrible that you have fallen in love? You should be over the moon,' she managed to say through a mouthful of toast.

'I know, I know,' groaned Jeremy, 'but it is not part of my plan. I do not want to get involved with anything other than my work. You know we have talked about this so often, Sally. I feel it is important that I focus completely on my job. We have got *Hamlet* coming up, and that will be tough for all of us.'

'But dearest, life can never really be ordered and controlled like you are suggesting, and in fact, having someone in your life can add to your understanding of yourself and others, and help you with your performances.' She watched her friend fiddle unenthusiastically with his food. 'Don't you want that?' she couldn't resist asking.

Jeremy smiled. 'Not really hungry – here you are, I know you are dying to have it.' He passed her his plate. 'The other thing we haven't mentioned is the whole issue of being gay. I don't understand how this has happened to me, when I have never fancied a man before. Why now, suddenly?'

Sally thought about this as she ate the last piece of toast. 'But have you ever really fancied a girl? Anyone?' she asked.

Jeremy finished off the wine in his glass and poured another. After a couple of sips he answered Sally with a sigh. 'No.'

Sally suddenly had a vision of Mack for some bizarre reason. She had fancied him when they had met again when she was home in Cheltenham. He had never got in touch afterwards, and yet Sally had felt there was a real connection between them. But then like Jeremy she was not really interested in anything at the moment except acting. So whose fault was it that Mack had not been given sufficient reason to call?

'It is so hard to deal with these intense emotions, isn't it?' she said softly. 'But I really believe you must go with your heart. Eddie obviously feels the same about you. But what will his parents say? Surely they will not understand their son and heir being gay? Oh Jeremy, I just don't want to see you get hurt. Go gently and don't rush things – and be careful.'

Jeremy leaned over and gave Sally a big hug. He felt so safe with her. He loved the fact they could talk about anything and share intimate secrets about themselves. Would he have that with Eddie? Just the thought of him made Jeremy's stomach do a somersault. It was no good, he knew, trying to discuss anything rationally; he had to pursue this thing to whatever conclusion occurred. He was completely smitten.

He left Sally with a promise to go slowly and embrace his newfound love with caution. However, as he walked home in the cold November night, he was already planning how he could meet up with Eddie as soon as possible.

After Jeremy had left, Sally cleared up and started to take her make-up off when the door opened and her sister bounced into the flat, followed by Simon carrying a bag of beers.

'Hi, Sally, didn't expect you to be up. Still, just as well you are, as we would probably have woken you up anyway. Sit down, Simon, and give me the beers, and I will stick them in the fridge. Would you like some scrambled eggs on toast?' Dora suggested as she made her way to the kitchen. But before Simon could answer, Sally piped up, 'Actually I just used up all the eggs. Jeremy came back for a drink and we had poached eggs. Sorry.'

Dora made a face. 'Oh pooh. Well, that is a bummer. Have we got any bread left? We can have toast and Marmite or something then.'

Simon flicked open the top of a can and joined in the discussion. 'Don't worry about me, darling. Beer is fine. Come on, don't fret. Come and sit with me.'

Sally could guess where this was leading and she followed Dora into the kitchen as her sister went to put the beers in the fridge.

'What are you doing?' she whispered. 'You are surely not considering letting Simon stay the night by any chance?'

Dora turned and studied her. 'What is this all about – the older sister taking care of her younger sibling's moral welfare? I don't know if he is going to stay the night yet. It depends. But if he does, that is really my business, don't you think? Come on, Sally, I am old enough to decide these things for myself.'

Sally snorted. 'You are eighteen, for God's sake! I was still a virgin then.'

'Well, I'm not,' replied Dora, relishing the dropping of this bombshell.

Sally was absolutely dumbfounded, but one look at her sister's smug expression made her determined not to reveal the extent of the horror she felt.

'Oh I see. Well then, I guess you know what you are doing. How many men have there been in your short life?' she asked with no attempt to hide the sarcasm.

Uncomfortable now with where this conversation might go, Dora did not answer immediately. While she was deciding how to deal with this rather tricky subject, luck intervened, and Simon appeared in the kitchen doorway.

'Come on, girls, give it a break, I am trying to chill out here. Are we going to have a cosy threesome?' he sniggered.

'Oh grow up, Simon,' snapped Sally. 'I will leave you both to it. Good night.'

She marched off to her bedroom and slammed the door, then regretted the gesture. They probably thought she was jealous. Simon was always trying it on with her, and now he was hanging around her sister. How pathetic was that? And what the hell was Dora up to? Had she really lost her virginity already? Sally was outraged and yet she realized that it truly was none of her business, was it? She thought about their parents and wondered if they knew about Dora. Thinking about them made Sally feel so homesick and alone. Talking to Jeremy earlier had caused her to start thinking about her own life and what she really wanted from it. Now she began to feel there was a chasm between her and Dora. Their lives were no longer under the auspices of their parents. The family had changed and she had to change also – but how? She suddenly felt very tired and resolved to have a long talk to Dora about everything and get things straight between them. Life was difficult enough without arguments with her sister.

As she hit the pillow, Sally heard music coming from the other room and Dora's throaty laughter. Oh God, how was she going to face them both in the morning if Simon stayed? Sally accepted that she was being ridiculous and getting herself in a tizzy for no good reason – except there *was* a reason: Dora's welfare. Just because she had had a few drinks, did her sister really have to stoop so low as to sleep with a slob like Simon? The answer was probably yes. If that was the case, then the less she knew about it the better. She would get up early, and if Simon was here she would make herself scarce and get out quick.

Sally managed to smile to herself as she felt sleep starting to take her away from all this pettiness. *Come on, girl, you have dealt with worse than this in your life*, she told herself. *Get a grip* . . . but her body was gone, drifting into blissful unconsciousness. She would save the gripping for another day.

Chapter 27

A Man for All Seasons ended this coming Saturday, which would mean a busy night for everyone getting the old set out, and the new one in. However, it was a little easier this weekend as they had three weeks' rehearsal for *Hamlet*. The actors were given a special dispensation to have the night off, and Sunday and Monday morning too. Several of the cast had decided to go home to family and loved ones.

Jeremy immediately rang Eddie and told him the good news.

'Fabulous.' Eddie was pleased. 'I have such a plan for the weekend you will not believe your eyes. How about I come over Saturday morning and pick you up? Presumably you will finish even earlier because you are not in *Lysistrata*, are you?'

Jeremy had not even thought of that! 'Yes, you're right – I will check today just to make sure. I can't wait. Talk to you later.'

'Oh yes, my lovely man, this is the beginning of a beautiful thing. Bye!'

The phone went dead in his hand but Jeremy held on a

little longer, trying to feel Eddie through the handpiece. 'Silly me,' he whispered. He then set off to find Heather, and as usual found the poor woman struggling with piles of props in her room.

'Oh, Jeremy – perfect timing. Can you help me get these boxes off my desk, and find a space in a corner somewhere? It's murder in here on Get-out Weekends. Would you like a coffee? The kettle has boiled – it's over there by the sink, and there is fresh milk in the fridge.'

Jeremy agreed to all demands and five minutes later the pair of them were sipping coffee on a relatively empty props table.

'So how is the world treating you, my dear?' asked Heather, who liked to keep tabs on everybody if she could. 'I notice you have not been in the pub much lately. Are the lads giving you a hard time still?'

'No, thank God, they have learned to leave me alone, especially as I am the official cleaner of the boys' dressing room in return. So we are all happy. No, it's just because I wasn't in this week's production, and you didn't overload me with prop-finding or other such chores that I have been getting out and about a bit. There is some lovely countryside outside Crewe.'

Jeremy took a swig of coffee before asking his question. Crossing his fingers under the table for luck he went on, 'Heather, I don't want to appear cheeky but as I am not in the last performances on Saturday, and if I make sure I have done all my duties, is there a possibility I could leave lunchtime on Saturday?'

'Cor, you are pushing your luck, mate,' chuckled Heather. 'However, in my great wisdom I see no reason why not. But how will you make it worth my while?'

Jeremy stood up and went and rinsed his mug in the sink, creating a moment of drama with the silence. He then turned slowly and announced, 'You have a choice of chocolates, ciggies or wine. Name your price, Heather Rollings.'

'Chocolates, please – and make it a nice big box,' she added.

'Naturally, my dear, that is a deal.' Jeremy blew her a kiss and practically skipped out of her office. He then went to the Green Room to call Eddie back, hoping there was no one around while he did so. With luck, the others were all still in bed. He was in luck; the room was empty, though it smelled of last night's stale ready meals, and Pot Noodles. But for once Jeremy didn't notice: he was a man on a mission. He dialled the number and waited nervously, picturing an enormous entrance hall and the butler, as described by Eddie, gliding serenely across the marble floor to answer the telephone.

'Crewe Hall, who is calling, please?' The tone was perfect.

'Oh, good morning, it is Jeremy Sinclair here. I am one of the actors at Crewe Theatre this season. I was hoping to talk to Eddie if that is possible?'

'I am afraid he is out with His Lordship, sir. They have a shooting party this morning followed by lunch. Can I take a message?'

'Yes, thank you. That would be great. If you could just tell Eddie I have arranged a tour of the theatre for him on Saturday, if that is convenient, and could he ring me as soon as possible and confirm.'

'Of course I will do so, and thank you for your call, Mr Sinclair.'

The phone went down. Well, I have done all I can, thought Jeremy. It is now in the hands of the gods. Two more days to wait – and oh, the anticipation! He made his way back upstairs to the dressing room thinking to have a clear-up but also to look at *Hamlet* and start to accustom himself to the script. To his joy and delight he had been summoned to Giles Longfellow's inner sanctum a few days ago and Giles had offered him the role of Laertes. Jeremy was over the moon and said so.

'Thank you so much, sir. I am very excited about the production and will not let you down.'

Giles looked at Jeremy from across his huge mahogany desk, which was his pride and joy, and steepled his fingers under his chin. This was his favourite pose, denoting thoughtfulness and good nature, the all-giving master.

'I hope not, Mr Sinclair. I hope not.' He bestowed a smile upon his minion, and then turned to the papers on his desk. Jeremy had been dismissed.

He went back to the dressing room and did his usual clean around and collected dirty mugs. Bloody boys! He got his script and a couple of bits and pieces he would need at the weekend, then took the mugs up to the Green Room, where he tried to call Sally at her flat. There was no answer but as Jeremy came back down, they met mid-stair.

'Hi, darling, what are you up to this morning?' he greeted Sally. 'I just tried to ring you to take you for an early lunch or brunch, what do you say?'

'Actually, that would just hit the spot, Jeremy. Thank you. Can you wait while I dump this laundry back for Janie for ironing? Dora was supposed to do it last night but she had a visitor.' Sally sounded fed up and weary.

'Ooh, tell all,' said Jeremy eagerly.

'Wait till we are sitting down,' said Sally and went on up to the wardrobe department with her bundle while Jeremy carried on down to the stage door to wait for her. Gladys was ensconced in her corner with her knitting as usual.

'Morning, young sir. How are you doing, my son? You've

had a bit of time off this last couple of weeks. That must have been nice for you.'

'Yes, it was lovely, Gladys, and I will be off early Saturday too. I am waiting for Sally to take her to lunch as the poor girl will be working non-stop.'

'She's a lovely lass, that Sally – so different from her sister. Chalk and cheese, that pair.' She sniffed. Gladys's sniff was infamous and could tell a thousand tales. Jeremy was just about to ask her to illuminate, but Sally appeared at his side.

'Ready when you are. Hi, Gladys, we are going into town: do you want anything brought back?' asked Sally.

'Nah, you are all right. Enjoy your lunch. See you later.'

The pair set off down the hill to the town square.

'Where shall we go?' asked Sally.

'I know,' said Jeremy, looking very pleased with himself. 'They have opened a lovely little café just off the square. It does amazing all-day breakfasts. Follow me.'

Once they had got sat down and Sally had ordered a 'full English', and Jeremy scrambled egg and smoked salmon – a real luxury – the pair attacked a pile of toast washed down with huge mugs of tea. Jeremy let Sally settle down before he asked, 'So what's the trouble?'

'Why do you think there is trouble?' replied Sally still munching her hot buttered toast.

'Well, you look tired and stressed, which is understandable with these schedules, but getting to act in between is usually the sweetener – and you don't seem very sweet, my love,' noted Jeremy, sitting back as his food arrived.

There were a few moments' silence while the plates were put on the table, and Sally took advantage of the time to try and get her thoughts in order.

'When Dora came to stay with me it was partly for support,

but also a way for her to discover new things she might like to do in the future if she abandons this idea of Business Studies. She was always very keen on design and fashion, and very good at drawing and art. It was her idea to try and get a job in the wardrobe department, which she did. But now she has decided she wants to be an actress.' Sally took a big mouthful of bacon and sausage.

'Well, that is OK, isn't it?' responded Jeremy, trying to understand. 'You won't be in competition. You are both very different.'

'That may be so out in the big, wide world, but here in a small company like this, we all knew where we stood when we took the job. There were parts we would like to do, and hopefully if we proved ourselves, those parts would follow. I know there are people in this company who will play dirty, given half a chance, to get what they want, but I just didn't expect it from my sister.' Sally could feel tears pricking the back of her eyes and took another mouthful of food to distract her.

Jeremy looked shocked. 'What are you talking about, Sally? What has happened to make you say this?'

'Obviously you have not been around for any of this production. In fact, did you even come to the first night? Oh yes, of course you did – you wouldn't miss hob-nobbing with the great and the good of the repertory system in this country. Did you get any work offered to you?' She waited for his reply.

'No, I didn't as a matter of fact, and I left early anyway. But come on, Sally, don't start having a go at me again. I am in love for the first time in my life – cut me a bit of slack.'

Sally smiled at her friend. 'Yes, yes, OK, you are right – now is not the time. Well, on that first night it was a riot. You saw what we looked like. All that hair and see-through costumes. I felt like a stripper, to be honest. Charmaine looked rather fetching though, because her wig was dark and she asked for a bit more coverage with the costume. So there we were, Dora and I, in our matching strawberry-blonde wigs and diaphanous gowns, doing our thing. I was thrilled because I got a round of applause for my song, and I know I made the best of a bad job of a rather dull character.

'Anyway, we all go upstairs to meet the bigwigs – pardon the pun – and to work the room. But of course, now we are without our hair no one recognizes us, so we have to be very clever and make sure at the top of any conversation that the director in question knows exactly who we were. I was doing OK, but you know me, I get so intimidated by all that stuff, and after half an hour I went and sat down with Janie and we just watched all the shenanigans. Suddenly I saw my sister giving this man the full beam of her headlights; he was obviously completely smitten and hanging on her every word. They chatted for quite a while, and then Dora turned and spotted me watching, and suddenly she was kissing him on both cheeks and was off to the other side of the room. Call me suspicious but I smelled a rat, and decided to go and ask Dora what she was up to. I caught her about to leave for the pub with Simon and Peter.

'"Hi, Sally, we are off to the pub. Why don't you come with us?" she said, practically pushing the boys out of the door.

'"Yes, I will. OK, let's go," I said and followed her out.

'We didn't talk much until we got to the pub, and while the boys were getting the drinks we found a table at the back. It was very busy and all the locals were congratulating us and blowing wolf whistles, et cetera. I had to stop Dora doing a tour of the room otherwise we would have been there all night, and I was knackered and still needed to find out what she had been up to before the boys came back.

'"Who were you talking to in there?" I asked. "It all looked very intense and then suddenly you left him. Who was he?"

'"Oh, some director – nobody important, I don't think. Anyway, he was telling me how much he loved my song and what I had made of a difficult part. He was basically suggesting I might like to go and do a season at his theatre, which was nice. I just can't remember which theatre though. I am hopeless."

'Then the boys arrived with the drinks and Simon congratulated Dora on her performance in the bar! I asked him what he meant and he started telling me that Dora had nailed this director from Nottingham Playhouse no less, and he had offered her a job. Well, you can imagine how my ears pricked up.

'"Was that the man you were talking to – and you said you couldn't remember his name?" I asked, and Dora looked really nervous.

'"Um, yes, I guess so – but it was no big deal. He won't remember my name."

'"Oh yes he will," said Simon, "because he checked you on the programme and everything. Mind you, he was looking at the wrong name, wasn't he, Dora?"'

Jeremy looked at Sally and said, 'I don't think I want to hear what is coming next.'

'Can you believe it? Simon goes on to tell us that the guy had got the wrong actress – it should have been me – and that Dora made no attempt to put him straight. Dora then pretends it was all a big mistake and says that she was going to tell the man, but she couldn't find him later on. It was so embarrassing, and Simon was loving every minute, so I just told Dora we had to go and made her leave.'

As Sally ate her breakfast she remembered the walk home to the flat and the scene that followed. They had gone into the flat, stuck some money in the meter and got the fire going. Both then went and changed into their big woolly dressing gowns and Sally had put the kettle on. Tea made, the girls had huddled in front of the fire and Sally had challenged her sister.

'You let that director from Nottingham Playhouse think you were me, didn't you, Dora?'

'Well yes, but I wouldn't have kept it up. I was going to tell him at some point.' But Dora could not look her sister in the eye.

'And at what point would that have been, I wonder? On the first day of the new season when you had signed and sealed the contract? How could you do that to me? I am your sister, Dora! I brought you here to Crewe to help you find yourself, and you have done nothing but try to muscle in on my job. And now you have taken a job away from me. What is your problem? What have I ever done to you to deserve this?' Sally had been shouting and pacing the floor.

Dora waited a few moments before giving her explanation.

'Sally, this is not personal. I do love you, and I am grateful for everything you have done for me. But I do want to get on in my life, and I have decided that acting is something I love doing. But unlike you, Sal, I am the sort of person who goes for it, no matter what. I grab what I can in the moment. You are very happy to troll along with everything and everybody, enjoying the whole company thing. Well, that is not me, I am sorry. I want to be Numero Uno, the centre of attention, and if an opportunity presents itself to me like tonight, I take it. Does that make me a bad person?' She had looked up at Sally who was still pacing. Sally was so confused and hurt and angry, she barely knew how to answer.

'At this moment, I don't know what to think, Dora. But I am your sister, and I would have thought, in this case, there might have been a degree of loyalty?'

'But, Sally, you will get so many offers from this season, I know it. This one just seemed to have my name on it, and I honestly thought you would be pleased for me.'

Sally had felt her anger rising like bile in her throat, and had shocked herself by how much dislike she was feeling for Dora. Her sister was playing the manipulative card, turning it all onto Sally. It was late, and Sally had the good sense to know that this problem was not going to go away any day soon. She needed to really think about the consequences, not just with regards to her position in the company and how to maintain that position, but her relationship with her sister, which could be damaged irrevocably.

'Let's leave it there for now, shall we?' Sally had said. 'Goodnight, Dora, see you in the morning.' She had gone to her room and quietly closed her door, just catching Dora's rather faint, 'Night.'

Sally finished her story, including what had happened at the flat the previous night, and her 'full English' all at the same time. Picking up her mug of tea she regarded Jeremy over the rim as he sat back in his chair. He looked a little shell-shocked.

'And on top of all this she slept with Simon?' was his first comment.

Sally burst out laughing. 'Oh, Jeremy, I do love you! Trust you to pick up on the least important issue of the whole mess. Yes, she brought him back to the flat. I was so cross, and then she had the gall to brag that she had lost her virginity much sooner than me!'

'She is a right little hussy in the making,' tutted Jeremy. 'But seriously, she is something else, Sally. I am disgusted and absolutely on your side. Where *is* the loyalty? But you are right, this problem is not going to go away, and you don't have many choices. Can't we send her home?'

'With what excuse? I can't tell my parents we have had a big falling-out. It will destroy them, especially my mum. I think I am just going to have to keep a sharp eye out and unfortunately learn to fight for my corner.' Sally gave a long sigh. 'It feels so much better to have someone to talk to about it all. Thank you. At least if you share the knowledge, you might have some suggestions as we go along. Now I must go and give my Welsh mountain pony impersonation with my traitor of a sister at my side. Oh dear. What next, eh? Are you OK though? Sorry it has been all about me. Taking things slowly, I hope?'

Sally peered into Jeremy's face, looking for signs of a lie, but he just gave her a charming smile that told her nothing, and said, 'Don't you worry about me, my pet. I am doing fine, but will be away this weekend in Manchester, so do try and keep everything together until I get back.'

'Yes, sir! But please remember, Jeremy, I want you to play Hamlet in my Players piece, and I would appreciate some input from you when we rehearse, although I know you are going to be up to your eyes with fight scenes, and mad scenes, and what-have-you. Gosh, it is going to be so exciting. So just go easy and make sure you are rested and raring to go.'

Jeremy laughed and gave his friend a big kiss and a hug. If the truth be known, he was feeling very guilty, because the last thing he would be on Monday morning was fit and raring to go after a weekend of wild lovemaking – he hoped!

Chapter 28

Lying in bed on Saturday morning, enjoying the luxury of not having to get up early, Jeremy had slept dreamlessly, but now his head was filled with the weekend ahead. What was going to happen? How would it happen? Did he really want it to happen? He had tried to focus on his scenes in *Hamlet*, but Eddie's face would spring up in front of his eyes. Jeremy knew in his heart that he had to go with these feelings, no matter what. He would worry about everything else later.

He got up and dressed in record time in an old T-shirt and jeans because he had decided to go to the theatre and get ready there as it was warmer. He had already packed his holdall – a new one he had splashed out on for the occasion. Good luggage said a lot about a man. He had a fleeting memory of his mother standing at their front door with an old suitcase done up with string, and frayed on the leather corners. They were all going on holiday to Devon. He had had a little leather case as well, which he had filled with crayons and paper and his favourite toy cars. He could see his mother's face beaming at him as he climbed into the family Ford, his dad already at the wheel studying an atlas of Great Britain, and sucking on a boiled sweet.

'They are for the journey,' scolded his mother. 'Your dad is dreadful, Jeremy, he eats all the sweets before we have even started the trip. Now come on, let's get going.'

Jeremy felt a pang of guilt as he shut his front door and set off for the theatre. God knows what his parents would make of him now.

The front of the theatre was still locked as it was early, but Jeremy made his way round to the stage door and found that the cleaners were already in.

'Hi, Alice, how goes it?' He waved to the girl on the stairs scrubbing away. He squeezed past her and went on up to the dressing room. The familiar smells hit his nostrils as he ascended on high: greasepaint and sweat, and cheap perfume, with the added touch of fried food. Lovely!

Alice had already cleared up the dressing rooms, so Jeremy was able to shower and change at a leisurely pace. He dried his hair and regarded himself in the mirror. His hair had grown quite long, as he had intended for Laertes, and he liked the fact that it softened his face. He was by no means handsome, but he was attractive and, as his mother would always say to people, 'He will grow into his face!'

He checked his overnight bag and squeezed in the bottle of very expensive aftershave he had bought himself for this weekend. A tingle ran down his spine, a tremor of nerves. *Please make everything go well*, he prayed, to no one in particular. It was hardly a matter for the dear Lord, he reminded himself.

Just then, he heard a shout from downstairs and recognized Eddie's voice.

'Coming!' he yelled, and took the stairs two at a time.

Eddie was standing in the stage doorway with the sun

glinting on his immaculately cut hair. He looked like an angel to Jeremy.

'Hi, Eddie, how are you?'

Jeremy moved towards him but stopped when he heard a wheezy voice comment, 'Lovely morning, Mr Jeremy. You're in early, aren't you?'

'Gladys! Gorgeous Gladys, good morning to you. Yes, I am up bright and early so that I may show Mr Graham here the wonders of our theatre before the horde arrive. Is that OK with you?' Jeremy gave her his most brilliant smile and Gladys grinned back.

'Of course, you go ahead. Be careful when you go onstage though because the lights are not on yet. Do you know where the workers are?' she asked.

'Yes, I do. I can switch them on easily. Thanks, Gladys. Come on, Eddie, follow me down to the land where magic is made.'

'Magic, my arse!' Gladys commented under her breath as the two young men bounded off.

By the time they arrived at the pass door it was indeed absolutely pitch black. Eddie grabbed Jeremy round the waist and pulled him towards him.

'Not here,' whispered Jeremy. 'There may be someone from the crew here already. Just hang on. OK, grab my hand and follow me across the stage. I have got a surprise for you.'

Jeremy felt his way along the back wall of the stage and down to the corner where there was a pass door leading out to the auditorium and the boxes. A door on the right opened to some steps winding round a corner to another door on which was written in gold embossed letters *Royal Box*.

Jeremy gently pulled Eddie inside. 'I thought this was very appropriate for an aristocrat like you. I have often wondered just how many secret trysts must have taken place in here over the years.'

Eddie moved closer to Jeremy. 'Are you suggesting a tryst right here, right now?' he murmured as they stood facing each other, breathing hard. Then, very slowly, each started to undress the other. Not a word was spoken. And finally they faced each other completely naked. Their eyes had hardly left each other's. Jeremy wanted to scream with anticipation. He was shaking now. The two young men were standing nose to nose, but Jeremy was completely frozen like a statue. Eddie traced the line of Jeremy's jaw with his thumb, and when he took his face in both hands and drew him into a kiss, Jeremy thought his head would explode. Colours whirled before his eyes and he struggled to catch his breath; he seemed to have been holding it for hours. Eddie pulled back just enough to give Jeremy some space, and then his tongue gently teased its way between his lips once again. Oh, so slowly . . . Eddie pursued his probing, becoming more insistent; demanding attention. Jeremy could feel his whole body pulsating with the passion he was feeling, this overwhelming need. Slowly, so slowly . . . he unfolded his whole being to Eddie's will, and sank to the ground.

'Are you OK?' murmured Eddie, gently releasing his arm from underneath Jeremy's back. 'Ooh, ouch! Sorry, but my arm has gone to sleep.' He giggled and sat up. 'We had better make a move, hadn't we, J? Someone is bound to be down soon.' He reluctantly stood up and started to sort out his pile of clothing.

'Shit – yes, you're right. What am I thinking, lying here like an idiot.' Jeremy pulled himself up to a sitting position and rubbed his face. He sighed, 'Oh my God, Eddie, I am in such a daze I can hardly function. Help me!' He looked up at Eddie standing on the edge of the blue circle of light coming from the stage, and put out his hand. He couldn't see Eddie's face and he felt a momentary slither of panic down his back. It was gone in a moment, as Eddie pulled him to his feet and planted a big smacker on his lips.

'Stop it, you! We must get out of here quickly.' Jeremy pulled on the rest of his clothes just as a voice boomed out from the lighting gallery.

'Who's there? That you, Eric?'

Jeremy recognized the voice of the Will Black, the head carpenter.

'No, sorry, Will – it's me, Jeremy. I lost the bloody switch. I am such an idiot – I was showing my friend round and couldn't find the switch for the working lights, but it is done now though.' He had managed to get to the back of the stage by this time and find the switch.

'Everything OK with you, mate?'

Jeremy searched the darkness above them and then heard Will coming down the ladder at the side. He quickly improvised for Eddie. 'See, Eddie, this is where all the hard work is done. Will Black is the man who makes it all happen up there in the gods. Will, may I introduce Eddie Graham. He is a friend who wanted to see how everything works backstage.'

Will Black shook Eddie's hand and slapped Jeremy on the back, saying, 'Bloody actors are useless! Still, you do all right, matey. Nice to meet you, Eddie. Now if you will excuse me, lads, I need to get on.' He strolled off across the stage like a huge bear.

'God, he is enormous,' whispered Eddie. 'Wouldn't want to bump into him on a dark night.'

'Come on, you,' said Jeremy. 'Let's get out of here, for goodness sake.'

They arrived at the stage door to find Gladys happily sat with her knitting and a huge mug of tea.

'Right, we will be off now then, Gladys,' announced Jeremy.

'It was very interesting seeing everything onstage,' added Eddie. 'Thank you for giving me a tour, Jeremy.'

'Well, you have a nice weekend, won't you,' said Gladys. 'Going somewhere nice, are you, boys?'

Jeremy gave her a second look to see if she was suggesting something else, but her face was inscrutable.

'Oh, just a trip to Manchester. Eddie is returning the favour by giving me a tour of the city.'

'Lovely, dears. Well, see you later – and be good.' The big woman could not resist a huge wink which made Jeremy wince with embarrassment.

'Thanks,' he stammered. 'Yes – right. Come on then, Eddie, let's go!'

Once they got down the road they burst into a fit of giggles.

'She is a witch, I swear it,' chuckled Jeremy. 'Will she tell everyone, do you think?'

'Oh, who cares. We are not doing anything wrong, are we? Come on, let's get this weekend started.' Eddie grabbed Jeremy's hand and pulled him up the street warbling a rendition of Doris Day singing 'Once I Had a Secret Love'.

Chapter 29

Sally yawned and stretched, then sighed. She could hear Dora banging about in the kitchen making coffee. God, I would love a cup, thought Sally, but that means facing my sister. It is too early for discussions of any sort, let alone family confrontations. Although as she lay here, this morning, Sally wondered if there was any point in bringing up the whole thing again. It was a fait accompli as far as Dora was concerned. Would it not be better if Sally just got on with her own life? And if that meant being less than open with her sister, so be it. She thought about home, and her parents, and how trusting and loving her childhood had been; Dora's too, for that matter. When had things changed? Why did they change? Sally loved her sister and would always love her, of course, but now there was a beat missing somehow, and she wasn't sure she could find her way back to how it was before. Her thoughts were interrupted by a knock on the door and Dora's head appeared.

'Fancy a coffee?' she said, and came into the room with coffee and toast.

'Wow, what a treat, Dora! Thank you. To what do I owe this attention?' asked Sally, sitting up in bed.

Dora looked contrite. 'I have behaved badly, I know, sis, but I honestly didn't mean to cause you grief. I just didn't think as usual, I suppose.'

'No, you did not, and yes, it has upset me quite a lot, as a matter of fact. But I have decided to leave things be, because to be honest, Dora, there is too much going on in my life at the moment and I don't want to fall out with you on top of everything else. But please do try and think about other people's feelings and remember that you are here because of me.'

'I know, you are right and I will try harder – but please understand, Sally, I am serious about wanting to try a career as an actress, and hopefully that will not mean we are in competition.'

Sally caught a look in Dora's eye. What was it, a challenge?

'What are you doing today – apart from two shows, I mean?' asked Sally. 'Only I was wondering if we should try and set up a rehearsal for my Dumb Show asap, and I have just remembered that Rupert and Isabelle arrive some time this weekend.'

Dora looked at her blankly. 'Who?'

'Our stars! How could you forget? I think Giles wanted me to greet them and make sure they are OK. Mind you, I have got enough to do as usual with two shows, plus the get out, and preparing for the big "meet and greet" on Monday morning. Can you help me at all, do you think?' Sally gave her sister her best pleading look.

'Oh well, I suppose so, but Simon has organized for us all to go to Manchester tonight to a club, and I have invited Mack up for the night – thought it would be a nice surprise for you, actually.'

'Mack? As in Mack McKinney – Muriel's Mack?' Sally was stunned by this news. 'Whatever brought this on?' she pressed. 'And what has Mack to do with me?'

'Oh come on, Sally, don't pretend you didn't fancy him when you were there in the summer. I suggested he might like to come up and visit one day and he seemed really chuffed to be asked.' Dora disappeared into the other room, leaving Sally to gather up her thoughts.

Mack here? She had to admit the idea was not unattractive to her, but she couldn't quite work out how Dora was involved in all this. She followed her sister into the kitchen.

'Did you see Mack then, when I had gone?' she asked. 'I didn't know you knew him that well.'

'No, I don't know him that well, but Muriel told me you had got on well, and I thought as you have been a bit tense the last couple of weeks, it might do you good to see someone from home. Simon was organizing this club thing and it occurred to me that you might like someone to go with. Oh for goodness sake, Sally, it is no big deal, just a bit of fun.'

'Keep me happy and out of your way, you mean?' snapped Sally, suddenly feeling very manipulated again. 'I really do not need you to organize my life, Dora. Please stop!'

'Fine,' returned Dora. 'You are such a drama queen, Sally. It doesn't matter. You stay here and practise your little Dumb Show while the rest of us have a life. Blimey, even Jeremy has gone away this weekend – and good on him.'

Sally was suddenly reminded that indeed she really was on her own this weekend, as Jeremy was away finding true love. So there you go, Sally! Miss Goody Two Shoes again trying to do the right thing. Well, sod it! She would at least have a heads-up before Monday on what to expect from the new 'stars'. Avoiding any more conversation with Dora, she got dressed and made her way to the theatre, just stopping at the corner shop for milk and biscuits and a bottle of wine for later. Come midnight they would be gagging for a drink.

As she was crossing the square she saw Peggy struggling with her weekend shopping and went to relieve her.

'Oh bless you, darling,' Peggy huffed and puffed. 'Bloody shopping always does my head in on a Saturday, but if I don't do it now there will be nothing for Sunday lunch, and His Lordship would be very cross indeed. Come on, let's have a coffee and a bun before we shut ourselves away for the rest of the day.'

Sally followed Peggy across to the tearoom round the back of the Memorial.

'You are so right, Peggy,' she said, putting the bags on the floor and plonking herself down at a corner table. 'There is something about Saturdays that is really depressing, because everybody else seems to be getting ready for a night out, and they are out and about shopping, and having fun, and the likes of you and me are preparing to hide away in the dark until ten thirty tonight doing two shows. I mean, don't get me wrong – I love performing – but sometimes it would be lovely to have a normal weekend, wouldn't it?'

Peggy chuckled. 'There is nothing normal about this game, dearie. Now what are you going to have?'

Once they had ordered coffee and two Eccles cakes, Peggy had a confession to make.

'I suppose you have noticed that young Sarah has been hanging about round Percy, haven't you?' she said.

Sally answered carefully, 'Well yes, she does seem to be overly attentive, but I suppose that is normal in younger actresses. She is probably learning a good deal from Percy.'

Peggy snorted. 'She is taking the silly old fool for a ride, and

I am getting fed up with it. Listen, Sally, I have had to deal with this all my life with His Lordship. Always young women, and that is why I even tried to put a stop to it by spreading rumours that he liked the boys! But it never worked. Normally I turn a blind eye, but this one just won't give up, and I think that Percy must be going through a midlife crisis because he is besotted. I have to admit it is getting to me, Sally, and I don't know what to do.' Peggy sniffed and held her paper serviette to her nose.

Sally wanted to reach across the table and give the woman a big hug. Instead she said gently, 'Oh now, Peggy, I think you are getting your knickers in a twist for nothing. I know she is pushy, that Sarah, but Percy is not a fool. He knows the score.'

'Well, you would think so, wouldn't you, dearie? But there is no fool like an old fool.' Peggy popped the last morsel of her Eccles cake in her mouth and chewed thoughtfully. 'What can I do?' she whispered.

Sally was suddenly very angry with all these girls making waves. Well, two girls – Sarah and Dora as it happened.

'Do you want me to have a word?' she suggested. 'I am very happy to warn her off – and maybe we can turn her attention elsewhere. Who else can help her career? What about Robert?'

'Huh! He is another one who spends all his time playing games,' said Peggy. 'He's not to be trusted at all, dearie.'

Sally thought about Jeremy and his little secret and made a mental note to warn him to be careful.

'OK then,' she said aloud. 'I will deal with this, Peggy, and don't you worry – we will get Miss Sarah Kelly to see sense.'

When Sally got to the theatre she was accosted by Heather, who was going mad trying to find one of the blonde wigs which had gone missing.

'If those boys have had it away as a joke I will kill the little sods.' She shook a finger at Sally. 'Do you know anything about this?'

'No, you daft thing,' laughed Sally. 'Give me a break, Heather, I have got enough on my plate. Do you know where Giles is, by any chance?'

'Yes, he is in his office – but he is with Lord Graham, so watch out . . .'

Sally made her way to the front of house and up the stairs to the Royal Circle where Giles's office was situated. She knocked on the door and waited. After a few moments Giles himself opened the door. He seemed less than pleased to see her.

'Yes?' he barked. 'I am very busy, so if it isn't important can it wait until later?'

Sally heard the sound of someone clearing their throat and a waft of cigar smoke curled round the door.

'No, it is fine, I will come back later but I do need instructions about the arrival of Rupert and Isabelle.' She turned and went away feeling very miffed. What on earth was the matter with everyone? They all seemed to have agendas that had nothing to do with getting the show on the road. She decided to seek out Sarah and give her a job to do. It might not ultimately help keep her away from Percy, but it would make Sally feel better! She found the young lady in the Green Room making coffee. Sally noted there were two mugs.

'Hi, Sarah, are you busy?' she asked.

Sarah stirred the coffee and smiled sweetly. 'I was just going to take this to Percy, as a matter of fact.'

'OK then, when you have done that, can you go down to the stage and help Heather find a lost wig? She is going mad.'

'Actually, I know where the wig is,' answered Sarah. 'I

caught Simon wearing it after the show last night, so I took it off him and kept it in my dressing room.'

Sally was rather nonplussed. 'Oh right, good. Well, can you take it to Heather and then see if Janie needs help to start putting costumes in skips?'

Sarah nodded and set off with her two cups of coffee. Sally couldn't resist calling after her, 'I don't think you have time to drink that with Percy, do you? Best get a move on.'

The sound of voices coming from the stage door reminded Sally that it was nearly time to get ready for the afternoon performance. She ran up to the dressing room and spent five minutes doing a warm-up for her voice. Suddenly, she found she could forget all the petty ups and downs and focus on herself. She must not forget this was what she was here for; to learn to grow as an actress. She had a great deal to get through in the next three weeks, so no distractions.

Her serenity was interrupted by the arrival of her sister. 'Sally, look who is here!' yelled Dora and stepped back to allow the surprise guest to enter the dressing room.

'Hello, Sally,' said Mack.

Sally was struck dumb. The room was full of this gorgeous handsome man who was smiling at her and moving forward to give her a kiss on the cheek.

'Mack – what a surprise! Oh my goodness, I am gobsmacked. Why are you here?' The question was out before she could stop herself.

'Charming,' he laughed. 'I am not quite sure how to respond to that.'

'No, sorry, I didn't mean to be rude, it is just such a surprise. Actually Dora did mention it this morning, but I have been so busy it completely went out of my head. It is lovely to see you. Are you going to watch the show? Shall I get you a ticket?' Sally could feel herself wittering on and tried to pull herself together. Bloody Dora had done it again!

But Mack seemed to be taking it all in his stride. 'Don't worry about me,' he said. 'I will have a wander round the town, and probably get something to eat, and then we can either meet between the shows or after. It is not a problem. I know you are very busy, so just do your thing and we will see what happens later.'

'Thank you, Mack.' Sally breathed a sigh of relief. 'I must say there is a lot to do, and, Dora, you should have been here an hour ago.' She turned her attention to her wayward sister. She was not going to let her get away with this disruption. 'You had better get up to the wardrobe department a bit quick.'

Dora had the grace to do as she was told, and Sally left Mack wending his way back to the stage door. By the time she had changed and got her make-up on she was exhausted!

Chapter 30

By the end of the second performance Sally was feeling like death. She was so tired, and the last thing she felt like doing was going clubbing.

'Oh come on, sis, don't be a spoilsport. You have got to come.' Dora was standing in the doorway dressed to the nines. 'What will poor Mack think? He has come all this way to see you and you are being a party-pooper.'

'You invited him, Dora, not me,' Sally retorted. She was well aware that Mack was waiting downstairs with the others, but she just couldn't face him. 'Tell him I am truly sorry, and that we can go and have a pub lunch or something tomorrow. I presume he is sleeping on our sofa tonight?'

'Who knows?' Dora giggled. 'Things might change in the night, sister dear.'

'Oh, don't be so stupid and childish. What is the matter with you, Dora? I hardly know the guy, for Christ's sake. Why are you pushing him in my face?'

Dora just waved her hand and disappeared down the stairs, calling, 'See you later!'

Sally was in a really grumpy mood now. Left on her own, she almost wished she had gone with them all. Almost. Then Janie appeared in the doorway with a load of dirty washing. 'Anything for me?' She stopped and noticed Sally's long face. 'Everything all right?' she asked.

'Oh yes, fine. It is just Dora is getting on my nerves. She sort of set me up tonight with this old friend from home. He is the brother of my best friend from school, but I don't really know him that well. Anyway, he is very nice and everything, but she invited him up here for the weekend, and then expects me to drop everything and go out clubbing. She can be very irritating at times.'

Janie nodded. 'She is still very young, Sally. Don't let it get to you. Come on, come and have a glass of wine with me and Heather while we finish clearing up. Gwendoline left early tonight with Geoffrey, so work that one out. Mark my words, it is all going to end in tears.'

After Janie had left, Sally pondered on her situation. Why was she being so dismissive of Mack? The last time she had seen him she was full of passion and longing, and now suddenly she was talking about him as if he was a complete stranger. Yet if truth be told, Mack had crept into her thoughts many times over the last few weeks. She had gone over and over their last evening together. She had even managed to pluck up the courage to send him the odd postcard of Crewe, with a reasonably bland comment like *So this is show biz!* but he had not replied, and as the days passed Sally had put him to the back of her mind and concentrated on the job in hand. Now he was here and she was just too tired to respond.

Sally finally crawled into bed about 1 a.m. and fell instantly asleep, not waking until nine the next morning. Wondering what was going to greet her on the other side of her bedroom door, she donned a dressing gown and pulled open the door quietly, creeping into the sitting room to find a body filling the sofa. She had left out a pillow and blankets last night, hoping that Mack would feel welcome. He had made full use of the sofa, and was sprawled over it with his feet hanging over the edge.

Sally tiptoed into the kitchen and put the kettle on. She was hoping that she could get some work done before everyone woke up, and then enjoy the rest of her Sunday with Mack, catching up on news from home. She made herself coffee and toast and honey, and crept back to her room. Now that Giles had done her the honour of offering her the job of directing the Dumb Show in *Hamlet*, Sally was determined to make her mark and do him proud. She had discussed masks with Gwendoline, who was happy to oblige, and Dora had promised to make white robes for the actors – though whether that offer still held was anyone's guess.

Sally spent the next couple of hours reading the text, and also acquainting herself with the part of Ophelia, since she was the official understudy, as well as director of the Dumb Show. Her thoughts turned to *Hamlet* and Rupert Hallam, who had been in the news a good deal lately as the new heart-throb, due to his role in an ongoing series on TV. Isabelle James, his opposite number, had just won a BAFTA for her performance in a very moody film about incest. Sally had not seen it but all the reviews raved about her performance, and there was much comment made about her nude scenes. She had apparently had to undress through most of her scenes. Well good luck to her, thought Sally. If you've got it, flaunt it! The phone rang suddenly and she was up and out to the hall, quick as a flash.

'Sally? It's Giles Longfellow here. I am sorry to trouble you on your day off, but I think I did mention I might need your help today with our new arrivals. I am still in the countryside, but apparently Rupert has arrived at the theatre and no one knows what to do with him. Can you get down there and ask Gladys to open my office so you can pick up the keys to his flat, which are on top of my desk. The address is number 1, Greenbanks – you know that block of new flats down by the river? Take a taxi and keep the receipt, and I will reimburse you. If you could just get him milk and bread and stuff and see him in safely, I would appreciate it.'

'Yes, that's fine, Giles. I will go now.' Sally put the phone down with a sigh. So much for her day off and a pub lunch in the country.

'Problems?' A voice at her elbow startled her.

'Oh gosh, Mack, you made me jump! Sorry, did I wake you? I have got to go to the theatre and play host to our new arrival, Rupert Hallam. Help yourself to tea and coffee, et cetera. I should be back within the hour. I was going to suggest a pub lunch, but I don't know how much time we will have left. It's eleven o'clock now.'

'Don't worry, I will hang out here and wait for you,' he said. 'I take it Dora is still asleep? Shall I wake her up in a bit so we can all meet up together?'

'Yes, why not,' replied Sally, without much enthusiasm. 'I'll see you later. Oops, I had better get dressed,' she added, realizing she was still in her pyjamas.

Sally threw on an old jumper and some jeans and gave her hair a quick brush. Looking at her reflection in the mirror, she could see the brush had done nothing useful, so found her favourite hat and hid the mess underneath. A tiny voice did hint she might have wanted to try a bit harder as Mack was here and they might go out later, but it was quickly squashed by a glance at the time. Sally grabbed her bag and left the flat as Mack was putting on the kettle.

When Sally arrived at the stage door she was greeted by Gladys looking very overexcited and decidedly pink in the cheeks.

'Oh, Miss Sally, thank goodness you got here. Poor Mr Hallam has been waiting so patiently and me not knowing what to do for the best. Mr Hallam, this is Sally. She is the ASM and knows all about everything.'

Rupert Hallam turned to shake Sally's hand, saying languidly, 'Thank God you have arrived. I was starting to think that everyone had forgotten about me.' He stuck his nose in the air.

Sally replied, 'Oh, not at all – and I'm so very sorry you've had to wait.' She turned immediately to Gladys. 'I need the keys to Mr Longfellow's office, please, so I can get the keys to Mr Hallam's accommodation. If you don't mind waiting a few more minutes, Rupert, we will sort this out, and I will take you to your flat. Can you also get me a taxi, please, Gladys, to Number 1, Greenbanks.' Inside, Sally was fuming. This guy was so aloof and full of himself. Well, we'll soon bring him down a peg or two, she promised herself.

By the time she got back to the stage door the taxi had arrived and she and Rupert were able to set off immediately. He did not say a word on the journey over and Sally was in no mood to try and be friendly. The taxi dropped them off and Sally made her way to the front entrance of Greenbanks. It suddenly occurred to her that she had no means of transport back to her flat, so that meant more grief. She managed the locks, and finally opened the front door to a very smart and obviously expensive first-floor flat. It had a glass window right across one wall and a leather sofa, and a glass dining table and four chairs. Sally couldn't help thinking, 'Oh, this is lovely!' Then realized she had spoken out loud.

'Yeah, not bad, I must say,' agreed Rupert Hallam, putting his bag down and going into the bedroom. Sally decided to investigate the kitchen, which was very modern and had every gadget imaginable. Lucky sod, she thought to herself. She dumped the carrier bag with the groceries on the counter.

'Well, I will leave you to settle in then,' she declared frostily. 'I have written out a list of useful numbers for you, including mine and the stage manager's. Her name is Heather Rollings and I am sure she will be calling you later.'

She had started to make her way to the door when Rupert stopped her.

'Listen, I apologize if I was a bit curt earlier. It's just all a bit overwhelming, to tell you the truth. Don't suppose you know where to get some food? Is there a pub you all go to? I guess there is no one about because it's Sunday.'

Sally suddenly felt a bit sorry for him. He looked very for-lorn standing there.

'Yes, absolutely right. Sunday is a dead day but we all love it. It is the only time we have off, really – the rest of the week is full on.' Sally wasn't quite sure what to do next. Leave, or invite him to join them in the pub. Her good nature getting the better of her, she decided to give Mr Hallam a second chance.

'As a matter of fact, we were thinking of going for a pub lunch so you are welcome to join us. I share a flat with my sister Dora, and we have a friend visiting from home, so please – do come if you would like.'

Rupert gave her a beaming smile that completely changed his face from moody and mean to young and boyish – and *very* good-looking, Sally had to admit.

'That would be really cool. Thank you so much.' He picked up his rucksack, found his wallet and started to leave. Sally remembered his keys and handed them to him at the door.

'Won't get far without them,' she grinned. 'Oh actually, can we use your phone to call a taxi? It is not far but a pain to walk it, and time is marching on if we want to get to a pub before it closes.'

'Be my guest,' replied Rupert, pointing to the phone.

Sally rang the cab company then tried her flat and luckily got hold of Dora.

'Listen, can you and Mack be ready to come down when I ring the doorbell? We can take this taxi on to the pub and charge the theatre. I thought we could go to the Cross Keys on the Nantwich Road.' Dora agreed and Sally put the phone down. 'Right – all sorted, let's hope the taxi gets here quickly.'

While they waited Sally explained who she was exactly, and how she was the understudy for Ophelia, and about her Dumb Show ideas. Rupert seemed genuinely interested and admitted that this was his first theatre role since drama school and he was very nervous.

'Do you know Isabelle?' asked Sally.

'Not really. I have met her at a couple of film things, but that's all,' replied Rupert. 'She is scarily beautiful though,' he added. Sally caught the admiration in his voice and thought that was par for the course; two beautiful young things together. She knew where that would lead.

When the two of them arrived at Sally's flat Dora was at the front door with Mack, bursting with excitement.

'Hi there! I rang Janie and Peter and they are joining us, and Simon may raise himself from his pit, so we should have a good laugh.' Dora clambered into the car leaving Mack to find his own place in the front, as it happened. It was only as Dora settled back in the seat that the penny dropped and she recognized Rupert. For one blissful minute there was silence and then she was off again.

'Oh wow, hi! You are Rupert Hallam, aren't you? I am such a fan and I think it is brilliant that you have given up your career to come here and do *Hamlet*.'

Rupert burst out laughing. 'Hang on a minute – give up my career? I do hope that is not how the rest of the world sees it, or I am finished. I have given up nothing, if you don't mind. It is an honour to be doing this production, and part of my heritage as an actor.'

Dora had the good grace to apologize profusely, and then shut up, as indicated to her by Sally making a zipping gesture across her mouth. The rest of the journey passed in relative silence, apart from Mack asking the driver various questions about local sights. The pub was on the edge of town so was nearly like a country pub. It served good wholesome dishes like shepherd's pie or Sunday roast with all the trimmings, and it was cheap. The gang were just in time to order food, and while they were doing that, Rupert went and bought everyone drinks, plus a couple of bottles of wine for later.

Sally joined him to help carry the drinks to the table. 'Nothing like bribery to get the cast on your side,' she quipped.

'Oh now, come on, Sally, don't have a go at me. I am trying my best to get off on the right foot, that is all.'

Rupert paid the bill and followed Sally back to the others. Janie and Peter were there already and had commandeered a table. Introductions were made and everyone got down to serious drinking. It turned out to be a lovely afternoon. Actors very rarely have trouble making friends. In fact, they tend to love everyone instantly, and it is only later that they see the cracks and start bitching. Rupert was very good company, Sally noticed. The aloofness she had seen at the beginning of the day had gone completely, and in its place was a joky, open young man enjoying the company, and loving the limelight – which was inevitable, thought Sally as she watched Dora hanging on his every word and flirting outrageously. Even Janie was doing her best to get his attention with all her talk of costumes and fittings.

'One of the perks of my job,' she piped up. 'Measuring the inside leg of handsome young actors.'

Peter pretended mock horror and everyone laughed. 'No leg could match up to that of your beloved boyfriend, Janie, my dear,' he leered, and he gave her a squeeze.

Simon arrived just as last orders were being called and found himself getting a round. Dora offered to go halves with him but he refused. Sally's sharp eyes picked up a look between them and suspected that things were not very happy. Sally had spent quite a good deal of the lunchtime observing everyone. She loved people-watching and would always try and sit in a corner if she could. She had inevitably found her-self comparing Mack and Rupert. Both were good-looking, confident men, yet so different. Mack was impressive just by his physical presence. He was by far the tallest of the bunch, and seemed like a gentle giant. His hair was thick and long and very shiny, and when he laughed he revealed strong white teeth. He was a very attractive man and not at all cowed by a load of actors wittering on about themselves. On the contrary, he seemed to really enjoy their anecdotes and stories, and even added a few of his own. Sally wondered if she was being fool-ish not getting to know him better. He had come all the way to visit her, after all.

By comparison, Rupert was very much the face of the

moment. He seemed much slighter than he appeared on the television screen. He was not quite as tall as Mack, but still about five foot eleven. He had a perfectly chiselled jaw, and his mouth and lips were perfect – almost like a girl's. His face was saved from being too pretty by an aquiline nose and high cheekbones, and those deep, penetrating dark eyes. He had the long floppy hair of an actor which he constantly kept flipping back out of his eyes. For all his good looks Rupert was definitely one of the lads, and seemed immune to Dora's attempts at flirting. Just as well, thought Sally, noticing Simon getting grumpy in the corner. Even Mack tried a couple of times to attract Dora's attention, to no avail.

As soon as they were thrown out of the pub Dora invited everyone back to the flat.

'But we have work to do and washing to sort, so let's leave it for now,' said Sally.

'Sis, what have I told you about being a party-pooper. We have got to finish Rupert's lovely wine he bought and the football will be on soon so the boys can put their feet up and watch telly just like being at home.'

This brought a roar of approval from the male contingency and Sally knew she was defeated. The afternoon passed very quickly, with lots of cheering and rowdy jokes. Janie managed to drag Peter away at five, and Rupert called a cab.

'Mustn't mess up my first day with a hangover,' he grinned to Sally at the front door. 'Thanks so much for today, Sally. I feel as if we have known each other for ever. Promise you will keep an eye on me? I sometimes find it hard to stay focused and then I fuck up.' For a moment he looked very serious.

'We won't let you fuck up, don't worry,' she promised. 'I will be your shadow, never fear.' She leaned over and gave him a kiss on the cheek and Rupert responded by giving her a big hug.

'Thanks again, Sally.' And he was gone.

'Well, aren't you the dark horse, getting a snog in so soon.' Dora was standing behind her in the hallway.

'Don't be stupid,' Sally sighed. 'Let's just get an early night, shall we, as it is a busy day tomorrow.'

'Oh yes, miss, whatever you say, miss. Actually, Mack and I might go out for a drink later, seeing as how you have ignored him most of the weekend, and he goes back to Cheltenham tomorrow.' The girl turned and flounced off into the sitting room.

Sally suddenly felt very tired and decided enough was enough. She went into the sitting room and started to clear away. Simon was asleep on the floor and Mack was dozing on the sofa.

'Where's Dora gone now?' asked Sally, working her way round the room. 'We need to tidy up and send people to their homes ... Simon!' She gave him a nudge in the ribs which produced a groan of protest.

'Time to go home, Simon. Come on, please.'

Dora appeared at her bedroom door. 'Actually I am knackered now. Do you mind if I just have a quick nap before we go out, Mack?'

Mack stood up and then realized there was nowhere to go.

'Sure thing, whatever,' he said. 'If Sally doesn't mind me watching TV, and taking up space in her sitting room tonight.' He turned to her, looking like a lost dog.

'Of course I don't mind, Mack, you are our guest. Though God knows we have hardly been the most attentive hosts, have we?' she said loudly enough for her sister to hear.

Simon had dragged himself to his feet and was looking for his shoes. When he had finally left, and there was silence from Dora's bedroom as she took a nap, Mack sat back and fixed

Sally with his big brown eyes. He had a way of looking at one very directly; his gaze was like his camera lens, thought Sally.

There was a long pause and Mack seemed to be gathering his thoughts together. Finally he said, 'Are you pleased to see me? It is just that I feel I am intruding on your life somehow. Dora made me think it is what you would have wanted. She can be very persuasive at times.' He smiled shyly. 'We have had a couple of nights out together since you left, and to be honest I am not sure that was such a good idea.' He hesitated.

'What do you mean?' asked Sally with a growing sense of foreboding. 'When you say you went out together, do you mean as friends or . . . something more?'

'That's just it, Sally. You see, she invited me to come and stay here when we were out one night in Cheltenham, and I think I misunderstood the situation – and now I don't know how to extricate myself without embarrassment all round. Shit, I feel such a fool.' Mack ran his fingers through his hair with frustration.

'I am sorry, Mack, but I don't understand what you are trying to say. Are you and Dora an item?' Sally nearly choked on the word. Surely this could not be happening? Had Dora managed yet again to crash through her life and create chaos? Could Mack be such a bastard, able to replace one sister with another? Sally wanted to get up and rush out but Mack seemed to read her thoughts and placed his hand on her arm.

'No, Sally. I thought Dora was trying to help. I have wanted to contact you so many times over the last few weeks but I just couldn't pluck up the courage. I know how much this job means to you and I didn't want to get in the way. But to be honest I can't stop thinking about you and our date together. I thought you and Dora had devised this plan between you so we could meet up again, but the way Dora has been behaving

I think she thinks I fancy *her*. I am sorry if that sounds arrogant or offensive but it is not at all what I intended. I just wanted to see *you* again, Sally.' Mack seemed to run out of steam then and sat back looking wretched.

Sally's heart took a huge leap and wiped out any fatigue she had been feeling.

'Oh Mack, I *am* pleased to see you – you have no idea. I am sorry I have been so grumpy and dull, but I really have had a hell of a time, and I apologize for not ringing you. But as you have so rightly understood I am trying hard to get to grips with this job and my career. I have so many mixed feelings about it all now, and no one to talk to about it all.'

Mack suddenly got up, came round and took Sally in his arms. He then kissed her with such ferocity she was completely taken aback, and when he stopped she practically dropped into her seat again.

'What happens now?' asked Mack slightly breathlessly.

Sally looked up at him and felt a surge of excitement. She wanted to drag him into her bed right now – but the thought of her sister in the other room was not conducive to her sense of romance. *Dora*. She could not bring herself to think about what her sister had had in mind. Certainly nothing as unselfish as helping Sally find love. But these thoughts were for another time. She stood up and gave Mack a hug.

'Much as I would like to seal our pact, I really don't think now is the right moment, Mack. Can we arrange for you to come up to stay another time, and maybe we could go and spend a night somewhere away from Crewe. Away from Dora,' she added.

Mack looked disappointed but he answered with a smile in his voice, 'I will wait for as long as it takes, Miss Thomas. Meanwhile, I will dream of you tonight and of things to come.'

They took their time saying good night. Sally loved kissing Mack – he was so good at it! Finally he drew back breathless and shaking slightly with desire.

'That's enough, Sally. I can't take any more. It is torture not being able to make love to you. I want you so badly. Are you sure I can't change your mind?' He moved towards her and Sally put out her arms to stop him.

'No – please, Mack. I want us to be alone and private. That will not be the case when Dora wakes up, believe me.'

'OK, I concede defeat but if you don't mind I will go now and get the late train back to Cheltenham. It will give me time to cool off and have a good think.'

They shared one last lingering kiss and then he was gone. Sally ran a bath; she lit lots of candles and soaked in the soothing water until she was prune-like. Not a good look, she smiled to herself, and stepped out into her towel. She was so tired she just lay down on top of her bed and fell fast asleep. She woke later and crawled under the covers, going straight back to the Land of Nod, dreaming that Mack was in bed beside her, wrapped in her arms . . .

Chapter 31

'Good morning, everyone. May I take this opportunity to extend a special welcome to our two newcomers, Rupert Hallam and Isabelle James.' Giles Longfellow paused long enough for the cast to recognize their new stars, and sensing that there was not going to be a round of applause forthcoming, started one himself.

He then continued, 'It is no secret that this production of *Hamlet* is my pet project, and one I have dreamed of creating for a long time. But I also hope that you, the cast and crew, will become as enthused as I am and realize the importance of the production's success. Not just for me or you, but for the future of Crewe Theatre. You see, I want this theatre to be firmly on the map as an important contributor to the arts in the UK. I am hoping to take this production to the West End eventually, and with luck, it will be the start of many such transfers and collaborations with different producers. Thanks to Lord Graham and his enormous generosity, we have been able to get the ball rolling with *Hamlet* – and may this be just the beginning of a new golden age for this theatre.'

Giles paused again, this time to compose himself. He really did feel quite emotional about the whole thing and, if the truth be known, he was also a little fearful of the outcome. This was his opportunity to shine. He had been working towards this moment for many years now, and was only too aware that the one thing that could let him down was himself. He and Teddie had been seeing a good deal more of each other, due to the fact that they were in close proximity and able to meet easily under the pretext of discussing the finances of the theatre. This had led to many a late-night supper, and the two men had grown closer in every way. His Lordship was still obliged to keep a low profile in his personal dealings with Giles, as he still had Her Ladyship to consider. Lady Tanya Graham knew the score only too well. She had fallen in love with Teddie Graham when they were both still at their boarding schools. Her family owned a huge estate in Northumberland, and over the years several of the landed gentry in and around the area would entertain each other and naturally keep an eye out for any of the younger members' future couplings. Same old, same old . . . Put the right two together, create an heir and a spare, and then all would be hunky-dory.

Tanya had always adored Teddie. He was such fun, and somewhat less pedestrian and conventional than some of the other suitors she was forced to endure. The two of them shared a sense of humour and did not take any of the rigma-role too seriously. They managed to laugh their way through the hunt balls, croquet parties and polo meets, and became firm friends. Inevitably they became lovers, and then engaged and married. It was a smooth transition and they were a very glamorous couple for the first few years on the circuit. Teddie loved to party, and there were many occasions recorded in *Vogue* and *Tatler* to keep his reputation going. But then they had their two children, Edward and Tilly, in quick succession, and suddenly Tanya found herself settled in Crewe Hall up north, while her husband spent a good deal of time at their flat in Chelsea. She actually quite enjoyed the early years with the children. They had a wonderful life in the countryside, and there were always holidays to look forward to: a chalet at Klosters for the winter ski season, or a villa in the South of France for the summer. Tanya was well aware of the situation. She would always be Lady Graham, and as such would enjoy a life of luxury forever – but she would no longer enjoy her conjugal rights with her husband. He would discreetly pursue another avenue. Should she decide to take a lover, that was acceptable, as long as it was never discovered or flaunted in public; appearances were everything.

The couple had lived this way for years, and mostly it worked very well, especially as Teddie tended to keep his other life down in London. Recently, however, he was spending a great deal of time at Crewe Theatre – and when Tanya was introduced to Giles Longfellow at the first night of *A Man for All Seasons*, she immediately knew the reason why. Her heart sank. The saying not on your own doorstep echoed in her head. She was far from pleased, and resolved to keep her distance from the theatre as much as possible. As far as Giles Longfellow was concerned, Tanya was polite but distant, and Giles very much understood his place in the scheme of things; he kept a low profile with the lady of the house.

Giles's relationship with Lord Graham was a distraction that he could have done without really, as he had a good deal on his plate and his career was very much at stake with this season at Crewe. But as usual, his emotional needs overruled his commonsense and he could not resist his trysts with Teddie, be they in a club in Manchester, or late at night in his office. He could no longer live without the thrill of being with his lover.

The only person who knew what was going on was Robert, who had once been the object of his affection. Their romance had almost ended before it began last year, here at the theatre, because Robert could not handle the intensity with which Giles fell in love. For the first few weeks the two men had shared every living moment together. They locked themselves away in Giles's office every lunchtime and ate each other for lunch! They became the laughing stock of the cast and crew, who got fed up with interrupting them in dark corners of the theatre, the most popular being the Royal Box, no less. Finally it was Percy and Peggy who took control and told them it had to stop as it was affecting the whole company, and not for the good. Giles accepted the ultimatum quite easily, and was soon back in his old routine, and directing the next production with great aplomb. Robert, however, was not so easily consoled, and disappeared back to London, never to be seen again.

Percy had announced his relief to Peggy, saying, 'I could never get me head round the lad – something not quite straight there. Very ambitious too, you know. Wouldn't surprise me if we see him again one day, Peggy. I get the feeling he won't let Giles off the hook that easily.'

So it was no surprise when Robert appeared at the first read-through this season, having been introduced as the director's assistant.

Robert was indeed using his power and knowledge to further his career. He got on fine now with Giles, and no longer fancied him, but he was going to use him as much as he could to gain advantages in the pursuit of his theatrical career. *Watch and learn* was his motto these days.

Giles rounded off his introductory speech by explaining that Robert would be taking rehearsals in the rehearsal room next door at the same time as Giles directed the play on the main stage.

'Robert will take individual scenes with you as required, and also oversee the fight sequences. May I also remind you that the lovely Sally Thomas will be directing the Dumb Show, and she will give you your calls accordingly. So now, no more talking, let us read this wonderful play. Heather, start the clock.'

Sally listened intently to the read-through, not just as an actress and understudy, but out of a natural curiosity to see how the company coped with the language of Shakespeare.

Rupert Hallam was a joy. He had obviously worked hard already on the text, and he had a fine sense of the play. He made the words jump off the page, and even found the humour in *Hamlet*, and what he could not find he managed to create. Isabelle, however, seemed completely lost and over-whelmed by the dialogue. She read her lines like a child, in a dull monotone. When she was not actually in a scene she spent the time playing with her hair and fidgeting with a cigarette, which she smoked intensely, sucking in the smoke as if her life depended on it. Rather the other way round, thought Sally to herself, having given up smoking at college, after realizing that the people in the know were right, and not only did smoking ruin your voice, but it could basically kill you.

Percy Hackett was in his element as Polonius, and it was obvious Peggy would have her work cut out supporting him through the play. Sadly, Peggy was too old to play Gertrude, which was a role she had played several times over the years. 'Still, it means I will be nice and free to keep an eye on my

Percy, if you know what I mean,' she said with a big wink in Sally's direction. Geoffrey was playing Claudius the King, and Charmaine was Gertrude, his queen.

'Now we will see all the Royal Shakespeare training coming to the fore,' said Gwendoline, with a touch of sarcasm in her voice. She and Geoffrey were now a definite item, but Sally knew she was very insecure. Geoffrey's wife had appeared at the theatre last week with their three daughters and made a very public scene; she had basically banned him from seeing his little girls. He was clearly very upset and Gwendoline was not able to easily distract him. She was also painfully lacking in any understanding about how a father feels about his children, and she and Geoffrey were finding things very difficult.

'He will go back to the wife, you mark my words,' commented Percy in the Green Room one morning. 'All the sex in the world can't wash away the guilt of leaving the children.'

Peggy turned round and studied her wayward partner. 'Oh? And you are such an expert then, are you, dearie?'

'Well, I don't have kids but I do know a bit about life, Peggy, and in the end loyalty and family count for a lot, don't they?'

Peggy held his look and smiled slowly. 'It is good to hear you say that, my old ducks, because sometimes I do wonder,' she said.

Percy crossed to her and gave her a hug. 'We are all right, girl, don't you fret. Now get my coffee and let's do some line learning.'

Sally had had a little time to study Ophelia and was keen to have a go. Hopefully there would be a chance for her to stand in for Isabelle over the next two weeks of rehearsal when the actress had costume fittings and suchlike. Sally was also very curious to see how Robert conducted his rehearsals. She found him difficult to pin down. Sometimes he was very friendly and rather camp, and yet at other times he was very aloof and cold. He certainly had the ear of Giles Longfellow, and Sally had tried to discover the nature of their relationship. Peggy had told her all about last season, but Sally wondered if Robert still held a torch for Giles.

'He watches Giles all the time,' she commented to Peggy. 'I find him quite tricky to communicate with, don't you?'

'Doesn't bother me, darling, I just get on and do my own thing. All the shenanigans that carry on after hours go over my head.'

Except those related to Percy, Sally thought to herself. That is a very different kettle of *poissons*!

Sally's attention turned to Jeremy. Her dear friend looked decidedly the worse for wear today. He was very pale and sweating profusely. She caught his eye and smiled encouragingly, but he just shook his head slowly and pointed to his glass of water. When they broke for lunch Sally went straight over to him and asked him if he was OK.

'No, I feel terrible and want to be sick, quite frankly. Oh God – I will be back in a minute!' And he was gone. Sally decided to get the full story later. She crossed to the props table which had been set up ready for the afternoon rehearsals and found Dora deep in conversation with Rupert.

'But does *Hamlet* know for sure that his mother is involved with murder?' she was asking him.

'Hi, guys. How's it going?' Sally decided to intervene.

Rupert turned to her with a big smile on his face and said, 'Sally! How are you? Do you want to discuss anything with me? Dora is grilling me on my motivation already,' and he laughed.

'I like to know everyone's motivation,' responded Dora, flirting outrageously with the leading man. She addressed her sister. 'How about you, Sally dear?'

'Some people would call that being nosy,' replied Sally, a little more tartly than she had intended. 'Dora, would you like to help me with the masks? I want to be able to explain to the cast what I will be doing with the Dumb Show when we discuss the play in a minute.'

'Oh, isn't it lunchtime yet?' sulked Dora. 'I'm starving, aren't you, Rupert?' She fluttered her eyelashes at the young man, who was just about to be accosted by Isabelle.

'Rupert, darling,' she practically purred. 'Can we go through some lines as soon as possible? I am *sooo* scared.' She took his arm and leaned into him, flicking her mane of hair out of her gorgeous green eyes to look up at her co-star invitingly.

Oh dear, thought Sally very ungraciously. You have serious competition for the femme fatale role, Dora! To the group she said, 'Come on, Dora, we have work to do. Good luck, you two – see you later.' And she dragged her sister away.

'Oh wow!' grumbled Dora. 'That Isabelle really is a piece of work. She can't act for toffee, but she certainly knows how to get the blokes going with all that bloody hair-tossing business.'

Sally stopped and took her by both shoulders. 'Dora, look at me and listen very carefully. Don't start all that sort of nonsense. You are very minor in all this, and if you want to continue in this company you need to know your place. You do *not* chat up the leading man or slag off the leading lady. Do you understand? You get on with the job and mind your p's and q's.'

'Oh, please don't treat me like a child, Sally. I know my place, but believe me, by the time I have finished here, and people see what I can do, my place will be very different. I just think it is unbelievable that girls like Isabelle get jobs when they blatantly can't act!'

'Well, that is the nature of the beast and always has been, to a certain extent. So the sooner you accept that fact, the happier you will be about it all.'

'But it is so unfair,' wailed Dora dramatically.

'Oh please. Who said anything in life was fair? You just have to work with it. Believe me, if life was fair I would be playing Cleopatra at the National!' Sally snapped.

'Ooh Sally, dear, your mask has dropped. Surely my mild-mannered sister is not showing signs of malice?'

Dora sensed revenge, but was stopped in her tracks when Sally turned and pulled her towards the exit with, 'Ah yes, talking of masks, come with me and find them.' That finished the conversation for the time being, but Sally knew her sister only too well: during the weeks to come, Dora would be on the war-path, and the fight for Rupert's affections would be fierce, she had no doubt. He was very lovely though, Sally had to admit, and her own heart gave a little flutter at the thought of his smile.

Jeremy felt much better after he had been sick. He had left Sally in such a rush, leaving his poor friend wondering what was going on, not that he didn't think for one minute that Sally was not on to him. It was just a question of how much he actually told her about Eddie. Jeremy whispered his name: Eddie . . . He looked at himself in the mirror above the basin, and saw the desperate longing in his eyes. 'What a pathetic sight,' he told himself. 'God, you need to pull yourself together.' He splashed cold water over his face and laughed quietly. Oh boy, had he fallen hard. One minute he had been a man with no emotional ties – now he was in knots!

'What's so funny, Jeremy?' Simon asked as he came into the Gents and went for a pee. 'What do we think about our leading lady then? Bit of all right or what?' He joined Jeremy at the basins and washed his hands.

'A tad out of your league,' teased Jeremy. 'But you never know, she might be into a bit of rough trade.' He made his way out of the door followed by Simon still doing up his flies as they bumped into Robert.

'Well, well, what have you two been up to? Simon, I didn't know you were that way inclined!' Robert said, noting Simon's zip.

'Yeah, very funny,' muttered Simon, pushing past him.

'Charming,' said Robert to Jeremy as he too tried to pass. 'How was your weekend, Jeremy? From what I saw, it was very full on.' He gave a theatrical wink. Jeremy cringed. He and Eddie had bumped into Robert in a bar on Sunday night and it had all been very awkward. All he needed was someone like Robert knowing his private affairs.

He just nodded and said, 'Yes, it was quite a weekend,' and carried on past him.

Robert watched him go with a smile on his face. Knowledge was power, he reminded himself.

Jeremy decided to go up to the dressing room for the duration of the lunch-hour and keep well away from anyone likely to interrogate him. He felt bad about not going to find Sally to explain his behaviour, but he knew she would understand, and he would talk to her later. He just needed a bit of time to sort out his thoughts and feelings. Everything had happened so fast that he was still reeling.

Chapter 32

When they left the theatre on Saturday afternoon, Eddie had driven them to Manchester.

'This is going to be a sort of Magical Mystery Tour,' he had announced in the car. 'Just sit back and enjoy the ride!'

Jeremy was in heaven. He watched the countryside speed past on the motorway, and every now and then he would turn to Eddie and catch his eye, and they would smile at each other. Their brief coupling in the theatre was still lingering. Jeremy could smell Eddie on his T-shirt. He was tingling with the need to touch his new lover. As if he could read his thoughts, Eddie put a hand on Jeremy's thigh and caressed him. His hand was gentle at first then more urgent, travelling further up his leg, kneading his flesh beneath his jeans. He finally found Jeremy's hard-on and laughed gently.

'Oh, so you want more, do you? That is good to know. Shall we stop somewhere and sort you out?' Jeremy was embarrassed and did not quite know how to react. Eddie seemed so experienced and well versed in all this seduction business, yet he was so young.

They had come off the motorway at the next junction and found a field. Eddie parked behind a hedge and made swift work of taking Jeremy to heaven. Jeremy could not have imagined the excitement of this fast love in a car, in a field, in the middle of the countryside. It made him want to scream with pleasure. His whole body was on fire and wanting more and more.

'Now come on, J, you will just have to wait until we get to our destination. Let's get back on the road or we will be late for the other delights I have in store for you.' And with that Eddie backed out of the gate and set off once more for the bright lights of the big city. They arrived in Manchester an hour later, and Eddie displayed a comprehensive knowledge of the back streets. They finally arrived at the front of a huge Victorian house, in a quiet street very near the city centre.

'Follow me,' he ordered, bounding up the front steps and ringing the bell.

'What about our bags?' Jeremy called out.

'Just leave everything and someone will come and deal with them,' replied Eddie. 'Come on, J – hurry up!' Just at that moment, the door was opened and a young man dressed like a butler appeared on the threshold. 'Welcome to the Queen's Hotel,' he said. 'Do you have luggage?'

'Just a couple of bags,' Eddie told him.

'Very well, we will collect those and bring them to your room. Would you like me to park your car, sir? We have a car park at the back for residents.'

'Yes, please.' Eddie took Jeremy's arm. 'Come on, you. Just wait till you see this.'

The butler stood back and let them pass, and then followed them inside.

The place was like a film set, thought Jeremy. The hall was

straight out of the television series *Upstairs Downstairs*. A grace-
ful staircase led upwards from an original black and white tiled
floor. A massive chandelier hung over the proceedings, the
hundreds of crystal teardrops sparkling above them. But the
most bizarre sight was of a huge gilt-framed portrait of the
Queen, in her ceremonial robes, which hung above the fire-
place to the right of the door.

Jeremy could hardly stop himself from bursting into laughter. He tugged Eddie's sleeve and pointed at the painting,
sniggering, 'You can't be serious. That is outrageous! Our
poor monarch would die if she knew she was presiding over a
gay hotel in Manchester.'

'Oh, never mind that. Come on, we need to sign in.' Eddie
skipped off down the corridor ahead.

Jeremy dutifully followed him, and like Alice in
Wonderland found himself in another world. The reception
desk was vast and had once been mahogany, he guessed. Now,
however, it had been gilded to within an inch of its life. It sat
in a sea of deep red wallpaper and twinkling rococo fixtures
and fittings. No one in this house had ever heard the expression 'less is more'.

The butler handed Jeremy a quill pen with peacock feath-
ers and said, 'Please fill in your details, sir. It is for two nights,
I understand?'

'Oh here, let me,' said Eddie, taking over. Jeremy was still
open-mouthed at his surroundings.

'Shall I give you a credit card?' added Eddie, taking out his
wallet. 'By the way, is George around yet?' he enquired.

'Not yet, sir, but he sent his regards and looks forward to
seeing you later in the bar for a cocktail. Now would you care
to follow me, please?' The butler glided off towards the
staircase, the two lovers in his wake.

At the top of the stairs they turned left and stopped at the first door. Written on it in very elegant gold script was *The Blue Room*. The door opened to reveal a blue room indeed. It was like being in the centre of a Wedgwood plate! There was a roomy canopied double bed with silk sheets, and an enormous blue and gold eiderdown. Jeremy had not seen an eiderdown since he visited his granny as a schoolboy. The lampshades either side of the bed were blue and gold silk, and the wardrobe and dressing table had been painted Wedgwood blue with white trimmings, as were the walls and all the plasterwork. It was incredibly ornate. The butler opened the door to the bathroom to reveal a classic Victorian bathroom, with black and white tiles and a large free-standing slipper bath with all the brass fittings. The toilet had the obligatory mahogany seat, and the pull chain was a twisted rope of fine coloured silks, with a huge tassel to finish it off.

The butler then explained where the fridge was hidden inside a tallboy, also painted blue and white. The matching TV looked most incongruous perched on top of the chest of drawers. Jeremy wondered what Josiah Wedgwood would have made of it!

'If there is anything else you require, please do not hesitate to ring the bell,' the butler said smoothly, and he indicated yet another bell-pull with the attendant tassel.

'Thank you, that is fine,' said Eddie, giving him a generous tip.

'Thank you, sir,' said the butler solemnly, then added with a wink and a wiggle, 'Have fun, you guys.'

Jeremy threw himself on the bed and let out a scream of delight. 'Eddie, this is unbelievable! How did you know about this place?'

Eddie was busy opening a bottle of champagne which had been left for them in a splendid silver bucket.

'Ah, I have friends in high places. Or should I say low places,' he laughed. 'Here, let's have a toast. To love at first sight.' And they touched glasses with a very satisfactory ping from the crystal flûtes provided.

'Everything is so over the top, yet somehow fits,' remarked Jeremy. 'Who owns it?'

'A lovely man called George Delaware. He and his partner Dale have been here for yonks. I don't really know the details, but apparently George used to be a bit of a gangster in the old days – part of the Manchester mafia. Did you know that in the fifties and early sixties, George Raft – an actor and alleged gang member in America – came over to Manchester to see if there was room for his lot up here, and they were sent packing by the good old northerners, who had their own mafia, thank you very much, and didn't need the likes of the Americans to help them make their millions. George told me all this once when I was here.'

Eddie took a swig of champagne then put down his glass and turned to his lover. 'Now, Mr Sinclair, I require you to make slow passionate love to me before dinner.'

And Jeremy was only too happy to oblige.

The rest of the afternoon and early evening were spent making love or drinking champagne. Jeremy decided to try the bath and lay up to his neck in bubbles. There was an extraordinary array of toiletries in the bathroom and he was determined to work his way through the lot. While he was soaking, Eddie watched TV or came into the bathroom to annoy his lover with attempts to seduce him.

'Leave me alone! I can't take any more!' cried Jeremy.

'Oh really? I don't believe that for a minute.' And Eddie whipped off his clothes and joined him beneath the bubbles.

After several of these forays Jeremy finally managed to finish his bath and get ready for the night ahead.

'What exactly do you have in store for me?' he asked delightedly. Eddie was proving to be full of surprises and all of them good, so far.

'Well, we will have drinks with George, then dinner in the restaurant, and then we will adjourn to the club next door, which is also part of the hotel and owned by George. So basically, we do not have to stray far to take our pleasure,' grinned Eddie. 'Pretty clever, don't you think, Mr J? Everything close at hand.'

'It is wonderful. *You* are wonderful. But you still haven't told me how you knew about this place,' said Jeremy.

Eddie looked at him for a minute and then seemed to make a decision. He sighed and said, 'My father has several queer friends. Obviously it is not something he wants to advertise and my mother does not allow them at the house.' Jeremy was about to interrupt but Eddie stopped him. 'Yes, I know what you are going to say, J – that she is a bigot and that it is not for her to judge people, et cetera. Unfortunately, the world is a cruel place, and people *are* ignorant and bigoted, including my mother. When you think it has only been since 1967 that homosexuality was made legal. That is a mere fifteen years ago, Jeremy, and it is still a big thing for a lot of people. You are lucky because you work in a profession where people don't care about things like that. Well, obviously there are a lot of queers in the theatrical profession, which helps, but in the big world outside there is still a great deal of prejudice. My father has started a campaign against discrimination of homosexuals, but it is a real uphill struggle and none of his so-called 'posh' friends want to know.'

'Is your father a homo then?' asked Jeremy. Eddie paused very briefly before he answered.

'No, definitely not – which makes it incredibly difficult for me. I mean, how can I tell him I am queer?' There was a catch in Eddie's voice and Jeremy took his hand.

'In fact, I don't think I will ever be able to be open about it, Jeremy. Well, certainly not in my family circles. I am expected to marry, and have an heir to carry on the Graham title. I have seen it with some of my father's friends. They are really queer but all married. I have seen them here in this hotel, but no one says anything. You wouldn't believe it in this day and age, but there is still a terrible stigma about being homosexual.'

Jeremy took Eddie in his arms and held him close. 'Come on, mate,' he said tenderly. 'Don't get upset. You have a friend in me now, and we will sort it out. Meanwhile, you have promised me a good time, so let's go and get a few cocktails inside us then we won't care about anything.' They kissed passionately and almost succumbed to their growing lust but broke away laughing, promising each other to save it all for later.

When they arrived in the bar it was already buzzing. Unlike a normal cocktail bar in a small hotel where couples sit discreetly chatting in whispers, here the conversation was loud and frequently interspersed with whoops of delight and screeches of laughter.

The barman was naked except for a jockstrap and a black bow tie. Jeremy could hardly contain himself and each new revelation was fuel to the fire. He wanted to be shocked or surprised. He certainly had had no idea that hotels like this existed. He was still wrestling with his feelings for Eddie which had sprung from nowhere seemingly. What would his father think, he wondered, if he announced he was queer? His father enjoyed comics like Larry Grayson, but just dismissed them in general as 'poofs'. Did his dad even know what a homosexual was? He had never had a conversation with his parents about things like this. It had been bad enough when his father brought up the subject of sex and 'taking precautions'. Jeremy had begged him not to continue, assuring him that they did all this kind of stuff at school and he really did not have to bother. Even at school no one mentioned homosexuality as such. There was gossip about a boy who had just joined their class from a private school where there had been a big scandal about abuse. But all that meant to Jeremy and his mates was that a teacher had been a paedophile. Even this expression was not totally clear to them. Girls got flashed at by dirty old men, so the assumption was it must be the same dirty old men who did whatever they did to girls *and* boys. But it was not regarded as anything to do with their take on life in general. Certainly not a life choice a young man might make.

'Jeremy, did you hear me?' Eddie's voice cut through his musings.

'Sorry, I was miles away. What did you say?'

'Would you like to try the house cocktail? I am assured by this charming barman that it is excellent.' Eddie gave the barman his most alluring smile and it occurred to Jeremy that he might have been flirting with him. He felt a flash of unease. Jeremy was discovering emotions he had never felt before. So maybe this 'unease' might better be described as jealousy. This was certainly not an emotion he wanted to feel too often.

He shook himself mentally then turned to Eddie and said, 'Yes, a cocktail would be lovely. This bar is pretty amazing.'

The bar was not large but it felt womb-like as the walls were a dark pink flock with the ubiquitous wall lights and drapes of silk where necessary. The bar was mirrored glass, and mirrors lined the wall behind it so customers sitting in the cubicles were reflected in them, doubling the amount of people, which made the room feel even fuller. Everything glowed in a pink light. Life was rosy!

'Good evening, you young things.' The voice told a tale of cigarettes and red wine and late nights.

'George, how lovely to see you.' Eddie jumped off his bar stool and embraced the man in front of him. Jeremy thought he was pretty impressive. He was tall, over six feet, and broad in the shoulders. He had a fine head of black hair but the black was out of a bottle and rather overused, Jeremy decided. The man was dressed in a dark red velvet smoking jacket with a white shirt underneath sporting a large frill down the front. He had black trousers and what appeared to be velvet mocassins with a coat of arms in gold thread sewn on the fronts.

'So this is Jeremy,' said the deep throaty voice. 'Pleased to meet you.' Jeremy took the outstretched hand and shook it. The hand was big and warm, and the handshake almost painfully strong.

'Great to meet you, George. Eddie has been telling me some fantastic stories about you.'

George looked at Eddie and then back to Jeremy and lowered his voice to say, 'Hopefully not too many stories – always better to keep things close to the chest. Careless talk costs lives, as they used to say during the war.' He paused for a fraction of a second and then burst into laughter. 'Only kidding, chuck, only kidding. My bad boy days are long gone.'

Jeremy was not so sure, and had the distinct feeling that he would not want to cross Mr Delaware. However, it was smiles all round now and the drinks flowed. Jeremy explained to George some of his life as an actor and invited him and Dale to come to the first night of *Hamlet*.

'We'll see,' said George. 'Dale is not very good at sitting still for long. You'll meet him later – he is DJ tonight in the club. He loves it, up and down like a sailor on shore leave. Well, my pretty babies, I am going to leave you to have your dinner, and then maybe we can meet up later with Dale for a nightcap. Have a good night and be happy, boys.' He kissed them both farewell and drifted off to a table of screaming queens who were obviously regular guests of the hotel.

Eddie and Jeremy adjourned to the restaurant which was yet another fantasy of colour and bad taste. This time it was about black walls and lamps that hung from the ceiling above each table, creating a pool of light by which to eat. However, it was incredibly difficult to see anything and Jeremy got quite hysterical with laughter as he peered through the darkness trying to talk to Eddie.

'Stop it, J, you will offend our host. It is supposed to be very atmospheric,' said Eddie, trying very hard to read the menu.

'It is certainly that – to the point of being almost stratospheric.' Jeremy groped for Eddie's leg under the table. 'Very good for touching up your date though, which I guess is what it is all about really.'

Eddie giggled and moved closer to Jeremy and they spent dinner behaving outrageously under the table. It added a whole new meaning to the words 'table manners'.

'God – if my parents could see me now they would disown me,' said Jeremy, stuffing his face with avocado dip. 'Have you eaten here before?' He was beginning to think that Eddie had been living this life for quite a while.

'Only once, with a friend from school,' Eddie replied. 'But nothing romantic like this.' He leaned across the table and licked some dip off Jeremy's cheek. 'Can't wait for the strawberries and cream,' he whispered.

Jeremy had another pang of unease. Something made him think that Eddie was telling him what he knew Jeremy wanted to hear. But he brushed aside the still small voice of suspicion. After all, what did the past matter? This was now, and he knew that Eddie was in love with him and they would be together for ever. This was his destiny. It was meant to be.

By the time they had finished dinner both of them were very tipsy. They arrived back at the cocktail bar to find George and friends equally well oiled.

'Here they are, love's young dream,' announced George to the table. 'Boys, meet my Dale,' and he practically shoved poor Dale in front of them for inspection. He was not at all what Jeremy had imagined, if indeed he had imagined anyone at all, but it certainly would not have been anywhere close to the vision in front of them. Dale was tall and elegant as a willow, with long blond hair nearly to his shoulders. He had piercing blue eyes, and very defined cheekbones. He was like a model, thought Jeremy.

'Hi, pleased to meet you,' said Dale in a soft voice, almost lisping. 'I hear you are coming to the club later. I will play a song for you if you tell me what you would like to hear.' He lifted a long delicate hand to his face and brushed some hair from his eyes. Then he turned and pranced off like a race horse.

'Don't mind Dale,' said George. 'I told you he can't keep still. Now sit yourselves down and have some of this champagne.'

They sat down and introduced themselves to the rest of the table. Eddie seemed to be in his element, and entertained them all with jokes and stories for the next hour. The irony was not lost on Jeremy, who for all his training as an actor, now felt completely useless. Yet somehow it didn't matter. His ego did not feel threatened and he was happy to bask in his lover's reflected glory. He was on a high, not just from the champagne, but from Eddie's attention. He had never felt so complete as a man. He just wanted to spend every minute with this guy and feel his energy inside him. He was lost to the world that night. When they got to the club Jeremy danced for hours. He gave himself to the thudding bass beat and just let rip. He had never really danced in his life, and he made Eddie laugh with his attempts at Disco dancing. There were bodies all around him and he could feel their heat. Different men passed by, and would kiss him or touch him up as they danced past. He loved the attention and yet always looked for Eddie for assurance. Eddie was equally busy moving around the dance floor flirting and touching up dancers. The two of them danced with another boy for quite a long time. It got very steamy and there was talk of going back to the room for a threesome, but Jeremy suddenly got cold feet and backed off. Eddie danced him into a corner and kissed him passionately.

'Don't fret, J, you are the only thing in my life now. We don't have to have any diversions or side orders if you don't want them. I am happy with just you and me. Let's go back to the room now and make love all night. Come on, you gorgeous man, I am feeling so randy!'

Jeremy was so drunk by this time he could not have done anything much in the way of dancing or flirting. When they got to their room he fell across the bed and passed out. The next thing he knew, Eddie was undressing him very slowly and whispering in his ear, 'You are gorgeous and wonderful and useless and drunk, but I love you, Jeremy Sinclair. Just get your clothes off and you will soon feel better because you will be feeling me beside you.'

Jeremy giggled and freed his foot from his trousers and

made a grab for Eddie who rolled away off the bed and out of reach.

'That's more like my J. There is hope for you yet. OK, I am going to take my clothes off now, and then we will see who is too drunk to screw.'

'Not me!' cried Jeremy, suddenly coming back to life. 'Ready or not, here I come,' and he sprang up, grabbed Eddie and threw him down on the bed, pinning him against the bed-head. He searched Eddie's face for several moments, trying to read every little tic or twitch. He looked deep into his lover's eyes and saw himself reflected there. He was giddy with lust and every muscle was taut with anticipation.

'I love you, Eddie,' he said very slowly, then lowered himself down and found Eddie's mouth for a deep kiss that took him away to paradise.

Chapter 33

Sunday was indeed a day of rest for our two young lovers. They missed breakfast and lunch, and finally opened an eye around two o'clock. Several glasses of juice and two pots of coffee later, Eddie announced that they should go for a walk.

'It's cold out there,' grumbled Jeremy, still snuggled under the sheets.

'But it is not raining, and the sun is visible. Come on, you wuss, get your kit on. I want to take you by the canal, and then I thought we could have an early dinner at an amazing Chinese restaurant I know called the Mandarin. It is incredibly famous in these parts and has been going for years.'

Jeremy really had no say in the matter and decided to succumb to whatever Eddie had in mind. His brain no longer seemed to function on a practical level any more. It was all about sensations and emotional highs, and living every moment with this incredible boy. Jeremy felt so old compared with Eddie, and yet there was only two years between them.

Eddie, however, seemed to have lived more lifetimes in those two years than Jeremy would ever do in twenty.

The boys set off in their winter woollies and walked briskly along the canal. It was pretty bleak even with the sun shining on the dark water, but Eddie seemed to love it.

'I reckon this will be very popular one day,' he said. 'The old warehouses and cottages will all get gentrified – you just wait and see.' By five it was dark, and they made their way into the centre of Manchester to the Chinese restaurant, which was packed already even at this early hour.

'Everyone here is Chinese!' exclaimed Jeremy.

'Exactly,' replied Eddie with a grin.

The menu was extensive and Jeremy lost the will to live just trying to read it, so once again he put himself into the capable hands of his lover. Eddie went to town and they really had trouble finishing the banquet, especially when it came to the chicken feet – a 'speciality of the house'.

'Oh, Eddie, this is really stuck in my craw,' groaned Jeremy, practically gagging. 'I can't eat it, I am sorry,' and he virtually spat it out into his napkin.

'I must say, you do look rather purple,' chuckled Eddie. 'Don't want to kill you off so soon in the relationship. Come on, let's go grab a taxi to the hotel and have a cocktail.'

By the time they got back, Jeremy was so full of Chinese he just wanted to lie down and go to sleep.

'Oh, don't be such an old misery guts,' retorted Eddie. 'Get in the shower and you will soon feel like a new man.'

Jeremy did as he was told and stood for a good ten minutes letting the hot water caress his back and shoulders. He suddenly called out to Eddie, 'You are right, I do feel like a new man. Got anyone in mind?!'

The next thing he knew, he was being scrubbed with a

loofah and Eddie was whispering in his ear, 'Haven't got any new men, but this one has plenty of wear left in him, so shut up and enjoy!'

Later, they strolled into the bar feeling on top of their game. As per usual the bar was full to bursting, and the conversation as loud and shrill as ever. Eddie waved to George, who was holding court at a big centre table. They decided to sit at the bar for a while and ordered champagne cocktails.

'Oh, this is slipping down a treat,' said Jeremy. 'Please order me another immediately.' He leaned across and was about to plant a kiss on Eddie's cheek when a familiar voice stopped him in his tracks.

'Well, well, what do we have here, love's young dream? I didn't think you had it in you, Jeremy. I was obviously completely wrong.'

Jeremy turned to look up from his bar stool into the amused eyes of Robert Johnson.

'Robert! What a surprise. This is my friend Edward. Eddie, this is Robert Johnson our assistant director.'

'Hi, would you like a drink, Robert?' asked Eddie innocently enough.

'No, I am fine, thanks. I am joining some friends here in a minute. Actually, Jeremy, I am joining Giles and his friend Lord Graham.' He had turned to Eddie as he said this. Eddie kept his cool but Jeremy just froze. 'Do you know Lord Graham, Edward?' asked Robert, pointedly holding the boy's gaze.

'I should do,' replied Eddie. 'He is my father. Can't think what he would be doing here of all places.'

'I am sure he would be saying exactly the same about your presence here, don't you think?' taunted Robert.

'In that case, maybe it's a good idea we keep this meeting to ourselves. Come on, Jeremy, we were just going anyway. We only stopped by for a quick drink, looking for an actor friend of Jeremy's.'

Jeremy rose and squeezed past Robert, who was standing very close to both of them.

'Sorry, excuse me,' he stuttered. 'See you tomorrow at the read through.'

Robert's smile was practically reptilian. 'You certainly will, my dear. Enjoy the rest of your evening. A pleasure to meet you, Edward,' he called back over his shoulder – and then he was gone.

Once back in their room, Jeremy and Eddie discussed the seriousness of their situation.

'We haven't done anything wrong, for God's sake. We are both over age, and why shouldn't we be having a drink here. Doesn't mean we are queer necessarily?' suggested Eddie.

'Oh come on, Ed. Did you see a single straight man in that room? I don't really mind because no one will care what I get up to, but you are a different matter. Your father will go mad if he discovers his son and heir is a homosexual.'

Eddie thought about this for a few minutes. 'Yes, you are right. But then what was my father doing there?' he added.

'I suppose Giles must have suggested they come here and your father's curiosity got the better of him. You said he is fairly relaxed about the queer thing, and maybe he wanted to see a bit of the life for himself.'

'Suppose so,' pondered Eddie, but he did not sound convinced. 'However, it's not a conversation I want to pursue at this point in time, so let's hope Robert keeps his mouth shut.'

'I wouldn't bank on it,' said Jeremy. 'He is a weird one and very difficult to read. He was quite pleasant to me at the beginning of the season but has cooled off since it became clear I did not fancy him. Having said that, he never really comes on to anybody too strongly, and he spends quite a lot of time flirting with the girls, so maybe he is playing a game all round. He definitely has Giles's ear though. Not quite sure why yet. Maybe when we see what he does as a director on *Hamlet* with Giles, we will spot the talent. Who knows? I will keep a very close eye on him in future. That's all we can do for now. Come on, let's watch some TV. I am knackered, and tomorrow is a big day for me.'

'Ah, my poor baby. OK, we will chill tonight, and you can show me your version of "An Actor Prepares" – as long as it involves lots of sex!'

The weekend ended perfectly for Jeremy on Sunday night with, indeed, not much sleep but lots of lovemaking.

'This has to last me a while,' he murmured to Eddie as they started to drift into blissful sleep. 'Good night, you beautiful man.'

Eddie turned and kissed him on the forehead. 'Sleep, perchance to dream . . .'

The next morning they ate a huge cooked breakfast in rather a subdued mode.

'Will you be around at all this week?' asked Eddie.

'I doubt it very much. Rehearsals will be full on because there is a hell of a lot to get through. Mind you, after I am killed there may be some time. But don't worry – I will ring you whenever I can.' Jeremy smiled across the table.

'Well, just remember I will mostly be out in the middle of nowhere on a bloody tractor. Best time to get me is before seven or after five. But then you are onstage. Shall I call you at your digs around eleven?' Eddie suggested.

'Yes, that might be best. Oh Eddie, this has been so wonderful I don't want it to end.' Jeremy took Eddie's hand across the table.

'Don't fret, there will be many more weekends – and even better than this,' Eddie promised, squeezing his lover's hand. 'But come now, we must get you back to the state of Denmark, where something is rotten and where princes come from. You have battles to fight, my love.'

Chapter 34

'We have battles to fight, literally and figuratively,' announced Giles after lunch. 'So I would like Rupert, Jeremy, Simon and Pete to go with Robert to practise sword-fights next door. Isabelle and Sally, we will make a start on all Ophelia's scenes, and Charmaine, Percy and Geoffrey – please be standing by to do your scenes. I am sorry if there is a bit of a wait, but it would be good just to run through what we are going to do with Polonius, and the whole ghost scenario. Everyone else, please do not wander far from the theatre as Gwendoline will want to do some fittings. It is going to be a very difficult show from the point of view of costumes, as many of you are doubling up in parts. I may have to employ one extra actor to play the ghost and cover. Still, that's enough to be getting on with for now, so off you go.'

Sally gathered her script and made her way down into the stalls to sit with Giles, but he had decided to stay onstage as Isabelle was already starting to cause concern with her nerves.

'I feel so vulnerable, Giles. The stage seems vast at the

moment and I am worried I will not be able to fill it.' She was clutching her script tightly to herself and puffing on the inevitable fag.

'That's OK, darling, we have plenty of time. Sally and I will join you, do not worry.'

The three of them sat in a huddle and started to work through the dialogue. It was painfully obvious, after only a few minutes, that Isabelle did not have a clue what she was saying, or indeed what any of the play was about. Sally's heart sank as she envisaged days spent with their leading lady giving her instruction on Shakespeare and his dialogue. Thank God she herself had learned the part already.

In the coming days it became very apparent to everyone that Giles was right: the production was going to be incredibly complicated with so many people doubling up as courtiers and small characters who came and went. Simon and Pete were hysterical, standing in the wardrobe with Gwendoline and Janie trying to fit them.

'Why don't we just wear different hats, or wigs?' joked Simon. 'Why, look yonder, sirrah! Behold, there is the watchman in his pink hat!' He then pulled on another hat from the pile in front of them. 'Nay, sir, this is not your hat. This belongeth to old Yorick, methinks.'

Pete by this time had pulled on a long robe and answered in a falsetto voice, 'Oh dearie me, alas alack, poor Yorick is long gone. But looketh over there, I see a ghost naked. What? Is it come to this? A naked ghost? Bringeth me the wardrobe mistress that she may see the error of her ways!'

By this time they were all laughing so much they did not see Robert watching from the doorway.

'I am glad you are all so confident about your performances that you can afford to stand around making jokes. Simon and

Peter, I want you onstage in five minutes to go through the fight scene.' He turned on his heel and left the room.

'Oops!' said Pete.

Sally was in a complete panic. She had had no idea how much work would be involved in setting up the Dumb Show with such a shortage of actors. In fact, she was forced to take some theatrical licence and have ladies playing men. She even had to put herself in the piece, which meant having to learn a huge speech. This did not last long, however, as she was wanted almost all the time to rehearse with Rupert. Isabelle was proving a complete nightmare. She could not seem to learn the lines at all. Rupert was having trouble going through each scene as they had to stop all the time, so he too was starting to panic, and relied more and more on Sally to provide his lines. At one point they were in the ridiculous position of Rupert and Sally rehearsing in one room, and Giles and Isabelle in another so that Giles could help the girl learn the lines as she went along. Truth be known, Sally was in seventh heaven; she loved every minute of her time with Rupert. He was so giving as an actor and warm and affectionate that by the end of the first week, she was truly smitten. But it was not to last. Giles called her into his office on Saturday morning and said, 'Sally, you are going to have to put Dora on the book with Rupert and get on with your Dumb Show. I need to know that that is one thing that is sorted.'

Sally was gutted. 'But I can do both,' she pleaded. 'I can get Dora on the case, and I have been thinking that she will have to do my big speech anyway, as I am tied up with Rupert and his scenes.'

'Sally, you are not tied up at all. May I remind you that *Isabelle* is playing Ophelia, and will shortly be taking her rightful position opposite her leading man. She has come on in leaps and bounds and I have to say, with no disrespect to you at all, that when Rupert and she are together, the chemistry is phenomenal. Now, please can you call Dora to the stage.'

Sally had to hold back the tears that were threatening to spill down her cheeks. She knew Giles was right, and she was only the understudy, but it still hurt that all her hard work was dismissed in a minute. Bloody Isabelle would step in, and thanks to everyone around her, holding her up and supporting her, she would come out of this with glory. She started to run up the stairs to the dressing room to have a good cry.

'Sally, are you OK?' asked Rupert as he came down the stairs towards her.

Oh God, no, this is all I need, thought Sally. *Please leave me alone.*

'Are we not going through the scene again?' he went on, unaware of any problems.

'Yes, I think you are going to do it with Isabelle. I need to get to my rehearsal for the Dumb Show. Sorry, Rupert, I must dash.' Sally tried to ease past him but he took her arms and stopped her.

'What's wrong? You are crying. Here, have a tissue.' He produced one like magic and gave it to her.

'I am so sorry, Rupert, you shouldn't have to concern yourself with me. You have enough going on in your life. It's just all getting to me, I guess. There is so much to do and not enough time. Please don't worry, just concentrate on your role.'

'Well, I was hoping you might have me round to your place tonight so we could consolidate everything we have worked on, and then I can introduce Isabelle to the scenes tomorrow.'

Sally sighed. She could not think of anything more perfect, but it was not to be.

'I think Giles wants to do that now, Rupert. But find me

later if you have any problems.' She pulled away and ran upstairs.

Sally spent the rest of the day gathering her cast together and nailing the Dumb Show. She was determined to sort it out and get back to Rupert and Ophelia. A nagging voice inside her was pointing out that she was not giving her Dumb Show the attention it required. The whole project had been so exciting at the beginning, and her debut as a director had fired her up. Now, however, all she wanted to do was get it over with so she could return to the intimacy of the rehearsal room and Rupert. She had put Dora in her role, but soon realized that it did not work, as her sister just did not have the vocal ability to hold the speech together. She herself would have to do it. She reluctantly told Dora to go off and join Rupert and Giles.

'Oh my God! This is brilliant,' enthused the other girl. 'I can't wait to work with Rupert – he is so gorgeous. Maybe Isabelle will be taken off, and *I* will be there to take over. I must make sure I know the part inside out. You will have to help me, Sally.'

'I will do no such thing,' her sister retorted angrily. '*I* am the official understudy, and if Isabelle was off *I* would take over. Just remember, Dora, you are only filling in for me while I sort out the Dumb Show, then I will take over again. You are just there to read the lines, thank you, so don't get any ideas above your station.'

'Ooh sorreee!' mocked Dora. 'Talk about getting on your high horse.' And she flounced off.

Sally went to find Jeremy as much for moral support as for his input into the Dumb Show.

'Now calm down and let's go through this slowly,' he said wisely. 'You are short of actors, are you not? Well, I had a thought this morning while chatting to the redoubtable Peggy. She would be perfect as the Player Queen. Let's face it, she may be getting on in years but her voice is very youthful, and one won't see the rest of her because she will have the mask on. Then you have got me as the Player King, so that will all work. You have Sarah and Dora – and even Robert if needs be. You will have to be First Player, and if you did have to cover Isabelle, then I guess I could learn the bloody speech.'

Sally gave her friend a grateful hug. 'I knew I could rely on you. Thanks so much, Jeremy – that is perfect. So can we rehearse now, do you think, or what about I cook lunch on Sunday and you come round and we go through all the speeches, and then I can put everyone else in next week, as and when they are free?'

'Ah now, weekends are going to be a problem from now on, I am afraid,' said Jeremy, looking sheepish. 'I will be seeing Eddie every weekend so will not be around.'

Sally looked at him. 'Wow, is it that serious? You have only known him a few weeks. Don't you think you should take things slowly?'

'No, I really don't,' he replied. 'This amazing thing has happened to me, Sally, and I am going to run with it. We are in love and I have found my soulmate. Nothing else matters.'

'What about your acting?' asked Sally carefully, remembering all their late-night discussions about their career prospects.

'What about it? As you said, it can only help me as an actor to have experience of these incredible emotions I am going through just now.'

'Yes, I can see that,' she agreed, 'but won't you feel the pressure of work if you are out gadding about all weekend? You were certainly in no fit state last week after your time off. I just don't want you to screw up this part, Jeremy. You have been longing for this job, so don't blow it because you are too exhausted to give it your best shot. Remember, all the agents are coming, and the producer of Isabelle's film and God knows who else. This is the moment you have been waiting for. We both have,' she added, suddenly reminded that she too had been working towards this production and now found herself pulled in all directions.

'Please don't worry, Sal. I am fine – I couldn't be happier. Now come on, let's go and find Peggy and talk to her.'

That night, everybody seemed to have the same idea and ended up in the pub. It was one of those spontaneous evenings that always go well. The one consolation during these two weeks of intense activity was the fact that there was no evening show. The actors could afford a night on the tiles and still recover, though some took longer than others, as Simon liked to point out every so often.

'I am a delicate little flower really,' he would say. 'I only drink because I am so insecure and fragile.' He would then spend the rest of the night trawling the pub for an unsuspecting female to massage his ego! Dora had long ago given up on him, and was far too busy pursuing her career as an actress through foul means or fair. Sally watched her sister now, flirting at the bar with Robert. Lately she had spent a good deal of time with him, much to Sally's dismay. She waved to Dora, who came bouncing over to where Sally was sitting waiting for Jeremy.

'Hi, everything OK, sister dear? It is good fun tonight, isn't it? Must go – Robert has got the drinks in, see you later.'

'Just be careful,' warned Sally. 'He is very slippery and will sell you out as soon as look at you.'

'I don't know why you are so against him,' replied Dora. 'He has been very kind to me, and given me lots of good advice about theatre and directors and stuff. He is quite sexy too, in a dark, brooding kind of way.'

She giggled and Sally looked up sharply. 'Oh Dora, please don't tell me you have slept with him.'

'No, he's gay, silly – well, I think he is. Maybe he swings both ways. I wouldn't say no if he asked me.' Then she added, 'Oh, don't be so stuffy, Sally. Relax. It is only a bit of fun. Haven't you slept with someone for a laugh?'

Sally sat there in the pub with her half a lager and lime and tried to understand what had happened to Dora to turn her into this frivolous wayward girl.

'I can't believe you are saying these things, Dora, I really can't. Is no one safe from your clutches? Why would I sleep with anyone just for a laugh? I am not a prude, but I am not a tart either. You sound like a slapper!'

Dora laughed. 'Oh come on, please – it's 1982. I am my own woman and I do what I like, when I like, with whom I like. It doesn't mean anything and that's the way I like it. I don't want to fall in love and find myself committed to a deep relationship with all its problems. I want to be a star, Sally. There – I have said it. I want to be a huge star and I am going to do it, you just watch me.'

Sally suddenly felt very old and tired. She dismissed Dora's declarations as typical youthful bravado. Her sister was just going through a phase. But she could not help but feel hurt and alienated by Dora's behaviour. She was still miffed about Mack, but had chosen not to bring up the subject because she didn't want to make matters worse. A part of her felt she was over-reacting. Dora had meant no harm. However, another part of Sally felt betrayed by her sister, who would probably have slept with Mack without a second thought, had she had the chance.

The more she thought about it, the more she felt betrayed. Best to forget all about it and hope that one day it would all be water under the bridge. But now, here Dora was again, challenging Sally's integrity and career as an actress. Sally had to admit she was a little overwhelmed by her sister's ambition.

Was that what it was all about – naked ambition? But then she remembered Jeremy's face today when he was talking about being in love, and how vulnerable he had seemed. That was also a dangerous route to take, in her book. The two of them had always agreed that emotional stability was important to survive the pressures of the business, but that stability could come from friendship, which was more reliable than using precious energy on romantic involvement. Sex was important, but not vital. Sally smiled wryly to herself; she should be so lucky! She had hardly been feeding her emotional or artistic soul in the last three months. Even the excitement of the first nights, and going onstage to face the audience had faded under the weight of everyday life in a repertory theatre. It was mostly drudgery, if the truth be known. Where was the spark?

She had often thought about Mack since their last meeting, but somehow she was still not ready to add him into the equation. It would just complicate matters. Better that she deal with the job to the best of her ability, and then meet Mack with a clean slate. She had rung him and they had chatted happily about general stuff in their lives. In fact, Mack was not going to be able to visit for a few weeks anyway as he had been commissioned to deliver three large sculptures for an exhibition in Italy.

'My first real international showcase,' he said happily. 'I am gutted we can't meet up yet, but believe me, when we do, we can celebrate in style.'

She smiled dreamily to herself at the thought of being with him.

'Penny for them?' Rupert broke into her thoughts as she finished her lager and lime.

'Oh, just trying to work out how to fit everything in. It's a nightmare, isn't it? How did your rehearsal go with Isabelle?' Sally asked, curious to know the answer.

Rupert made a rueful face. 'Well, all right, I suppose, but there is a long way to go. She is trying really hard, and she is so sweet one can't get angry with her.' He turned to look round the bar and spotted Isabelle, who was surrounded by adoring males, all hanging on her every word. She looked a little the worse for wear.

'She should really go home to bed by the looks of her,' said Sally, feeling deflated. She had hoped that Rupert might suggest coming back to her flat to go through the lines as he had mentioned earlier.

'I think I had better be the gent, don't you? Get her home. Hopefully we can run some lines tomorrow, Sally. Thank you for being such a brick.' He kissed Sally on the cheek, and she got a brief whiff of his cologne, and then he was gone. She watched him scoop Isabelle up and carry her, in a fireman's lift, out of the pub. Everyone was whooping and hollering and cheering. Sally decided she had had enough for the night and left soon afterwards. She had to admit she was exhausted, and as her mother always used to say: 'Things always look better in the morning after a good night's sleep.'

As she lay awake in bed that night, restless and unable to drop off, Sally tried to stop the negative thoughts from spilling over her sleepy head. Then very slowly, her thoughts turned to Rupert. But what about Mack? She tried to focus on him, but it was Rupert's face that floated before her. In fact, her whole body tingled, and she felt herself falling into his arms as he lifted her up and carried her away.

Chapter 35

By the end of the week Sally was seriously pissed off. She felt completely abandoned by everyone. Giles and Robert were always having private meetings in the office, and the cast were fretting about all the costume changes and paying very little attention to the text. Jeremy was really irritating her, as he gazed endlessly into space with an inane grin on his face. As soon as he could after rehearsals, he was on the phone at the stage door to Eddie. She had hoped he would be around to support her, not just as a fellow actor, but as a friend. She was also aware that Dora had completely taken over her duties as understudy, and every time Sally visited the rehearsals she watched with growing anger as her sister flirted with Rupert. The only consolation was that Isabelle stood between Dora and the object of her desire. The actress might not have the means to absorb the text of one of Shakespeare's greatest plays, but she sure knew how to fend off female competition. Sally had hardly had a chance to talk to Rupert as he was spending every minute of the day, and possibly the night, with his co-star. This was the nub of the matter. To Sally's dismay it seemed that romance had blossomed between the two leading actors and she was devastated by the thought. How could Rupert fall for such an obvious ploy? He had seemed so sensitive and caring when they had talked, and now here he was blatantly indulging his carnal needs like any other bloke. The trouble was that for all the sexual chemistry that might be going on offstage, the onstage performances were still lacklustre, and it seemed to Sally that Giles was not able to inspire the actors to do better. This was the other problem for Sally. She could see that Giles was losing his grip, and Robert also was very anxious. The two of them seemed to have lost the plot. Well, it was a bit late now!

Sally decided to corner Robert and see if she could find out what was going on. She met him at the stage door one morning early and offered to make him a coffee.

'Thank you, that would be very welcome,' he said and followed her up to the Green Room.

'I think I may even have some chocolate biscuits squirrelled away for emergencies,' said Sally as she put the kettle on.

'Is there an emergency?' asked Robert. Sally turned and caught him watching her very carefully.

'No, not exactly, but things do seem a little – how shall I say? A little fraught.' Sally busied herself with the coffee. She did not want to overstep the mark. Robert could be very tricky and she had no wish to jeopardize her position.

'Fraught?' Robert rolled the word round his tongue. 'Fraught. Yes, you could say that, I suppose.' He pulled out a chair from the table in the centre of the room and sat down slowly. Suddenly he seemed frail; all the swagger and posturing was gone. Sally finished making the coffee and placed a mug on the table in front of him. She fetched her own mug and the biscuits and sat down beside him. They remained in silence for a good five minutes, then Robert seemed to gather himself together. He picked up the coffee, took a few sips and then turned to Sally.

'So, do you have any bright ideas as to how we can ease the situation?'

Sally was not quite sure how genuine the question was, or whether there was a hint of sarcasm. She decided to opt for the positive.

'Oh, I didn't mean to criticize or anything. It is just that obviously we all want the play to be a great success – for Giles and the theatre – and if there is anything I can do to help, then I am very happy to be of service. I have managed to nail my Dumb Show at last, though what will happen when we get onstage with that truck, God only knows.' The designer had decided that a part of the scenery would be built on a moving truck which could be wheeled on and off. This was going to be particularly dramatic in the grave-digging scene as there was a grave built into the truck part so *Hamlet* could jump into it. However, the truck was also onstage during the Dumb Show and, in fact, Sally was contemplating using it as a way to get her actors off at the end of the scene. She had in mind a final tableau which would then disappear as the truck was pulled off the stage in a blackout. However, in order for this to work it was imperative that all the actors were firmly on the correct bit of the stage, or someone might well get left behind or worse still, disappear into the grave!

Robert smiled and agreed that, 'It would indeed be interesting to see what happens. But what exactly do you feel is not working as far as the play is concerned?'

Sally knew she was on the spot. It was not her place to pass comment on the directorial skills of Giles Longfellow. She weighed her words very carefully.

'Oh goodness, I wouldn't dream of suggesting there is anything not working, not at all. But I have spent quite a good deal of time with Giles and Rupert and Isabelle, and it has been quite frustrating at times when the text is not clear, or the lines are slipping. You know what it's like, Robert.' She tried to put the ball back in his court, but he was refusing to co-operate.

'Yes, I understand it has not been easy, but Giles tells me Isabelle is finally making progress and hopefully with a few runs of the play under her belt she will pull it out of the bag.'

Sally decided to change the subject. 'I gather we have a few important folk coming to the first night?' she said. 'Even a West End producer, with a view to taking the play into Town?'

Suddenly Sally saw Robert shut down in front of her. She had gone too far. There was no way he was going to share with her – a mere ASM – any information like that.

'We will have to wait and see. Now I must get on. Thank you for the coffee, Sally, and I look forward to seeing your Dumb Show.' He stood up and was once more in control as he left the room without a backward glance. She had been dismissed. That is all very well, she thought, but it does not change the fact that things are not right, and I am going to make sure my actors are given the best chance there is to shine.

She went in search of Jeremy, who was usually in early. Sure enough he was up in his dressing room going through his lines.

'Hi, how are you?' he asked as Sally stomped through the door.

'Not happy!' she exclaimed. 'Jeremy, if we don't pull our fingers out, this production is going to sink without trace. What are the fight scenes like? Are you happy with what Robert has done with them?'

'What has brought all this on?' asked Jeremy. 'Since when have you been in charge?'

'Oh, stop it! I am not in charge but I am worried that we are not up to speed. I have just tried to get Robert to give me a clue as to what is going on, but he was very tight-lipped.'

'Why do you think there is something going on?' replied Jeremy. 'Has something happened?'

'No, not really, it is just that Giles and Robert seem to be constantly whispering in corners, and I know that there are problems with Isabelle which do not seem to be getting any better.'

'Oh really? I thought she *was* getting better. Dora seems to think she is going to surprise us all on the night.'

'Huh,' replied Sally, unable to hide her disapproval. 'What does *Dora* know about anything?'

Jeremy laughed. 'Oh dear, sisterly affection, eh? Are you sure it is not you who is seeing the world through very jaded glasses at the moment?'

'What is that supposed to mean?' retorted Sally. 'I have been working my butt off to make this play work and no one appears to notice or care. Dora seems to think she is now Isabelle's understudy, which is ridiculous, and Giles won't let me get back to the job I started. I was helping Rupert, and it was going really well until . . .' She stopped suddenly, aware that she wanted to burst into tears.

Jeremy got up and gave her a hug. 'Come on, Sal, don't give up now. You are being brilliant and once we have opened the play it will all calm down. I know you must be upset about Rupert and Isabelle, but—'

Sally cut him off. 'What do you mean? Why would I be upset? Upset about what? Just because the two stars are shagging each other? It is just a shame they don't put the same energy into their performances as they do in bed.' Sally knew she was being unfair but she just could not help herself.

'Well, well, Miss Thomas, I never thought I would see you crack. Don't tell me you have become emotionally involved with a fellow actor. That is not how we decided it worked. Were you not giving me hell just last week, for not focusing on my performance?'

'Oh, don't be ridiculous, Jeremy,' Sally snapped. 'That was a completely different thing. You are madly in love with Eddie and risking everything else. What is there to compare with me? I am not madly in love with anybody.'

'No, but you are infatuated with Rupert, and don't try and deny it. I am your best friend, remember?'

Sally opened her mouth to protest and then changed her mind. It was the truth. Jeremy had got it right. Everything she was feeling was down to Rupert. She felt so stupid and angry with herself for letting her feelings get the better of her. The ridiculous thing was that Rupert had no idea how she felt about him. As far as he was concerned they were great mates, and that was all. How could he know she was so destroyed by his affair with Isabelle? How could she feel so betrayed by him? There was nothing *to* betray. She had created the whole thing in her head and now it was spoiling everything.

'Oh, Jeremy, I feel such a prat.' Fortunately, she managed to stop the tears. The last thing she wanted at this moment was to let Jeremy or anyone else know how she felt. She would deal with it in private.

'Come on you, cheer up. You have done a fantastic job with the Dumb Show, and everyone knows how much you have contributed to Isabelle's performance. With any luck she will go missing and you will get a go. Imagine that.' Jeremy kissed her on the cheek and turned back to his script.

'Are you going away this weekend again?' asked Sally.

'Yes, of course. Why do you ask?' Jeremy waited.

'Oh nothing really, except I thought I might have a big Sunday lunch to get everyone together for the last week before we open. Bit of bonding, you know.' She smiled.

'Sorry, got my own bonding to do.' Jeremy grinned meaningfully back at Sally.

'Great,' said Sally to herself and left the dressing room. She decided to go and visit the girls in Wardrobe for a cheer-up and a gossip. She found Gwendoline sewing beads onto a gorgeous silk gown.

'Is that for our leading lady?' enquired Sally as she came in the room.

'Yes, and she is thrilled with it,' said Gwendoline, looking up at Sally. 'I just hope she stays thrilled enough not to lose any more weight because I have to keep taking it in.'

'Blimey, if she lost any more weight she would disappear when she turned sideways,' snorted Janie, who was ironing in the corner. 'Mind you, I joke – but bloody hell, girls, she is something else isn't she? You know she keeps making herself sick. Practically every time I go in her dressing room she is puking in the toilet. I reckon she has got a problem.'

'What sort of problem?' asked Sally.

'You know what I mean – an eating-disorder type of thing. Anorexia, I think they call it. I was reading about it the other day in a magazine. Lots of film stars have it because they have to be so thin for the films. They either don't eat at all, or eat and then make themselves sick afterwards. Some people have even died, it gets so bad.' Janie was warming to her subject. 'Mind you, she probably gets sick from all that dope she smokes as well. What?' Janie looked up from her ironing to see Gwendoline and Sally staring at her open-mouthed. 'Oh, don't tell me you didn't know? She is always rolling joints and stashing them in her make-up bag for later. Pete reckons that is why she can't learn the lines. He says she is basically stoned all the time. I am surprised Giles hasn't noticed – or Rupert, for that matter. Let's face it, he is such a lovely guy and so obviously not into drugs, yet he spends all his time with her. Did I tell you I caught them at it in the dressing room the other day? God, it was so embarrassing.'

'I thought you said she spent all her time with her head down the toilet,' Sally said rather sullenly. 'What a busy girl she is.'

Janie laughed. 'Go on, Sally, tell it how it is!'

'Sorry, but it does make me cross, Janie. People like her always seem to get away with murder, don't they? Not much talent but all the luck in the world, and mugs like us prepared to cover for her. Anyway, enough of all that, I came here to be cheered up and get the gossip. How is Sarah these days?' For some reason Sally had suddenly thought about the girl and her dealings with Percy. Peggy seemed happier of late so maybe things had gone back to normal.

'Funny you should mention her,' said Janie. 'She is not my favourite person and she owes me money as it happens, but she is very quiet these days. I think something has happened.'

'She owes me money as well,' joined in Gwendoline. 'And I believe she has had money off most of the boys. She seems to have eased off on Percy, I noticed.'

'I know Peggy was worried about all that,' said Sally. 'Do you think Sarah was actually sleeping with him?'

'Yes, I do. She is a right little madam,' blasted Janie. 'And I tell you what I think, that she tried to get money out of Percy because he was in a right state a while back and asked Pete about loans and such from the bank, and when Pete asked him why he needed the money, Percy got all tearful and admitted he was a bad boy sometimes and girls took advantage – but he wouldn't actually own up to it being Sarah. But let's face it, we all know she has been all over him like a rash. Even Peggy knows the score. I reckon Peggy has fronted her up and told her to get lost and that is exactly what she has done. Can't blackmail Percy if the wife knows all about it, can she? So now she is keeping her head down – looking for the next victim, I expect.'

'I always suspected it was Sarah who told Geoffrey's wife he was having an affair.' Gwendoline let this statement hang in the air and all three girls digested the information.

Sally found herself thinking what a sad world it was when people spent so much time and energy being horrible to each other.

The silence was broken by the arrival of Dora.

'Hi, guys! Just been told I have to try on Isabelle's costumes in case I have to go on. How cool is that . . .' She stopped as she caught her sister's glare across the room.

'You have to go on? Dora, how many times do I have to tell you *I* am Isabelle's understudy?'

'Don't blame me, sis. Giles sent me here. Talk to him.' Dora crossed to Gwendoline and started to undress.

'Oh, don't worry, I will,' Sally hissed and marched out of the room.

Chapter 36

Sally was fuming as she strode across the stage towards Giles Longfellow's office. This was beyond endurance. Never mind the fact that her bloody sister was trying to usurp her role, Sally had a contract with the theatre that stated that *she* was the official understudy. As she approached the door to Giles's office she could hear raised voices. She knocked loudly and the shouting stopped immediately. There was a pause and then the door was opened by Robert who looked at her briefly and then pushed past her and left.

'Sally, come in, come in.' Giles looked decidedly ill at ease and was mopping his brow with a silk handkerchief. 'Please sit down, dear. What can I do for you?'

Sally took a deep breath and jumped straight in. 'I am very disappointed to discover that somehow my sister Dora seems to have replaced me as the understudy for Ophelia. I have a contract which states I am employed as an ASM, and to play small parts and understudy. Why have you not allowed me to continue in this capacity?'

Giles let out a long sigh. 'Oh, Sally, my dear, do we have to go through all this now? I am so stressed, as you can appreci-ate. I value your time and your talent enormously, but you can't do everything. You have been engaged with the Dumb Show, which I hear is fabulous, and you have had your usual duties to perform finding props, et cetera. I felt it was impos-sible for you to understudy as well.'

'But you could have talked to me about the situation,' said Sally. 'You agreed I could put Dora on my other jobs, and once I had set up the Dumb Show I would have been free once again to work with you and Isabelle. I have arranged the whole thing to fit round my duties, and there is not a problem. Please, Giles, it is only fair you give me back the job. Apart from anything else, Dora is not experienced enough to hold the performance together, no matter what she thinks.'

Giles regarded Sally for a few moments and then remarked, 'Do I suspect a trace of filial jealousy?'

'Oh, for goodness sake!' cried Sally. 'I am so sick of people always resorting to that old chestnut. I brought Dora here to work. I am proud of what she has achieved and happy for her, but that is not the point. I am the understudy *and I want my job back.*'

Giles laughed, a deep throaty sound that resounded round the room.

'Well done, you! OK, Sally, you win. You are the official understudy and I will check with the printers that your name is in the programme. Make sure you let Gwendoline know about costumes and then meet me onstage to go through all the Ophelia scenes with Isabelle. I might as well tell you now that there is every possibility that you *will* have to go on at some point, as the girl has some medical problems that may need attention. Obviously we just hope and pray she is fine for the first night. Please keep all this to yourself,' he added.

'Of course,' replied Sally, trying to keep calm and hoping Giles would not notice the flush of exaltation she could feel spreading over her whole face. 'Thank you, Giles, I am very grateful.' She moved as swiftly as possible, without looking as though she was rushing, to the door. She just wanted to get away before he changed his mind!

Once outside, and out of earshot, she let out a whoop of delight and went to find her dear sister. Dora was still in the wardrobe department trying on costumes. Sally made sure she was very calm and businesslike. It would not do at all for her to look as though she was enjoying her assignment.

'Dora, can I have a word outside? Would you excuse us for a minute, ladies?'

Dora followed Sally out and up to the dressing room. 'So what is so secretive we have to come up here?' she asked.

'I have just been talking to Giles and we have agreed that it is only right and proper that I get my job back as understudy to Isabelle. So I—' Sally was interrupted by a very petulant Dora.

'Oh come on, Sally, that is not fair! I have worked really hard the last couple of weeks. I am perfect for the part, and Rupert and I have a very special bond.'

'I am sure that is true, sister dear, and nobody is denying you have worked hard, but unfortunately you do not have a contract, as I do, stating that you are the understudy. I too have worked hard for the last few months with this company, and it is only right and proper I get the perks of the job. Your turn will no doubt come one day if you continue to pursue your chosen career with the zeal you have shown so far.'

The two sisters stood facing each other eyeball to eyeball; neither wanted to be the first to break the spell. Finally they both had to turn to face Janie, who announced breathlessly,

'Sally, you have to come quickly. Isabelle has collapsed!'

They all rushed downstairs to the stage where a very dramatic scene awaited them. Rupert was bent over Isabelle, who was lying on the floor surrounded by various members of the cast and crew. Robert was pacing back and forth, and Giles was standing at the edge of the group looking lost.

'Has someone called an ambulance?' ordered Sally. 'Come on, guys, move out of the way. Give the girl some breathing space.' She knelt down beside Rupert and tried to work out what was happening.

'The ambulance is on its way,' called Gladys from the pass door. 'I will bring them straight down luvvie, don't you fret.'

Sally displayed her First Aid technique to great effect, and having felt Isabelle's pulse and established there was nothing too serious going on, she announced, 'I think she has just fainted. Someone get me a towel soaked in cold water . . . Oh, you got one – thanks, Heather.' She took the towel from the stage manager and laid it across Isabelle's forehead just as the actress started to stir.

'There you go . . . Everything is all right, Isabelle, you just fainted.' Sally spoke softly to the girl as she slowly came to, and became aware of her surroundings.

There was a commotion from the other side of the stage and two paramedics marched across to them.

'Is this the lady? Can we have her name, please? Isabelle. OK, Isabelle, can you hear me?' The two medics proceeded to put Isabelle back together again, and everyone drifted away. Sally took Rupert by the arm and led him towards the edge of the stage.

'Would you like me to make you a cup of tea?' she murmured. 'What happened?'

'Don't worry about me – I'm all right. It was just a surprise.

One minute she was fine and the next she was on the floor. God, I hope she is going to be OK.'

'I am sure she will soon recover.' Sally had a thought. 'Has she eaten anything today?' she asked.

'I don't know. No, I don't think so. We didn't have time for breakfast this morning.'

Sally gritted her teeth at the thought of the two lovebirds tumbling out of bed. 'Does Isabelle eat properly, Rupert?' Sally wondered if he had any idea about the girl's eating problems.

'Yes, I guess so. I mean, we all eat at strange times here, don't we? I haven't really noticed, to be honest. Why do you ask?' He looked at Sally enquiringly.

'Oh, no reason, just that Isabelle is very thin, and you know what actresses are like about their figures. You can never be too thin. But sometimes it can be dangerous. She needs all her strength at the moment with the hours we are working.'

'Yes, I suppose you are right,' said Rupert, looking as though he had no idea what Sally was going on about.

'Now come on, let's go and find Giles and get some work done. I can take up my role again as understudy.'

Giles, Rupert and Sally worked all afternoon. It was a fabulous rehearsal and by the end of the day Rupert was flushed with excitement.

'Let's go to Mrs Wong's and get some chips,' he said. 'That was fantastic, Sally. I really feel as if I have turned a corner and I know I will be able to help Isabelle too.'

Oh great, thought Sally. All this effort for someone else to get the glory. But out loud she agreed. 'You certainly have cracked it now. That last scene is going to be so moving.'

Before they left the theatre they got an update on Isabelle. Apparently the hospital was going to keep her overnight for tests but she would be back tomorrow.

'I suppose I should go and visit her,' said Rupert as they made their way next door to Mrs Wong's.

'I am sure she will be fine and probably sleeping, so I don't think you need worry too much,' Sally reassured him. 'Heather has gone to the hospital with her stuff for the night, so I would relax and just enjoy your chips. Shall we get a bottle of wine as a treat?' They got takeaway in the end, and bought a bottle on the way to Sally's flat where they spent a wonderful evening chatting about nothing in particular. They really did get on so well and Sally was glowing with contentment.

Suddenly the door opened and Dora appeared, weaving her way across the room.

'Oh wow, what are you two up to, eh? When the cat's away in hospital? You are a quick worker, Rupie boy.' Dora plonked herself down on the sofa and started to take off her boots.

'Dora, you are drunk. What have you been up to?' said Sally, trying to change the subject.

'Oh, just drowning my sorrows with the lads, now I have been relegated to general dogsbody again by my scheming sister. So Rupert, what are you doing here? You didn't answer my question.' Dora had managed to get her boots off and was now splayed across the sofa watching Rupert who was sitting nearby on the carpet with his glass of wine.

'I am enjoying a glass of wine with your lovely sister. Is that not allowed?' asked Rupert, completely unaware of the under-currents swirling around him.

'Do you want a sandwich or something, to mop up the booze?' Sally was hovering at the kitchen door, desperate to create a diversion. She knew what Dora was like in this mood.

'No, thanks. I am going to bed in a minute. What are you two going to do?'

Dora leered at Rupert who quite innocently replied, 'I am off too in a minute – got another hard day tomorrow. Isabelle is going to be back in the morning, so we are all good to go.' He got up and finished off the last of his wine. 'I will see you tomorrow, Sally, and thanks again for today. You have been a star.'

He went to kiss Sally on the cheek and Dora chimed in, 'I bet you are disappointed, aren't you, Sal? Isabelle is going to be OK. How very annoying!'

Sally was leading Rupert to the door as quickly as she dared. She tried to sound light-hearted as she replied, saying, 'Oh, Dora, stop it! Of course I am delighted that Isabelle is recovering. We had a lovely time this afternoon but that is all part of the job. Thank you, Rupert, for working with me today. I look forward to putting it together with Isabelle tomorrow.' She closed the door with a sigh of relief, and then turned to her sister.

'What the hell is the matter with you? Why are you being such a bitch? I am beginning to wonder whether you should think about leaving, because quite frankly I have had enough of your machinations, and insults, and bad behaviour.'

'Oh, give me a break,' responded Dora, sitting up now and ready for a fight. 'Who are *you* to decide whether I leave or not? I have the theatre to think of, and my responsibilities to the rest of the cast. I happen to care about them, you know,' she said hotly.

'Oh really? So then why don't you get on with the jobs in hand and stop giving me a hard time? I don't want to fight, Dora. I don't understand what has gone wrong between us. We were having such fun in the beginning.' Sally went to sit beside her sister on the couch.

Dora looked sullen.

'It is just so frustrating sometimes watching you at work and wanting to be doing it myself. I just want to get on, Sally, and you are so happy to plod along and take things as they come.

I want to *make* things happen. Then you have taken away the one thing I was really into, and now I am back to square one.' Dora was pacing the room now like a cat. She is very beautiful, thought Sally. Much more like an actress ought to be than me. Maybe she is right and I am ruining her chances but not making the best of my own.

Out loud she said, 'I am sorry about the understudy thing but you have to understand I have looked forward to that since the beginning of the season. I didn't know you were going to come here and turn into an aspiring actress overnight. I don't want to be the enemy.' Sally suddenly felt exhausted. 'Look, please let's try and have fun like we were before. You will get a great part in the next production, I am sure. Giles really likes you, and I will remind him you are keen to work as an actress.'

'We are doing Victorian music hall next, you idiot! So I get a couple of solos. Big deal – that is not going to show off my acting skills, is it?' Dora complained.

Sally was defeated. 'OK, sorry, I forgot – but please just be patient, like we all have to be. Why should you get everything all at once?' With that, she took the wine glasses into the kitchen and left Dora to ponder life's foibles.

As she crossed the living room to go to bed Dora stopped her and gave her a hug. 'OK, sis, a truce. I will try not to wind you up or give you a hard time.'

Sally gave her a hug back and said, 'Thank you, dear, that makes me very happy. Now I need to sleep. I will be so glad when this production finally opens. Night night.'

But as she undressed in her room, Sally wished she felt better about her situation with Dora. She still loved her sister, but she didn't like or trust her very much, and that felt so sad. Her every instinct told her things were never going to be the same between them again when this job finally came to an end.

FINALE

The walk down

Chapter 37

Let's all go down the Strand –
Let's all go down the Strand!
I'll be leader, you can march behind
Come with me and see what we can find!

The first dress rehearsal of *Hamlet* was an absolute disaster. It lasted four hours, and by the time the curtain came down, everybody had lost the will to live. Giles told everyone to go home and sleep on it. 'It' being any version of terrible acting that any one of them could muster.

Sally had a nightmare that she was buried in the grave onstage and nobody could hear her shouting to be set free. She woke the next morning in a terrible sweat, trembling with panic. It took half the morning for her to shake herself free of the sense of doom that hung over her. When she got to the theatre for the note session she could almost smell the clods of earth descending on top of her again.

'All right, Sally?' The familiar voice of Heather cut through the day dream.

'Oh God, Heather, I had the most terrible nightmare last night,' started Sally, but Heather broke in with: 'Me, too. I was the stage manager of this awful production of *Hamlet*.' She burst out laughing and after a couple of seconds Sally joined her, relieved to be able to understand, finally, that it had only been a nightmare.

'Oh dear God, what a night! What are we going to do, Heather? Four hours of unadulterated crap. The bloke playing the ghost was like something out of a Disney cartoon, and when Peggy nearly did the splits as the truck went off – well . . .'

It had, indeed, been an unforgettable moment. Having warned everybody so many times that they must make sure they were standing on the upstage part of the truck, behind the carefully drawn luminous line, it was with growing horror that Sally watched Peggy take up her final position for the Dumb Show tableau, with one foot on one side of the line and one on the other. As the truck slowly moved back upstage, so did Peggy's legs move apart, one going upstage, the other down. Just as disaster seemed inevitable, the actress hauled her downstage leg from the ground and toppled slowly into the gap where the grave would have been. As the black-out descended Heather rushed onto the stage and dragged her off. The incident would definitely go down in the annals. Poor Peggy was hysterical, refusing to go onstage ever again.

This morning, Sally went straight to her dressing room with a box of chocolates she had bought on the way in.

'Oh bless you, darling, what a lovely thought. I must say I was beside myself last night, but I am back to my old self today. Nothing like a good night's sleep and a few whiskies to put me straight. Percy said he thought I was going to lose my virginity all over again, cheeky sod!'

At that moment, Percy appeared at the connecting door, saying, 'Bit of a no go last night, eh? Reckon we will have a few cuts, don't you, love?'

'Oh Percy, who knows? Maybe it will all come together. It was the first dress, after all,' said Sally, trying to be optimistic. 'Come on, let's go and hear what our director has to say.'

Giles Longfellow faced his cast and crew with remarkable stoicism.

'It was not good,' he began. 'However, there were moments when I could see the light, and although we have a good deal to embrace I think we can do so with positivity. I am not going to give individual notes just yet. The first thing we are going to do is run the play sitting here now and get the lines right. You have to understand that there is no way in a Shakespeare play that you can make up the words if you forget them. Everyone has got to be word-perfect. After that I will decide what to rehearse first this morning. Right, Heather, start the clock.'

After the word run Robert took the boys away to practise the fights and Giles got hold of Henry Hooper who had been cast to play the ghost. He was an old actor who lived locally and had been delighted to be asked to appear. It was an unmitigated disaster, however, and Giles was forced to ask him to leave.

'It has just not worked out. I am sorry, Henry, but we will give you your wages and hopefully there will be another opportunity to use you.' Giles had no alternative but to play the part himself.

It was also agreed that some of Sally's dialogue in the Dumb Show would be cut. She was not surprised and set to work chopping and changing the script as subtly as she could. In the midst of all the activity, Isabelle announced to Giles that she had to go to London for a medical issue and would be away for the night. It would mean she was not available for the second dress rehearsal.

'It is fucking unbelievable!' Giles raged to Edward Graham. The only light in Giles's life at the moment was his meetings with Teddie. They had arranged to have dinner in the Queen's Hotel in Manchester. It was rare for Lord Graham to allow himself to stay in such places, but being midweek it was relatively quiet and George Delaware, the owner, was very discreet and made sure he chose the staff on duty who would deal with the room service. He just loved the fact that his hotel entertained a Lord and nothing was too much trouble. Discretion was very much the order of the day with His Lordship, and George had been rather thrown when his son Eddie had tipped up. The first few times George had assumed the boy was with friends of a certain persuasion, but when he had spent his first long weekend with a rather attractive young actor called Jeremy, George began to think he might have a problem with the father and son.

George had opened his club after his last stint in prison. He was well known to the Manchester police as a villain of long standing, but few people on either side of the fence knew George was homosexual. Had anyone in the police known this before 1967 they would no doubt have added that felony to the list. Fortunately for George, the Sexual Offences Act was passed in 1967 and it was no longer illegal to be a homosexual. However, George realized it would be many years before certain sections of society were ready to accept gay men. 'Gay' was a word that for many years had suggested someone with a racy lifestyle. Slowly it became a more pleasant way of describing a man – or woman, for that matter – who was homosexual, which was such a clinical term. George had spent the last twenty years defending his gay customers and yet at the same time promoting them. His club became a refuge in the late 1960s for men who could not 'come out' as it were. It was unbelievable that even now in 1982, men like Lord Graham had to hide their true sexuality. But the Queen's Hotel had also become a leading light in gay clubs. Men from all over the world would visit and stay in one of the elaborately decorated rooms. Nowadays the police regularly visited too, either for personal reasons or for information. George had retained his ability to keep his ear to the ground. What he didn't know about what went on in his city wasn't worth knowing.

George's latest campaign was to bring to the attention of the gay community a very dark and forbidding phenomenon that had first reared its ugly head in America last year. It was an unknown disease which presented itself in the early stages as flu, but as the months and sometimes years went on, it developed and attacked the immune system, until the patient ultimately died. The *New York Times* had reported in July last year that there appeared to be a new form of illness which presented among gay men. There was a rush of young gay men turning up at hospitals in the city of New York all with the same symptoms. They dubbed it the 'gay cancer'.

George knew only too well how ignorance could cause panic, and the public always reacted before knowing the facts. He himself had witnessed an incident recently in a gay club in London where a young man was eating in the restaurant and another customer called the manager and suggested there was a problem because the young man in question had lesions on his skin and could infect the rest of the customers. It had been a very unpleasant situation and in the end the young guy was forced to leave. George had followed him out and they had gone for a drink, and the young man told George his sorry tale. His name was Barry and he was twenty-three. He had been on a holiday in New York four years ago, and as is usual for a young guy, had spent many hours in the clubs. About two months after he returned to England, he developed flu-like symptoms and went to his doctor, who basically just told him to take aspirin and hot drinks. Then two years later he noticed that his glands were swollen and he kept getting mouth ulcers and night sweats. He was referred to a hospital and after several blood tests was told he had HIV or AIDS. There was no cure, the doctors informed him, and they could not estimate how or when death would occur, except that research to date was indicating the disease attacked the immune system so he should be careful not to go anywhere near people with infections of any sort. The boy was distraught. His family had thrown him out when they discovered he was gay. Other friends said he had brought it on himself for being a 'poof' and would have nothing to do with him in case they caught it. He was in such a state he was talking about suicide.

George took Barry back to Manchester and put him to work in the hotel. He then sat down and found out as much as was possible about the disease so far. He quickly realized it was a deadly foe and that there was going to be a huge outcry as more and more men and women died. He was appalled that the gay community were attacked for bringing it upon themselves, and it was only after hours of reading reports and actually speaking to doctors in the USA, that George got the real facts, or as many as were available at the time. AIDS was the general term used to cover the illness, though it was a much more complicated scenario involving the immune system. The disease was capable of infecting anyone, but because it entered the body through the blood it was passed on through sexual encounters, or infected needles as used by drug addicts. Obviously those most at risk would appear to be gay men and addicts who used dirty needles.

George was now on a mission to educate the gay community. He started with his own staff and explained all he knew about the disease. He tried to impress on all his friends the need to wear protection when having sex. This was not just another venereal disease: this was a death sentence. He watched over his customers like a shepherd with his flock. Sadly, and tragically, so many of the younger guys just did not listen, and brushed off the advice as old men panicking. 'It won't happen to me,' was the inevitable cri de coeur.

One man who was beginning to face up to his fate was Robert Johnson. George had known Robert for several years and they had once been lovers. Robert had contracted HIV three years ago and was made very aware that his time was limited. He and George had spent many hours talking about his dilemma, and George had watched helplessly as his friend became more and more bitter and disillusioned with life – or the life he had left.

Last year, Robert went to work at Crewe Theatre and began an affair with the director there called Giles Longfellow. The couple seemed well suited, and when Robert brought Giles to meet George they had all got along very well. George had begged Robert to tell Giles about his illness but he refused, saying it would only mess things up for him. Robert seemed so much more positive about his situation and was talking about going to London with Giles and becoming a director. George let his pleasure in seeing Robert feeling better take over his commonsense, which was to advise Robert to come clean. But suddenly everything changed again. Robert turned up at the Queen's one night in a terrible state. It was all over with Giles and he was heartbroken. George spent days with Robert cajoling him into a better frame of mind. Slowly Robert responded, but he was never the same again. He remained withdrawn and watchful. He was cynical and aloof. He liked to stir things up for people. Why should they be happy when his life was so fucked up, was how he described his motives to George.

Now another problem was looming on the horizon. Robert was back at Crewe, working as assistant director to Giles Longfellow, who was currently having an affair with Lord Graham – whose son Eddie was also turning up at the Queen's with a young actor based at Crewe. None of this boded well, and George was on the alert to pick up the pieces . . .

Chapter 38

'Shall we make the first night black tie?' mused Giles, as he and Robert sat having a sandwich for lunch in his office. 'It would make it a really special occasion, the like of which has never been seen before in Crewe.'

'I think that is pushing your luck, my dear,' replied Robert. 'How many men own a dinner-jacket these days? Why not just put "dress glamorous" and they can decide for themselves? We tell them to come dressed in style for our Victorian music-hall shows, don't we? The audience always love dressing up for that.'

'Oh God, we have got that to contend with in two weeks' time!' exclaimed Giles. 'I can't believe the time goes so quickly.'

'Except during our production of *Hamlet*,' commented Robert, bringing Giles back down to earth with a horrible bump.

'Christ, yes, we must lose another fifteen minutes, Robert. Have you got any suggestions? Actually, I have one: to cut down the sword-fight between Hamlet and Laertes, I do think it goes on too long for that point in the play. We are nearing the home run and we should be speeding up the pace. I also feel that the boys need to pick up their cues in all those bitty scenes with Fortinbras and stuff.'

'Marvellous overview of the great play by our director,' sneered Robert with a big dollop of sarcasm. '"Bitty scenes with Fortinbras and stuff." What the fuck does *that* mean?'

Giles regarded Robert across the desk and sensed there was more to this outburst than appeared on the surface.

'Is something wrong, Robert?' he asked.

'Where to start?' the other man returned. 'The production stinks, Giles, and it is *your* fault because you have taken your eye off the ball and spent too much time shagging His Lordship.'

Giles finished chewing his sandwich, wiped his mouth on his paper serviette and took a sip of coffee. When he finally spoke, his voice was almost a whisper.

'How *dare* you talk to me like that. Who the fuck do you think you are? You are only here because I felt sorry for you after everything that happened last year. You have no qualifications to direct and certainly no right to talk to me as you do. What is your problem, Robert? You ponce around being patronizing to the actors most of the time, you nitpick at every opportunity, and to be honest, your directorial skills are pretty shabby – and now you have the gall to blame me for mistakes in this production!'

Robert held his ground. 'Yes, I do blame you, Giles. Who else is there to blame? I have done my bit, whether you like it or not, and as for my personality faults – well, tough, no one is perfect. But you are the director at the end of the day. You cast the play, you agreed design, and you are the head of this whole caboodle. So yes, the buck rests with *you*.'

Giles absorbed the blows and contemplated his next move. He knew he had failed miserably to pull the production together, and he also knew that his emotional life had once again distracted him from the job in hand. This was to have been his big chance. How ironic was it that, years ago, Teddie Graham had bailed him out of trouble so he could pursue his career once more, and now it was Teddie who was the cause of the trouble. Robert knew too much about him for Giles not to acknowledge some of these facts, but it would make him weak, and Robert needed no encouragement to take advantage of him in the vulnerable position he had put himself. He chose his words carefully.

'I am truly sorry that you feel this way and maybe I have made mistakes, but now is not the time to upbraid me for them. We have two days to the first night, Robert – can we not work together to put the show on, and then discuss our differences? I am assuming you will not want to work with me after this and do not see a future for the play in London?' He looked questioningly at Robert, who was still standing tense and straight-backed in front of his desk. Robert now relaxed and moved to the big wing-chair in the corner of the room and sat down slowly. He took out his cigarettes and lit one, inhaling the blue curling smoke and holding it in his lungs for a moment before releasing the smoke in a thin stream through pursed lips.

'Ah, now we come to the crux of the matter, Giles, my dear. If you are happy to admit mistakes so am I happy to admit lack of experience in the directorial stakes. You and I know I will not get employed by anyone else after this, so we are stuck with each other. I have every intention of going to the West End with this production, and you and I will do everything in our power to make that happen, won't we?'

Robert took another drag of his cigarette and waited for Giles to answer.

'Robert, is this a game of some sort? What are you trying to say? On the one hand you think I am useless as a director, yet on the other you are suggesting we can pull this off between us and continue to work together. I really don't see how that is going to happen. I have to be completely honest and say I am not sure I want to work with you any more after this.'

'I don't think you have a choice,' said Robert very quietly. 'Giles, you and I were once in love, and then you dropped me for the sake of idle gossip and your career prospects. Pretty pathetic excuses for destroying someone's life, don't you think? But to be fair when I came to you this year and suggested we work together, you gave me the opportunity to follow my dream and become a director. I am not going to let you drop me again as casually as you did last time. Especially as you seem intent upon ruining your chance of a lifetime for romance. So if you need a little persuasion, let's talk about Lord Graham and his son Eddie, shall we? Eddie has followed in his father's footsteps and I am not talking about agricultural college. Young Edward is proving quite the "gay young thing" in social circles in Manchester, especially in the Queen's Hotel. I know you enjoy the delights of this venue as I introduced you to George and his happy band. I also know that you enjoy many a night with His Lordship under the protection of George. All well and good, you may say. But I do not think His Lordship would be happy to know his son is indulging his passion for young men's flesh under the same roof, and risking the family name in doing so. I would be happy to have a word in his ear should you and I not find a way to carry on. Surely it is much better all round, that we keep these things in the family, so to speak. We should all be looking after each other and our reputations, don't you think?'

Robert sat back and waited for Giles to respond. He gleaned enormous satisfaction from watching the man sweat. He could see the thoughts running through Giles's head. The panic and fear in his eyes. Let someone else feel helpless and abandoned like he had been. He lived every day now with the promise of death and it made him intolerant of those who took life and good fortune for granted. Those people who walked through life taking what they wanted with no thought of what havoc they might wreak on others' emotions. Giles was a weak man who always managed somehow to wriggle out of trouble. Well, lucky him! This time he would find it a little more difficult and maybe his misfortune would be lucky for Robert. It was too late to save him from the fate that so cruelly awaited him, but not too late to make whatever was left of his life worth living.

Robert saw Giles swallow hard and his Adam's apple rose and fell in contradiction to the feigned outward calm he was presenting across the desk. Giles then rose and came round to the front of the desk and leaned against it.

'Well, well, life *is* full of surprises. Why don't you and I go now and get this play ready for a spectacular first night in Crewe? Who knows where it may lead us.' He walked to the door and held it open for Robert, who rose from the chair like a bird of prey and crossed the room in one fell swoop, to pause and peruse his prey before making his exit.

Chapter 39

The first night was a huge success, much to the amazement of the cast. The run-up to the big night had been unbelievably fraught with drama, never mind the drama onstage. The biggest problem had been Isabelle, who just seemed to go to pieces. Sally and Rupert spent every minute with her encouraging her and feeding her and trying to make sure she kept the food down. She would use any excuse to get to the toilet, but Sally would refuse to budge from her elbow. Rupert was remarkably calm and together. He was obviously besotted by his leading lady, much to Sally's disgust, but she understood that without him beside her, there was no way Isabelle was going to get on that stage.

The rest of the cast had come together in the last two days, and decided that in spite of their director's lack of guidance, they were bloody well going to do this, and the energy onstage was terrific. Jeremy was sick with nerves, not just because the audience was full of important people from the world of theatre and film, but because Eddie was going to be sitting in the Royal Box with his family. His Lordship was coming with his whole family, Tanya and Tilly and Eddie. He and Eddie had talked about the night and how they would keep their affair under wraps.

'For God's sake, you must not come too close to me or I will give the game away. I know I will just want to kiss you!' exclaimed Eddie. 'We must make sure we are always in a group together. Will you peep through the curtain at the beginning and blow me a kiss?'

Jeremy laughed. 'Oh yes, that would be just great, me standing behind the curtain blowing kisses. "What are you doing, Jeremy?" "Oh, just waving at my lover in the Royal Box!" Can you imagine how that would go down with Giles Longfellow?'

'Well, frankly, he is the one person who *would* understand. Did you see him in the bar at the Queen's last weekend, by the way? I was wondering who he was with that night. I asked George, but he didn't seem to know. Perhaps he has a secret assignation sometimes. We could investigate.' Eddie giggled.

'We have enough trouble keeping our own assignations secret without worrying about other people,' said Jeremy.

Dora, meanwhile, was obsessed with the guest-list for the evening, and how she was going to get herself introduced to the producer of Isabelle's new film.

'If I can just get him in front of me, I know I can win him over. And did you know there is a casting director from *Coronation Street* coming, Sally?' Dora looked at her sister, who was busy trying to make posies of wild flowers for Isabelle to carry on in her mad scene.

'Why would you think I care about *Coronation Street*? I do not want to be in a long-running series – it would ruin my career. You just get typecast.'

'Oh, don't be so bloody pompous, Sally. Work's work – and

it's better to be out there being seen. No point in sitting in your little garret room acting to the mirror. Where is that going to get you?'

Sally did not bother to answer her sister. They did not agree on anything these days. She had not had the time to work things out between them, but she knew that something would have to be done. She was nervous about seeing their parents while the situation was like this. It would only take a minute for their mum to realize that something was wrong, and she would be so upset. Sally had actually put their parents off coming to see *Hamlet*, telling them it was not much good, and that she and Dora were just too busy to enjoy their visit.

'All right, my darling,' Patricia had said. 'But we really do want to see you both very soon. We miss you!'

Giles and Robert worked together, and it had been agreed between them that Giles would discuss the future with Robert after the opening night. In his heart Giles knew it was make or break time, and he would do anything to keep Robert quiet. If he had to agree to giving him a job once the play went to London, so be it. It was worth it to prevent Teddie from finding out about his son. Of course it would all come out eventually, but now was not the time.

The curtain went up and *Hamlet* hit the stage. Rupert was magnificent, and whenever she had a minute during the play, Sally watched him from the wings. He soared, there was no other way to describe his performance. The scenes with Ophelia were magical. Rupert seemed to imbue Isabelle with all his energy and magic. She looked amazing with her golden hair like a waterfall down her back, and with her long slim legs draped in fine silk which clung to her body, she resembled a young fawn. Charmaine was another surprise on the night. Her Gertrude was full of hidden depths and feral sexuality.

Sally was also impressed with her friend Jeremy. His Laertes shone a brilliant light. Sally had never seen him so strong onstage. He had grabbed the role and brought a new dimension to the stage.

'I do so hope he gets a wonderful job from this tonight,' she remarked to Heather. 'He deserves a break.'

'Don't we all,' the woman sighed.

It was a strange evening for Sally because she did not have much input as an actress, and all the fuss about being seen by the right people was out of her reach. But she didn't feel envy or jealousy. She just wanted the team to do well. Her time would come, she felt sure. The more she watched Dora's intense quest for recognition, the less she craved it. She just wanted to be taken seriously as an actress and play wonderful parts in great plays. Not much to ask!

The curtain came down to thunderous applause. In the bar afterwards the actors mingled with the regular audience and tried their best to present themselves to anyone of importance who might give them a job. The big producer had left straight after the performance, but not before going to visit Isabelle in her dressing room to congratulate her. Sally happened to be passing her dressing-room door and heard Isabelle say, 'Thank you, darling, but it was nothing. I just love Shakespeare and adore working on text. I guess I have a natural instinct for words.'

Sally wanted to be sick! What a load of old tosh. She went to congratulate Rupert who was surrounded by a group of schoolgirls getting his autograph.

'Look at you, you big Hamlet you,' she laughed. 'I can see your head getting bigger by the minute.'

'Sally! Give me a kiss, it is all down to you. You have been my guiding light. Come here, I love you!' He wrapped his arms around Sally in a big hug and then planted a kiss on her lips. She longed to cling to him forever. He felt so good.

She pulled away, however, and said, 'See you in the bar?'

'You bet, lovely lady. I will see you there.'

Sally looked for Jeremy to congratulate him but he had already gone to the bar apparently, according to Geoffrey who was making his way up to the Dress Circle bar.

'Great night, Sally. We pulled it off!'

'Yes, we did. Congratulations, Geoffrey.'

Sally made her way through the crush to the bar to grab a drink. Suddenly Dora was in front of her flushed with excitement.

'Hi, Sally, isn't it great? Everyone loved it. I have just met the casting director lady and she is going to call me about doing an audition for *Coronation Street*. Isn't that fantastic?' Dora didn't wait for an answer, but carried on past Sally, waving at someone across the bar. Jeremy was just ahead of Sally, about to lean into the bar and grab a glass of champagne.

'Get one for me,' she called out. The noise was unbelievable and she had to shout her request a second time. Jeremy smiled at her and passed her a glass and then got one for himself, and turned to give her a kiss.

'Well done, Sally, the Dumb Show was a triumph.'

'Well done you, more like. Jeremy, you were amazing – you were on fire!' They hugged each other.

'Oh, look at the luvvies,' sneered Robert. 'Daaarling, you were maaarvellous! God, nothing changes.'

'Oh, shut up, Robert. Just for once stop posing and join in. It was bloody marvellous and you know it,' said Jeremy. 'Here, let me get you a glass of champagne.' As Jeremy turned back to the bar, someone pinched his bum.

'What the ...?' he started, only to stop immediately as

Eddie appeared at his side. 'Don't do that,' Jeremy hissed. 'That is exactly what we discussed we would not do, you stupid boy!'

'Hello, Eddie, and how are you this evening?' enquired Robert, stepping between the two men. 'Did your family enjoy the play?'

Eddie gave him a charming smile and replied: 'Yes, thank you so much, Robert. You must be so proud of your very talented cast.' He turned and beamed at Jeremy. 'You were wonderful.'

'Oh yes, they were *all* wonderful. Well, I must go and mingle. No doubt we will meet again – soon, I expect,' Robert held them both in his gaze for a moment and then moved off.

'He is impossible,' said Sally. 'Here, Jeremy, can you nab me another drink. So how are you, Eddie? Oh, here is your father.' Sally stepped aside to allow Lord Graham to get to the bar. 'Please, Your Lordship, let Jeremy do the honours. Jeremy, make that two glasses of champagne, please,' she shouted over the hubbub. 'Sorry, we haven't been introduced. My name is Sally Thomas. I am a member of the company, and Jeremy is my best friend.' She turned back to take the glasses from Jeremy, who having realized who they were for, was panicking silently.

Eddie made the introductions, again formally, and they all politely chinked glasses.

'The sword-fight was wicked,' enthused Tilly. Then: 'Have you ever made a mistake and stabbed each other?'

Jeremy laughed. 'Not yet, touch wood. And thankfully Rupert and I get on very well, so there is no danger he will stab me on purpose. I am sure there must have been times when actors didn't like each other and things could have got a little ... difficult.'

Eddie joined in. 'Well, we always hear about actors being bitchy to each other, don't we?'

'Oh, I think that aspect is exaggerated,' replied Sally. 'Certainly in this company we all pull together, don't we, Jeremy?'

'Really?' said Eddie. 'That's not what Jeremy told me the other day. Your leading lady has been a nightmare, I gather.' Suddenly realizing he had said too much, he whipped round to see if his father was listening. Lord Graham had, in fact, been accosted by a local dignitary and missed the conversation. Breathing a sigh of relief, Eddie took his sister's arm and said smoothly, 'Well, we have to go, don't we, Tilly? Where is Mother? Lovely to meet you all and well done. Come on, Father.' They disappeared into the throng and left Jeremy and Sally staring at each other.

'Do I suspect a faux pas here?' asked Sally. 'I take it Lord Graham does not have any idea that you two are an item?'

'Oh my God, no! That would be a disaster. Can you imagine the repercussions? Poor Eddie would probably be disinherited.'

'But surely he is going to have to come out one day?' said Sally. 'He can't pretend for the rest of his life.'

'Lots of people do,' replied Jeremy sadly. 'I don't know what is going to happen – I just know I love Eddie so much I couldn't live without him.'

Sally squeezed his hand and said kindly, 'Come on, let's go and join the others. I feel a Mrs Wong coming on.'

They crossed to where the rest of the company were beginning to assemble ready for a mass exodus to the pub.

'Hi, guys,' said Pete. 'We cracked it, didn't we? No thanks to the management, but—'

'Ssh, Pete!' cautioned Janie. 'The management is about to give a speech.'

Giles Longfellow was tapping his glass and getting nowhere in his attempts to silence the crowd, until finally Simon put two fingers in his mouth and produced an ear-splitting whistle. The rest of the cast whooped with delight.

'Ladies and gentlemen, it gives me great pleasure to stand here tonight and express my delight and gratitude to the citizens of Crewe for making this evening possible. To the members of the council who work with us on a daily basis to keep our theatre running. To all the members of staff front of house for their hard work, and to all the wonderful cast and crew for their tireless commitment. It has not been easy but I think I can honestly say tonight has made it all worthwhile. And finally I would like to extend a huge thank you to Lord Graham for his support. Nothing would happen without his generosity. Thank you, sir, and thank you, everyone. Enjoy the rest of your night!'

Jeremy looked across the room to see Eddie, flanked by his mother and father, shaking hands with Giles and making their goodbyes. He caught Eddie's eye and his lover flashed him a heart-melting smile.

'Quite a boy, isn't he?' said a voice at his elbow. Jeremy looked at Robert and tried to gauge what he was driving at, but it was impossible to read the man. Jeremy was always left with a feeling of unease, as if Robert were about to divulge a terrible secret. But then it was true, wasn't it? He did know a terrible secret and if he did divulge it they would all be ruined.

'Coming to the pub, Robert?' was all he said and he made his way to the door.

Chapter 40

Sally sat opposite Giles in his office and tried to take in what he was telling her.

'I am afraid Isabelle will be leaving at the end of the week. This, of course, means a huge upheaval for the cast, and we will have to rehearse you in. For you it is an even bigger challenge, but one I know you will embrace with your usual professional approach. It is an extraordinary situation, I must say, and I feel very frustrated that my hands are tied.'

'But what about her contract? Can she legally just bunk off like this?' Sally could feel her anger bubbling up.

'Legally it is not credible, but the circumstances are so unusual I have agreed to her dismissal. The trouble is, Sally, between you, me and the gatepost, Isabelle is a liability. The fact we managed – *you* managed – to get her on at all is a miracle. Her agent can provide a letter from a specialist confirming that she needs medical attention as soon as possible, so what can I say?'

'But she is going off to Hollywood to make a film,' protested Sally. 'Is that a euphemism for "medical attention" or is that simply taking the mickey? I can't believe people can get away with these things.' She was growing angrier by the minute, and Giles was irritating her as well, because he was being so pathetic.

'I know, I know, it is a hard pill to swallow. But the good news is, you are going to be playing Ophelia! Now I have called the company for two o'clock to explain everything, and by then we will have a rehearsal schedule worked out. It is going to be very tough for everyone, as we have to start the next production at the same time. Thank God it is Victorian Music Hall. Not too much to rehearse, just learning the songs really. Timothy is so good he will soon have everybody off their song-sheets, and Sarah is going to help me stage some of the numbers.'

'Sarah?' said Sally. 'Why Sarah?'

'Oh, she has done a lot of Music Hall and I went to see her at the Leeds Variety last year. She was wonderful. She came to me earlier in the season and asked if she could assist, and now it will be a great help, because I will be rather busy for the first week sorting out your performances. By the way, I have given Dora your big number since I thought you will not be so free to rehearse. So I hope you don't mind that I have given her "Burlington Bertie". Is that OK with you, dear?'

'Yes, of course.' But Sally wanted to weep. She had been so looking forward to doing that number and had already learned it. She was going to be sidelined again. Still, it wasn't all bad. She was going to play Ophelia with Rupert for a whole week! The thought drove everything else from her mind.

'Right – well, I had better get off to Wardrobe and sort out costumes. Thank you, Giles, I will not let you down,' she told him.

'I know you will be marvellous, and by way of reparation I

have invited a top London agent up next week to cover your performance. He is going to come with James Langton, who I know is an old friend of yours.' Giles looked very pleased with himself.

'Oh, that *is* fantastic news!' exclaimed Sally. 'Thank you so much, Giles.' And she practically hopped with joy out of his office.

The rest of the cast were thrilled with her news, although they were not so thrilled by the thought of more rehearsal.

'I will do my best to learn it all quickly,' Sally promised them. 'Listen, I know most of the play because I have been working on it.'

'Can I take over all your stuff then?' chimed in Dora, always quick to jump on an opportunity.

'Yes, you can,' said Sally. 'We will need to work on that, obviously. We will have to co-ordinate times with Timothy and his rehearsals. Congratulations, by the way, Giles has told me you are going to do "Burlington Bertie".'

Dora had the grace to look slightly sheepish. 'Oh thanks, Sally. I am sorry you have missed out but you are going to be brilliant as Ophelia.'

'I hope so,' her sister said.

Rupert was beside himself when Sally found him in his dressing room.

'How can she do this to me?' He was nearly in tears. Sally wanted to console him but she was actually annoyed that he seemed more upset for himself than for the situation, and the fact that the stupid cow had dumped everyone in the prover-bial, not only him, for her own selfish reasons.

'How can she do this to *us*, you mean,' she chided. 'Come on, Rupert, the girl is a mess and has completely lost the plot. She has got away with murder. Giles has released her from her contract so she can gallivant off to Hollywood. She is completely selfish.'

'I know that, Sally, but I love her. We were going to get a place together. We had the West End production to look forward to – what will happen to that now?'

'I am sure they will find it very easy to engage another actress. Hopefully one with more talent than Miss Isabelle James.' Sally no longer cared what Rupert thought of her harsh words regarding the love of his life.

'Please don't be mean about her, Sally. This is very hard for me. I know you will be brilliant as Ophelia, and believe me, I will give you all my support, but just understand how I am feeling right now.'

Sally looked at Rupert sat there feeling bereft. She longed to hold him and comfort him, but the actress in her took over. There was no time for all that now. She had a performance to create, and he was going to help her no matter how heartbroken he was. This was her time now, and she was going to make the most of it.

'Come on, you. Time enough to weep later – we have work to do,' she told Rupert.

Isabelle had the good sense to keep well out of everyone's way, and only came into the theatre at the last minute to get changed and ready for the show. She seemed to sleepwalk through her performance, as though she was already on the plane to La La Land.

'Good riddance, I say,' remarked Gwendoline. 'You are going to be so much better, Sally. Now try this dress on and let's see what has to be altered.' The alterations were all straightforward but when it came to the floaty number there was an underwear problem.

'The thing is, whatever you put on by way of underwear

will show through this material. Isabelle didn't wear anything underneath. Are you happy to do that, Sally?' asked the wardrobe mistress.

Truth be told, Sally was horrified at the thought of wearing a see-through dress with nothing on underneath. But a little voice was telling her to get over herself. She was an actress, and she would do whatever it took for the good of the scene. She could quite clearly see the benefit of being naked under the dress, not just for the line of the dress, but basically for the whole atmosphere of the scene. She would feel so much more vulnerable, and it would help the madness and the feeling of loss somehow; she knew she had to do this.

'Yes, that's fine,' she said firmly, hoping to convince herself in the meantime.

The rest of the week was crazy. Sally hardly ate or slept. She started to watch Isabelle from the wings but decided it did not help her. She was better off just creating her own performance without any other influences. Rupert was wonderful as ever and they were able to create a real energy between them. By Saturday night everyone was quite happy to bid farewell to Miss James. There was even relief for Rupert, who had struggled all week knowing she was leaving but needing to keep everything smooth as they had to work together. Isabelle had a studio car coming to pick her up after the show and drive her to London, as she was booked on a flight the next day to LA.

'I won't have time to shop or anything,' she whined to Sally, who wanted to be sick.

To save Rupert facing a lonely Sunday in Crewe Sally had invited him to lunch. Dora decided she would cook and let the actors chill out as she put it. It turned out to be a very good idea as Sally was so nervous she could think about nothing except the play, and Rupert was beyond conversation as he wallowed in his misery. Dora drank copious amounts of red wine as she stirred her chilli con carne and couldn't care less about anything. Every now and then she would burst into a chorus of 'I'm Burlington Bertie, I rise at ten thirty,' and strut around the living room. She even managed to glean a smile from Rupert.

'That's better!' she exclaimed. 'Right, you guys, come and eat my chilli, and all will be well.'

Sally watched Dora flirting with Rupert and tried to be generous of spirit. Her sister was not a mean or malicious person. She was just young maybe? Sally thought back to their childhood and how most of the time they had been very happy as sisters. Sally was always the sensible one though, the older sister in charge. She had a mental picture of Dora standing on a low wall outside a holiday cottage singing at the top of her voice, and their parents rushing out and blaming Sally for letting her sister climb up and put herself in danger. Looking at her sister over the table at lunch, Sally felt a surge of love for Dora and made a mental note to make sure that once she had opened next week, she would talk to Dora about all the goings-on so far, and try to mend some bridges.

By seven o'clock on Monday night Sally was a wreck. She could not stop shaking. She sat in her new dressing room, recently vacated by Isabelle, and brushed her hair slowly, trying to restore some calm. The cast had all been round with little gifts and cards, which had made her cry!

'Five minutes, everyone. Five minutes.' Heather's voice through the Tannoy was strangely reassuring. There was a knock on the door.

'Come in,' she called out.

The door opened to reveal Giles Longfellow with an enormous bunch of lilies followed by Robert with a huge box of chocolates.

'Good luck, my darling,' Robert said as he leaned over and kissed her on both cheeks.

'Yes, good luck, dear. I know you will be marvellous.' Another set of kisses from Giles and they were gone.

'Beginners for Act One, please. Beginners for Act One.'

Sally was not on straight away, but she could not bear to sit up here in the dressing room on her own, so she decided to go and stand in the wings. She stopped at Rupert's door and knocked.

'Come in.'

Sally popped her head round the door. 'Just wanted to wish you good luck and apologize in advance for any cock-ups.'

Rupert rushed to the door and opened it and gave her a big hug. 'Oh Sally, I am sorry, I should have come to you, but I have been going through my lines again. Please don't worry about tonight – you are going to be wonderful. You have been all along, let's face it. I am so looking forward to acting with you. Good luck.' He planted a huge smacker on her lips.

Sally stood in the darkness of the wings and wrapped her cloak around her. She could feel the audience like a living breathing creature waiting out there to devour her. From where she was standing she could see the first few rows, and the lights onstage shone on the faces of the people watching. Eventually she heard her cue and walked into the light. She was hit by the warmth onstage after the draughty wings. It was the heart of the building, its soul – and she was slap bang in the middle! She had a split second of sheer panic as she opened her mouth to speak and her mind went blank. It felt like an eternity, a huge empty space and everything seemed to be moving in slow motion. She saw Jeremy, as Laertes, her brother, coming towards her, his mouth moving but no sound coming out. She wanted to scream and as she took a breath . . . her words flowed out with ease. She was off and running!

'You did it! Well done – it was terrific!' Jeremy was hugging her and Sally was numb. She could hardly remember anything about the play.

'I am just so relieved I got through it,' she said. 'Oh Jeremy, was I really all right?'

'You were better than all right, you were brilliant – such a relief after Madam. Suddenly the play makes sense.' He kissed her on both cheeks, lifted her off the ground and twirled her round. 'Come on, get changed. We are taking you to the pub!'

When they arrived at the pub everyone was there including Giles and there was a bottle of champagne on ice waiting for her to open. Bob, the landlord, came and gave her a kiss and opened the champagne for her, saying, 'Well done, lass, I hear you were grand.'

There were cheers all round, and Sally was completely overwhelmed by everyone's kindness.

'What it is to be loved,' remarked Dora at her side. 'Well done, sis, you were brill.'

Sally found Rupert sitting at a table with Geoffrey and Charmaine and Peggy and Percy. They all congratulated her, and she bought everyone a drink before finally sitting down. Suddenly she was completely exhausted.

'Oh my goodness, I am so tired all of a sudden,' she said.

'That is normal, my dear,' offered Peggy. 'It is all the adrenalin you have used tonight. Worse than a car crash, they say. You will soon get used to it. It was a bloody good night though, wasn't it, Percy?' She nudged him into a response.

'Not half, my love. You played a blinder, no doubt about it. Now come on, drink up, and I will get you another.'

'No, not for me, thank you, Percy. I am going to go home and sleep. Hopefully Giles will let me have a late call tomorrow, just for once. Rupert, I have to thank you most of all for being so kind and helpful despite your broken heart.' Sally looked across at her leading man, who was getting quietly sozzled. He grinned at her and blew her a kiss.

'See you tomorrow.'

She found Dora, who was not yet ready to go, and gave her instructions not to wake her in the morning. Then she bade a final farewell to her companions at arms and went home. It was a clear and starry night. There was frost already on the trees, and all the cobbles were twinkling as she walked across them. It looked like fairyland. Snatches of Ophelia's song ran through her mind and she hummed to herself. She wanted to do it all over again, right now, even though she was practically dead on her feet. She had loved being onstage and feeling the audience with her; almost leaning in to her to catch her words. She had reached out to the back of the circle, and sensed the back row. Every corner of the auditorium was hers to play. She had given her all, and the audience had embraced her and taken her to their hearts. She loved being an actress!

By the time she climbed the stairs of the flat she was freezing cold and could not stop shivering. She made a hot chocolate and undressed as quickly as she could, donning a jumper over her pyjamas and a thick pair of socks on her feet. Slowly she calmed down, and the warmth of the drink spread through her body, right down to her toes. She didn't even bother to clean her teeth as her head hit the pillow and she fell deeply asleep – with no 'perchance to dream' about it!'

Chapter 41

Giles watched the frozen fields speed past through the window of the train. The sun was coming up a deep red splashed across the horizon, cracking daybreak like a golden egg across the landscape. Robert was sleeping opposite him and Giles took the opportunity to study him. They had been lovers for a while last year, but Giles had found Robert to be very intense, and rather negative in his approach to their relationship. Giles had tried to talk to him, and get to know what he was like, underneath the rather cold and brittle exterior, but did not get very far. Certainly Robert had secrets and held them very close to his chest. They had decided to part and Giles did not see Robert again for months, until he turned up at the theatre one morning, and basically asked for a job. Giles felt guilty enough to agree, and thus began Robert's new career as assistant director. Giles had regretted his decision almost immediately, as it was obvious that Robert did not have the intuition or natural instincts that make a good director. He was also difficult with the actors, who did not respond favourably to his patronizing, and often plain rude, remarks.

Since their confrontation in his office last week Giles had done some serious thinking. He knew just how serious the situation would be if Teddie discovered his son was gay: the repercussions would spread across his own life as much as the Graham family's. Over the past months Giles had fallen deeply in love with Teddie Graham, and as so often happens when one is blinded by emotion, he had hidden his head in the sand as to where they were going with their relationship. Giles could not think beyond the now. He just wanted things to stay the same forever. Robert had brought him up short with a jolt. Not only was his personal life threatened, but his professional life too was in jeopardy. So here he was on his way to sign a contract with one of the biggest producers in the West End for a three-month run of his production of *Hamlet*. Robert would also get a credit as assistant director and work with him on the production. Teddie would remain in blissful ignorance of his son and heir's sexual proclivities, and Giles could enjoy his lover's attentions indefinitely.

Robert coughed and stirred. 'Oh sorry, I must have dropped off. What time is it?' he asked.

'Not a problem, we have two hours to go yet. Go back to sleep, dear boy.'

'I have a headache, as a matter of fact. I think I will go and see if I can get an aspirin.' Robert rose and started for the buffet car. 'Do you want a coffee or anything?' he asked.

'Lovely idea – yes, please, and a ham and cheese roll would be even more perfect.' Giles grinned. 'A secret treat of mine.'

'Coming up,' said Robert and set off in search of supplies. He returned later with the coffees and two rolls, and as he sat down he grimaced.

'Something the matter?' asked Giles, taking his roll and greedily unwrapping it.

'I think I must be getting the flu or something. I ache all over and I have got terrible mouth ulcers. I am going to see my doctor on the way back to the station this afternoon, as a matter of fact – see if he can give me something to stave off the worst of the symptoms.'

They lapsed into silence as they ate their breakfast, and shortly after that Robert was asleep again. Giles continued to watch the world go by, until he also dropped off. Both men were awoken at the same time as the train hooted its arrival into Euston. They took a cab to the Charing Cross Road, to Wyndham's Theatre, which also housed the offices of their producer. Robert was still struggling to feel better, and Giles suggested he go straight to his doctor.

'Listen, it is not as though you really need to be here with me,' he pointed out. 'You have seen the contract and you know the contents. I am not going to have you written out at the last minute or anything.' Giles laughed tightly. 'Can't afford to do that, can I?'

Robert nodded. 'Very well then, I will accept your suggestion and go now – and then meet you at the station this afternoon at four fifteen at the barrier.'

'Absolutely. See you then,' acknowledged Giles, and strode off towards the theatre.

Robert hailed a cab. 'St Thomas' Hospital.'

'Right you are, guv.' The taxi driver looked in his mirror and decided this was not a passenger who wanted to chat, so he put his foot down and kept his mouth shut!

Robert sat back in the cab and tried to stop the thoughts from swirling round in his head. It was always like this when he went to the hospital for tests. Nothing could stop the rot, he knew that. Would the doctor be able to tell him how long he had? He decided he would go to the Terence Higgins Trust after the hospital. This was basically an advice centre set up in July by the partner of a man called Terence Higgins, who had died of this disease. No one really knew what caused it, or how to cure it. The doctors could only monitor patients like himself and struggle to find a solution. But Robert knew he was getting worse. Soon he must take himself away somewhere to die.

The counsellor had told him last time that he *must* tell all the men he had had sex with what was going on, but he just couldn't do it. And yet, he had to tell Giles, for Christ's sake. Now there was this stupid business with Lord Graham and his son. Robert had not intended to involve them in his campaign to make Giles employ him. It had been a spur-of-the-moment thing because he was angry. He had watched Giles and Lord Graham being fêted at the Queen's Hotel by George Delaware and he had been jealous. After all, it was he who had introduced Giles to the hotel, and now he had been swept aside by titled gentlemen. Then he had seen Eddie at the hotel, and they had got together one night. The boy was uncontrollable. Robert had given him a serious talk about protection and too much careless sex, but who was he to talk? They had all partied together that night. It had been wild. None of these guys seemed to know anything about the disease that was stalking them. He had had a couple of conversations with some friends about the symptoms, and yet there was nothing concrete to work from.

Robert had never, in the whole of his life, felt so alone and abandoned. He would tell Giles tonight when they got back to Crewe, he decided, and if Giles was unable to find any compassion for him, so be it. He was fucked anyway.

Giles lifted the glass to his lips and savoured the moment; another wonderful lunch with his colleague Mr Langton, courtesy of the British Drama League.

'Here's to Hamlet, Prince of Denmark. May you be the Prince of Shaftesbury Avenue!' announced James Langton, enjoying the toast. 'It is good to see you, Giles, and how delightful that I will be seeing my protégés on Friday night at your theatre.'

'Yes, it all turned out very well, did it not?' replied Giles. 'Sally has proved invaluable as a company member and Jeremy is a splendid actor with a formidable career ahead, I think.'

'But you had problems with your leading lady, I gather?' asked James, who loved the gossip. 'She was on drugs and all sorts, I hear.'

'Well, I don't know about all that side of it, but as far as her acting skills went she was a non-starter. She had no idea about text or stagecraft. Los Angeles is welcome to her, as far as I am concerned. We are already inundated with suggestions for Ophelia for the production in Town. I hope we can use some of the cast from Crewe as well, although it is always difficult with London producers as they want to be in control of everything. Mmm . . . this wine is absolutely first-class, James. Good choice. Now tell me your news. How is your wife?'

Giles meandered through lunch getting pleasantly pissed and arrived at the barrier in Euston station in good time to meet Robert and get the train home. To his dismay Robert never appeared, and he was forced to board the train alone. He was concerned at first, but shortly after Watford Junction he was lost to the world in an alcohol-fuelled coma and did not wake until the guard announced their arrival at Crewe.

Robert lay in his hospital bed staring at the ceiling. He had asked the nurse if she would be so kind as to call Crewe Theatre and explain that he would not be returning for some time due to ill-health, and to ask Giles Longfellow to call him as soon as possible, on the hospital number. So here he was, waiting for death to come. The doctor had looked at the lesions which had appeared on his legs and taken more blood tests.

'I am so sorry, but there is nothing we can do for you except keep you comfortable, and in as little pain as possible. Do you have anyone you would like us to contact in the meantime?'

Robert told him that all that was being taken care of by the nurse, and said that hopefully, his friend from Crewe would ring, and would be able to make a visit. No, there was no family member he wished to inform.

So now he was alone, and acutely aware of his body. There is something about lying in a hospital bed with few distractions that encourages self-examination. Robert could feel a tingling in his toes and in his mind's eye he traced a route up his legs past the lesions, which he had tried to ignore, up through his groin which was aching, no longer with lust or love, just regret at what had been. Across his stomach which was churning with fear, up through his chest and heart, which was hurting with sadness and self-pity, up through his neck which ached, and into his mouth which was ulcerated and dry with panic. His brain was jampacked with too many thoughts jostling for position. He tried to swallow and drew in a sharp breath of pain. Then the tears flowed, slowly at first and then in a torrent – unstoppable, like his demise. Did anyone care?

Chapter 42

Sally spent the week in a dream. It flew by way too quickly for her. Every night she learned something new about a scene or an emotion, and every night she drew closer to Rupert. Her initial nerves, about being naked under the dress, were soon forgotten, but there had been one moment in the wings when Rupert had come up behind her and put his arms around her, and she could feel him hesitate as he became aware of her nakedness through the dress.

'Wow!' he whispered in her ear. 'You feel amazing. I could stand here all evening and explore you.'

Sally shivered and moved away quickly, wrapping her cloak around her. 'It is so cold in these draughty old wings,' she whispered back. 'I can think of better places to be.' *In my bed, she thought. Holding me, making love to me. All thoughts of Isabelle expunged from your mind.*

Onstage, she and Rupert were a good team, and had created a chemistry between them, even if it was not quite as charged as before. Friday night had been a scary evening, when James Langton arrived with the agent from William

Morris. The latter was a very charming urbane man who pulled no punches. After the show they met in the bar. Giles had arranged a light supper to be served, and had gone to town with smoked salmon and oysters, and champagne. Jeremy and Sally and Rupert were invited with Giles, James and Peter Stone, as he was introduced to them. He was very laidback and looked just like Sally had imagined a big London agent would: wearing a trendy, expensive suit, handmade shoes and silk shirt, and with distinguished grey hair and a slight Californian tan.

'A pleasure to meet you both, Sally and Rupert. And you are Jeremy – that's right, Laertes. A very exciting and enlightening performance, if I may say so, young man. You have a future ahead of you. Would you like to do more Shakespeare?'

'Oh, absolutely,' enthused Jeremy. 'I would love to get into the RSC and do a season at Stratford. That is my goal.' He laughed nervously, wondering if he had gone too far, but Peter seemed to be genuinely interested.

'And you, Sally, what are you hoping to do after your season here?'

Sally found it more difficult to express her desires. She had been so sure when she left drama school that she would work her way up through rep to a play in the West End, or maybe join the company at the National, but since she had been watching Dora work the system here, and all her talk about exposure on TV, she was not so sure where she belonged. Did she have enough talent, as Jeremy seemed to possess, to crack the big companies? She suddenly felt very shy, and hesitated before she replied. She looked at them round the table waiting for her to speak.

'I am not sure, to be honest. In the last three months working here, so much has happened to me, and I probably need time to absorb everything I have experienced. I know I am a good actress, but maybe not good enough.' She looked round the table and smiled. 'Not exactly selling myself, am I?' she said.

Peter Stone answered her. 'No, you are not, but I like your honesty, and you have an understanding of yourself and the business which is intelligent and useful. Too many young actresses just think their looks will see them through. There are many ways of getting a foot on the ladder, young lady, but many of those ladders lead to nowhere. If you are really serious about staying in the game you have to want it more than life itself, and accept that it is ultimately down to luck. You must have heard the cliché "right time, right place" – but that is exactly what it boils down to in this game. Now enough talk, let's eat this delicious supper you have provided, Giles.'

Everyone relaxed and the evening seemed to go well. Giles and James were an odd couple, and Sally wondered if they had ever had a relationship, but when she whispered her query to Jeremy, he giggled into his napkin, replying, 'He would never come out of the closet, Sally. Do you remember when we were at the British Drama League? He went on and on about the wife, even though he was desperate to get into my knickers, I now realize.'

'I am so naïve,' sighed Sally. She watched Rupert talking to Peter Stone about films in the pipeline, and casting opportunities, and could see how well he played the game. He was flirting with Giles and Jeremy, and at the same time being the serious Young Pretender to the throne. Everybody put on a face – except her! Once supper was done, Sally was more than ready to leave, glad of the excuse of two shows tomorrow as it was Saturday, and tomorrow night was her last performance.

She thanked Giles for the lovely dinner and the opportunity

to see James again. Made her farewell to Peter, who gave her his card and said, 'Ring me and make an appointment when you are back in Town and we can see what's on offer.' Well, at least she had not been a complete failure. She gave Jeremy a big kiss and said goodbye. Thank God Giles had ordered her a taxi, and she was able to sit back on the short journey home and try to assess the night. She started to fall asleep and decided to leave it all for the morning. Too much to cope with now.

She was relieved to find Dora in bed asleep, as she had wondered whether her sister would wake up and give her a grilling about the night. Needless to say, Dora had begged Sally to ask if she could come to the supper as well to meet Peter Stone, but Sally had refused point blank.

'You will just have to wait your turn. I am sure it will come soon enough. Isn't that casting woman coming to watch you next week?' she had asked.

'Well yes, but that is not the same as a top London agent, is it?' Dora sulked. 'Anyway, I get the message.'

Sally woke early on Saturday. She got up and made a cup of tea then sat in the kitchen trying to sort out her thoughts. She found the card Peter Stone had given her and turned it over and over in her hand. She would go and see him, she decided, as soon as she finished here. She needed an agent, that was for sure, because she was not capable of doing all the chat-up stuff. Yet she just had a gut feeling that Peter Stone found her a little dull for his style of agency, and maybe Dora would be more to his liking. She got up to go and get ready, leaving the card on the table.

When she arrived at the theatre, she found a huge bunch of flowers at the stage door.

'Here, you must have a secret admirer, love,' grinned

Gladys. 'I can't find a note anywhere.' It was accepted by everyone in the theatre that there were no secrets from her, at least not anything that could be pried open to divulge a name. It was all fair game to Our Lady of the Door.

'Oh wow! How lovely. I will have another look and let you know,' said Sally with a wink. She also had several cards in her pigeonhole which was a new experience for our budding actress. She loved opening them. They were all so different and always kind. She made sure she responded wherever there was an address, and sent one of the little postcard-sized photos she had had printed before she left home. It was her mother who had suggested she do them.

'Oh, Mum, don't be daft!' she had retorted. 'Who is going to want a picture of me?'

'Your fans, you stupid girl. You wait and see, they will be thronging round that stage door like bees to a honey pot.'

Well, that hadn't quite happened, but Patricia had been right about the fan letters and Sally was very glad she had taken her mother's advice. The thought of her mother suddenly made her very homesick. Unfortunately, her parents had not been able to come this week as Dad could not get the time off from school, and Mum was nervous about coming up on her own. It was a big blow, but Sally had stuffed her disappointment to the back of her mind and got on with the job. There would be other times. In fact, it now looked like they would come up to watch the Christmas show, *Wind in the Willows*, because both Sally and Dora had lovely parts. Sally had been cast as the water rat and Dora was the gaoler's sexy daughter. So the plan was for her parents to come to the last show on Christmas Eve which finished early so they could drive home and be back for Midnight Mass, followed by champagne and hot mince pies; then a bit of a sleep-in, before indulging in a perfect family Christmas Day. Jeremy was going to pick them up on the motorway somewhere very early on Boxing Day morning so they would be back for the two o'clock matinée. God forbid anything went wrong, as most of the leading players would be in the car. Short and sweet though the holiday might be, it was worth every wink of sleep lost to Sally, who could not conceive of Christmas anywhere else on earth. She was also secretly hoping that she might be able to see Mack. He had rung her to wish her luck, explaining that he would be away until Christmas, but would make sure they met at some point during the holiday. Her Christmas reverie was interrupted by Jeremy, who was in early, as usual.

'Good night last night, wasn't it?' he said. 'That Peter Stone seems to have his finger on the pulse. And guess what? Giles has invited me and Eddie to have dinner with him tonight in Manchester, so I will be off for another night of debauchery.'

'Not with Giles, surely?' asked Sally. 'He wouldn't let himself be that vulnerable to a cast member, would be?'

'Well, he already has to a certain extent, because we have seen him several times in the club with His Lordship and Robert.' He stopped short. 'Oops, I have just committed a huge boo boo! Sally, you must swear on your life not to tell anyone. Please swear. It is the best-kept secret in the gay world that Lord Graham and Giles Longfellow are a couple.'

Sally was completely dumbstruck. 'I can't believe it,' she whispered. 'But what about his wife, Tanya, and his daughter? What about Eddie? Oh my Lord, Jeremy, does his father know his son is gay? What happens to the Graham line if Eddie is the only son and heir? Difficult to continue if you are gay.'

It was something that Jeremy and Eddie tried not to think about too often.

'Will he get married and have an heir and a spare like his

father has done, do you think?' she continued. The complications were growing by the minute. 'Would he have to give you up for the time being?'

Jeremy sighed and ran his fingers through his hair. 'I just don't know, Sal. It is my worst nightmare. Let's face it, the aristocracy have their own rules. It is a bit like the mafia. They have the money and the power. Eddie may well be forced to make decisions against his will, and you can bet your bottom dollar I will be out of the picture.'

'So why do you think Giles wants to see you this weekend?' asked Sally.

'Probably to warn me off, I don't know. Maybe he is going to talk to Lord Graham – who can tell? It is a bit scary, I admit, and I haven't been able to get hold of Eddie since yesterday to see if he knows anything. In fact, I am going to the pub now to use their telephone. Gladys does not need to know about this conversation. I am hoping to catch Eddie at lunch. I'll see you later.' He kissed her on the top of her head and left.

What a tangled web we weave, thought Sally.

She made her way up to Wardrobe to search out Janie. They had decided to give a party tonight by way of saying goodbye to Rupert and 'well done' to Sally. It was going to be hard for Sally but she was prepared – had been all along in a way. Through this week she had wondered if there was a smidgeon of hope that she might be in with a chance, as ever since their moment in the wings when Rupert had put his arms around her, she had felt a frisson between them. Maybe tonight she would ply him with drink and seduce him. The problem was, she would have to have had a few drinks herself to find the courage!

After the show tonight Pete and the boys planned to go back to her flat and get everything ready for the party. Sally had made a big shepherd's pie, and there were lots of nibbles, and they had all clubbed together for the booze, but the champagne that Sally had bought was going to be the surprise. Janie had also hinted that she had a surprise too, so it was going to be fun.

The matinée was full of schoolchildren, which was always hard work, because they would chatter all the way through the play, and whoop and holler at any suggested sexual innuendo. Sometimes the actors just longed to go to the front of the stage and yell 'SHUTUP!' But this company had mostly been very good about their behaviour, although the skeleton of Yorick was sometimes written on, and displayed to the rest of the cast onstage by Rupert turning his back on the audience. The first time he did it, Pete and Simon giggled so much they both jumped into the grave and stayed there until they could control themselves. The Ghost, while waiting in the wings one day, had decided to lift his gown and flash his parts at Charmaine, who was just about to go onstage. She was so shocked she practically leaped ten feet in the air and landed with a bump on the stage. There had been strict instructions from Giles that there were to be no dirty tricks on the last night as it was very unprofessional, and the audience tonight had paid their money like everyone else and deserved a good show.

Well, we will see, thought Sally nervously.

Sally spent the time between the shows packing up. She would be out of this dressing room and back up with the girls next week. She wondered if Dora would be in here as she was headlining in the music hall. They were certainly chasing each other. Maybe they would share a dressing room for *Wind in the Willows*, although the role of the rat was considerably bigger than the washerwoman's daughter, so it would seem fair Sally got the dressing room to herself. Oh stop it, you silly cow, you are turning into a right old diva. This is Crewe Repertory Theatre, not the Haymarket.

'Beginners Act One, please,' came the call. Everybody involved in the play came down to the stage and had a group cuddle. It was such a lovely moment, and the kind of thing that only happened in the theatre – real company spirit. Sally went to her usual corner to catch the beginning of the play and Rupert came to give her his customary hug.

'Mmmm, you feel better than ever tonight, Miss Thomas. The vibes are positively jumping.' He kissed her ear, and Sally had to hold herself together so as not to melt in his arms. It must be all the adrenalin coursing through her body that created this sensual thrill. *Use it well, Sally, make it work for you onstage.*

She turned round and embraced Rupert, clinging to him so he would remember her through her thin silk dress. 'Good luck. It has been an amazing experience for me, I will never forget this moment.' She kissed him gently on the lips and then pulled away. 'Off you go – the curtain is rising!'

The performance went like clockwork. Everybody upped their game. The only mishap was that having never injured each other in the duelling scene, Rupert nicked Jeremy on the neck. There was real blood! Although it looked very dramatic from the wings, and poor Heather was trying to get first aid organized *and* stay on the book, disaster was averted as Jeremy pulled a silk hankie from his pocket and used it to good effect to stop the blood. Thank God for the hankie. Later that night, a toast was proposed to the indomitable Gwendoline, who had a policy of always secreting hankies on her actors for just such emergencies.

As soon as the curtain came down, the boys were off to set

up the shindig. The crew were in, already tearing down the walls of Elsinor. It was an easy get out tonight as there was no real set to erect for the Victorian Music Hall. So they had high hopes of making the party before all the food and drink had gone, which is what usually happened, though Sally and Janie had made a pact to hold some back for the workers.

It took Sally a bit longer than usual tonight to get ready. She had a shower and reapplied her make-up, because she wanted to look her best. She had saved a new dress for tonight and even managed to hide it from Dora. It was a little low at the front, and Sally was not sure about flashing her cleavage – but it was now or never! She waited for Janie and Gwendoline to finish putting the washing in, so they could walk up the hill together.

'Where's Geoffrey? Isn't he going to escort us ladies then?' enquired Sally as she appeared at the door. Gwendoline managed a tight smile and replied, 'He has escorted his opposite number, the Queen of Denmark, to the party. Felt he couldn't leave her to walk on her own. So come on, girls, let's give it all we've got.'

Chapter 43

The party was in full swing when they got back to the flat. The music was very loud, and could be heard halfway down the street, but everyone reckoned that for one night only, Crewe and their downstairs neighbours would have to put up with it. Sally put her shepherd's pie in the oven to warm up, with mountains of garlic bread to sop up the drink later. She dropped her stuff in her bedroom and then went to find Rupert. She should have known he would be pinned in a corner by her dear sister. Where Sally had gone for cleavage, Dora had gone for a plunging backless dress. She looked stunning, and Sally's heart sank. *Here we go again. I can't compete with that.* She went to the kitchen to get a drink and Janie caught her grim expression.

'Not fed up already, surely?' she commented.

'Oh no, just feeling inadequate as usual. Darling Dora has set her sights on Rupert tonight – she obviously has intentions of giving him a good send-off.'

Janie came and gave Sally a hug. 'Listen to me. You have a bond with Rupert, you always have, and that counts for a lot.

I don't know if it can go anywhere – let's face it, a week ago he was wildly in love with Isabelle – but don't let Dora muscle in on your night, and it *is* your night, Sally. You have been a triumph in every way on this production, and saved a lot of people's arses. You go for it and enjoy. You look gorgeous. Now please find my errant boyfriend, and tell him I need him for five minutes.'

Sally did as she was told and sent Pete to the kitchen. She then made her way to the corner.

'Hi, guys! Wow, Dora, you look amazing. That dress is almost finished,' she quipped.

'Yes, very funny, sister dear. But I could say the same about yours,' Dora threw back.

'Now, girls, please no scrapping. This evening is all about feeling the "lurve" in the room.' Rupert was laughing at them.

'Can I get you another drink?' suggested Dora.

'Or would you like some of my homemade shepherd's pie? You must be starving,' ventured Sally.

Rupert raised his hands in surrender. 'I give in! Both, please.'

Sally and Dora exchanged murderous looks and went off to the kitchen. Rupert meanwhile went in search of male support and found Geoffrey and Jeremy in deep conversation about the play.

'Oh, we will miss you, Rupert,' said Geoffrey, 'even though the competition has been gruelling, hasn't it, Jeremy?'

'Indeed it has – from both sides of the fence,' teased Jeremy. 'You had the pick of the bunch.'

'Oh don't,' groaned Rupert. 'Sally and Dora have been on the attack already. I am beginning to wonder if this would be my chance to have a random night with two sisters. What do you reckon?'

'Oh, too much information!' chorused the other two. 'We will await the results, like two sad old farts.'

'Actually, I must say my farewells, Rupert, as I am off to Manchester tonight,' Jeremy told him. 'So good luck, mate, and I hope we meet again very soon. Maybe even in the West End, fingers crossed.'

'Absolutely – wouldn't that be great? We could knife each other to pieces every night!'

Jeremy went to find Sally and accosted her on the way to the kitchen. 'Hey, Sal. Sorry I have to go so early, but Eddie is picking me up in five minutes. Have a great night and see you Monday morning. Love you.' He gave her a kiss and loped off.

Peggy and Percy were tucking into the shepherd's pie at the kitchen table when Sally came in to get her share for Rupert.

'This is spot on, girl,' mumbled Percy through a large mouthful. 'You're not only a lovely actress, but a consummate cook. You'd better watch out, Peggy, you have got competition.'

'Yes, dear – in your dreams. Well done, Sally, it is lovely. Come over here, I want to ask you something.' She beckoned to Sally, who crossed the kitchen and knelt down at Peggy's side.

'What's up?' she asked.

'Have you see that Sarah tonight anywhere?' Peggy whispered.

'No – come to think of it, I haven't. Did she say she couldn't come?'

'No, but I tell you what, she is up to something. Every Saturday night I notice she is gone a bit quick, and I just wondered where she goes. You mark my words, there is something going on.'

Sally filled her plate and went in search of her man. Rupert was surrounded by the boys and they seemed to be having such a wonderful time she felt a smidgen of guilt at breaking it up, but once the boys saw the grub they were off!

'Well, you certainly know how to clear a room,' laughed Rupert. 'Ooh yummy, is this for me? Sally, you have been so outstanding on everything to do with this job. I really couldn't have coped without you. I hope we can stay in touch. Do you think Giles might ask you to understudy in the West End? Wouldn't that be great? Maybe I should mention it to him.'

'Well, it is a kind thought,' agreed Sally, 'though it would be great to have a real part in something next. Who knows?' She knocked back her drink, and decided now was the time for the champagne before everyone was too plastered to enjoy it. 'Will you excuse me a minute, I have a hostess job to perform,' she said and reluctantly turned away to see Dora bearing down on him with a bottle of champagne, no less, tucked under her arm.

'Um, just a minute, my girl. That belongs to me and is going to be opened when *I* say the word and not before. So give it here and go and find some other form of alcohol with which to seduce your prey.'

'My word, aren't we the Diva tonight? Here, take your miserable champagne. I don't need any help to seduce a man.' Dora sashayed across the room and joined Rupert and the boys, who had returned with their spoils.

Well, that should keep her out of trouble till I return, thought Sally.

When Sally got back to the kitchen she was greeted by the sight of Janie and Gwendoline laying out an incredibly beautiful cake onto a plate.

'Oh my goodness, where did *that* come from?'

'Oh no! You were not supposed to come in here until we

were ready to present this to you and Rupert. Janie made it and I supplied the ingredients,' said Gwendoline.

'Oh, girls, what a wonderful idea. And it's great timing, because I was just about to open the champagne I have bought as my surprise. So we can have cake and champagne to finish off the evening with a bit of class.'

Sally got all the glasses laid out on the side while the girls finished arranging the cake.

'Shall we carry the cake in last?' said Gwendoline.

'Absolutely,' nodded Sally, 'and I will now go and give everyone a glass of champagne and prepare them for your entrance.'

She managed to get everyone next door to be quiet, and not sip the champagne until she had said her few words, but first she went to the kitchen door and announced, 'Ladies and gentlemen! Pray silence for that talented duo in the wardrobe department, with yet another side to their talent. Let them eat cake!'

The girls entered to wild cheers, and applause at the sight of this huge cake. On top they had written:

To Rupert and Sally
What a pair!
With love from the cast and crew, November 1982

'Would Rupert and Sally please like to come and cut the cake,' said Janie, producing two big knives, one for each of them.

Rupert spoke first, saying, 'I never imagined it was going to be as good as this. All the ups and downs – and that was just my sex-life! No, seriously, we have had our problems, but you have all been so supportive to me and I hope we all meet again one day in the future. But can I say a special thank you to Sally here. She has been my rock.' Rupert leaned over and gave Sally a big smacker on the lips as everyone cheered with delight. Perhaps Dora less so!

Sally responded with a short and sweet: 'Thank you so much, everyone. I am completely overwhelmed. No job will ever compete with this. Thank you.' She swallowed hard, and raised her glass of champagne to the room. 'Cheers, everyone, and good luck always!'

The toast resounded around the room, and then in a flash all was back to normal and the business of eating and drinking was resumed.

'Let's hope once the champagne dries up they will start to leave,' said Sally, who was feeling a little tipsy.

'Oh, don't worry, they will go soon enough, but you and I have some serious drinking to do,' Rupert said. 'I have never seen you drunk. It could be quite a surprise, a bit like your lack of underwear in your Ophelia costume. That was so arousing – but you already know that, don't you?' He held her gaze.

Sally did not look away but murmured, 'Yes, it was very exciting – one of those rare unexpected moments. I love them, and I love to be surprised.' She turned away to give someone a piece of cake.

Rupert slipped his arm around her and drew her to him, whispering, 'Perhaps I can surprise you again tonight?' It took all of Sally's self-control not to let out a whoop of delight right there. Instead she looked him straight in the eye and whispered back, 'Show me.' And then she walked away, hoping Rupert could not see how her legs were trembling. The next half an hour seemed like an eternity, but eventually everyone was gone except Sally and Rupert and Dora. Oh yes, Sally had forgotten about Dora!

'This is cosy,' the girl said, opening the last bottle of champagne – the one Sally had been saving to take to bed with Rupert.

'Where did you find that bottle, Dora?' she asked carefully.

'In your bedroom, for some reason in an ice-bucket ready to go.'

There was a deafening silence. Then Rupert spoke very quietly, but steadily. He said, 'Ah yes, Dora, you have caught me out. I was going to spend some time drinking that with Sally tonight before we say our goodbyes. We have been through a great deal, as you know. So no offence to you, but we will say good night now and go in the other room, if you don't mind.'

Dora was dumbstruck, probably for the first time in her life. She had nowhere to go with this. So she stood up and put the bottle down on the table, but kept her own glass in her hand.

'Good night then. I am sure you won't begrudge me this one glass. I raise it to you both, and wish you health, wealth and happiness.'

And with that she went to her room without a murmur.

Sally turned and looked at Rupert. 'I can't believe you did that,' she breathed.

'Needs must sometimes. Now come on, take me to your room so we can have that talk, or whatever ...' There was a very naughty twinkle in his eye, or so Sally hoped, because quite frankly she was two sheets to the wind and her own eyesight was blurred. She hoped Rupert's sight might be similarly incapacitated for the rest of the evening, should she have to take her clothes off. But stop! She was getting above her station.

They adjourned to the bedroom with the bottle. Rupert placed it by the side of the bed and proceeded to take his clothes off.

Sally was taken aback. 'What are you doing?' she asked rather foolishly.

'Isn't it obvious? I hardly think lying in your bed in my brown boots and Levis is very suitable.' He had stripped to his pants, and then pulled back the sheets and got into bed.

'Come on then, chop chop, we haven't got all night. Well, we have – but I have no doubt that at some point you will fall asleep on me.'

Sally was now completely thrown. She had never undressed in front of anyone before. All her drunken sessions had been with as little light as possible, and as many clothes on as she could reasonably get away with. This was a nightmare. She sat on the edge of the bed and turned on the lamp her side of the bed.

She had pulled off her dress before she realized she would have to go and turn off the main light, thus exposing her fat stomach and unattractive tights. But at least the tights kept the fat on her legs enclosed and gave them a nice smooth shine. So she was going to have to make a dash for the switch and hope he wasn't looking. Fat chance of that: he was sitting up sipping his champagne waiting for the floorshow!

Oh well, here goes nothing, she thought. She had a gorgeous bra on at least, which she had had to go and buy to complement the low dress and get a good cleavage. Janie had chosen it, otherwise she would have been in her usual Marks & Spencer white matching sensible underwear. It was a black lace half-cup bra and she wore a matching black lace thong, which had been annoying her all night, because it was right up her bum! She tried to walk with her stomach turned away from the bed, which gave her a strange look of a lost spider! When she got to the light-switch she lifted her arms above her head in a kind of mock stretch, which gave her the opportunity to breathe in deeply, and hold her stomach in for the final moment in the light. Then, thank God, the light was off and there was only the rosy glow from her little bedside light. She managed to hold her breath all the way back to the bed, where she slipped niftily between the sheets.

'Well, they weren't exactly the most seductive moves I have seen in a bedroom, Sally,' came Rupert's voice, 'but I guess you have yet to perfect them for professional purposes.'

'What do you mean by that!' she exclaimed, stung. 'You think I do this all the time? How dare you suggest I am a slapper – like some girls you know,' she said pointedly, then regretted it.

'No,' Rupert said calmly, 'I mean when you have to do love scenes on camera, you twit. It is horrible, believe me, Sal. You feel such an arse in front of the crew, and everyone is scrutinizing your bits, et cetera. It's a nightmare. So all I am saying is you should practise a bit more and have your moves ready.'

'Sorry, I didn't understand what you were driving at, but I can assure you, Rupert, I will not be asked to do those sorts of scenes. I am just not pretty enough. I know my limitations. I am a character actress – I will always be the fat friend, or the mixed-up one who is useless. Honestly, I don't mind. As long as I can play good parts in prestige productions I will be happy. Give me some champagne, you greedy pig, you have already drunk half the bottle. It was me who was supposed to show you I can get drunk.' She grabbed the bottle, poured herself a glass and threw it back, then poured another.

Rupert was leaning on one elbow watching her with a smile on his face. 'You are such good value, Sally, do you know that? I love being with you, it makes me smile all the time. Isabelle was hard work and I am supposed to be in love with her.'

Sally sighed inwardly. Oh god, I knew *she* would have to come up eventually, but how am I going to get rid of her from the conversation.

'Don't you think, maybe, it was more lust than love? I mean, she is a gorgeous girl and everything, but she is so self-obsessed, Rupert – how could she love anyone back? And all the anorexia and bulimia and the drugs; it is not good for her certainly, nor you. You don't need that kind of image just as you are about to crack it big on the West End stage. You need a nice calming influence – like me.'

Sally couldn't believe she had just come out with that statement, and was about to take it back when Rupert leaned over and kissed her. She waited for him to draw away again, but he didn't. Instead he moved over to her and slowly began to explore her with his tongue. It was bliss. Sally loved kissing and was always disappointed when boys used to stop as quickly as they could, in order to get to the next part of the proceedings, which was usually to grab a breast. Not so young Rupert. They seemed to kiss for hours, only coming up now and then for air. But suddenly everything changed, for both of them. Sally could feel her need growing inside her. All the doubts and hurts and worries were disappearing, and leaving in their place a hunger. A huge desire to feel another human being. To touch skin and taste salty kisses and burn from his touch. Rupert had slipped on top of her and seemed to have discarded his pants on the way.

'What about precautions?' she managed to mumble through the kisses.

'Taken care of,' Rupert's voice was low and urgent. 'Sally, you are a beautiful person.' He gently found her g-string and removed it, and then unclasped her expensive lacy bra with one deft flick of his fingers. But he did not clutch at her boobs, he just kissed her all over, exploring her body. Sally was shy at first because she did not want him to be disappointed. Isabelle she most certainly was not! But whether it was down to the champagne, or Rupert's power of seduction, slowly she opened up to him. She wanted to explore his body, was hungry for more.

'Hey, take it easy,' he panted, 'we have got all night, you know. I want to savour this. Miss Sally Thomas, a tiger in bed.'

'Stop, Rupert, you are embarrassing me now. Please let's just do it!'

'What a quaint turn of phrase for the excellent lovemaking I had in mind. Do it! Sally Thomas, just lie back and enjoy, you deserve it . . .'

Chapter 44

'You will both have to have blood tests.' Giles sat back from the table in a private sitting room of the Queen's Hotel and watched the two young lovers try to absorb the devastating information he had just imparted to them. There was no other way of doing this except with the brutal and honest truth. All of them, including himself, were in mortal danger. He had discussed it endlessly with Teddie, who had gone off to London immediately to see his private doctor. But this was not something that could be cured with money.

'So is Robert going to die?' whispered Eddie.

'I am afraid he is very close to the end, and I was going to suggest you both went to visit him to say goodbye. I will pay the train fares for you. You could go down tomorrow and come back Monday morning. Do you have anywhere you can stay tomorrow night? If not, I will pay for a B&B – there are plenty in the vicinity of the station. Now, is there anything you want to ask me?' Giles was acutely aware that Eddie was going to have to talk to his father, and God knows how Teddie Graham was going to deal with the fact that his only son and heir was gay; or indeed, that his own secret life was now threatened with exposure.

'Are we going to die?' Jeremy was holding himself ramrod straight, and his face was white and pinched. He let out a little moan and then covered his mouth with his hand. 'Oh God, what am I going to tell my parents!'

'I suggest you say nothing to anyone at this juncture,' advised Giles. 'First things first. You will go and have blood tests on Monday morning, and then once we have the results we will know better what we have to do. I am so sorry, boys. It is the most frightening and threatening thing to happen to any of us. Everyone in the gay community is going to have to stick together and beat this.'

He got up from the table and bade them both good night. It was already the early hours of Sunday morning and the boys were exhausted.

'Come on, Eddie, let's go to bed and try to get some sleep,' Jeremy said. 'I will look up the trains for tomorrow.'

They passed the bar on the way to their room, and heard all the laughter and screams of delight that accompanied a Saturday night at the Queen's Hotel. How different was life going to be for so many people if this terrible disease got a grip?

They undressed and prepared for bed in silence. Once under the covers they lay side by side, each with his own thoughts racing through his head. Then very softly Eddie began to cry, just sniffles at first as he brushed away a tear, but then he could not hold in the sobs that racked his body. Jeremy took him in his arms and rocked him gently, ignoring his own tears, wet on his cheek.

'Shush now. Come on, Eddie, all is not lost. We may be OK. Come on, be strong. We will fight this together. Please don't cry, my love.' Jeremy held his lover until finally Eddie fell asleep. Jeremy turned over and tried to fall asleep himself, but his mother's face was right there in front of him; her warm, lovely smile reassuring him when he was frightened, or insecure as a child.

'It is all right, Jeremy dear. You will be fine. Mummy loves you very much. You are a very good boy.'

The boys found themselves a room in a B&B near Euston the next evening. It was not the most salubrious of areas, but this particular establishment was down a side street up near Camden Town in a shabby Georgian terraced house. The room was clean and the landlady a very jolly lady, born and bred locally.

'Just make sure you have no visitors. All right, darlings?' She wagged her finger at them. 'There are plenty of "ladies" out there willing to oblige you with a bit of fun, but they do not belong in my house. Do you understand?' She stood in front of them with her hands on her hips waiting for their response. It would have been funny if things had been different, thought Jeremy. He smiled at her and promised.

'Oh absolutely. We have no intention of bringing anyone back. We just needed a place to sleep tonight before we get the train back to Crewe tomorrow morning.'

They had arranged to go and visit Robert that evening. Neither of them could talk about it or what they were going to do or say. Jeremy had so many questions for Eddie, as he had had no idea that Robert and Eddie had once had an affair. Or was it just a one-night stand? How many others were there? But he could not bear to open that can of worms just yet. There was too much at stake. For now they were simply doing what Giles told them.

They had been given the number of a new organization

called the Terence Higgins Trust, which offered advice to anyone who needed it regarding the disease.

'Let's see Robert first and then we can ring them and ask questions,' said Jeremy.

'I hate hospitals,' muttered Eddie as they made their way through Reception on the ward at St Thomas'. It was not a good place to be, Jeremy had to agree. The neon lighting was harsh against the dark windows and outside, a cold damp December evening was pressing up against the glass. The nurse showed them to a side room on a ward.

At first, Jeremy thought the bed was empty as there was no sign of a body under the covers, but as he moved further into the room and round the corner of the end of the bed, he gasped, and pulled back. Robert's head was just visible above the sheet but it was more like a skull. The skin was stretched so thinly across the cheekbones and the eyes were sunken, lost under the brow, like two black stones at the mouth of a cave.

Jeremy had to use every ounce of strength to pull himself together.

'Hi, Robert.' He tried to smile. 'We have come to say hello, and to wish you better. I am so sorry this has happened.'

Robert opened his mouth and tried to speak but there was nothing. He then pushed the covers down and struggled to lift his arm.

'What do you want?' asked Jeremy. 'Water? Hang on, I will get it for you.' He went to the cabinet at the side of the bed and found a beaker with a spout. He leaned in to Robert and tried to place the spout in his mouth. He felt so clumsy and was terrified he would break Robert's arm trying to sit him up, as it was as thin as a twig, and covered in sores. He could feel the revulsion in himself, then the fear that he would, somehow, be infected. He pulled back and said, 'Shall I get the nurse? Sorry, I am being useless, aren't I?'

Robert shook his head, and a ghost of a smile brushed his lips. He looked past Jeremy to Eddie, who was transfixed. He could not move from the end of the bed.

'Robert . . . I am so sorry. I . . . Sorry, I can't cope with this, I . . .' Eddie turned and fled from the room.

Taking a deep breath, Jeremy took Robert's hand in his and squeezed very gently.

'Take care, lots of love.' He could feel Robert trying to squeeze his hand back, but the tiny, bony sticks that were his fingers just lay inert. It was like touching a skeleton, and Jeremy had to grit his teeth to stop a scream pushing its way up from the pit of his stomach. This was his worst nightmare. He managed to extricate his hand and step back. Every fibre of his being was pulling him towards the door. He just wanted to follow Eddie and run. Run for his life, literally.

'Goodbye, Robert,' was all he could murmur, and he slowly moved backwards towards the door, keeping his eyes on the man in the bed until the very last moment, when he turned and staggered from the room. Eddie was nowhere to be seen so Jeremy went to the exit, hoping to find him on the way. He discovered Eddie outside, sitting on a wall, hugging himself for warmth.

'I am so sorry, but I just couldn't take it, J,' he said hoarsely. 'He was like a skeleton, there was nothing left of him. Oh my God, what a horrible way to die. It's like he just disintegrated. Fuck this!' He stood up and paced in circles.

'Come on,' said Jeremy. 'Let's get out of here. We need to eat.'

They found a little trattoria and had a plate of pasta and a carafe of red wine.

'So tell me about you and Robert. When did that happen? Before me or after me?' Jeremy was determined to keep calm and objective, although his heart was pounding. What other secrets had Eddie been keeping from him?

Eddie did not answer straight away but sat very still staring at Jeremy. Finally he said, 'I love you, Jeremy, I really do. You are the first person I have ever felt really close to in my life. But I love sex. I love the excitement of pulling someone. That first kiss. I can't help myself, and it is going to destroy everything for me in the end. Robert was just a fling. He was at the Queen's one night with a whole load of faggots, and they were all such fun and there was lots of champagne flowing and we had an incredible night. It is what I love, Jeremy, and I have basically been doing it for the last three years. I am not proud of who I am or what I am becoming, and my love for you has made me realize it is not the way to live my life. So now I am going to reap the terrible rewards of my actions, aren't I? I am probably going to die a horrible death like Robert.' He took a sip of wine to stop himself from bursting into tears.

Jeremy pushed his plate away. He felt sick. Sick and incredibly hurt and shaken. How could he have not seen what Eddie was like? He had had his suspicions when Eddie had first taken him to the Queen's and everybody seemed to know him. But this was a whole different person talking now in front of him. The boy was in a different league. Jeremy had thought theirs was a romance. A love story. The two of them finding each other and building a life together. But how could that ever happen if Eddie needed these 'diversions'? It was never going to happen now anyway, because they could both be infected with this deadly virus.

'I cannot understand how you can say you love me and then go and have an orgy with other men. Sorry, Eddie, I am obviously not in your world. I am disgusted. I feel betrayed and demeaned and very foolish. How naïve am I? You must have had a laugh about good old Jeremy coming out of the closet.'

'Stop it, J! Please, I love you. I know I am a mess but I can change. I *want* to change – that is the most important thing. If you are there for me, I can do anything. Please, Jeremy, don't abandon me now,' he implored.

Jeremy could not deal with any of it; he was just lost. He called for the bill and they went back to the digs. Jeremy lay on top of his single bed and tried to put his thoughts in order. Eddie lay beside him on the other bed, waiting.

'Look, I am sorry, Eddie, but I don't know what to think at the moment,' he said in the end. 'Let's just get through the next twenty-four hours and then we can see where all this is going. It's a fucking nightmare at the moment, that's for sure. Good night.' Then he turned off the light and lay in the London night feeling as though he was hurtling down a ravine into nothing but blackness.

Chapter 45

Sally woke with a start and lay still, listening in the dark for a few seconds before she dared move, or dared to remember last night. Had it really happened? Suddenly the bed shook as something heavy beside her moaned softly and then settled down once again. Sally turned over as slowly as she could so as not to disturb the covers, and came face to face with the sleeping Rupert. Her heart did a somersault and she had to stop herself from planting a kiss right there on his luscious lips.

Then the panic set in. What must she look like? Last night's make-up streaked the pillow and she could smell her own stale breath. This was not how she wanted Rupert to see her when he opened his eyes.

She slid from the bed and tiptoed round the bedroom collecting her dirty washing, and then opened her chest of drawers very carefully and retrieved her one pretty nightdress. She slipped through the bedroom door, closing it silently behind her, and set up camp in the bathroom. It was still early so she had time to make herself look presentable before Rupert or Dora surfaced. She had a lovely scented bath, washed her hair and lavished half a pot of Dora's body lotion over herself. She even put some mascara on as her eyes were looking decidedly piggy this morning. When she felt presentable, she went into the living room, tidied up a bit and washed up last night's debris, by which time she was wide awake and starving. However, she didn't want to start breakfast without Rupert. Yes, Rupert – right. She crept back into the bedroom to find him quietly snoring in blissful ignorance of the world around him. Sally climbed back into bed and moved as close as she dared so that when he did awake, she would be in grabbing distance. She lay there for ages and finally dozed off herself, to be suddenly awoken by a yelp as Rupert jumped out of bed.

'Oh shit – what time is it?' he said, looking round the room and trying to understand where he was. 'Sally, are you awake? Listen, what time is it? I have to get the train to London this morning, and I have probably missed the only direct one there is!' He was pulling his jeans on and searching for his socks and shoes. Sally scrambled from the bed feeling her world beginning to crumble.

'But you never said anything last night. You never said you were leaving today. What about all your packing and everything?' Sally stood in front of Rupert and took his arm to keep him still. 'Why didn't you tell me?' Her eyes were bright with tears.

Rupert stopped and looked at the girl in front of him in her crisp white nightie, and light dawned.

'Sally, I am so sorry – it never occurred to me. I have been packing all week and I have got a mate at the Manchester Library Theatre who was driving down this weekend to take a load of my stuff for me, so now I just have a couple of cases. The thing is, I wasn't expecting to be here – you know, this morning. So I need to get back to my flat and pick up my stuff, and leave the keys, et cetera.' He looked again at Sally's face and realized he had made a huge mistake. Completely misread the situation. He took Sally's hand and led her to the bed, and they sat down on the edge.

'Sweetheart, I had a fantastic time last night, it was a hoot. You are my best mate and I know we will be friends forever, but I hope you feel the same, and that you didn't think there was anything else ... well, anything stronger. I mean, last night was great but maybe we shouldn't have confused the issue – you know ...'

Sally was hardly listening to him. There was just a loud buzzing in her head. Why didn't he just go? She hated him, hated herself for being so stupid. God, she must look ridiculous sitting here in her fucking virginal white nightie! She wanted to scream and kick and punch him, and everyone! *Just leave me alone*, she wanted to shout, but she only managed to stammer, 'Don't be daft, of course I understand. It was great fun. Thanks. But you must go. I think you will be OK for the train if you hurry. Do you want to ring for a taxi? I can do it.' Sally went and dialled for a cab and managed to pull herself together. She put the kettle on and filled mugs with coffee.

Rupert joined her in the kitchen.

'Five minutes for the cab. Here, have a sip of coffee while you're waiting.' Sally wandered into the lounge and plumped a few cushions and generally made sure there was a huge space between her and Rupert.

'Sally, I do hope we will keep in touch. You've got my number, and hopefully you might consider understudying in the play? It would be great to have you in the company.' Rupert waffled on until he was saved by the doorbell. 'Ah, that will be the taxi. Well, goodbye for now, Sally, and thank you again for last night.'

He advanced towards her and Sally felt herself go as stiff as a board. She practically pushed him away from her, saying as brightly as she could, 'Yes, it has been a wonderful experience all round. Thanks, Rupert, and good luck.' She turned to open the front door, and as he passed her Rupert leaned in and gave her a kiss on the lips.

'Maybe another time, another place?' And he was gone.

Sally turned and ran to the toilet, where she threw up. She sat there on the bathroom lino for a long time, sobbing into the roll of toilet paper. If only I could throw up my heart and start again, she thought to herself. It can't get much lower than this. How did I get it so wrong?

Chapter 46

'Good morning, everybody. It's another Monday, and another opening of another show. I hope you are all well rested and ready to raise the roof with our Victorian Music Hall delights!'

'Blimey, whatever she's on, I want some,' whispered Simon to Pete as they swigged their habitual post-weekend Lucozade.

Sarah continued with obvious delight, revelling in her new-found role as director.

'There is an air of the Butlin's Redcoat about her though,' commented Charmaine, none too kindly.

'I have been asked by Giles to mention a couple of things this morning. Sadly, Robert will no longer be with us for the rest of the season due to ill-health. We will be sending him some flowers from the company, and Heather will be coming round with a card for you all to sign. We wish him well. Secondly, Giles will be commuting between London and Crewe a good deal, finalizing the plans for the production of *Hamlet* in the West End. He apologizes profusely, but what with the run-up to Christmas, and losing Robert as his assistant, he is very pressed for time. However, I will be stepping in wherever possible, so if you have any queries, please feel free to ask me. Finally, I have the casting for *Wind in the Willows* which I will pin on the noticeboard. So now, down to business. There will be a vocal warm-up with Tim, and then we will start the technical dress rehearsal and work through the numbers. Hopefully there will be time for a dress rehearsal tonight, then one tomorrow afternoon as is normal, and then – curtain up! Throughout the day Gwendoline will see you about your costumes, and anything you have offered from your own wardrobe should be given to her today. Thank you! I will be in the Royal Box if anyone wants me.'

Sarah swept off the stage as though she had owned and run the theatre all her life. Sally watched her take her large briefcase and script up to the box, calling to Heather to bring her a coffee.

Sally followed Heather to the props room. 'Blimey, this is a bit of a turn-up, isn't it?' she asked Heather, who was trying to find a clean mug in the sink.

'Bloody Lady Muck,' grumbled Heather. 'It has been a nightmare taking orders from her. She has got Giles wound round her little finger. Mind you, that was not difficult as he is in a terrible state. Have you seen him? I don't know what the matter is, but something is up. He was in Manchester all weekend, only got back this morning, and now he is holed up in his office with Lord Graham. Anyway, Sarah has taken over and that's that. Be interesting to see if she really does know what she's doing. Tim says she is spot on with all the musical stuff, so let's hope so. Now how are you, my little flower? You are looking a bit forlorn this morning.'

Sally really did not want to tell anyone of her humiliation, so she explained away her abject misery as a bit of a cold.

'Well, take care of yourself because we are going to need

every hand on deck this week with all the comings and goings.'

Sally then went to find Jeremy who had seemed very distracted at the company meeting. He was in his dressing room, clearing up as usual after the others.

'God, Jeremy, do you never stop tidying up?' Sally embraced her friend.

'It makes me feel better,' he explained. 'I need to have calm and structure in my surroundings, especially when my life is falling down round my ears.' He crumpled suddenly and sat down with his head in his hands.

'Whatever is the matter?' asked Sally, alarmed, pulling up a chair beside him.

Jeremy began to cry. He was taking in air in great gulps, trying but unable to stem the flood. Sally held him, and passed him a tissue from time to time, but there was nothing else to be done except let the man cry it all out. Finally, Jeremy sat back exhausted. Sally fetched him some water and he drank it gratefully. They rested for a few moments in silence until Jeremy seemed to make a decision and started to speak, his voice thin and shaky.

'Sally, have you by any strange coincidence heard of HIV or AIDS?'

'No, I don't think so. What are they?'

'Basically it is a disease a bit like cancer. It attacks the cells in the body and destroys its immune system. It is relatively new in this country and doctors don't know much about it at this stage, but the trouble is, it is a killer. Once infected, a person will almost surely die.' Jeremy bit back another surge of tears. 'It seems to be transmitted sexually, but they don't know for sure, so everyone is panicking and frightened to touch anyone or share anything. It is horrific, Sally. They think it is spread by gay men, but I have been talking to doctors in London and they are saying this is not true, and people must have all the facts before they accuse people of causing such havoc. But so far it seems to be only gay men who are dying, and ...' He started to weep again.

Sally stopped him, saying, 'Hang on a minute, Jeremy. Please, just slow down. What are you trying to say - that you have caught this virus? And what about Eddie – is he involved in all this? Come on, just take it slowly, and tell me everything.' She held Jeremy's hand and did not let go until he had finished talking her through everything that had happened, including the visit to see Robert.

Sally tried to understand exactly what Jeremy was saying. 'So you have both had a test and it is highly likely that you could develop this virus and die?' Her voice petered out to a whisper.

'They have to monitor us over the next few weeks,' replied Jeremy.

'What about your parents?' ventured Sally. 'Have you talked to them?'

'No, of course not! How can I, Sally? They don't even know I am gay, never mind a potential victim of some fucking killer disease. And can you imagine what it is like for Eddie? If Lord Graham finds out his son is gay, he will go crazy! It is the worst possible mess, and I have no idea what we are going to do.' Jeremy broke down again.

'What are we going to do, Giles?' Edward Graham was sitting opposite Giles Longfellow in his office. Giles was clasping his head in his hands, wishing it would stop thumping.

'I will be ruined!' Teddie went on. 'Never mind dead! Oh Christ Almighty. We are not promiscuous, Giles, so how did this happen?'

The other man groaned. 'How many more times do you want me to have to grovel, Teddie? I had an affair with Robert last year, and I had no idea he was infected. For whatever reason, he didn't see fit to tell me. Please God we are clear. We will know soon enough. Just try and hold yourself together until we know for sure.'

'If Tanya found out I had been having this affair with you, she would divorce me,' said Edward, running all the possible disasters through his head.

'I doubt it,' retorted Giles. 'I think you will find she knows all about you, Teddie, dear boy, and chooses to look the other way. She has no intention of rocking the family boat because of your peccadillos!'

'You may well be right,' sighed Edward. 'But what about the children? Poor Eddie will never forgive me.'

This was the moment Giles had been dreading. He had discussed the matter with Jeremy and Eddie, and they had all decided that it would be Giles who broke the news to Lord Graham of his son's affair with Robert and his subsequent relationship with Jeremy – and where that left them in this horror story.

Giles was often criticized for being a weak man in many respects, but he accepted his responsibility to his friends and loved ones, and in this case his love for Edward Graham overcame any qualms he might have had about facing this head on.

'Teddie, there is no easy way to tell you this. But I want you to know how much I love you and will always be there for you and Eddie. You are going to have to spend a good deal of time with your son over the next few days and weeks, and it is going to hurt you so much I can hardly imagine how you will cope. But you will because you are a strong and loving man. Teddie, my dearest heart, your son is also gay. He is having a relationship with the young actor from our company here called Jeremy – you have met him. Tragically, last year Eddie had a fling with Robert Johnson, so he too is under threat of this insidious disease, as is his lover.' He was stopped by a bloodcurdling cry and groans from Lord Graham. The sounds were primeval. He was like a wounded animal at bay.

Giles went to get him a brandy. The man was rocking backwards and forwards in the chair, moaning and whimpering, and calling out his son's name. Giles made him drink the brandy and waited for it to take effect. He was trying to decide the best plan of action. Should he take Lord Graham home, or keep him in a hotel or his flat, until he was calm and in control, and they knew for certain what their futures were going to be? Eddie was back at Crewe Hall, he knew from Jeremy, and it was probably not a good idea for father and son to meet there. So there were not many options. He had not had time to consider his own predicament, which was pretty grim by any standards. But he refused to think about that now. He had to sort out Edward.

'He can't be gay,' Edward was muttering to himself. 'I won't let him be gay. The Graham name must go on. He will do as I tell him and marry, and have a son and heir as I did. He will stop this nonsense right now.' The more he talked himself up, the angrier he was becoming.

Giles took him by the shoulders. 'Teddie, look at me. Look at me! Can you hear yourself? Really hear? Your son may be dying – *you* may be dying. Right this minute we all need each other. We need to love and support each other, do you hear me?' He looked into his friend's eyes and could see only panic and fear and loathing.

'Damn you, Giles! I blame you for this. You are a weak man who has always followed his cock! Why couldn't you just keep

your dirty habit to yourself? We could have been so happy forever with our secret. Now my son has fallen, and it is your
bloody company of actors who have done this. They have
seduced him!' He started to moan and berate Giles again.

Giles took no notice of the accusations because they were
so ludicrous, but he could not help but feel a tinge of sadness
at how quickly Teddie resorted to type, and how quick he was
to stereotype actors. Theatre was to blame for corrupting society with the gay community. All ills rested at their door. The
hypocrisy made him sick.

'Listen, Teddie, you have to pull yourself together and
decide what to do for the next couple of days. I don't think
you should go home. Why don't we go down to London and
stay in your flat until we are sure of the outcome of the tests,
et cetera, and let Eddie and Jeremy cope with their situation.
And then we will have to face whatever life is going to throw
at us.'

Giles suddenly felt so tired, and defeated, and sad for them
all.

It was Life or Death, simple as that.

Chapter 47

Sally went and sat at the back of the stalls in the dark to think. She was overwhelmed by the events taking place around her. Her own heartbreak seemed so unimportant in the great scheme of things, and yet it had left her feeling vulnerable and useless. All confidence in herself was gone. Yet now she was faced with the possibility of losing her closest friend and was completely incapable of helping him in any way. Everything was out of control; even their work was in danger from an ambitious young woman who was the Pretender to the throne. Sally watched her shouting commands to Jeremy onstage. Sarah Kelly was like an eagle in her eyrie swooping down every now and then to chivvy the actors along. Poor Jeremy, thought Sally, how can he concentrate on singing at a time like this? How long would he have to wait for the results? And what on earth would happen when Eddie was discovered to be gay by his father? Sally thought about Eddie and his promiscuous lifestyle. Jeremy was completely out of his depth on that score. Could the two of them ever have had a chance in the long run?

Her mind turned to Dora and her life, and suddenly Sally had a terrifying thought. What if Dora had slept with Robert? She could be in danger of this dreadful virus as well. Sally got up and immediately went in search of her sister. She found her in the wings, waiting to go on for her number. Now was not the time to ask intimate questions.

Jeremy was coming off shaking his head and swearing to himself.

'That was good,' said Sally, hoping to encourage him, but he was having none of it.

'It was crap. Look, I need to get to a phone and find out if there is any news.' He started towards the exit and the stage door.

'Why don't you come and use Heather's phone? It is more private and I can stand guard,' suggested Sally. 'Let me help where I can. I know I can't do much, but I love you, Jeremy, and want to be there for you and Eddie.'

'Thanks, Sally, I appreciate it. Lead on.' He followed Sally out of the wings to the office.

After several attempts to find Eddie, to no avail, Jeremy decided to go and see Giles. 'Do you know where he is?' he asked Sally.

'Not for sure, but I assume he must be in his office because I have seen him in the building,' she answered.

'OK, I will go and see if I can find him. If anyone calls for me I will be back in fifteen minutes or so. Can you cover for me, please, Sally?'

'Of course. Go on – go.' Sally went back to the stage.

'Ooooh! What a beauty, I've never seen one as big as that before.
  Oh! What a beauty, it must be two foot long or even
more . . .'

Simon was giving his all to a huge marrow which was being constructed onstage by the crew as he was rehearsing. Geoffrey and Charmaine were standing by waiting to go on next, and Sally overheard them discussing their new director.

'I think she reckons she is running the National,' moaned Charmaine. 'She keeps giving me detailed notes about my motivation. My motivation is to sit quiet and still while you sing to me! Do I need to have a discussion about what my thoughts are as you warble away?'

'Probably best not to know,' replied Geoffrey solemnly. 'I can only imagine what *you* must be thinking about. What you are going to eat for tea? Why you are here at all?'

Charmaine laughed at this. 'Oh now, Geoffrey, don't be so hard on yourself. I enjoy listening to your voice, I really do.'

Sally could not help but stifle a giggle and the other two turned round guiltily.

'Oh, Sally, don't do that! You gave us a fright.' The two of them looked like naughty school children.

'Sorry, guys, but you are a hoot. Sarah is certainly making her mark though, isn't she? Are you coping with it OK?'

'Oh God, yes!' exclaimed Geoffrey. 'We have been doing this too long to be put off by anything less than an earthquake. We do it ourselves most of the time anyway, don't we?' They all laughed and Sally watched as the two of them went onstage to set up for their number.

Heather appeared at her side and said, 'Sally, can you go over to the workshop and oversee the marrow? It needs adjusting or something, according to Simon. See what he wants, will you?'

Sally saluted and disappeared.

'Has anyone seen my tiddler?' Pete's voice whispered in Heather's ear. She spun round. 'I beg your pardon?' she gasped. 'What on earth do you mean – and is it rude?'

'That is the name of my song,' chuckled Pete. 'I need a jamjar and a stick with a long bit of string attached to it with a little fish on the end of it. And yes, it *is* rude.'

'Blimey, bring back *Hamlet*,' said Heather. 'All I had to find was a skull! Right, come with me, young man and we will sort out your tiddler, if you'll excuse the expression.'

On the way to the workshop Sally suddenly remembered Dora and did an about-turn towards the dressing rooms instead. She found her sister pacing up and down going through her song.

'Sorry to interrupt,' said Sally, 'but can I have a word?'

Dora stopped singing and faced her. 'Yes, but make it quick. I have to go and do a chorus number in a minute.'

Sally took a deep breath. 'Dora, I am sorry to pry but it is important. Did you sleep with Robert?'

The girl sighed heavily. 'God, Sally, we are not still on that, are we? For Christ's sake, what does it matter to you?'

'Nothing.' Sally pushed on. 'It is just something I need to check. Please just trust me on this – it is important.'

Dora said very slowly and clearly, 'No, I did not have sex with Robert Johnson. There, are you happy now? I can't believe I am even bothering to answer you.'

Sally gave her a quick nod and sped out of the room before Dora could ask any awkward questions. She still needed to see how Jeremy was getting on, but Heather found her first, and asked about the marrow.

'Oops, I forgot. I am so sorry – I will do it now. It is just there is so much going on I can't keep up with it all!'

'Tell me about it,' said Heather grimly. 'It is supposed to be the season of comfort and joy, but there seems little evidence of that around here. By the way, just to add to the chaos, we have to get someone to organize a "secret Santa" jobbie for between the shows on Christmas Eve. We always have a bit of a tea and buns and prezzies. I know, I know, now is not ideal but it is only three weeks away. Shit – look at the time! I need to call the company onstage, excuse me.' She hurried off like the white rabbit in *Alice in Wonderland*, shaking her head and muttering to herself.

Sally was forced to follow her to the stage where Sarah was waiting with a sheaf of notes in her hands.

'Right, everyone, I am pleased to say we are in good nick. So I propose we break for lunch then start the technical rehearsal at two o'clock. As I said before, with a bit of luck we may get a dress rehearsal in tonight, or at least half a one. So tomorrow morning around eleven we can finish it and then break, and then start the proper Dress at two o'clock, ready to open the show at seven thirty. Thank you, everyone, it is going to be fabulous.'

Sally had hardly rehearsed her number at all, but she was not too bothered as she knew exactly what she was doing with it and did not need Sarah Kelly's input. She did, however, need a dress – and a period dress at that. She knew Janie had put one aside for her but she had not yet tried it on and it might be a good idea to do that now. She met Janie coming down the stairs with an armful of costumes.

'Can I try on my dress any time soon?' Sally asked her.

'Yes, of course. Do you want to do it now? If so, just follow me.' Sally did as she was told and followed Janie to the wardrobe department, where Gwendoline was overseeing Pete while he tried on a pair of short trousers for his Tiddler number.

'Pete, you look most fetching,' chuckled Sally. 'What do you think, girls? Could you have that in your bed?'

'Please spare me,' Janie replied. 'It is bad enough having to listen to him playing with his tiddler!' They burst into fits of the giggles.

'Yeah, yeah, very funny, girls. Mock a man trying to do the best for his art.'

'Art!' screeched Janie, and this brought about further squeals of laughter.

'Sorry to interrupt, but could I have a word please, Sally.' Giles Longfellow was standing in the doorway and the whole room went silent.

'Yes, of course,' said Sally. She followed Giles out of the room without a backward glance.

Not a word was spoken all the way to Giles's office. He showed Sally into the room and shut the door.

'Please have a seat. Would you like something to drink?' He was pouring himself a very large brandy as he said this.

'No, thank you,' said Sally, and waited for Giles to speak.

He sat down opposite her slowly. He looked old and grey, and there was none of the dashing entrepreneur about him today. He swirled the golden liquid round the brandy glass and peered into it like a fortune-teller hoping for inspiration.

'You are Jeremy's closest friend, he tells me.' Giles spoke without looking at her. 'I understand he has told you about Robert and his illness.' He paused and took a sip of brandy. 'He has also told you of his involvement with Eddie Graham and the obvious problems this creates. Do you have any idea how serious the situation is for everyone?' He gave Sally a piercing look and Sally held his gaze. She could see the pain in his eyes but also something else. Giles was frightened. Deep down to his bones he was scared. The fear was rolling off him, Sally could almost smell it.

Why was she here? She could not understand why he had asked her to see him.

'I am a little confused as to why you have asked me here, Giles. Yes, I understand that there are serious issues concerning Jeremy and Eddie and possibly yourself, but what can I do exactly?'

There was a long silence and then a groan from Giles.

'Because Eddie has contracted this virus and he will probably die, and he is your best friend's lover. Jeremy is devastated and you are the only person he has in his life to turn to, so I am asking you to take care of him through this. We are all devastated and the whole dreadful business touches so many lives. I won't go into the details if you don't mind, as they are confidential, but I would also ask you to keep this private. I know you can be trusted, Sally, and I value your discretion enormously, and your support. It is going to be exceedingly tough on Jeremy for the next few weeks so I just wanted to make sure you would be there for him.'

'Of course I will. Thank you so much for telling me and for trusting me. I do hope you all get through this and I am so sorry to hear about Eddie.'

Sally decided the best thing to do was to get out quick. She left the office and ran down the stairs as fast as she could. She was so shocked she really could not take it all in. Where was Jeremy now? She needed to talk to him. She went straight to the boys' dressing room but only Simon and Pete were there.

'Have you seen Jeremy?' she asked.

'He had gone to the shop to get some lunch,' said Pete.

'Thanks,' replied Sally and was gone. She raced down the stairs and out to the stage door. 'Gladys, have you seen Jeremy?'

The big woman was eating a hot pie and could not answer immediately. Much to Sally's frustration she had to wait while Gladys chomped her way, huffing and puffing, through her mouthful of steak and kidney.

'Pardon me, luv, sorry 'bout that. Blimey, it was 'ot! Now then, what was you asking? Oh yes, young Jeremy. Well, he came running out looking something terrible. White as a sheet. I told him to go to the pub and buy himself a brandy. So I think that is where he has gone. Nothing serious is it, luv?' But she was talking to herself because Sally had already gone.

Sally found Jeremy sitting in the corner by the fire surrounded by hearty happy lunchtime drinkers. He was hunched over his glass, staring into the flames. Sally managed to grab a spare stool and dragged it across to sit down beside him. He hardly acknowledged her presence.

'Jeremy, I am so sorry. What is there to say? It is terrible news. Please look at me, come on, you need to talk. Shall we go somewhere more private?'

'Eddie is going to die and I can't take it in. Why has this happened? Am I being punished? Sally, I am OK, I am not infected, and nor are Giles or Lord Graham. I can't comprehend it. We are spared, yet Eddie has to die. What am I going to do? I can't tell my parents and I have got to get through Christmas Day. Oh God, I can't do it.'

Sally could feel his shoulders starting to shake and knew she had to get him out of the pub. She hauled him up, saying, 'Come on now, let's just go somewhere private. Hang on a few more minutes, and then you can cry all you want, my friend.' She literally dragged him out of the pub and managed to get him to walk back to the theatre.

'Now let's get past Gladys without an enquiry. You just have to hold your breath and stand up straight and walk quickly.' Jeremy did everything he was told and the two of them hurried past Gladys with a wave. The latter was not too bothered as she was now engaged with a large portion of steamed roly poly pudding, which was also very 'ot!

Sally got Jeremy sat down in her dressing room and shut the door so they would not be disturbed. There was still half an hour before the technical rehearsal started.

'Look, we are going to have to find a way to get you through this show starting with two o'clock today unless I tell Sarah you are ill. I could do that and then you could go home.'

'I don't want to be on my own,' cried Jeremy. 'I want to see Eddie but his father has forbidden it. Sally, they have taken Eddie away to a nursing home somewhere. They are telling people he has terminal cancer, but he might live for ages yet. I don't know much about the illness, but Giles had been telling me and George Delaware that the virus could lie dormant for years before it presents itself. I want to talk to Eddie and make him see that we can still be together. I won't leave him. I love him, for God's sake.'

'OK, let's get this straight. Lord Graham won't let you see Eddie ever again?'

'Yes – he is crazy! He told Giles it was my fault his son was gay, never mind caught this terrible virus. Nothing could be further from the truth, Sal. I feel like a teenager compared to Eddie. He has betrayed me and our love. He has been having affairs for the last three years. He says he wants to stop now he has met me, but who knows. Anyway, all that is irrelevant now. I just want to see him and talk.'

'Can't Giles help you see him? Surely if he and Lord Graham are so close he would have some influence?' she suggested.

Jeremy blew his nose and sat up, trying to pull himself together.

'To be honest, I think this whole thing has split them up. Giles seems completely lost. Lord Graham is battening down the hatches and closing all possible means of this leaking out to the press. Can you imagine what they would make of it? I reckon Giles has been given his marching orders as well. So one way or another, we are all fucked.'

'I think Eddie will find a way to contact you,' said Sally thoughtfully. 'He will not want to leave it like this. Just try and sit tight for the time being and see what happens. You have got so much on your plate, these next three weeks, Jeremy. I know it is tough but you must be strong and you must not let it stop you doing your work. You know what we have always told each other. Work comes first.' Sally stopped as she saw the tears welling up again in Jeremy's eyes. She gathered him to her and held him tight. 'You can do this,' she whispered. 'We will do it together.'

Chapter 48

'Ladies and gentlemen, for your delectation and delight please put your hands together and welcome a young and perfectly formed songstress born to soar to the heights of sublime ecstasy . . . Miss Sally Thomas!'

The audience cheered and whistled as Sally was lowered on a swing to the centre of the stage where she sang 'The Boy I Love is Up in the Gallery'. She wore a gorgeous pale blue and cream lace dress with mountains of petticoats, and little leather boots which peeped through the folds of her gown as she swung backwards and forwards. With all the drama that was going on in real life it was a relief to be here for five perfect minutes every night and sing her heart out to an adoring crowd. She had had more fan letters this week than any other time. It certainly helped her through the days rehearsing with Jeremy, who wandered about in a coma.

His poor performance as the all-important character, Badger, was so disappointing for her, and the rest of the cast, because they had all been so looking forward to *Toad of Toad*

Hall. Simon was creating a wonderfully evil leader of the weasels, and Percy was sublime as Toad.

'This part was made for you,' said Sarah, clapping her hands after a particularly good run-through.

'Don't know whether to take that as a compliment or not,' whispered Percy under his breath to Peggy.

She gave his arm a squeeze and whispered back, 'You are too good-looking for the role really, my darling!' and they both laughed.

Sally was having a ball playing the water rat, Ratty. She was strutting about with a false moustache on, much to everyone's amusement. Pete was the perfect Mole because he was quite small anyway but he had already devised an amazing face make-up which blended down his neck and chest into his costume. It was a pain to put on every night, but the effect was incredible because it gave the animals real characters. Pete had to give lessons to everyone else in the cast and even got his name in the programme as animal make-up designer.

'Can't be bad to have another string to his bow,' commented Janie. 'We need all the help we can get in this game.'

Dora was a dream as the gaoler's daughter who disguises Toad as a washerwoman so he can get out of gaol. Gwendoline had made her a frock with the lowest bodice imaginable, and Dora's cleavage was very much on show, to the delight of the boys.

'Are you sure she can go in front of children dressed like that?' asked Sally. Janie and Gwendoline had a fit of the giggles.

'Well, it will make all the dads happy, won't it?' chuckled Janie. 'It's a laugh – children don't worry about a bit of cleavage.'

'A bit!' yelped Sally.

Jeremy, however, was giving a decidedly lacklustre performance as Badger.

'I am so sorry, Sally, I just can't stop thinking about Eddie. If only I could see him and talk to him.'

After a few days of this Sally had had enough and went to see Giles.

'Please, Giles, can you persuade Lord Graham to at least let Jeremy say goodbye properly,' she pleaded. 'We need him up to speed for this show.'

'I will do my best, but His Lordship will hardly give me the time of day either.'

If truth be known, Giles was at his wit's end. He and Teddie had had a meeting in London to discuss the finances of the theatre, and Edward Graham had basically told Giles that after this season he was withdrawing his support.

'But why, for God's sake? Just because you and I can no longer be together doesn't mean the theatre has to suffer. You know how much it means to me to keep Crewe going, and all my dreams for the future, and we are going to open *Hamlet* in three months' time, which will be a fantastic achievement. Please, Teddie, don't destroy everything I have. I have lost you, which is enough to bear.'

But Giles was wasting his breath. Lord Graham had shut down and was immune to all pleading. From the moment he had heard that his son had HIV and his predicament was life-threatening, something inside Edward Graham had also died. He could hardly face Tanya and Tilly, so he spent most of his time in his apartment in London. He rarely went out socially. Gossip was rife in the inner circles, but he had managed to keep it all from the press. He had sent Eddie away to stay with some friends in New York and had arranged for his son to see a doctor there who was an authority on this new disease. Any hope that could be offered would be welcome. But there had been none.

He was expecting Eddie home for Christmas and intended to keep him well away from that boy he thought he was in love with. Love! He was so bitter and angry with poor Jeremy for no good reason. He knew he was being illogical, and he even felt remorse at the pain he must be causing the boy by not allowing him to see Eddie. But he also felt repelled by him, by them both, for their obvious passion and pleasure with each other. Not his son! How did it happen? He could see the hatred and loathing in his wife's eyes and he knew she blamed him for everything. But then had he not been similarly over-whelmed with a passion for Giles? Did he not support being gay? It was no longer against the law. Society recognized it as acceptable now. Why did he feel this guilt? He must stand proud and face the world for himself, for his son. But in his heart he knew he was weak and that his life would be a hell on earth if he admitted his sexuality. Tanya had promised to stand by him for Eddie and Tilly's sake, but only if he never saw Giles again, or engaged in any extra-curricular activity. They would live the lie to the end and if, God forbid, Eddie's 'illness' should develop, then it was to be known as cancer and left at that.

If Eddie died . . .

'I have had a postcard from Eddie!' Jeremy was beside himself with delight when he cornered Sally early one morning. 'He has been in New York but gets back this weekend and wants to meet. Oh my God, I am so happy, Sally. I am so sorry I have been such a pain, and I promise I will make it up to you guys and give the performance of my life for you all. Old Badger will rise up and strike the Wild Wood!' He gave Sally a big kiss and skipped off to the dressing rooms.

Thank goodness, thought Sally. The euphoria may not last when reality sets in, but at least if it gets us through the play, that is something to be thankful for at least. And maybe the Christmas spirit will imbue us all with a little hope.

Christmas was bearing down upon them fast and the cast were becoming quite demob-happy. All the dressing rooms were festooned with paperchains and tinsel. Even Sarah had put some holly round her mirror and was hanging silver balls along the edge when Sally came into the dressing room one morning. The two girls were not exactly enemies but not friends either, but Sally had decided that Sarah had her feet under the table and if Sally wanted certain parts after Christmas she needed to stake her claim.

'Morning, Sarah, that looks very festive,' she smiled her greeting.

'Thank you,' replied Sarah, standing up and turning to face Sally. 'How are you finding life on the water bank? I must say, all of you have really taken to your characters.'

'Oh, we love it! Ratty was always my favourite as a child. Actually, Sarah, I have been meaning to ask you about the next couple of plays after Christmas. Will you be directing them?'

'Yes I will, as a matter of fact. Giles, as you know, has a lot on his plate with *Hamlet* so he asked me to take over. As you can imagine, I am thrilled. It is what I have always wanted to do.' Sarah said this as though in answer to any questions anyone might have had who was in doubt as to her intentions from the beginning of the season.

Sally nodded in agreement. 'Oh yes, that is obvious from the work you have done so far. So that's great then, you have your heart's desire, lucky you.' She couldn't help her last comment and it was out before she could stop it.

'It is not all luck, you know.' Sarah's answer was sharp. 'You have to fight sometimes for what you want. I take it you have not found *your* heart's desire, Sally. But have you really worked out exactly what that is yet?'

Sally began to feel uncomfortable. What did this woman want from her? It was really none of her business what her heart's desire was anyway. Deciding to change the subject, she put on a big cheesy grin and said, 'I would love to play Sandy in *The Prime of Miss Jean Brodie*. I take it Charmaine will be playing Jean Brodie? I would also love to play the lead in *The Boyfriend*. I am very committed to this season at Crewe, Sarah, and feel quite strongly that I can bring a good deal to the productions as an actress and a company member.'

Sarah watched her without any expression. She was giving nothing away.

'Well, it is good to know where you stand, and I am glad to see you still have ambition after the ups and downs so far. What about Dora? She is very popular with the audiences and very keen to make her mark.' Sarah could not resist throwing a small spanner into the works.

'Absolutely right,' agreed Sally, refusing to be drawn. 'There are certain roles she will be perfect for in the coming plays. However, she still has to get more experience before she can take responsibility for a leading role. But that is just my opinion,' she added with her most charming smile. 'Well, I had better get going or there will be no props ready for the dress rehearsal. See you later.'

Sally breathed a sigh of relief as she went down the stairs. Sarah was tricky, there was no doubt about it, and she really kept her cards close to her chest. But Sally was determined not to be put off. She had had a shitty time since Rupert left, and the only good thing was, they had all been so busy she had had little time to feel sorry for herself. But every now and then she thought about their night together and her stomach tied in knots. He had sent her a card from LA saying he was having a wonderful time. There was no mention of Isabelle, but why would he be that cruel to her? She was not a fool, and just wished he would leave her alone now. She could never be friends after what had happened, and she certainly did not want to understudy in *Hamlet* in the West End. That really would be going nowhere fast. The lowest of the low, watching *his* star ascend to great heights. They had asked Jeremy to go, and that was quite right. His Laertes was a brilliant piece of work. Sally was so happy for him, and hoped it would make up a little for his problems. He was still very quiet and withdrawn, and she spent any spare time she had keeping an eye on him and trying to raise his spirits.

Sally was concentrating on making *Toad of Toad Hall* a huge success, and she was looking forward to going home for Christmas Day. She was also hoping to catch a few moments with Mack. Everything that had happened with Rupert had rather taken over her thoughts . . . but Sally still needed to resolve her feelings about Mack. Somehow, he represented another way of life. But was that what she wanted? There was so much going on around her that was affecting her in so many different ways . . . and it was difficult to put it all together. She was longing to see her parents and just bask in their warmth and security.

Sally had managed to get gifts in between rehearsals and prop-collecting, and tonight she sat in the flat in front of the fire and played Christmas carols on the radio while she wrapped them all up. Dora had come home one night from the pub and interrupted her reverie.

'Oh my God, sis, don't tell me you have done all your presents already? What are you like?' She had slumped down onto the sofa, squashing some Christmas paper and decorations as she did so.

'Oh, for goodness sake, Dora, look what you are doing! Get up – you have wrecked my wrapping stuff. Come on, please, move your fat arse.'

'Excuse *me*,' huffed Dora, dragging herself off the sofa. 'I do not have a fat arse, if you don't mind. Oh come on, Sally, chill out a bit. You are no fun these days. Still pining for Rupie? Let's face it – that was never going anywhere.'

Sally refused to rise to the bait. She was just too tired and fed up with everything. She and Dora did nothing but bicker these days, and Sally was hoping that on Christmas Day they could keep it pleasant for their parents' sake.

'Have you heard from the casting woman at *Coronation Street* yet?' she asked, changing the subject.

Dora let out a scream of delight. 'Oh shit, yes! How could I forget to tell you? I have got an audition for a character in *Corrie* – a possible regular character. Can you believe it?' Dora was now jumping up and down, dangerously close to Sally's wrapped gifts.

'Hey, that is wonderful news, but please mind my parcels. Sit down over there, can't you, there's a good girl.' Dora actually did as she was told, and sat in the chair hugging herself. 'I can't believe it, but it would be so amazing if I got it. I go next week. What a Christmas present that would be, wouldn't it?'

Sally went and gave her sister a hug. 'I am really happy for you. Good luck.' She then went to the kitchen and started to make some hot chocolate.

Dora stood in the doorway and watched her. 'Are you really pleased for me?' she asked.

Sally looked at her. 'Yes, of course I am. Why do you ask?'

'Oh, I don't know. These days I just seem to annoy you all

the time, and things have not been going very well for you, have they? Did that agent ever get in touch, by the way?'

Sally concentrated hard on the hot milk. 'No, he didn't, but to be honest I didn't expect him to really. I was not his type of actress. He has offered Jeremy a contract, did you know? I think that is great news – just what Jeremy needs at the moment.' She forced a bright smile in Dora's direction and poured out the drinks, adding, 'Don't you worry about me, Dora, I will soon be catching you up. Think hare and tortoise.'

They laughed and said good night and each went to her own room.

Sally undressed, desperately trying to keep all thoughts of agents and jobs at bay. She did not want to think about any of that for the time being. She had received the letter from the agent Peter Stone with resignation. She had known it would be a no. She had not even expected him to contact her, and when she had had a moment of daring and decided to write to him, she couldn't find his card. Last time she had seen it was on the kitchen table, the night they had all met. So when she couldn't find it she took it as a sign it was not to be and let it go. She had been thrilled for Jeremy and decided she would tackle the whole agent thing after Christmas. If she got a couple of good parts she would write to various theatres and casting directors and agents, and take it from there. For now she just wanted to go home and sit in front of the familiar Christmas tree and pretend she was ten years old again.

Chapter 49

Giles scanned the room but could see no sign of Edward. Why would he? This was a crematorium in North London and Giles was here out of respect for his ex-lover and friend, Robert Johnson. Why the hell did he think Edward would be there? He shivered and pulled his scarf tighter round his face. It was a bitterly cold day, bleak and depressing, with a sky full of rolling black clouds. They seemed angry. Was that in support of the man lying in the coffin in front of them? Was Robert's anger creating this dark presence around them?

There were only a handful of people sitting there, and Giles did not know any of them, although he vaguely recognized a counsellor from the Terence Higgins Trust who gave him a nod. Please let it be over! Giles could not stop shaking and he knew it was not just the cold. These last few weeks had seemed a lifetime. A lifetime spent surrounded by unhappiness and betrayal. He just wanted to get through this. He would survive, of that he had no doubt. There was a tiny part of Giles that he never gave away to anyone, not even Teddie. Call it hope or ego or just plain self-preservation, but this tiny part of him was the spark that kept him going. He would rise up again from the ashes. Ashes – Christ, now was not the time to bring up ashes. The director of the funeral parlour had contacted him and suggested that he, Giles, might like to take Robert's ashes. Not in a million years! There did not seem to be any relatives until today, when apparently, a distant cousin had turned up and was happy to take the urn. She was a thin, grey little woman sitting at the back. Giles wondered if he should speak to her and offer his condolences. But what would be the point?

Poor Robert, he had been so flamboyant when he first arrived at the theatre. His particular sense of humour had appealed to Giles, the cutting, slightly sarcastic comments he would make about people. But their union had been awkward from the start and Giles had always had the feeling that Robert had another agenda. He was a closed book as far as his emotions were concerned. But then Teddie and Giles had become close once more, and these last six months had been the happiest time of his life. To have a partner to share things with and a job that he adored made for the perfect life. He knew he would never be able to find that again. He had to face the production of *Hamlet* on his own and he was not sure he had it in him any more. Large tears were rolling down his cheeks and Giles hastily wiped them away. He wanted to leave, but the service, such as it was, had begun. Someone sat down next to him and his heart sank. Who would sit down next to a total stranger when there were plenty of empty pews? He tried to shift away but that someone grabbed his arm.

'It's OK, Giles, it's only me, Jeremy. Are you all right? You look as if you want to run away,' he whispered.

Giles looked up and saw Jeremy smiling at him and he let out a huge sigh of relief.

'Oh my God, am I glad to see you. I just can't do this on my own. Thank you for being here. Did you come down by train? How are you going to get back?' he fretted.

'Don't worry about that now. Let's just get through this and then we can go and have a drink somewhere,' replied Jeremy.

In fact, Jeremy was on cloud nine as he was going to meet Eddie this afternoon at some flat in St John's Wood. When Eddie had rung and suggested they meet this Sunday it was ideal, as Jeremy already knew about Robert's cremation from George Delaware, who had called him.

'I am sorry to say we are not going to be able to come to the cremation as Dale and I are away that weekend, abroad. I do so hope you will go, Jeremy, and say a prayer for Robert on our behalf.' It was more a command than a request.

'Yes, of course, I will go,' he promised.

When Jeremy saw Giles sitting all alone, and looking so forlorn he was glad he was there.

After the service, the two men made a hasty retreat, found a pub and sank a couple of vodkas each.

'Poor Robert,' muttered Giles. 'He has died in vain so far. No one seems to want to address this terrible problem of HIV, do they?' He took Jeremy's hand. 'And yet his death has destroyed so many lives around him. Yours and mine, to name but two. Are you coping OK, dear boy?'

Jeremy thought it best to keep his visit to Eddie to himself, but it was difficult not to share his joy because he had been unhappy for so many weeks.

'I am surviving, Giles, but it is very hard. What about you?' he asked.

Giles stared into his vodka then threw it back and ordered another. 'I am bereft, dear boy. Rock bottom. I just don't know how I am going to pull it all together after Christmas.'

'But we have *Hamlet* to look forward to. Please remember, Giles, how important this production is going to be. It is everything you have worked for and it is going to be fantastic. Please, Giles, you have to make it work for the likes of me. I am relying on you to make me a star!'

'You are right, of course, my boy. I will do my best. With your help, I hope?' He looked into Jeremy's face for confirmation. Suddenly Jeremy thought of Sally, how they always talked about their work, and how it should always come first, and he suddenly did feel stronger and more positive.

'Bloody right you will succeed, Giles. Failure is *not* an option. Broken hearts are one thing, but broken dreams are not allowed. We will overcome!'

Jeremy left Giles having one for the road, and boring some poor barman with his version of *Hamlet*, and made his way to the address he had been given in St John's Wood. He arrived outside a rather impressive block of flats which must have been built sometime in the 1930s. He took the lift to the fourth floor and, catching sight of himself in the glass panelling, became aware of just how nervous and excited he was, as he had pink cheeks! He paused at the front door and took a few deep breaths before finally ringing the bell. He then stared straight ahead of him, not moving a muscle, until the door was flung open and Eddie was there before him, alive.

'J, I can't believe it is you at last!' Eddie pulled Jeremy through the door and they closed it with their bodies as they leaned against it to embrace. They kissed long and deep, and when they finally broke away both men were flushed and breathless.

Eddie led Jeremy into a beautiful 1930s-style living room full of period furniture and antiques.

'Wow, this is fantastic. Who does it belong to?' Jeremy

wandered around examining everything and picked up a photo in an Art Deco frame. 'Oh, I see,' he said softly. 'It belongs to your father, doesn't it?' He turned to face Eddie. 'Does that mean he has forgiven you your heinous crimes?' The sarcasm was not lost on his lover.

'I am so sorry about everything, Jeremy. Please let me explain things properly. That's why we are meeting, isn't it?' He turned away, and had a coughing fit. It was a horrible sound and Jeremy suddenly felt frightened.

Eddie went on breathlessly, 'Please, sit down. Would you like a drink or coffee or something?'

'A glass of white wine would be good, thank you,' said Jeremy and he sat down on the edge of one of the perfectly upholstered sofas as though he was waiting to be called into the doctor's surgery.

Eddie brought him the glass of wine and put the bottle in a silver wine-cooler on the side.

'One glass is never enough,' he smiled. He coughed again and it racked his body. Jeremy noticed for the first time that his friend had lost weight.

'Are you ill?' he said curtly, trying to hide his terror at what Eddie was about to tell him.

'Gosh, J, you sound like a headmaster,' Eddie laughed.

'I am sorry, Eddie, but this is agony. You obviously have something to tell me and I am guessing it is not good news, because apart from anything else you look bloody awful. And sorry, I didn't mean . . .' Jeremy could go no further; he could not stop the tears from flowing.

Eddie came and sat beside him and held him. 'Don't, Jeremy, please. Don't make this any harder than it is. I love you so much, it just does not seem right that we cannot be together, but the truth is, my dearest love, I am dying and—'

'*Nooo*, don't say that!' wailed Jeremy. 'You can't die, Eddie! Please don't say that!'

'Listen to me, J, please. This is very important to me and to you. There is nothing we can do. My father will not let me see you again after this. My mother actually arranged this for me. She hates the whole mess but she understands how much I love you and that I need to say goodbye.' Jeremy tried to speak but Eddie stopped him. 'No, please, you must let me finish. I have presented with the first symptoms and now who knows? It could be months or years before the next phase. But the prognosis is not good. I don't want you to spend the next years of your life worrying about when I am going to pop my clogs. You have a fantastic career in front of you, Jeremy, and if you love me you will make sure you do everything in your power to embrace your success. I will hear all about it, believe me. I will be following you all the time. My father will never let us be together and we will never be reconciled. His hypocrisy is beyond belief. The pain he has caused my mother all these years, and now he castigates me! However, it is something we aristocrats have to do . . . stick together. So they will all gather round me and that will be that. It is shit, there is no other word for it. A wasted life, but *please*, Jeremy – promise me you will not waste yours.'

Jeremy sat there on the sofa in his lover's arms and just wanted to die, right there. If there had been a poisoned chalice he would have drunk deep and died happy.

'Do you promise me then?' Eddie's voice hung in the air.

Jeremy shuddered and gathered himself up off the sofa. There was nothing more to say; he was exhausted. He stumbled against a chair and reached out to Eddie, who took his arm and steadied him.

'You will write to me or phone me sometimes?' asked

Jeremy, clutching his stomach as if it were going to drop on the floor. He was just full up with pain and hurt, and wanted to scream his agony to the world.

Eddie held him tight and steered him to the front door. 'I will always love you, Jeremy. You showed me what real love is, and for that I thank you. Please be strong for me, and remember wherever you are I will be watching you.'

They kissed one last time – a gentle, tender kiss – and Jeremy drew strength from his lover and was able to ride the lift down to the ground floor with dignity. He went out into the freezing December evening grateful for the darkness to hide his tears. So many tears and so much pain. Jeremy walked all the way to Euston, by which time it was nine in the evening. He was too cold to care, but once on the last train back to Crewe he started to unthaw and as he grew warmer, his heart grew colder. *Life's a bitch and then you die!* Except the wrong people seem to die, always the wrong people.

He would work hard for Eddie; he would make him proud, and show his fucking father what his son loved about him. He hoped Lord Graham suffered for the rest of his life the guilt of destroying his only son's chance of happiness. Please let Eddie live a long life, prove them all wrong. He was a shining star, he couldn't die!

Chapter 50

Christmas Eve was finally here! Sally woke early with just the same sense of excitement she had had as a child. She was all packed and ready to go. Her parents would be arriving during the day and then they would watch the last show before driving their daughters home for the holiday. Christmas morning in her own bed! It was almost too much to bear, thought Sally happily. The week had flown by, and everyone at the theatre had been in a constant state of goodwill. Presents appeared on dressing tables and the boys bought everyone a chocolate Father Christmas. Sally had organized the girls' presents to the crew and front-of-house staff. She had found a stall in the market which sold homemade soap. So everyone got a little bar of soap in the shape of Santa Claus and a sack of gold money. Chocolate, of course.

Dora had had an early Christmas present in the form of an offer from Nottingham Playhouse for their next season.

'The job that should have been mine,' remarked Sally to Janie as they were ironing costumes.

'Do I detect a hint of the green-eyed monster?' teased Janie.

'No, not really. It's just I wish she showed a bit more

gratitude. Let's be honest, she did lie to the director of Nottingham Playhouse at that repertory conference and lead him to believe he was talking to me! She seems to be blissfully unaware of just how bloody lucky she is. Even the powers that be at *Coronation Street* are willing to wait for her to get her Equity ticket and then give her a job.'

Sally suddenly realized how curmudgeonly she sounded and stopped herself, saying contritely, 'Oh, I am sorry, Janie. I must sound like a right old miserable twisted sister. But each time I give Dora the benefit of the doubt, she goes and does something else. She pinched that business card of the agent Peter Stone that I had left on the kitchen table a while back and rang him and made an appointment to see him. I know she is perfectly entitled to do so, but it is so insensitive of her. She could have asked me first if I minded.'

'And do you mind?' ventured Janie.

'Do you know what? Yes, actually, I do ...' Sally was pleased for Dora, of course, but she could not deny a touch of envy. Her younger sister's life seemed to just progress with such ease. Everything always falling into place.

'I suppose the thing that galls me is that she just takes it all for granted.'

'Oh, come on, Sal. Everyone hits a bad patch eventually and it is how you deal with the knocks that counts.'

'I don't wish her any bad patches,' sighed Sally. 'Just wish she was a bit more grateful. I am sick to death of being the second-class citizen – the sad sister who is always one step behind. I seem to be getting nowhere fast.' Sally was very close to tears and Janie knew it.

'Hang on a minute, girl. You have gone from ASM to leads in three months. Not bad going, is it, eh? I am thrilled you will be playing Sandy in *The Prime of Miss Jean Brodie* – and has not Miss Sarah Kelly hinted that you could be leading the ensemble in *The Boyfriend?*'

Sarah had, indeed, told Sally that she and Giles thought she was the best person for the role of Polly Browne in *The Boyfriend*, the last production of the season. Sally had been thrilled to bits at the time, so why was she feeling so down now?

'Listen, we are all tired and emotional. A day off and some Christmas pud and you will be feeling as right as rain,' advised the ever-optimistic Janie.

On the quiet, Sally was also very worried about Jeremy. He had told her about his trip to London and she had had to admit it was very hard on him.

'You poor thing, it does seem as though the rich close ranks under fire, doesn't it?' she had consoled him. 'All I can say is that time *will* heal. You will survive – and you *must* survive because you have an incredible career ahead of you. A new agent, a role in the West End – what more did you ever dream of? I wish I was so lucky.' Sally couldn't resist her small moment of self-pity.

'Oh, Sally, don't say that. You are doing fine. You have made the right decision to stay at Crewe and play proper parts instead of understudying. It would have driven you mad, and you would have had to put up with Rupert.'

'I suppose you are right,' she replied a little sadly. 'I wonder who will play Ophelia this time?'

'Forget it! Whoever it is will be a one-hit wonder and forgotten about by the time you are accepting your first Emmy. Now come on, let's clear up the Green Room because, let's face it, no one else will.'

Patricia and Douglas Thomas arrived at the theatre just before curtain up on the matinée. Dora and Sally met them with shrieks of delight at the stage door.

'It is so good to see you,' said Sally, running into her dad's arms. 'We have to go and do the show now, but you know how to get to the flat, don't you?'

'Yes, of course,' replied Douglas. 'We can go and start packing the car with Dora's stuff, can't we? Then your mother and I will be at the stage door at four o'clock to take you to tea before the final show. She wants to go and buy some supplies for the journey home as well, I think.'

'OK, then we will see you later,' called Dora over her shoulder, already on the way to the dressing room to get changed. She added to Sally, 'I will never get all my stuff in the car, so do you mind hanging on to some of it until I get a place in Nottingham, then I will come and get it?'

'No, not all,' said Sally, carefully putting on her moustache. 'You know, I will miss being Ratty, but maybe not the facial hair. Perhaps that is why I can't get an agent, because they think I am a hairy actress!' She burst out laughing, and Dora joined in, until they were both laughing so much their make-up was running.

Sally gave her sister a hug and said, 'I will miss you, Dora, even though you have been a pain in the butt. Just try and think about other people sometimes before you go off on one.'

'Yes, sister dear,' Dora giggled. 'I love you too, and I am truly sorry for all the grief I have caused.'

Sally smiled, and they left it at that. However, in her heart of hearts Sally knew that things between them would never be the same again. She would never be able to fully trust Dora, and she knew that Dora would be living on a different planet this time next year. It was sad but true, and Sally surprised herself by her cynicism. Probably best to get on and take everything with a pinch of salt.

The rest of the day went like clockwork. The girls took their parents to the pub for tea, and had pie and chips, and then did the last show to a full house of screaming children. As the curtain fell there was a stampede for the dressing rooms, with poor Heather trying to remind people that they must be back on Boxing Day for the half, at two o'clock.

'Why do I bother?' she shouted over the noise to Sally. 'Have a great Christmas Day, pet.'

Sally went to find Jeremy, who was struggling to the stage door with a huge bag.

'We will see you at Junction Six bright and early on Boxing Day. Have a lovely Christmas Day, my darling.' She gave him a big kiss.

'You too, Sally. I hope Santa brings you something gorgeous!' Then: 'Bye, Gladys, don't eat too many mince pies or you won't fit through the stage door!' Jeremy planted a smacker on the big woman's cheek and was gone.

Sally found her parents waiting by the car which was piled high, but with room for them all to squeeze in.

'I have got all the food and drink with me in the front,' explained Patricia. 'Just ask me when you want something. Now come on, let's get going. I loved your moustache, Sally.'

They all climbed in, and Douglas tooted a farewell to whoever might be listening, and they were off!

The comings and goings on a Saturday night in the theatre were always chaos. No one would have noticed anybody slipping through the big dock doors at the back of the auditorium where all the scenery was kept. Gladys had already gone home and locked the stage door. The remaining crew would switch off all the lights except the safety ones, and then leave through the small door in the dock doors.

Gradually the noise died down, and after the final calls of

'Good night' and 'Happy Christmas' had floated past the stage door, silence fell like a huge blanket over the theatre. The figure in the dark anorak and hood sat for some time in the Royal Box, just listening to the silence. The stage was lit by a vague blue light, casting a sheen across the floor, making it look like a lake. The rows of red velvet seats appeared tiny from the box. The figure brushed the nap of the ledge, and his skin tingled as the velvet pricked his fingertips. A door banged and made him jump but soon there was silence once more. It was a dead silence, with no reverberations, echoes or resonance. The figure closed his eyes and tried to imagine he could hear the audience; the murmuring of an expectant and excited crowd, a laugh ringing out now and then. But there was nothing. The theatre had shut down for the holidays. It was sleeping now, dreaming of all the shows and drama that had filled its walls. It was resting, ready for the next onslaught.

'Life goes on,' murmured the man. He took a swig from the bottle of champagne he had by his side, and coughed as it went down the wrong way. His cough bounced off the walls of the auditorium like a joke from the stage and came back to hit him like a stone, reminding him of the evil that was inside him. He grasped the brass railings of the box until the hacking cough stopped raking across his chest. He was left breathless and feeling sick. He tried another sip of the bottle, this time taking it more slowly. The bubbles made his nose itch and he smiled to himself in the darkness. He reached into his pocket for the envelope, and as he pulled it out, he realized it was all scrunched-up. He laid it on the edge of the box and tried to flatten it out. Then from his other pocket he took the bottle of pills and put them on one of the little gilt chairs. He suddenly clasped hold of the envelope again, thinking that no, it wasn't safe to leave it there. One gust of air would send the missive fluttering down into the stalls below, and it would be lost.

I need a table. He looked around the box. It was like a toy house with the tiny gilt chairs and the heavy brocade curtains either side, held open with gold and silver tassels. Then he spotted a table near the door, beautifully inlaid with pale wood, and carried it down to the front of the box. He placed the pills and the bottle of champagne on it and then sat down again, holding the envelope. Careful not to tear the letter inside, he pulled out the headed notepaper and began to read:

Hi, everyone!

Well, I certainly messed up, didn't I, but who was to know there would be a bloody virus that could kill you just for having a good time!

The trouble with contracting a terminal disease is that you have to live with it until you die, and I am not prepared to do that. Sorry, guys, but why should I stay alive a bit longer to keep you happy?

Mind you, my father probably can't wait to get rid of me as I am such an embarrassment to the family, but I know Jeremy will be upset, and for that I am truly sorry. J, my darling, you are the one reason I would choose to stay alive. But it would be no life, Jeremy. You taught me how to love another person more than myself and I am so grateful. But now I can see the horizon, I just want to get on with it and not hang around and disintegrate before your very eyes.

Enjoy your lives!

I do love you, Mother, and I am sorry if I have disappointed you.

I love you, Tilly, and say again: enjoy your life. Grab it and hold it tight. I know you will be OK and I will be watching over you, never fear.

Dad, I do love you and I know you love me. Why couldn't you have been honest? With me, with Mother, with Tilly – but most of all with yourself? There is no shame in loving a man, you must believe that. But what you did was lie and cheat to do it. Please learn from me. Ha! That would be something, wouldn't it? A lesson learned from your promiscuous gay son? But I have been honest, in the end, with everyone, and God knows I have enjoyed my life, albeit short and sweet.

Now there is just this bloody death business, so the sooner I get it over with, the better.

Lots of love to everyone,

Eddie x

The young man carefully folded the letter and put it back in the envelope addressed to Jeremy Sinclair. He laid it on the table, then unscrewed the bottle of pills and tipped them out. With the help of the champagne, he managed to wash down the entire pile of white tablets. Then, feeling tired, he folded his arms on the edge of the balcony, slowly laid down his head and closed his eyes. He wanted to remember his visit to this box with Jeremy. It had been the happiest moment of his life when they first touched each other. He could smell the scent of Jeremy's skin and feel the softness of his lips as he kissed Eddie . . .

Chapter 51

'Ladies and gentlemen, it is with enormous sadness and regret that I have to tell you that Lord Edward Graham's son, Eddie, committed suicide on Christmas Eve, here in this theatre. It is for this reason that the police are still here, as some of you may or may not have noticed. The theatre will be closed until further notice. I apologize for getting you back here, but I did not know myself until last night when I returned from the break. I suggest we use the time wisely though, and start with a read-through of *The Prime of Miss Jean Brodie* in the rehearsal room. Heather, if you would be kind enough to organize some coffee. I will need the whole company to stay in the theatre, as the police may want to speak to you all, at some point, regarding this dreadful business.'

After Giles had left the Green Room, no one spoke for ages. Heather bustled round getting mugs and coffee sorted, but most people just stood or sat in a daze. Suddenly Sally asked, 'Has anyone seen Jeremy?'

There was no answer.

She left the room and rushed to his dressing room where she found him sitting with a bottle of vodka open beside him.

'Oh, Jeremy, I am so sorry. You must be devastated. Come here.' She made to take him in her arms but Jeremy stopped her.

'Please, Sally, I know you mean well, but just leave me alone for now. Giles has given me permission to miss the read-through.'

'But I am worried you . . .'

'Please, Sally – just go. I promise you I am not going to do anything foolish. I just need to absorb this, and work my way through it.'

Sally nodded and backed away. She was desperate to console him, he looked so frail, but she did as she was told and left Jeremy to his mourning.

She called into Wardrobe to see Janie and find out if she knew any more details.

'Well, not really. We only came in this morning. Apparently he was just sitting in the Royal Box dead. They don't know exactly for how long, or anything. There was a suicide note, which the police took away.'

'Oh God, how sad. Anyway, I had better get going. See you later.'

The read-through was a disaster. Jeremy was not there, and nobody was concentrating, so Giles broke early.

'I think we can leave this for today. But I want everyone here tomorrow morning bright-eyed and bushy-tailed.'

Sally managed to grab Giles by the arm as he was leaving. 'Sorry to bother you, Giles, but do you have any more infor-mation? I am so worried about Jeremy, you understand. Someone said there was a suicide note?'

'Yes, Sally, of course you are worried. I do understand, but

I can't help really. You need to speak to the police about the suicide note, I should imagine. Come with me and I will introduce you to the man in charge.'

Sally followed Giles down to the stage, where there were police and people in white boilersuits everywhere. He went to find Detective Sergeant Derek Bush, who was in charge. While she was waiting, Sally glanced up at the Royal Box, and the memory of her first encounter with Giles floated into her mind. How happy and excited she had been that day. Giles had looked so grand and formidable up there in his eyrie. Why had Eddie chosen that particular spot to die, she wondered. How unbearable it must be for his loved ones. But not only was he dead, he had killed himself. He had chosen to die. He must have felt so alone.

Sally wondered if Jeremy would blame himself somehow. She must help him to understand it was nothing to do with him. He could not have prevented it.

'But if I hadn't left him on his own! I should have made him come with me, that day I saw him at his father's flat. I knew he was going to end up on his own. Oh Christ, why did I leave him!' he cried.

Sally and Jeremy were sitting in his dressing room. Everyone else had gone to the pub for lunch so it was quiet, and private.

'But, Jeremy, Lord Graham would never have let you take Eddie away. What would you have done, kidnapped him?'

'I know, I know you are right, Sally, but I feel so useless – like I let him down.'

'Jeremy, may I remind you that it was because of Eddie, and his behaviour, that you too could have been facing a death sentence. You haven't let anyone down!'

Jeremy looked at Sally for a few minutes and then got up and gave her a hug.

'You are a very special person, Sally, and a good friend. I can only say these things to you. I knew Eddie would take his life, because from the moment he was diagnosed I could feel it in him, sense his desire to do something positive about the situation. I know that must sound ridiculous because to most people suicide is a very negative response. However, to someone like Eddie, he was being positive. There was no cure for his illness so he would have had to spend the rest of his days waiting for the dreaded signs to appear, warning him of his approaching death. Does anyone want to live like that? I know one day they may find a cure and all the rest of it, but for now Eddie had nothing to do but wait. I have thought a good deal about him while I have been at home, and I have almost cried myself through it, Sally. My poor parents did not know what to make of me, I was so down. I know how lucky I am to be in the clear, and it has made me even more determined now to make a success of my career. I don't need anyone in my life any more. I loved Eddie more than life itself, and I don't regret a single moment I spent with him, but now I am on my own and going to make the best of it.'

He gave Sally another hug and said huskily, 'Come on – let's join the others in the pub.'

Everyone was a bit subdued, and the word was out that Jeremy and Eddie had been an item, so when they arrived at the pub no one quite knew what to say. Jeremy cleared the air by announcing that the drinks were on him, and they were going to toast his lover and wish him well, wherever he was. A big cheer went up and everyone's spirits rose. They were a team and would move on together.

Sally sat in the corner and watched the proceedings. Dora caught her eye and waved to her. Sally smiled and waved back and was reminded that they were back in action again now, so anything could happen. Dora had taken over Christmas Day with her high spirits, and wonderful news. Of course Mum and Dad were absolutely over the moon, and could not believe things had changed so much in just a few months. Sally could not help but feel that she herself had somehow let them down. She had stayed in much the same place, as far as they were concerned. Never mind that she had fallen in love and had her heart broken, discovered that she and her sibling were worlds apart, and decided that maybe she was not cut out to be an actress after all.

When Patricia had come to tuck her up on Christmas Eve, she said, 'I know we joke about things sometimes and you may feel we don't take you seriously enough, but you know you can tell us anything, my darling. We just want you to be happy.'

Happy! Wasn't that what everybody wanted in life? Was Eddie looking for happiness when he popped those pills? Was he searching for happiness when he was partying hard, and taking all those men inside him? Was Sally happy when she woke up beside Rupert?

Yes, I was, I suppose, Sally thought to herself. But I was also happy because deep inside me, I felt good about myself. Surely I can achieve that contentment without having to rely on other people all the time? I am quite content at Crewe, and I am going to enjoy each minute as it happens, and see where I go. As that agent Peter Stone said, it is all luck and karma, and being in the right place at the right time.

'Sorry to interrupt your day dream, sweetie, but I need you to help me clear the wing space for the next show,' Heather said.

'Just coming,' answered Sally and went to find Jeremy.

He was surrounded by the lads so she pulled him to one

side, saying, 'I just wanted to tell you I love you, and that we *can* do this!'

That afternoon, Giles assembled the cast and crew once again to tell them that the police had finished their investigation of the theatre and they were now free to continue their rehearsals. There was a round of applause and people wandered off to sort themselves out and get back to life as normal.

'Oh, Jeremy,' Giles called to him as he was leaving with the others. 'This is for you. The police no longer need it and it is addressed to you.' He handed Jeremy the envelope.

'But what about his family? Surely you should give it to his father?' Jeremy ventured.

'I have tried to contact Lord Graham on several occasions, but to no avail. It has been made very clear to me that neither he, nor the Graham family, want anything to do with me – or the theatre for that matter.' Giles smiled at Jeremy sadly. 'God only knows what is going to happen to us next season when His Lordship's grant is withdrawn.'

'I am sure we can think of something, Giles, and everyone will rally round. Don't give up hope yet, and just think: once *Hamlet* has had rave reviews, you will be flavour of the month!'

'Thank you for your vote of confidence, young man, it is much appreciated.' Giles watched the young actor join the gang, and thought for the umpteenth time how much he missed Teddie. But once again, Lady Luck had not left him completely. He had his production of *Hamlet* to keep him busy and he could do without romance for the time being.

Sally had invited Jeremy to supper at the flat. She had made proper dinner, and the two of them were sitting at the kitchen table finishing their bottle of wine when Jeremy produced the envelope.

'What's that?' asked Sally.

'It's the note Eddie left for me, and I thought I would share it with you.' Jeremy smiled shakily and squeezed her hand. 'I am not sure I could have read it on my own anyway.'

He slipped his finger inside the envelope, took out the sheet of notepaper and began to read his lover's last words aloud.

Chapter 52

April 1983

Sally gazed out across the rooftops of Venice. The beauty of the scene was overwhelming. It was another world. She thought back to Christmas, just three months ago. So much had changed in her life. When the season had finished at Crewe she had retreated home still reeling from Eddie's suicide and Jeremy's despair. She had so wanted to help her dear friend get through this terrible time, but in the end it had to be down to him. They had parted with promises to catch up after a break, Jeremy to his parents' home and Sally to hers. Dora had left to go to Nottingham and suddenly Sally was back to her childhood days being cosseted by her parents.

And then there was Mack. She could not believe how happy she had been to see him. He had come to the house and they had gone for a walk, and to her amazement Sally had poured out all her hopes and fears to him. He had wrapped her up in his love and coaxed her back to her usual sunny self.

She still had not decided what she wanted to do next though, and suddenly fate had taken over.

'I have been offered a three-month tour of Europe to teach and advise on sculpture for a new generation of city-dwellers,' announced Mack one day in the pub. 'God knows what it means, but I get paid to work my way round Europe. Why don't you come with me and give yourself a real break, Sally.'

Sally could not think of one reason not to say yes. And here she was in Venice, looking across St Mark's Square, feeling as if she was in a Canaletto painting. She was the happiest she had ever been in her life, but sometimes a nagging little voice would remind her that she had to decide what she wanted to do with her life. Her career. She suddenly thought of Jeremy and all the conversations they used to have about commitment to the theatre and dedication. She must send him a postcard. Maybe when she got back, she would ring him and see if he wanted to share a pad together. They had discussed it at one point . . .

'Hey, you – come back to bed. I need you.'

Sally turned and looked at the huge double bed, then the head of glossy black hair, beneath which she could see a pair of piercing blue eyes smiling at her.

Domani, domani – tomorrow, tomorrow – what would tomorrow bring?

Final Curtain

Read on to discover

Lynda Bellingham's

first novel

Tell Me Tomorrow

Chapter 1

Hertfordshire, Spring 1910

John and Alice Charles had three sons, loud, strapping lads always up to mischief, but only one daughter. She was called Mary, and she was the youngest of the family. John was the vicar of St James' Church in a small village called Allingham, not far from the historic town of St Albans in the county of Hertfordshire.

It was on a church outing to St Albans that Alice Cooke entered the young would-be curate's rather lonely life, and love blossomed. Alice was the daughter of a wealthy landowner in Buckinghamshire, and her marriage to John was deemed a drop in the social scale. Once it was clear to Alice's parents that she was determined to marry beneath her station, they sent her packing, albeit with a quite substantial dowry. However, Alice never saw her parents again. They regarded her as feckless, and a disappointment, and concentrated their hopes and ambitions on their two sons instead. As the only child of elderly parents who died when he was embark his career in the clergy, John was alone in the world. Alice was now abandoned, so the two young lovers made their world themselves, and thanks to Alice's optimistic nature and goodness of heart, between them they created a loving family.

Their daughter Mary had the advantages of being brought up with three brothers – and the disadvantages. She was protected and spoiled, but also very innocent, and unaware of life outside her family. But she had a lively mind and had inherited her mother's warmth and optimism. She loved to learn, and if truth be told she was the brightest of them all. However, life in those days was ruled by the men. Mary had to play a secondary role to her brothers even though she often taught them herself, as school was not something they went to willingly. There was many a day when cries could be heard from the scullery as one or other of the boys was beaten for playing truant.

But not today; nobody was going to be shouted at today. It was Sunday, Mothering Sunday to be precise, and it was a beautiful morning, with the promise of spring in the air. Mary had been waiting for this special day to arrive for ages. She had made a card for her beloved mother and helped her brothers to make one from them. The back door of the scullery was wide open as the girl searched the garden for early snowdrops and budding daffodils to put on her mother's breakfast tray. She could hear a lark showing off in the field behind the house, and paused to listen to the clear notes soaring above her. It was hard not to enjoy the promise of the day, outside here on the step.

But Mary was under a dark cloud that morning. Her mother, Alice Charles, lay upstairs grievously ill with pneumonia.

Mary was only ten years old but was already taking on the

household chores. With her father and three brothers in the house, the work never ended. Mrs Edge came in every day to help. She was a lovely round lady who lived in the village. Her duties covered everything from cooking a hearty tea for Mary and the boys, to arranging all the flowers in the church and leading the ladies of the village in the cleaning of the brass. She was a great comfort to Mary as her mother's illness took hold. The little girl was very much alone as John Charles did not seem able to cope at all with his wife's decline. He had always been a rather distant figure to Mary. He worked very hard, dividing his time between the church and his parish duties, and spent hours shut away in his study. He always had time for his wife, of course, for Alice was the light of his life, and she tried to ensure that the house was calm and tranquil. Not an easy task with three sons around. Now Mary was trying to ease the burden of her mother's care, so that her father could write his sermons, and perform his pastoral duties. But the house had lost its brightness since her mother had taken to her bed.

Mary had spent most of the night beside her mother, tending to her and trying to keep the fever at bay. She had just changed the bed-linen and Alice's nightgown. Having washed the other sweat-soaked sheets by hand and stuffed them through the mangle, she was hanging them out in the morning sunshine to dry. She felt a little faint from lack of sleep but paid no heed. Time enough to sleep when her mother was on the mend.

Back inside the kitchen, she put her posy of flowers in a tiny glass vase and placed it on the tray. Then she went to the range to pick up the heavy black iron kettle that was boiling on the top. She made some tea and spooned plenty of sugar into a cup. Mrs Edge said sweet tea could cure anything.

would make her mother feel better. She was not supposed to touch the heavy kettle, but these were difficult times, and all the child knew for sure was that she had to do her very best. She cut a slice of bread very carefully, with the sharp bread-knife threatening to do her mischief at any moment, and spread some butter and jam on the extra thick slice. How she loved the sweet-smelling sticky jam her mother made. It smelled of summer and strawberries and fun.

She carried the tray upstairs to her mother's bedroom. The curtains were closed and the room was dark and stuffy, and it smelled sour. Mary put down the tray and tiptoed to the bed-side. Alice was propped up against the pillows, her eyes closed, breathing with great difficulty. The little girl took her hand and squeezed it gently.

'Happy Mothering Sunday. I've got your breakfast, Mother. A nice cup of tea, and some bread and jam. Now you must eat it all up to make you strong.'

Alice Charles opened her eyes and smiled wanly at her daughter. 'You are a wonderful nurse, Mary,' she managed to whisper. 'I'll have it in a minute. But first, will you open the drawer in my bedside table, please, dear?'

The little girl did as she was told. Inside the drawer were some lovely lace hankies and a lavender pouch. Mary picked it up and smelled the wonderful fragrance. As she did so, Alice tried to turn her head but the effort was too much. She breathed hard and it caught in her throat as a gasp. Mary was frightened by the sound.

'Mother, please be still,' she implored. 'Please get better.' And she tried in vain to stop the tears that were desperately forcing their way down her cheeks.

Alice drew herself up, praying silently for the strength to do what she had to do, and said, 'Mary, dear, now don't cry. It is going to be fine. Inside that drawer you will find my prayer book. Please pass it to me.'

Mary found the book and put it in her mother's trembling hands. Alice opened the book at the first page and showed it to her daughter.

'Look here – see? I've written you a note. Promise me you will keep this prayer book with you always, and every night when you go to sleep, you will say your prayers and think of me. I'll be watching over you all the time, my dearest daughter. You will have a lot to do, but your father and your brothers need your help. Please don't be sad, I will be with you always in your heart.'

The dying woman made a last superhuman effort as she gasped, 'Now be a good girl and go and call your father to come quickly. I need to speak to him.' Then she fell back on the pillows, exhausted.

To Mary it seemed as if she had fallen asleep.

'Mother, please wake up, you haven't eaten your breakfast.' She shook her mother's arm and it dropped heavily off the bed and just hung there. The little girl slowly backed away from the bed and a scream rose in her throat.

'Father! Come quick!'

The funeral service seemed very long to Mary. She tried hard to sing all the hymns well for her mother, but she wanted to cry all the time. As she sat in a pew with her prayer book clutched in her hands, and her eyes screwed tightly shut, she prayed and prayed to God to make her mother come back. But He didn't. Mary would often talk to Him at night, after that. She never gave up asking, and she always kept her prayer book close by, along with the card she had made that day for her mother.

Mary now became a mother to her brothers even though she was the youngest. It was a lonely life, for her father could offer her little comfort as he was grieving himself, and the boys were busy growing into men. Mrs Edge still came in every day and helped with the chores, but it was clear to everyone in the village that the vicar wanted to be left alone. He performed his duties with care and diligence, but the spark of life had gone out of him.

Mary never really had time to make friends at school because as soon as the bell went, she was off home to cook and clean for the household. But it was not all bad. There was a farm just up the road from the vicarage owned by a couple called Ernest and Olive Cooper. They had two sons of their own who went to school with the Charles boys, and all the lads loved to play on the farm. Haystacks and cowsheds made great hiding places, and every summer the boys would spend long hot days in the fields. For Mary it was a magical place to go and be with all the animals. She loved the smell of Olive's kitchen where there was always an animal of some description in front of the range. Cats, dogs – even baby lambs. One afternoon there was a sheep giving birth and Mary sat with Olive who was keeping an eye on it, because it had been having difficulties. At last the lamb dropped to the ground as Mary watched in awe. The farmer's wife picked up the lamb and placed it under the mother's nose, rubbing it with the afterbirth.

'They need a bit of help sometimes, to understand what it is all about, God bless 'em!' she explained to the little girl.

But the ewe did not want to know. She butted the still wet and bloody lamb, and walked away. Mary was so distressed to see this that she burst into tears.

'Don't fret yourself, dearie,' said Olive kindly. 'I will take the lamb indoors and put it by the fire, and you can help me feed it by hand.'

Sure enough, they carried the lamb indoors and soon it was lying in Mary's lap in front of the fire, while she fed it from a glass baby bottle. It was love at first sight. Mary was round at the farm every minute she was free. The lamb grew bigger and bigger each day. Mary called her Alice after her mother. Her brothers teased her mercilessly and ran round her singing the old nursery rhyme:

> 'Mary had a little lamb
> Its fleece was white as snow.
> And everywhere that Mary went
> The lamb was sure to go.'

She even took it to school one day to show her class. Mary could never quite get over the way the mother sheep had rejected and abandoned her baby, but the farmer's wife was very matter-of-fact about it. She said it happened quite often.

'But how could you not love your baby?' whispered Mary.

'Well, there are some women as have the same problem, dearie. There's naught you can do about it though. You can't *make* people love you.'

Having three brothers meant that Mary was always learning all sorts of things, not all of them good either. They taught her to spit and she was really good at it. In addition, she could skim a stone across the pond with the best of them and ride a horse and drive a cart like a champion. Her happiest memories were of sitting on the hay cart at the end of a hot summer's day. The sun would be setting as they rolled back to Coopers Farm full of fresh air and cider and homemade pies. The boys would be fighting and scrapping on top of the hay like young lion cubs. She would sit up front with her eldest brother Joseph, lulled by the swing of the horses' rumps in front of her and the jangling of the harness and the screeching of the bats swooping around them in the dusk.

As they reached the farm gates, the last streaks of the red sunset collapsed on the horizon, and darkness would fall. The boys would walk Mary back to the vicarage and then they would go to the pub. The landlord of the Wheatsheaf in Allingham was well aware that the boys were not only too young to be drinking but also the vicar's sons, so the boys were given non-alcoholic ginger beer and big plates of shepherd's pie. At home, Mary would creep in and check on her father, who was usually sitting at his desk preparing a sermon or writing letters to do with parish matters. Sometimes she would find him fast asleep with his head on his arms. The Reverend Charles made Mary feel a little frightened because he was always sad and often stern with them. He just could not give his children the affection they needed, and while the boys had each other for comfort, it made the girl miss her mother so much, especially at bedtime when she could remember so vividly her tender embrace as she tucked Mary in, with loving words to help her dream wonderful things. Just before she fell asleep, Mary would remember her mother's words and slip out of bed to kneel on the floor and say her prayers, because she knew her mother was watching.

One morning Mary got out of bed and was horrified to see blood on the bed-sheets and on her nightdress. She checked herself all over for cuts and could find nothing wrong. In the bathroom, she suddenly felt her stomach contract in pain. She sat down on the lavatory and bent over to ease the cramps, but felt a rush of liquid between her legs and heard it splash into the bowl below. Looking down, she cried out in panic as the water in the bowl turned pink. Sobbing now with fear and disbelief, she grabbed a flannel and held it between her legs. What was happening to her?

There was a knock on the door and she heard Joseph's voice outside. 'Mary? Come on, girl, we want our breakfast. What are you doing in there?'

Mary tried to rise from the seat, but another trickle of blood stopped her in her tracks. She called out, 'Joe, something dreadful has happened. I am bleeding and I think I am dying. Please fetch the doctor.'

As a young man of nineteen, Joseph had already picked up a good deal of knowledge about the opposite sex. However, it was one thing to discuss the female anatomy with his friends, but quite another to speak of such delicate matters with his sister.

But he knew someone who could help. Telling his sister to stay calm and to hold on for a few minutes while he fetched help, Joseph sped off to Dr Jeffreys' house two streets away, and banged on the door. The doctor's wife, Lorna, answered his knock. She was a trained nurse and often stood in for her husband when he was too busy to deal with minor ailments that arose during surgery hours.

Blushing, Joseph explained to her what he thought was Mary's problem. Lorna Jeffreys was very understanding, and quite impressed by this young man's grasp of the sensitivity of the situation. Fetching her coat and hat, and an old but clean sheet, she followed Joseph back to the vicarage, where poor Mary was still closeted in the bathroom. Joseph led the nurse upstairs and tapped on the door.

'Mary, dear, don't panic,' he called. 'Mrs Jeffreys is here to help you. Please open the door. I will go downstairs and make us all a cup of tea in the meantime, and don't worry about breakfast. I will see to everything.'

Once Mary had heard her brother go downstairs, she opened the bathroom door and Lorna was soon attending to her, helping her bathe, showing her how to cut up and make a cloth pad and fetching her clean clothes from the bedroom. At the same time she was giving the poor girl a welcome lesson on the female anatomy.

'You must think me very foolish,' said Mary, as Mrs Jeffreys explained about her monthly cycle. 'I am so sorry to cause you all this bother. I just had no idea what was happening to me. Mother died two years ago now and my education mostly consists of housekeeping and reading books that my father suggests to me. There has been no room for girlish talk or another friend or their mother to teach me about such things.'

'Oh, you poor child,' said Lorna. 'Please don't apologize. It is a very natural thing to be worried when you start your cycle. But all is well now – and if you ever need to ask me anything again, anything at all, please do not hesitate to come and see me. I am very happy to talk to you at any time.'

With that the doctor's wife packed her bag and was gone, leaving Mary feeling as if her life had changed forever, and she was still not quite sure why.

Life went on and Mary toiled from dawn till dusk in the vicarage. She was quite content with her life, however, and loved nothing better than to see everyone round the table of an evening, eating the food she had cooked and laughing and animatedly discussing things going on in the world. She still visited the farm all the time to see Alice, her pet sheep. Mr Cooper suggested they might let her ewe have a lamb of its own one day soon.

The Charles boys were finding their feet now. Brother Joseph had been away in London studying to become an accountant and would come home on his rare leaves full of stories of drinking all night and dancing till dawn. Joseph was the only one of the three boys who had left home, albeit temporarily. Reginald was still at school and studying very hard. He had a rather serious side to his nature and his father had great hopes that he would follow him into the Ministry.

John Charles remembered his own years of study with great fondness, even though he had lost his parents so young. His meeting with Alice had changed his life completely. Not just because of her sunny disposition and warm and caring spirit, but due to her inheritance. Although John vowed he would never touch his wife's money, Alice had persuaded him to buy their first home – a small terraced house in St Albans – as a means of securing their future. When they left to take up residence in the vicarage at Allingham, the couple did not sell the house but found a lodger and his family. And to this day, the rent still provided extra income for the family – a welcome boost to the Reverend Charles's modest stipend.

Alice had turned the sombre vicarage into a house full of light and joy, and the sound of happy children. John Charles missed his wife with every fibre of his being every day of her passing.

Stephen was the youngest of the boys and closest to Mary. There were only three years between them. He shared her love of animals and the two of them spent all their spare time at Coopers Farm. Recognizing the lad's love of farming, Ernest Cooper encouraged him to learn all he could about animal husbandry. One day, as they were sitting in the farm's big welcoming kitchen, Stephen announced that he wanted to be a vet when he left school.

When he told his eldest brother of his hopes and dreams, Joseph gave him a friendly punch on the arm and said, 'That's a fine ambition to have, young Stephen, but beware you don't get led astray like me and spend too much time in the pub instead of attending to your studies.'

Their father had just quietly entered the room and overheard this – and they fell silent, waiting for a reproof. But he hardly seemed to see them and just turned and went out again without a word. Mary ran after him to make sure he had everything he needed. She hated to see her father so lost. When she returned to the kitchen, the boys had already forgotten the interruption and were laughing and joking as Joseph continued his tales of life in the big city.

One day, Joseph came home with a friend called Henry Maclean. Henry was in the Army and talked about how there was going to be a war soon, with the Hun, and everyone would have to fight for their country. All the brothers sat round the kitchen table listening to him and drinking beer, which Mary served them. She could only feel dread at the thought of a Europe at war, but the boys were bright-eyed and full of plans to join up. She was secretly entranced by Henry, who seemed different from her brothers somehow. More sophisticated and well-groomed. He had beautiful sandy hair that flopped in his eyes, and he had to keep brushing it out of the way as he talked. His voice was very mellow and he was well-spoken, but not too posh.

When Henry left that night, to return to his regiment, he squeezed Mary's hand and gave her a kiss on the cheek. The spot burned from the touch of his lips. She was so young, but already she felt the catch in her belly, the tightness in her throat – and the pain in her heart.

Henry Maclean was proved right. War did come – and it

spread across Europe like a huge black cloud, covering everything in a net of death and destruction. Hundreds of thousands of lives were lost. Stephen Charles was killed in battle, blown up in a German attack on his regiment, three months after he arrived in Passchendaele. Joseph somehow managed to survive but came home a broken man. The carnage he had witnessed left him shell-shocked and staring into a bottle of whisky. Reginald took all the pain and suffering as a sign that he should follow his calling and enter the Church – much to the delight of his father. The Reverend John Charles went straight to his wife's grave to share the good news with her.

Although devastated by the news of Stephen's death, John had somehow found a new strength during the war. He had worked tirelessly, travelling from village to village to take services in times of need; many of the clergy had joined up to provide spiritual support for the soldiers and to work with the wounded. Often with Mary at his side, Reverend Charles would seek out bereaved families and offer his help and comfort.

Mary herself felt that she had been pretty much deserted by everyone. She mourned her brother's death and prayed for his soul to that same God who had taken her beloved mother from her. She shed many bitter tears. But life had to go on and there was so much to do and so many people in need that she had to push her own hurt to the back of her mind and just get on with life. She worked with the Red Cross, helping to care for wounded soldiers, and she also taught classes in the village school when necessary. She grew up very quickly, as did so many young people at that time.

One summer evening in 1919, Mary was picking strawberries in the garden when she heard a motor car. This was a rare occurrence. She knew no one who owned a car except the doctor. She ran out to the front of the house and saw Joseph, looking very much the worse for wear, slumped in the front passenger seat of a Bentley. At the wheel was Henry Maclean. He looked just the same as always, if a little tired and lined around the eyes. Mary's heart skipped a beat. Joseph stumbled out of the car and staggered up the garden path, waving his arms in the air and attempting to sing 'It's a Long Way to Tipperary'.

'Joseph, calm down! What are you doing here? Whose car is that?' she asked, dancing excitedly round the two young men as they walked into the house.

'Got any of that homemade sloe gin, Mary?' Joseph hiccupped and fell into the nearest chair.

'I think you have already had quite enough,' she retorted.

'Oh, come on, old girl, don't be such a killjoy. Poor Henry here needs a drink. He has fought a war, for God's sake!'

Mary turned to Henry, who was standing in the doorway with his hat in his hand looking rather bemused.

'I am so awfully sorry,' she said shyly. 'Please do come and sit down. Of course I will fetch you a drink, and some food maybe? You look like you could do with a good meal inside you.'

'That would certainly be very welcome. Thank you, Mary.' He gave her a huge smile and her legs went quite wobbly.

An hour later, Henry and Mary were tucking into homemade soup and bread and cheese, followed by bowls of strawberries just picked from the garden.

'Oh my God, this is heaven,' said Henry through mouthfuls of food. Joseph was sprawled on the sofa now, practically asleep. He was red-eyed and unshaven and stank of whisky.

'I have made a bed up for you in Stephen's room. If you

don't mind, that is, sleeping in his room because he ...' Mary stopped and felt the tears fill her eyes. She hurriedly left the room and went into the kitchen to compose herself. She was leaning on the sink wiping away her tears with her apron when Henry came to find her.

'Please don't worry,' he said gently. 'It is so hard for everyone. We have lost so many of our friends and loved ones. Joe only gets drunk because he is grieving so much.'

Mary looked into Henry's eyes and could see the pain. 'Was it very bad?' she whispered. Henry didn't answer for a long moment and seemed to be fighting with himself for control.

'Yes,' was all he said, and then he took her in his arms and kissed her. Long and hard. Needing to feel her softness, her goodness and her innocence.

They stood absolutely still, holding each other. Mary wanted the moment to last forever, but it was broken by the sound of Joseph's snores from the other room.

'We'd better get him into bed,' she said, gently breaking away from Henry's arms. 'Would you be kind enough to help me?'

'Of course, come on.' Henry led the way and the two of them hauled Joseph off the sofa and somehow managed to push and heave him upstairs to his room, where Henry virtually threw him onto the bed. Joseph moaned and turned on his side and was fast asleep again before they had reached the door. They laughed and turned to go downstairs. A moment held between them. What now?

There was a bang from the front door downstairs and the Reverend Charles called out, 'Hello? Anybody home? Mary, where are you?'

Mary quickly moved away and went to the top of the stairs, calling out, 'I am here, Father. Henry and I have been putting

Joe to bed.' She ran down to give her father a hug and turned to indicate Henry as he came down to join them.

'Hello, my boy, good to see you home safe and sound,' the minister said. 'Terrible business – thank God it is all over at last. Are you staying the night? Has Mary fed you?'

'Mary has done us proud in every way, sir. She has kindly offered me a bed, and if you will excuse me, I will retire to it now. It has been a long day. Goodnight, Mary, and thank you for everything. Goodnight, sir.' He turned to go up the stairs and Mary put her hand on his arm.

'Wait, let me get you a towel.' She went to fetch it and her father moved off to the kitchen in search of his supper.

Mary came back with a clean towel and handed it to Henry, her eyes never leaving his face.

'Thank you.' He leaned in and softly kissed her on the lips before turning slowly and climbing the stairs. He might have been going to the moon. Mary felt so bereft. What could she do to keep him close?

'My dear, have you got my dinner ready?'

'Coming, Father,' came her reply.

After he had finished his supper, John Charles left the table, kissed his daughter goodnight, and retired to his study, where he shut the door.

Mary cleared away the dishes and went out into the back garden. It was a beautiful summer's night. The sky was so clear she could see every single star.

'Twinkle, twinkle little star . . .' Mary whispered to herself and she looked up at the window of Stephen's bedroom, as if she could transport herself to where Henry lay asleep. At the thought of him, a tremor ran through her entire body. She felt as if she was on fire. What was happening to her?

Sensing movement behind her, she turned – straight into

Henry's arms. He held her very close and she could smell him. Touch his skin with her lips. She caught her breath and tried to look at him but that meant pulling away, and she didn't want to do that. She wanted to stay close to him forever. Oh, but what about her father? She let out a little gasp of fright.

'What is it?' Henry asked.

'My father is in his study. He must not see me this way.'

'He just went to bed. I heard his door shut. I was lying awake thinking of you. I couldn't sleep, Mary. I had to hold you once again.'

Henry took her chin in his hand and slowly pressed his lips to hers. Oh so gently, did his tongue prise her lips apart, and play against her teeth. Oh so gently, did his tongue go deeper, teasing her tongue to respond. She seemed to be melting into his arms her body pressed into his, as he lifted her up in his arms and carried her towards the little summerhouse at the bottom of the garden. Never letting his lips leave hers for a moment, he lowered her onto the garden seat and started to unbutton her dress. Mary could feel nothing but the beating of her heart and a sound like rushing water in her head.

As he kissed her, Henry's hand moved down to touch her breast and then her nipple. He teased it between his fingers, making it hard, and Mary let out a moan of pleasure. Could anything be more wonderful than this? Henry had lifted her dress now and was exploring beneath it. He ran his fingers, feather light, up the inside of her thigh, pausing to stroke the soft skin above her stocking top. Her body jerked involuntarily as he found her secret place. She could not control the waves of ecstasy and opened herself to his fingers as they gently pushed into her warm moist self. With this exquisite sensation, her head lost the battle for logic or reason; her innocent young body responded naturally to his touch, to his closeness, and her very being demanded to be satisfied.

Her legs fell open to take Henry's body between her thighs. Her hands instinctively found his hard erect penis and fondled it. The anticipation was unbearable. She was gasping with need. And suddenly he was inside her, pushing urgently into her warmth and wetness. There was no pain, just the pleasure of being full up with his manhood. He moved and she moved with him. It was so natural, both these young bodies wanting affirmation of life after so much death. As their passion grew, their lovemaking became more intense and he penetrated deep and hard into her, touching her to the core. She followed his rhythm, and felt him spurt into her, her muscles clasping him as if her life depended on it. She let out a cry of pure joy and held him to her until they were spent. He looked down at her and smiled to reassure her all was well. She took his face in her hands and kissed every inch of it, laughing and crying all at once.

Eventually, Henry got up and dressed himself, then helped Mary gather herself together. They did not speak a word as they walked back to the house, under the starry sky, holding hands. Henry kissed her lightly at the kitchen door and went to his room. Mary stood at the kitchen sink drinking a cup of water and feeling every bone and muscle in her body tingle. This was what it felt like to be alive, she knew it! She wanted it to last forever.

But it was not to be. The next morning, when Mary woke up, Henry had gone. Joseph explained to her that he had made his apologies, but said he had to drive back to London to attend a job interview with a City bank. He sent his thanks to Mary for everything, and hoped they would all meet again soon. Mary had to run out of the room, so as not to give herself away. She raced into the garden and was violently sick under a hedge. A terrible blackness swept over her as she seemed to understand her fate.

Three months later, she was sat in front of Dr Jeffreys, white-faced and trembling, as he gave her the results of her night of passion. A baby, due to be born in the spring. Mary left the surgery in a daze. Despite the warm summer sunshine she was shivering and her legs felt weak; she had to sit down on the bench outside the doctor's house.

'Hello, Mary. Are you feeling all right, dear?' Lorna Jeffreys was looking down at her. The doctor's wife remembered so clearly their shared secret of all those years ago – Mary's ignorance of her body. Now she could see the naked shame in the young woman's eyes and her heart went out to her.

Putting her arms round her and lifting her up, Lorna said quietly, 'Come on, let's go and have a cup of tea, shall we?' She led Mary round the side of the house to the living quarters at the back of the surgery.

Neither woman spoke until they were sitting at the kitchen table with their tea in front of them.

Lorna broke the silence: 'Do you remember all those years ago, when I said that if ever there was anything I could do to help, you should call on me?'

Mary sighed deeply and searched Mrs Jeffreys' face. The woman had obviously guessed what was wrong, but there was no reprimand in her voice. No disapproval in her gaze. Mary started to cry. She felt so alone and so ashamed. What could she do? She was a fallen woman. This news would surely kill her father.

Charles had grown quite frail in the last few months, so much so that they had called Reginald down from his Theological College in Hendon in North London. The family hoped that it might be possible for Reginald to do his curate training with his father, at St James' Church in Allingham.

The Reverend John Charles was highly regarded in the Diocese, and the Bishop of St Albans was a close friend. The proposal had been discussed, and as things in the local parishes were still a little disordered since the war ended, it was agreed that John Charles could do with the help, and to have his son close by was the best thing to do for all concerned.

It was a comfort to think that her father would soon have Reg to support him. As Mary's tears slowly subsided, she was able to drink her tea and think more clearly.

'Is there anything I can do to help you?' asked Lorna, taking Mary's hand.

'No, not really. But thank you for all your kindness to me. I don't deserve it.' Mary stood up and made for the door. Turning, she told Mrs Jeffreys, 'I am going to talk to my brother Reginald; he will know what to do for the best. Thank you again. Goodbye.'

Mary walked home, consumed with her guilt and shame and fear. Her father must never find out. How could he ever forgive her? She thought of her dear mother and the tears sprang afresh. How could she have been so foolish? Reg would be coming home in the next few days to make arrangements for his training, and until then, she would have to keep her own counsel.

On reaching the vicarage, Mary went straight to her bed, telling her father that she had a headache. She hated to tell him a lie but needs must. Yet another sin to add to her long list. Before getting into bed, Mary prayed to her mother and begged her forgiveness. She held her prayer book to her heart and fell asleep with it in her hands.

'It's all right, I will help you. We will get through this together,' Reginald told his sister as he handed her a cup of tea; he and Mary were sitting in the front parlour. The vicarage was empty as John Charles had gone to visit a sick parishioner. Mary had poured out her story to her brother and was now once again collapsed in tears in her seat.

Although Reginald had always been the most serious of the brothers, he possessed a very kind heart. Deep down, there was a romantic streak inside him and he was currently in the throes of falling in love, thanks to a meeting with a girl called Leonora Matheson, who came to his college for Bible Studies. But now was not the time to confess these feelings to his poor dear sister.

'Leave things with me and let me have a think,' he said, handing Mary a large handkerchief so she could blow her nose. 'I have an idea already that could be a solution but I need to find out more. Take heart, dear Mary. God will find a way and He will forgive you. Now stop crying and go and make yourself busy.'

Mary did as she was told, but nothing could take away her deep shame and sense of foreboding. What did life have in store for her now, she wondered.

CBS◉drama

Whether you love the 1980s glamour of *Knots Landing*,
the feisty exploits of BAFTA-winning *Clocking Off*, the courtroom
dilemmas of *Judge Judy* or the forensic challenges of the world's
most watched drama *CSI: Crime Scene Investigation*, CBS Drama is
bursting with colourful characters, compelling cliff-hangers,
love stories, break-ups and happy endings.

Winter's line-up includes Amanda Burton in popular British drama
Waterloo Road, new seasons of *Judge Judy*, big hair and bitch
fights in *Dallas*, and the trappings of wealth in *Beverly Hills 90210*.

Also at CBS Drama, you're just one 'like' closer to your
on screen heroes. Regular exclusive celebrity interviews and behind
the scenes news is hosted on Facebook and Twitter with recent
contributors including *Taxi's* Louie De Palma (Danny DeVito).

www.cbsdrama.co.uk
f facebook.com/cbsdrama
🐦 twitter.com/cbsdrama

Sky: 149
Virgin: 197
Freesat: 134